LAST FLIGHT OF THE FALLEN VALKYRIE

©2003
All rights reserved.

No part of this book may be reproduced, stored in a retrieval system, or transmitted by any means, electronic, mechanical, photocopying, recording or otherwise, without written permission from the author.

Northwoods Books
In cooperation with PageFree Publishing, Inc.

ISBN 1-58961-133-0

This book is the work of fiction. Although the settings are in true locations of the world, the characters and events, except those actual events recorded as history, are fictional. Any resemblance to persons either living or dead is purely coincidental.

LAST FLIGHT OF THE

FALLEN VALKYRIE

by

THEODORE LOVECRAFT

To Patricia, with unending love and affection.

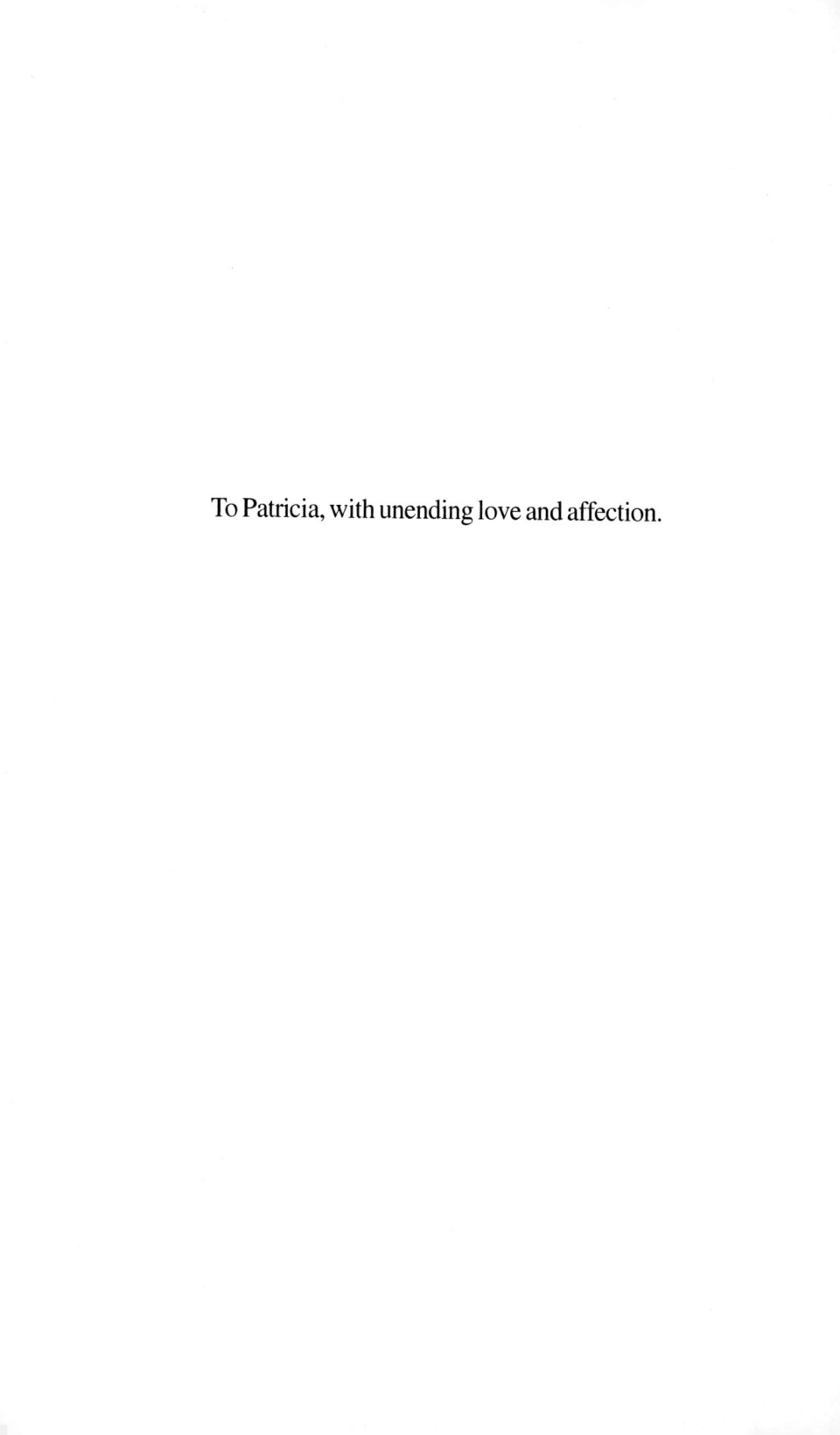

PART I

THE FALL OF THE VALKYRIE

CHAPTER ONE

Koblenz, Germany
December, 1918

    Dr. Horst Von Himmler was finishing up his evening rounds at Koblenz Hospital hurriedly. The Great War had now been over for more than a month, and the number of patients undergoing treatment for battle related injuries was declining steadily. The victims of the mustard gas and their ghastly sufferings, the memory of their miseries, were at least less fresh in Herr Doktor's compassionate mind.
    The gray bearded doktor, who walked with a pronounced slouch, his feet well separated with the toes pointed off to either side, dreaded this final call of the night. His patient had been assigned one of the hospital's few private rooms, for obvious reasons. Von Himmler, himself past sixty and in the prime of his long career in medicine, took a deep breath, which was normally not his custom, held his palm over his mouth and white whiskers, pinched his nose, and opened the door to the room.
    Henry Sturmer lay on his side in the narrow bed, a backgammon board at his right elbow. He was a man of about forty-five, with his dark brown hair parted down the middle and big, brown eyes like those of a puppy dog's, sad and forlorn. He hadn't been properly shaved in more than a week.
    "Evening, doktor, this- this still giving me lots of trouble. Lots of trouble."
    Von Himmler made his way around the foot of the bed and approached Sturmer's rear end, pocketing the note pad that he had held under his right arm, all the while pinching his nostrils tight with his left hand. Von Himmler gulped air through his mouth. He untied Sturmer's gown in order to examine his derriere.
    "Fistula in ano, Herr Sturmer, does not always heal naturally, I am

afraid." Sturmer turned his head way back. Doktor's voice sounded different than it had that morning. He sounded as though he might be getting sick, in fact. Von Himmler took in a great, gasping breath, and released his other hand from his nose in order to pry the buttocks apart. The patient whimpered. A bedpan had been strategically located there on the mattress. It was heaping with gauze. The nurses were attempting to soak Sturmer's leak into the pan, carrying it away from the skin and over the rim with the absorbent material. A creative idea, which unfortunately, was not working out particularly well; The sheet, doktor noted, was heavily soiled. Von Himmler adjusted his wire rim glasses pensively.

Fistula in ano was a very painful disease in which a communication at the side of the fundament opened through the flesh into the rectum, above the sphincter muscle that ordinarily kept it closed. This opening was generally the result of an abscess at the side of the large intestine. Sturmer was suffering from categorically the worst type of fistula, the opening being such that it constantly leaked out fecal matters through this hole or sinus, causing great pain, and rendering him disgusting to everyone whom he came into contact with.

"What can you do for me? When will I heal? You have got to help me!" Sturmer buried his puppy dog eyes into the sleeve of his gown and sobbed despondently. He had come to the hospital after his landlady and a group of fellow tenants had forcibly evicted him from the rooming house where he had been staying. Frau Krickstein complained bitterly that despite the great shortage of housing in the city, what with the return of thousands of soldiers from the front lines, Sturmer's unique condition was causing a daily fifty percent turnover in her clientele, resulting in half a dozen empty rooms each night. Her tenants left in droves, particularly when he came down for the evening meal.

"Surgery may be the only answer." Von Himmler covered the hairy buttocks. "For now, we shall wait and see if the air might not cure it. I will be back after breakfast." Sturmer wiped his red eyes on the corner of the sheet.

Leaving the drab, gray hospital corridors for the crisp winter air, Von Himmler permitted himself for the first time to look forward to the upcoming Yuletide- to a Christmastide to be spent in utter peace. He opened the case on his shiny, gold pocket watch and held its face up before a brightly lit storefront. A few minutes past ten; His wife, Hilda, nearly twenty-five years his junior, would be lounging on the dais in the parlour, reading. Their eleven-year old son, Wolfgang, should be fast asleep upstairs.

The doktor walked briskly through the narrow city streets, toward his modest home. He smiled thoughtfully. How nice for Wolfgang, to be racked by only the minimal pressures of excelling in primary school, and nothing more. Just two years before, for a period of weeks around the holidays, the doktor had real worries that the great conflict had reached such an impasse, with neither side able or willing to back down, that it became plausible to imagine that the war might become so protracted that his only son would face conscription into the military seven or eight years hence in order to serve *his* time at the front. With the certain evolution of the machinery of warfare, such duty would carry with it a likely death sentence. Looking back, those had been dark days, indeed.

In reality, though, the war to Wolfgang and most of Koblenz's other citizens had been fought entirely in the distant shadows. The military barges passing by on the Rhine and the occasional movement of German troops through the countryside nearby were the only reminders that an earth shaking conflict was taking place less than three hundred miles to the west. The RAF aerial bombardment of the previous February had caused little damage, and only five civilian casualties.

Back during the early days of the war, the German high command had foolishly used the town as its central command post for a time, directing the moves of over two million soldiers along the front through France and Belgium. Wireless communication was unreliable at best, and most information was still transmitted on horseback. The scheme was soon abandoned, following a series of costly defeats, and the generals left the safety of the Rhineland for positions much closer to the barbed wire, machine gunning, and 'round the clock artillery barrages along the endless miles of trench lines which defined the Western Front.

There! A big, dark supply truck rumbled rudely past, stinking the air and shattering the doktor's line of thought. Things would not be returning to normal in his town for quite some time, he was afraid. The Americans had chosen Koblenz as their post-war headquarters on the Rhine, an unpopular move with the local denizens. The townsfolk took immense pride in their picturesque but progressive village where the Moselle and

Rhine rivers meet. The Americans, with their distasteful habits of jamming the beer gartens and seemingly intentional late night maneuvering with their heavy vehicles in order to maintain their check points were certainly out of place.

Dr. Horst turned down his old cobblestone lane and approached his dwelling. Smoke from the coal stove poured out of the chimney and spiraled into the air, joining with those of his neighbors to form a massive plume high above in the moonlight. Hilda's feet would be warm and toasty, as was always the case at such a late hour.

Horst unlocked his front door and entered quietly. The house was small, owing to the sizable alimony payments granted to his first wife. A narrow two story, it was nonetheless beautifully decorated by Hilda, who had set off the modest pieces of furniture with print curtains in bright colors, and detailed needlepoint work throughout the house.

Wild flowers were her specialty, and Horst loved to inspire her each summer with long hikes through the woods together, where they would seek out the daintiest and most colorful specimens which Hilda would sketch while Horst held them patiently in his expert fingers for her, the hands of a surgeon clasping the fragile stems for many hours without so much as a twitch, for the artist whom he loved.

He delighted in looking upon her finished works, and felt that they somehow represented in their woven patterns the beauty of their marriage together, the strength of the thread binding them as one, so as to overcome the social stigma which always went with the territory when an older man left his loyal wife for a much younger woman.

Horst hung his greatcoat on one of the pegs in the entranceway. He followed the central hallway through the first floor. The parlour was to the left, the kitchen and dining area was off to the right, and the bath with water closet was to the very rear, next to the back door that opened out into the alley behind the house. There were two sleeping rooms and a storage area on the cramped second floor. The stairway was directly across the hall from the parlour.

Horst found Hilda dozing on the couch in the parlour, beside the coal fired heater. She opened her eyes and smiled sweetly at him. "Hello, darling," she said, stretching her arms and yawning. "Did your evening go smoothly for you?" Her husband leaned down and kissed her softly on the cheek. He had always been so attentive, so concerned with the little details in her life. His extensive schedule at the hospital kept him away from her for long periods of time. This extra vigilance was his way of making up for the lost hours. That was why she loved him so.

"The evening went very well," he replied. "And young Wolfgang, he is fast asleep?"

"Soundly," she said, her soft mouth puckering in her effort to tell him everything. "He studied for his tests, and then he waited up for you but I finally put him to bed. I did drill him and he only missed one answer, I believe. He is so smart! I fancy to think that one day he will be a physician, a surgeon, just like his father."

Horst beamed with pride. He hadn't given much thought to his son's future while war was still being waged. The new peace, as unsettling as it was in Germany, would enable him to dream of the security which he could now offer his family. They had grown accustomed to severe shortages, but now slowly, farm produce such as milk and eggs were coming back to the markets in greater supply. The money he was making was almost worthless, but the hospital was on the priority list for what food and other goods were available in the aftermath of the Armistice. He hoped that in the coming months, law and order would be established and his defeated Fatherland would be well on the road to healing its war-ravaged wounds. Surely, there would be no more war. Not for a score of generations.

"Come, really kiss me," said Hilda. He held her tightly and kissed her firmly. She always tasted so fresh, like his beloved Black Forest. He stood up to admire her calm beauty. Her blue eyes sparkled. Her eyebrows were high and narrow, and accentuated her bright eyes. Her wide set cheeks were proportionate to her rather high forehead. Her nose was narrow and longer than she liked. To him, it was unique, and not nearly as long as other women's noses that he'd seen over the years.

"We must make love, tonight," he whispered.

The man standing over her was not particularly desirable, at least not to other women, Hilda knew full well. His gray beard was unkempt, his hair disheveled, and the glasses which he wore were so thick that they magnified his eyes oddly- made his blue irises look large and rather dull behind the wire framed heavy glass. As for his body- it was soft and bulgy beneath the layers of clothes which he normally wore, and, to top it off, he was bull legged and his feet he often placed like a circus clown, pointed well off to either side. In spite of all this, the man was amazingly passionate, and with all of the lights off, he kissed and stroked and fondled and mounted her with great energy and drive, as if he were proving to himself more than to her that he could win this hopeless battle with Father Time and remain her source of companionship and strength indefinitely, or at least until she became old and infirm.

At that moment, Wolfgang sat straight up in bed, his eyes cold with fear. He began to cry out loudly.

"What the devil!?" his father exclaimed.

"I'll go to him," responded Hilda, scrambling into her slippers. "Horst, get yourself a beer." She jumped up and bolted from the parlour. Horst marveled at her fluid movements, even after twelve years of marriage. She had studied ballet into her early twenties. She seemed to fly up the stairway. Their son continued to wail.

Hilda opened the door to Wolfgang's room and switched on his electric lamp. She was startled when she first looked at him. His face was so rigid- the bones beneath his cheeks so high and tight, his lips pursed as though he had been sucking on a sour lemon right there in the bed. She put her arms around him. "Angel boy! Everything is all right. Your mama's here, shhhh!" The boy buried his face into his mother's breast.

"Mother, it was terrible!"

"Wolfgang," she soothed, stroking the blonde hair above his left ear. "You have had a nightmare. Look, the moon is bright. It disturbed your sleep, that is all." The boy settled down, fingering the tears from his eyes, squinting as he was in the stark light of the lamp.

"Mother, there was you, and father- and there was war here in Koblenz. There were soldiers marching through the streets, with guns and swords."

"But the war is over now, dear. The Americans- they will be gone, soon. They are with us now because it is required of them. Your father says they help keep the peace. You must know that they would rather be home? I even feel sorry for them, sometimes. Some of them don't look much older than you, don't you think?" The boy shook his head slowly.

"You know, Wolfgang, the mothers of those American boys cannot wait until they see their sons, again. I know I couldn't tolerate the thought of knowing that you were over in America, so far away from me."

"You never have to worry about that, mother! I will never, ever leave you! Especially to go to America!" The boy's voice was strong and assured.

"Now you go right back to sleep, my angel. You have a full day of school tomorrow." She switched off his light. "Good night."

Wolfgang pulled the quilts up to his chin. The moonbeams were bright against his window. The heavy curtains were parted several inches, permitting a stream of light to illuminate a corner of the bed and a narrow section of floor. He listened as the stairs creaked beneath his mother's feet. Soon, there were muffled voices downstairs. Father would want all of the details, no doubt. Wolfgang was glad that his mother had not asked him for every particular. He would have lied to her. He would not be able to recount the dream to her. There was blood, the splintering of bones, and an eruption of body fluid and bile. Wolfgang closed his eyes and drifted off to sleep.

The next morning, it was a Thursday, Wolfgang was up at his accustomed hour, well before dawn. The house was cold and drafty. He was drawn downstairs by the lights and the fire. His father stoked up the coal heater early most mornings, and then he would return to bed, leaving the empty scuttle next to the stove door. Slowly, the heat would fill the house. Horst also made it his practice to place a pan of milk (which he took from the hospital's stores when the shortages were pronounced) on top of the ceramic tiles on the stove, and Wolfgang gratefully found it steaming gently. He went quickly into the pantry off the kitchen for the cocoa and sugar and just when he re-entered the parlour, his mother unexpectedly burst through the front door.

"Good morning, darling."

"Morning, mother." He could see that it must be quite cold outside. She was apple cheeked, and there was a clear mucous coating at the base of her long nose, which she summarily wiped away with her kerchief, having taken it off the top of her head. Wolfgang was very aware of the white bag beneath her other arm.

"I thought we could use an apple streusel in this house- you have been studying so thoroughly, and your father has been working harder than ever." Wolfgang raced for the bag, his mouth already watering. Heidelhoff Bakery was three streets over and made the very best pastry in the city, according to his father.

"Thank you, mother! I will have a great big piece!"

"Let's make your cocoa first, dear," she said, switching the bag to her left hand. "You stir the pan while I go and cut the coffee cake."

As his mother went into the kitchen, Wolfgang walked over to the stove. He measured out the ingredients and dumped them into the milk pan. Barely two weeks until Christmas! What a wonderful feeling spread through him. There was sure to be a sweet smelling tree, and cookies, cakes and carols to be sung. It was his favorite time of year. And, it was all there in front of him- just like the warm streusel that his mother had brought back in with her into the parlour.

"I have the cup for your cocoa, Wolfgang."

The flakes of pastry melted in his mouth. The top of the streusel was swirled with the most delicious sweet, white frosting, and the apple filling was mixed with just the right quantity of raisins. His father was right, at that. This streusel was the best anywhere!

Just then, his father appeared fully dressed, coming from the base of the stairs. "Good morning, darling. And, good morning, Wolfgang my son."

"Did you sleep well, father?"

"Very deeply, my boy. I trust that you had no further nightmares?"

"No sir. I slept like a log."

"That is good, truly. If your mother will fetch me a slice of that coffee cake, I might just tell you about the little dream that I had last night."

"And what was your dream about, my darling?" asked Hilda with a smile. She handed him a piece of streusel.

"Well, let me tell you directly!" He paused for a bite of the pastry. "I dream, er," he swallowed, "I dreamt that right after Christmas, I took some time off at the hospital and we took a train over to Vienna."

"Oh father! Is that possible!? Do you think we really could?"

"I think it would do us all a great deal of good. I thought that while we were there, we could visit the medical college. Wolfgang, you could get a firsthand look at the lecture halls, the anatomy pavilion, and the laboratories. Why, I'm sure I could arrange for quite a little tour."

"Oh, Horst! That would be just wonderful! We could shop, and how lovely it would be to see the opera!" Hilda's eyes filled with tears. Herr Doktor felt like an older man with two children, looking on at the reaction of his little family.

"That settles it, then. We'll take the train the day after Christmas. I will make all of the arrangements this morning, from the hospital's telephone."

"Thank you! Thank you, father!" Wolfgang ran over and hugged him as hard as he could.

"Careful, boy! You'll break my bones! Now, upstairs with you! You've got to dress for school!"

Later that morning, Horst made his way into the administrative office at Koblenz Hospital. Fraulein Hanna, the pretty, brown haired secretary to the director sat busily at her typewriter, but immediately stopped her work and greeted him with a cool nod. "Good morning, Doktor Von Himmler, may I be of help?"

"Yes, fraulein. I am actually here to make use of the telephone, if it would not be of any great inconvenience?"

"Of course, doktor, the telephone is at your disposal. Doktor Schmidt is attending a civic breakfast at the moment. He would want you to make full use of his office." Horst nodded appreciatively.

"I have decided to take my family on a holiday to Vienna right after Christmas, if the train schedules permit it. I have a son who has a keen interest in the university, there."

"Particularly the medical college, Herr Doktor, I am told," added the fraulein knowingly. "And I am sure that you and your wife will find many other things to do, as well."

"Thank you, fraulein," he said. "Gemutlichkeit! I'm sure we will."

Horst spent the better part of the next hour in contact with old acquaintances at the University of Vienna, making out the itinerary for their trip. When he'd finished, he sat back in Dr. Schmidt's chair and sighed.

It seemed like only a few years had passed since he was a student at the medical college, there. What glorious days those were! What precious days! He closed his eyes and could clearly see the magnificent buildings- the great State Opera House, the grand Hofburg with its Imperial Library, the Rathaus. What would become of Vienna now that the war was lost? He shuddered to think of such a city losing any of its far-reaching influence. It would be the grandest of holidays to go back, with his wife and son.

There was a sharp knock on the door, and then a heavy set, well-dressed man in his early thirties entered the office, holding a monocle up to his right eye. Von Himmler, lounging as he was at the director's desk was glad that he was not Dr. Schmidt.

"Herr Doktor Von Himmler? You look very comfortable. The chair fits you well, eh?"

"Doktor Pfanmuller, how are you?" Von Himmler squirmed uneasily.

"Fine. Don't mind me, I have come in to use the telephone myself." Von Himmler leapt from the chair. "Of course, Herr Doktor." Horst had never learned to trust this man. He was sure that Dr. Schmidt would receive a distorted report from Pfanmuller- something to the effect that he had been found sleeping quite soundly in that comfortable chair.

"Have you been getting sufficient rest at night, Herr Doktor?"

"We're all somewhat tired, I suppose. I am taking my family on holiday to Vienna."

"That will refresh you. A glorious city to visit at the New Year."

"Yes, my wife and son are very excited. As for me, I'm not getting any younger. Now would be a good time to go." Von Himmler was not at ease, making small talk with a young man whom he considered to be entirely too ruthless. "Nice seeing you, Doktor Pfanmuller."

"Give my regards to your family, please." A flash of light glinted off the face of the monocle when he smiled.

"Thank you," said Horst, and then he strode past him.

That night, when the doktor returned home following his evening rounds, young Wolfgang was wide awake, waiting for him right at the front door. "Good evening, father!" There was a particular brightness in Wolfgang's eyes. Shiny expectations;

"Hello, son." Horst removed his coat and kissed Hilda as she came to him. "Get me a beer, dear. I'll take it in the parlour." Hilda uncapped the beer and brought it to him. Horst pulled his stein from the shelf above the stove and poured out a foamy head. Wolfgang could stand the suspense no longer.

"Are we going, father?" he cried out in a high-pitched voice. "Are we going to Vienna?"

"Of course, my son." And then the little family formed a tight little huddle and hugged in celebration. "Now, after I've had my beer, I'll tell you and your mother about the plans which I've made for us. But first, how about those tests, today? Did you do well?"

"Oh yes, father! The tests were easy for me!"

"Excellent! They were easy because you studied thoroughly. Your schooling is so important, Wolfgang. In fact, you'll learn just how important when we go to Vienna."

"And my husband. Where shall we stay on our holiday?"

"The Hostel," he replied. "It is right on the Ringstrasse."

"And father, the Opera House, will it be close by?"

"Yes, and it being the height of the Christmas season, the opera, and the rest of the city, for that matter, will be unusually busy. Vienna will be bustling, my dears! And, we'll be right in the center of it all! Herr Doktor Richtenstein, my school chum, is obtaining orchestra section passes for us. We'll have the best seats in the house for Wagner!"

"A Wagner, Horst?" cried Hilda. "What a happy Christmas for us! With luck, Doktor Richtenstein may have even examined the schedule for the opera before buying our tickets. Darling, does he know what your favorite movement is? Did you tell him that you just had to experience 'Ride of the Valkyries'?"

"I do not deserve it, Hilda, but Henry had the schedule and I advised him which night we would most like to attend."

"Father! I love you!" Young Wolfgang hugged him hard. "Father, what is a Valkyrie?"

Horst smiled, looking at his wife with a gleam in his eyes. "When our hero dies with his sword, he is escorted to Valhalla by a troupe of the most delightful winged creatures. These are the Valkyries."

"Father, may I be a Valkyrie?"

"My son," he replied with a laugh, "most Valkyries are female. For you, however, we will make an exception."

"Father, I will grow wings and fly. You will see." Wolfgang looked up at him hopefully.

"Now Wolfgang! To bed! We'll talk more about our trip tomorrow. For now, I need some time to talk to your mother."

The boy nodded, then headed towards the stairway.

"I'll be upstairs shortly, Wolfgang," said his mother. She turned to her husband. "You've made us so happy! You're so wonderful, Horst!"

"I suppose I am, er, wonderful." And the two of them fell into each other's arms in laughter.

For the remaining members of the American Expeditionary Forces stationed in Germany and throughout the whole of Western Europe, the Great War was still not entirely over. The German surrender on November 11th had brought an end to the fighting and horrible gassing along the front, but the subsequent allied occupation had created additional tensions, spawning a small but steady wave of isolated atrocities against the defenseless citizens of the defeated Fatherland.

Enacting the Armistice was a time consuming, thankless job. This task was assigned for the most part to men who had originally answered the call to arms intent on putting a swift end to the 'war to end all wars' on a continent a half-a-world away gone mad.

With the combat concluded, those doughboys assigned to remain in Germany would not be destined to receive the hero's welcome afforded their more fortunate, though equally deserving counterparts who quickly returned to the ticker tape and feasting in first, the eastern port cities of the U.S., and later, in the towns and rural villages across that great land. There would not be the same wild, thunderous displays of appreciation when the Second Infantry trickled homeward some months later. For even the victors in battle desired to put the inconveniences, heartache, and ugliness of mortal conflict behind them rapidly, in order that life be returned to that semblance called normalcy, taking hold the peaceful, rewarding future which their collective sacrifice had guaranteed.

Among the Americans stationed in Koblenz, primarily the Second Infantry, was the Second Motor Mechanics Regiment hailing from the upper Midwest. Shipped over in the autumn of 1917, originally seventy-two members strong, the regiment had suffered twenty-two casualties during the final thirteen months of the conflict amid some of the most intense fighting of the entire war. Now frustrated in their desire to return to the states, these men were allocated meaningless tasks which, when added to the whole of the operation, were designed to create a high profile of organized troops in the community and out in the surrounding countryside.

In the Blue Bird beer hall the night of December 13th, three Americans from the Second Motor Mechanics sat at a table near the entrance, celebrating the end of another pointless, twelve-hour tour. One of the soldiers, seated with his back to the door, drank steadily from a stein of dark, bitter brew, watching the beer maids in their ruffled blouses and velvet green skirts as they hoisted exceedingly full trays on their shoulders, picking their way through the aisle ways amongst the throngs of happy customers. He wore a big, strong face with bushy, black eyebrows and his nose was rounded, almost to the point of looking puffy.

"These German girls are strong and hardy!" he said loudly. "And, they can put up one hell of a fight between the sheets, eh?"

"Broomhilda!" shouted the second, and they roared with laughter. This man was broad shouldered, almost pudgy beneath his brown uniform. His hair was close cropped, his nose was long and his chin was short and jutted. His dark eyes darted nervously about the room. When he laughed, he cackled so infectiously that even the locals seated at nearby tables who spoke no English couldn't keep themselves from turning around and smiling.

"The French women are tops," said the third. "As you know, I fell in love twice in Alsace." He had a boyish look to him and his light hair was slicked back smartly. His hazel eyes were kind. He was thinner than his fellows and wore an ever-present smile on his thin lips.

"That's right, Dick," said the first, furrowing his heavy brow, "we remember well. The going rate was twenty francs each-"

"No, Sam," interrupted the second with a grin, "this devil whittled the price down to two for the twenty francs!"

"And all in the same night! Dick, you dirty, filthy, flea ridden dog, you!" said the first. "Now tell us, the truth be told, did you have two at once?" They roared with laughter, louder than before and Dick took a huge drink from his mug and didn't put it back down on the table again until his red face regained its original hue.

"I cannot, in good conscience hand out details of my wild nights in France on the grounds that I am a gentleman," Dick said grandly. "If the details were made available in all their splendor to the likes of you two north woods dandies, you'd conspire to pitch me into the icy waters of the Rhine with a sack of rocks lashed to my ankle out of shear, wanton envy."

"That will be the day," said Sam, the one seated with his back to the main doorway. "You know Dick, for a week or so, the big Finn, here, and I wondered what the hell was happening to all our brandy, eh Toivo?"

"We wondered, Sam and me, where all our brandy was going," echoed the Finn.

"Now Toivo, you fess up to Dick, here! You just tell him what was goin' on in the latrine- you know, with the brandy? Our brandy?" Toivo blinked and the expression on his mug went from blank to kind of a half frown.

Dick was smiling. He knew, of course, that this had been rehearsed for his benefit, and he eagerly anticipated Toivo's tale.

"I saw Dick with his bloomers down 'round his ankles. He was all stooped over, too, and pouring brandy onto his crotch and rubbin' it in all over his privates!" Toivo gasped for air as the three of them shuddered with glee. "His privates was all red, and swollen!"

"Horse dung! You're just full of horse dung!" Dick cried as he motioned for yet another tray of steins.

Sam said, "no question in my mind, Dick, that you were taking it upon yourself to kill off your French pox with our good brandy! You selfishly deprived Toivo, here, and myself, of several good drunks. And what did you accomplish in all this? You saved twenty francs, eh?"

"I get the total picture, Sam. You and Toivo are so damn tight with your billfolds that you'd actually dream up the fanciest of tales just so's I'd buy the next round of beer, out of turn I might add."

Sam drained the contents of his mug. He was working on a good drunk like the others and was fast getting in the mood for some female companionship. "One more round and then I'm headed down to the river. I don't know about you sorry sons-of-bitches."

"The river, it is," said Dick with a knowing nod.

"Sam's gonna see Sophie, tonight. The pretty, blonde haired one." Toivo looked at Dick. "What about you?"

"Nothing for me tonight, thank you; I think I'll just sip some schnapps."

The winter's night was clear and cold and Dick felt in his pocket for his full flask of schnapps on their way down to the red light district. The hour was late and on the street corners and in the alleys adjacent to the houses of prostitution, there was an unmistakable drunkenness in the air. American doughboys stood in small groups, drinking and smoking, and their mood was festive and spirited. Perhaps they anticipated their imminent return home, for rumors had spread that some of those soldiers still in Germany would be home for the holidays. One man's wishful thought, was Dick's view of it.

He stood off by himself, taking frequent nips from his flask while Toivo and Rutledge entered one of the whorehouses. These old, stone sided buildings stood here and there between the rows of warehouses. Pale red lights shown in the frosted windows, the only advertising required. Dick thought he detected a hint of Christmas in the air. More wishful thinking; He disdained visiting the prostitutes himself, having only recently recovered from a case of lice which had imbedded themselves in his crotch and had ferociously fought off his initial attempts at extermination. He finally did succeed in eradicating the parasites after shaving and treating the area with a diluted lye solution. This remedy had been taken in total privacy. Toivo's wheezing account at the beer hall was just mere coincidence. Dick was sure the flap on the tent had been tied down before he'd stripped naked. He had inherited the bugs while in love with two beautiful French girls east of the front and had promised himself never to go looking for love again as long as he was stationed in Europe.

A fellow private approached him on the street. The man reeked of beer and tobacco and he thrust his unshaven mug into Dick's face without invitation. "Evening there, bud. You take a roll in the hay tonight?"

"Not hardly," Dick replied, mildly irritated, taking a sip of the schnapps.

"What you got goin' there?" asked the soldier, gesturing at the metal flask.

"Here," Dick said, offering a drink.

"Thanks. How about a cigarette?"

"That will make it an even trade."

The soldier pulled out his tobacco pouch and papers and deftly rolled up two cigarettes, one handed. He offered one to Dick and they lit up together. "Where you from, friend?" Dick asked, pulling on the schnapps again and puffing merrily on the cigarette.

"I'm from Three Oaks. Three Oaks, Michigan; That's about thirty-five miles south of St. Joe." They shook hands.

"Dick Chapman, Chilicothe, Ohio. Second Motor Mechanics."

"Hank Warren, Second Infantry, at your service. What you got to go back to over in Chilicothe?"

Dick smiled, forgetting about Germany for a minute. He had a lot in common with this man standing beside him. They were both boys when they'd shipped over in '17, fresh faced and eager to get the job done.

Now, after withstanding the thunderstorms of death, they were tired, shadowy, unshaven and drunk most every night. Their only joy came from their memories, when their sheer innocence dictated the haphazard decisions of youth. They had been tarnished, like brass sprayed with water and allowed to set. Their lives would shine again, one day, but the grim spots were cast, and no amount of scrubbing would rub them away for good.

"Chilicothe is old Indian country. My folks have a farm just south of town. In the spring, after we go through with the first plowin', we wait for a good rain, us kids, then walk the furrows and you wouldn't believe the arrowheads! They pop up like dandelions."

"What do you grow down there?"

"Corn mostly; Winter wheat, alfalfa- we don't have a real big operation. My dad works about sixty acres. We've got eighty acres, total."

Dick handed Hank the flask.

"Sounds like nice country. Bet you can't wait to get back, huh?" Dick flicked his ash onto the cobblestones at the edge of the street.

"You said it, friend. You from a farm family?"

"Not exactly," replied Hank. "My gramps opened up a feather bone factory and my dad's runnin' the place, now. Biggest employer in town."

Down the lane, a brief altercation erupted between two soldiers. Voices were raised and there was pushing and shoving but no punches. Moments later, one man had his arm around the other.

"They're stinking drunk," said Dick with a laugh. "Just like me- 'cept I never been a mean drunk. Before I get to that point, I jus' throw up. What do you make in your feather bone factory?"

"Started by makin' women's stays outta turkey quills. Now we added pillows, quilts, upholstery stuffing, and we process down and ship it all over the country."

"I'll drink to that, Hank, especially to them lady's underthings." And Hank handed the flask back after taking another swig.

"Damn-it-all! Can you think of really being home at Christmas, bud?" Hank asked, and Dick saw that his eyes were coated with mist. "I sure miss everybody. We're nothin' but a pack of animals over here!" He gestured at the party in the street all around them. "Hell! You can just see why everybody hates our guts."

"The beer's good," Dick said softly. Hank smiled.

"You're right! The beer's damn good over here. I'm probably gonna miss this damn beer! They've had a thousand years practice over here makin' it."

"You gonna miss any particular whore, Hank?"

"Hell no! I can't believe they got whorehouses like this, right smack in the middle of town."

Another quarter hour passed, and Toivo walked up and joined them so discreetly that Dick barely noticed him. The conversation continued on for a few moments until Toivo pinched Dick's shoulder and pulled him aside. "Sam wants you."

"What the hell!" cried Dick obnoxiously. "Does Sam need help stickin' it in? Or maybe pullin' it out? What is he, stuck together with that poor bitch like a couple dogs?! Son-of-a-cur Toivo! What gives here?" Hank and Dick laughed so hard that they were in tears together, far gone in liquor on this icy December night, sharing the moment like two old friends.

"Toivo?" asked Hank, "what's a Toivo?"

Toivo thrust out his chest and glowered at the stranger. Dick stretched his arm out before the rooster chest, restraining his buddy. "Toivo Ahonen is a big, fucking Finn," he announced. "You'd best not be on his bad side!"

Toivo could stand this no longer. A great urgency took hold of him. His manner alerted Dick immediately to the fact that something was wrong and needed tending. "The back door," Toivo whispered. "Sam wants you to come with me to the back door."

Dick sensed that Toivo was quaking and uneasy and he shook Hank's hand and wished him the best and joined Toivo on a fast paced trot to the rear of the whorehouse. He was led through the dark shadows, past the back door to an old stone fence behind two bushy evergreens. Sam appeared from between the bushes.

"Dick," he said, "there's trouble here. We've got to move on out."

"What is it?" Dick asked. He felt quite drunk but was determined to clear his thoughts, to make rational decisions despite his stupor. "I'm in the sauce, Sam. Let's go sleep it off. The trouble will have gone far away come sun-up."

"Dick! You don't understand. Our girl's hurt. She hit- hit her head-real hard." Sam led him firmly by the arm around the corner of the stone wall. A girl with light hair lay on the cold ground, unconscious. Her dress was off and her heavy, white slip was pulled off one shoulder. She was wrapped in a wool blanket.

"My God!" Dick dropped to one knee and felt for her pulse. It was rapid. "She's really hurt, Sam. We have got to get her some help!" He pivoted and took one step towards the rear door. Toivo and Sam both stopped him in his tracks.

"Dick, the Madame knows us, and knows we were with the girl. You just can't go back in there."

"Well, we sure as hell can't just leave her here, either. She isn't in good shape at all." Dick rapped Sam on the chest, which was his habit when a good idea popped into his head. "Look, I'm going back out to the street. There's plenty of drinking going on out there, still. I'm sure somebody can give me directions to a doctor's house in the neighborhood."

"That should work, Dick. Toivo and I will be ready to hoist her." The alarm in Rutledge's face bespoke his perilous circumstance.

The sudden pounding on the front entrance below awakened Dr. Von Himmler instantly. He leapt from his bed, causing Hilda to sit up in alarm and rotate her hips, stepping into her slippers in one fluid movement. Doktor Horst, due to his many years as a practicing physician, was conditioned to be fully alert upon awakening from even the deepest of sleeps.

He tramped down the stairs, with Hilda gliding behind. This was not the first time that someone in need of treatment had beaten on his door in the wee hours by any means. Birthing babies was a typical occupation in the early hours, as was treating the more ghastly injuries resulting from the sport of bar brawling. Doktor Horst switched on the lamps and, without hesitation, opened his door.

Three American soldiers attired in their camel brown uniforms walked right into the house. One carried the limp body of a young, blonde girl, wrapped in a dark blanket. Doktor looked at the blonde tresses, which were stained with blood.

"Doctor Von Himmler," addressed one, and as he spoke, Von Himmler, who understood English well, surmised that they all had been drinking quite heavily. "We were told to bring- er, to bring her here- that you could provide medical care. Th- this girl needs help." The girl was laid carefully on the floor. Von Himmler said nothing, going to one knee. Hilda had gone for his medical bag and now she returned with it and as she set it down at his side, for he was determining the extent of the girl's injuries, her own left breast protruded from the neckline of her nightgown. She stood up quickly, re-aligning her clothing, and as she did so, she looked over at the soldier who had carried the girl in and he was staring at her chest with bloodshot eyes beneath his bushy, black brows.

Von Himmler, aware that the injured girl's breathing was shallow and that her pulse raced weakly, was not surprised to find a collapsed area of skull bone beneath the gaping wound which he now explored with his fingertips at the rear of her head. There was little, he knew, that could be done- the injury was surely a mortal one. He unsnapped his bag and, lifting her head, gently placed a white towel beneath the wound and carefully returned her head to rest upon the floor.

The soldier whom had originally spoken upon their sudden arrival was leaning over the girl with his hands on his knees, a look of concern etched on his young face. "How is she, doc? Is it real bad?" Von Himmler pouted, which he generally did when searching for the right words with which to hand out grim news.

"I am sorry. There is nothing that I can do," he said in excellent English. "The back of her skull is crushed. She shall never regain her senses."

Dick placed a hand over his face, turned and looked at Toivo and Rutledge and said, "this ain't so good, fellas. Not good at all."

"My God! Sh-she j-just fell back!" explained Toivo slurrily. "Sam says sh-she fell back!"

"Shut up! Stupid, little pig tailed slut!" bellowed Rutledge. "Look at the goddam mess she's gotten us into!" It was just then that the girl took her final breath.

"Doktor, there's nothing left to do?" asked Dick in disbelief.

Von Himmler wiped his bloody fingertips on a wet cloth that Hilda had somberly fetched for him. "We must call for an ambulance," he said firmly. "And, I must speak with the authorities. There will be an official inquiry made into this matter, I can assure you. The three of you had better have a good explanation at the ready for your role in this. From what I gather, you face some serious charges."

Rutledge's broad face reddened noticeably as the doktor chastised them. He suddenly reached out and grabbed Hilda's gown at the neckline and ripped a gaping hole in the fabric, exposing her breasts, and as she squealed and crossed her arms over her brown-capped nipples, he swung her around, his hammy hand about her waist, and clutched her back tightly to his chest with the one vise-like arm, freeing his other hand to squeeze and poke cruelly at that part of her breasts which she could not protect.

"You filthy American bastard!" cried out the doktor, enraged with the liberties that the soldier was taking with his attractive wife.

"Der swine!" shouted Hilda. "Horst! Be careful! Don't do anything rash!"

"You American swine!" continued the doktor, "you let go of my wife and get out of this house at once!!"

Rutledge threw Hilda into the grasp of Toivo and stepped up to the old man. Dick placed his arm between the two but Rutledge shoved him aside, closing in on Von Himmler menacingly. "Herr Doktor, the old codger that you are, seems to me like you still need a lesson in hospitality, eh?"

"Murderer," judged Horst, noting that the girl on the floor had turned blue with death. "How will it feel to dangle by your neck from a braided rope?" Each word he enunciated with such conviction that a volley of spittle misted onto Rutledge's stricken face. And then he laughed at Rutledge, and then looked at him in highhanded disgust.

The American tightened his right fist and stepped into the doktor with a fearsome blow to the abdomen, and followed that up with a whole series of punches, all to the midsection. Von Himmler reeled and would have gladly fallen under the torrent of blows, but Rutledge placed his left arm around the slumping shoulders, and then began upper cutting his right from down below, digging into the flabby underbelly over and over again.

"Sam! Stop!" yelled Dick, "you'll kill him, too!"

Hilda screamed and struggled in Toivo's arms and then, without warning, a considerable weight crashed down onto the big Finn, knocking him at once to the floor in a heap. It was young Wolfgang, who, having been awakened by all the commotion, had snuck halfway down the stairs and then just stood, like a paying customer in an overhanging balcony, witnessing the drama below. He had stood there enthralled by the scene at first, but his enchantment with the spectacle of three foreign soldiers brooding over the dying girl had given way to a helpless terror the instant they started to fondle his mother and then suddenly his father began absorbing the blows to his stomach and then the boy sprang into action, leaping down from the sixth stair the moment that his mother had screamed. He dove headlong at the big man holding his mother. He had landed on top of the massive shoulders, knocking both the man and his mother to the floor.

Wolfgang's fingernails were quite long and sharp, and now he dug them into the neck flesh of his mother's attacker with every ounce of his strength, twisting and gouging the skin folds in a wild frenzy. Toivo gathered himself and jumped to his feet, and all in one motion threw his attacker back against the thick, plastered wall behind him with a heavy thud. The boy crumpled lifelessly to the floor, coming to rest atop the fresh corpse of the young prostitute.

Hilda was hysterical. Her husband lay in the parlour, doubled up in the fetal position, moaning softly. Her young son lay motionless on top of the blue tinged blonde. She turned and faced her attackers like a mother bear whose cub has just been bludgeoned, fearless and full of hate.

"You will pay for this!!" she informed Rutledge, slugging his cheek with all of her might. He easily sidestepped her onslaught, and at the same time felt Dick's hand taking hold of his collar.

"Sam! Let's get out of here! Now!! Before the military police come!!"

Toivo was standing over the boy, praying that he was not too seriously hurt. A trickle of blood dripped from one small ear.

Dick opened up the front door and the three of them streamed out into the night. "Quick! Let's make some time!" As Dick dashed up the lane with Toivo and Rutledge at his heels, the desperate cry of the doktor's wife could distinctly be heard, sending an alarm out through the cold air. By the time Dick was completely out of breath, they were three blocks away and the cries for help were but a faint wail on the edges of the long moon shadows.

CHAPTER TWO

Chilicothe, Ohio
May, 1955

Dick Chapman looked out through the big front window wall of his hardware store in sheer disgust. A big wind had whipped up what had started innocently as a few sprinkles into a driving rainstorm, sending the late afternoon shoppers scurrying for cover out on Main Street, and bringing to an immediate halt any outdoor activities taking place anywhere in his city. 'Damn the rain, anyway,' he thought to himself. There goes the backyard barbecue party that his wife, Lucy, had been making preparations for all day long. It wasn't to be a social event by any means. The invites included their twenty-five year old son, Dean and his wife, Sherri, who in turn were escorting the guest of honor, Dick and Lucy's first grandchild, tiny, one-year old Todd. The next-door neighbors, the Prescotts, were supposed to drop by, as well as Dick's brother Vic and his wife, Nell. Just a cozy little Saturday evening get together with friends and family out on the patio, and now this downpour was threatening to wash it all away.

    The skies had suddenly grown so dark that as Dick faced the front window with his arms crossed, he could make out perfectly well a mirror image of himself in the glass, with the pelting rain serving as a backdrop from without. Dick was of medium height and build, and there was something strong and firm about him even as he advanced into the twilight of middle age. The busy work around his store, all of the hefting, carrying, and stocking had kept his upper body toned and rugged looking beneath his starched, white shirts, as befitted the handyman look of a hardware store owner. He was now fifty-six years old, and with his grayish hair thinning appreciably up on top, the heavy bags hanging like Christmas stockings beneath each eye, and the crow's feet at the corners of those eyes extending down along the ridges of his pale cheeks until they more closely resembled the imprints from a barnyard full of chickens, he looked every day of his age, and then some.

His life had been a struggle, but not without its just rewards. He had served his country in what had become known as World War I, although he would forever refer to it as the 'Great War', with distinction. Shortly after returning home from Europe, he had received his discharge, at which time he moved back to the family farm to help his father and two brothers with the chores. He had known since his mid-teens that the farming life would not be for him, but he was aware that the work ethic which it had ingrained in his every muscle and sinew would directly fortify his chances for success in any future endeavor that he might choose. Dick firmly believed that hard, physical toil during a boy's formative years was every bit as important as a good education in rounding out the young man into a productive and useful citizen. According to Thomas Edison, genius was one-percent inspiration and ninety-nine percent perspiration, and Dick was a true disciple of this premise.

Dean, his only son (they also had a twenty-eight year old daughter, Sandy, living in Pennsylvania with her husband), having just joined the ranks of parenthood the previous year, had benefited from his farming heritage. Dick had assigned his son a host of chores around the house as he grew up, and the sometimes overly stern father had made sure that the jobs were done right the first time. The boy had gone on to star on the local high school football team, and Coach Stubbs had gone out of his way on several occasions to compliment Dick on Dean's tireless efforts during the weekday practice sessions.

"Mr. Chapman, your son pushes his teammates so damn hard it makes my job a pleasure," Stubbs had said one Saturday afternoon after a big win. "You gotta be proud of Dean."

Dean had attended Ohio U over in Athens but a knee injury had ended his football career in early October of his freshman year. He stayed in school, and received his engineering degree. His football glory days had been cut short, but in spite of his bitter disappointment, he was able to channel his energies toward scholastic success. Dick always believed it was that early work ethic which had made the difference.

Dick reminded himself to broach the subject that evening when he saw his son. Baby Todd certainly wouldn't be taking out the trash for a few more years, at least, but Dick was curious to see how Dean planned to raise the little fellow.

Dick had left the family farm, then, and taken a job at the Aberdeen Dairy delivering milk, eggs and butter in town. He took over a regular route, and within three years, he had inherited a second one, as well. He worked long and hard for the next fifteen years, applying that work ethic which he pegged his future on. When the Depression loosened its grip sufficiently to permit Dick to take out a business loan, he jumped at the chance to open a hardware store in downtown Chilicothe. It proved to be the smartest move of his life.

The telephone rang. Dick spun around on his heel and made his way through his empty store. It was almost five o'clock. In another hour it would be time to close up shop. He picked up the black receiver, which was mounted on a support beam next to the cash register. "Chapman's Hardware, this is Dick speaking. Hello, Chapman's. Can I help you? Hello?"

Dick hung up. That was funny. That was the fifth or sixth such call that he had answered in the past week. There had been someone there- someone on the other end of the line. Sometimes he could hear breathing- it was faint but he could hear it. There was the rushing air sound, as the caller moved the handset from his or her ear back to the base of the phone. Then, the almost musical sound as the receiver was replaced on the cradle. And then, the click; "Has to be kids playin' around," Dick said to himself. The phone rang, again.

"Chapman's."

"Hi, honey. I just came in from the garage. I moved the lawn furniture in from the patio. I think my hair is ruined. Is it pouring downtown, too?"

"Poor Lucy," said Dick, his voice laced with exaggerated irritation to somehow make her feel better. "This has been one rainy spring. The farmers are prayin' their seed doesn't just rot in the ground."

"To hell with the farmers," she said. "What about my cookout? I've got the potato salad, the macaroni salad, the chuck wagon beans, and the jello salad all molded. I wanted to light the Japanese lanterns tonight. There aren't any bugs, and the air's real mild. It's raining cats and dogs."

"We can cook in the garage, if we have to," said Dick. "You never know, it might clear up." He squatted down and looked through the windows at the narrow band of sky that was visible above the roofline of the buildings across the street. It was pitch black. "Lucy, they got a tornado watch on or anything?"

"I've had the radio on. They said widely scattered showers."

"Sure, as in widely scattered over every square inch of southern Ohio."

"The grill and the charcoal are in the garage. Honey, would you pick up a case of beer on your way home?"

"Sure. Now don't you worry, doll, we'll have a good time come hell or high water."

"Most likely the high water, I would say." Dick chuckled at her wit.

"See you in an hour, then."

Dick hung up the phone and looked up as a customer came through the door. She was a young woman with an umbrella, which she collapsed down and shook vigorously over the carpet mat just inside the entrance. She then leaned the umbrella up against the sill of the front window.

"We've got the rain today, don't we?" Dick said with a smile. "How can I help you?" He decided that she must be in urgent need of something to brave such nasty weather.

"Hello." Dick didn't recognize her- probably her first time in the store. She was striking. Her eyes were deep green, her lips full and moist, and her cheekbones were well defined beneath her smooth, velvety complexion. She cut quite a nice figure in the little green dress that she wore. Her jet black hair was up in a bun. He figured it was nice and long when she let it down, most likely way past her shoulders. She leaned forward slightly as she adjusted the heel on her shoe. Dick saw lots of cleavage. He looked way down her dress, in spite of his gentlemanly instincts. He wasn't positive if she'd done that on purpose or not. Most likely she had. In any event, he very much liked the dress.

"Good afternoon," she said, her eyes glinting devilishly as they met his own. She'd adjusted that shoe on purpose, he decided then and there. "My husband sent me down here, although I, for one was pretty sure you'd already closed."

"Here til six Monday through Saturday, closed on Sunday," he advised her.

"I'm so glad." She smiled and looked down at the floor. "This is really kind of an embarrassment for me. You see, Jim, that is to say, my husband, is working on our toilet."

"God bless him," said Dick. "That's an honest project if ever there was one."

"Anyhow, he sent me down for a new wax ring- to seal the bowl at the floor. You carry those, don't you?"

"Of course. Now you wait right here. I'll go and get a ring out of our stock room." Dick walked quickly into the rear of the store, ducked under the 'employees only' sign, climbed a ladder back there, reached into a box on a high shelf, and came back with a toilet ring.

"It's two-nineteen, plus tax," he announced.

"Why you're fast for an-"

"Old man?" Dick asked with a mock frown. The young lady actually blushed.

"Excuse me, I didn't mean to imply that you're, you know, too old to do your job." She was feeling awkward, and in need of his help.

"Of course not, Mrs.-"

"Thomas."

"Mrs. Thomas. Dick Chapman at your service. No, in fact, I took your comment as a compliment. Thank you."

A look of assuagement washed across her features. "Oh, good!" she cried, "I have such respect for a mature man." She handed him three dollars as the cash register rang.

"That isn't to say that I might not be retiring in the next couple years."

"Oh, really?"

"Seventy-three cents is your change." He bagged the ring unconsciously. "Yes, I'm thinking of selling the place, actually. Been thinking about it for a while. Next week my son and I are heading up to Michigan's Upper Peninsula for a week of fishing. I'd like to retire while I can still enjoy things."

"Oh, say, that sounds like quite a nice trip. Jim and I made it to Mackinaw City once. We've heard upper Michigan can be a beautiful place." Dick smiled. Mrs. Thomas noted the far off look in the hardware man's eyes. He sure had big bags underneath.

"Guess I don't know what I'd do the rest of the year if I did sell out. I could fish plenty in this area, I know that. Got some great bass fishing in these little farm ponds around here."

There was a terrific clap of thunder and then the lights went out in the store. It was dark as night. Mrs. Thomas shrieked.

"Lord have mercy!" cried Dick. The young woman was groping in the sudden darkness like a windmill in a hurricane. She latched on to Mr. Hardware in her fright. She grabbed an overflowing handful of crotch and held on, obviously convinced that she was squeezing a fleshy knob of stomach at the belt line. Dick's eyes watered in the dark.

"Everything's fine, Mrs. Thomas," he managed to say. He eased out of her vise-like grip and located a flashlight beneath the counter. He switched on the beam and could see that the poor girl was, indeed, terrified of the storm.

"Heaven's sakes!" she cried. "I'm sorry, Mr. Chapman, for acting like such a baby." She smoothed out her dress as she spoke. "Lightning and thunder do scare the daylights out of me. And when the power goes off, why-" She put her right hand over her heart and tried to catch her breath. Dick had the light trained on her and once again admired the ample curves of her firm figure. The accidental fondling of his genitals had excited him. If he weren't such a damn gentleman he'd just walk over and kiss her hard and slowly hike up that dress and if she gave him the green light he'd go ahead and take her. LIKE HELL! He was a coward and had never had an extra-marital affair.

"I can escort you to the door, Mrs. Thomas." Dick made sure she had the bag with her. He approached her and placed his hand gently against the small of her back, training the flashlight at the ceiling as he escorted her out. Dick aimed the light at the exit. It appeared that the power would not be coming on anytime soon. He would let her out and then close up the place. They walked slowly to the door. She was really undulating her hips, exaggerating a full swing of her rear end from side to side with each step as though to clearly advertise her libido to him, letting him sense the ripe availability of her sex if he was man enough to conquer it. By the time they reached her umbrella, Dick had slipped his hand softly down her backside and onto her voluptuous behind. He let go of her when he discerned that she had not bothered to wear panties to his hardware store.

Outside, the sky was brightening up, though the rain continued to patter on the sidewalk.

"Do come back again, Mrs. Thomas," Dick said with a bow. "Hopefully on your next visit, our lights will stay on, at least." He opened the door for her as she extended the frame of her umbrella.

"Would you say, Mr. Chapman, that one size fits all, of these I mean?" she asked as she held up the bag containing the ring.

"You're darn tootin'. Standard size. If your husband has trouble with it, bring it back. Everything in our store is guaranteed."

"I'm so glad. I'll be running along, then. Thank you."

"Goodnight," Dick said, and then he closed the door behind her.

Dick let out a big sigh as he approached the phone. With the power out in the city, Lucy would really be throwing a fit. He dialed his home number reluctantly, with the assistance of the flashlight.

"Got the candles lit?" he asked her.

"Candles? That would be a charming touch. Honey, you're such a romantic. Hey, I think the rain is easing up."

"Isn't your power off? It's pitch black at the store. We had a major bolt of lightning downtown. I had a customer at the time-thank God there was only one! It was a real adventure, believe me." Dick put a hand on his groin and scratched.

"Have you called the Board of Light and Power?"

"No. I just figured they knew all about it."

"I'll call for you, dear. Why don't you close up. Don't forget the beer."

Dick locked the front door and, peering at his watch, was happy to see that he was only closing ten minutes early. The sky had lightened further, and now emitted an eerie, lemonade tinted light on the sidewalk and street. It continued to rain, but the droplets were much finer now. Their cookout might be salvageable, yet. Mrs. Thomas had one fine ass.

He still needed the flashlight while emptying out the cash register, then made his way toward the rear of the store and turned off the bank of light switches along the back wall. He guessed that the electricity would be on shortly- probably within an hour or two. The city's line crews were on call, and they liked the overtime.

Dick walked through the stockroom, past the bins full of plumbing parts, the cases of wood and masonry nails, and the racks of unsold garden tools and exited by way of the delivery entrance out into the alley behind.

He dodged the pools of rainwater that collected in the moonscape that was the parking area behind the store. His bulbous, 1953 black Buick was back there, the water beading on the well waxed exterior. He climbed right into the car and then slipped on the wire-rimmed glasses from the soft case in his breast pocket. Dick was nearsighted, and needed the glasses whenever he drove. He also wore them at sporting events, whenever he played golf, and at the picture show because Lucy refused to sit up front with him. His ophthalmologist had prepared him for the worst- upon his next visit he would require bifocals full time.

Dick stopped at Don's Party Store and picked up the beer, then headed straight home. The clouds were beginning to part and he was encouraged to see that people were out in their yards, already tidying up from the brief windstorm, picking up broken branches and raking the leaves that had swirled and landed on their neatly manicured lawns.

Lucy had the garage door open. As Dick pulled up the driveway, he spotted her as she made her way into the backyard with an armful of lawn furniture. Her retreating silhouette reflected that farmer's wife look of hers- stout and solid in her blue housedress, forward leaning and in constant motion. That wife of his sure worked like a horse. He loved her for it- almost the way he had loved her for sex in the old days. She had acted like a dirty girl back then, though he knew she only acted that way with him. She had been his naughty whore- exactly like the two girls in France he'd met during the war.

Dick climbed out of the car and pulled the case of beer from the rear seat. The air smelled fresh and clean from the hard rain, and the birds were singing happily up in the big elm trees that surrounded their two story, red brick bungalow. The Prescott's beagle dog, Roscoe, came from around the back side of their brick home and hurled himself savagely against the white picket fence which stood along the edge of the Chapman's drive, barking fiercely. "You son-of-a-bitch," said Dick.

"Roscoe!" came the cry from behind the lilac bushes beyond the property line, "You bad dog!!" As Dick watched, the animal seemed to lower his eyes somberly, then turned tail and disappeared into the greenery.

"At least you remembered the beer," said Lucy, wiping at her brow as she re-entered the garage. "You're just in time to wheel the grill out. We'd better get the fire started." Her light brown hair was somewhat wind whipped. Her pretty blue eyes were clear and strong. Some of the pounds which she had packed on over the years were nestled under her chin, and this served to further strengthen the resolve which was reflected on her wide red cheeks and full, ruby lipped mouth.

"Can't I have a beer first?" he asked in jest.

"After we light the charcoal," she retorted.

He set down the beer case, took hold of the handles on the old, square shaped grill, and wheeled it across the wet grass and onto the patio stones set in adjacent to their back porch. "Darling, the yard looks great," he said, aware that she had already strung the Japanese lanterns around the parameter of the patio.

Lucy gently pushed him aside with her elbow, her arms laden with the charcoal and lighter fluid. "Get out of my way," she ordered. "Now you go get that beer on ice- then bring us a cold one."

"Want to split one?" he asked.

"Yea, bring me a little glass."

Lucy heaped a pile of briquettes into the grill and saturated it with lighter fluid. The warm evening air was whisking away the moisture from the top of the gray patio stones at her feet. Unless another storm rumbled through, the evening would go as planned.

Dick returned with a cold bottle of Stroh's beer and a juice glass for his wife. He poured a miniature serving into the glass, complete with frothy head, and handed it to the wife, who sunk back into a lounge chair, the first break she'd taken in four hours, and watched wistfully as the briquettes which she had just lit roared in a spectacular ball of flame. A car pulled up their driveway and a good-natured beep-beep announced the arrival of its occupants.

Dick looked at his watch. "Must be Vic," he said, "six-thirty, sharp." Roscoe erupted with a fearsome barking growl along the fence line. Moments later, his brother Vic and sister-in-law Nell walked into the backyard. Lucy stayed put on the lounger.

Dick greeted his youngest brother with a playful hug around his neck. "Glad you could come, brother." Vic was taller and heavier, and having just turned fifty in late February, the bags under his eyes were much less pronounced. Twenty years ago he had moved Nell and their two young daughters off of the Chapman family farm after the other brother, Vern, was killed in a heavy machinery accident. Vic now ran a real estate business out of his basement. He was an ardent Cincinnati Reds fan. Dick rooted more for the Indians and their great pitcher, Bob Feller. He loved to needle Vic about the Reds' starting pitching.

"Hello Dick, you sweetheart," said Nell as he nuzzled up to her and kissed her hard on the cheek. Her hair was pure white and had been for fifteen years. She was particularly radiant in the summer when her face was browned from her work in her flowerbeds, contrasting with her hair to give off a very healthy glow. She wore little makeup, but always put on brilliant red Maybelline lipstick when she left the house.

"Sorry I'm not getting up," Lucy explained from her chair. "I had to rush and put everything away when the storm hit. My husband was working, as usual."

"He was probably waiting hand and foot on some sexy bombshell," Vic cracked, driving a hammy hand into the small of his brother's back.

"That probably deserves a beer," Dick replied with a soft smile. It was the first time in recent memory that his brother had been right on the mark. "Nell, I'm the bartender. Can I make you a good, dry martini?"

"I was looking forward to it all the way over here," she said, winking at Lucy. "Dick, your brother will just never be able to mix a decent martini. I've resigned myself to that fact. Thirty years of marriage and two grown children later."

"You and Vic just sit yourselves down, and I'll be back with the drinks."

"You need help, big brother?" asked Vic, which is what he'd always called Dick, even as he towered over him. Big brother gestured emphatically with outstretched palms.

"Relax. I mix one fast martini."

"So that's your secret!" announced Nell.

"And that ain't the only thing he's too quick at!" cracked Lucy, refilling her little glass with more of Dick's beer. They all chuckled as Dick slid through the rear door and into the house.

Roscoe was at the fencerow again, gnashing his teeth. Lucy jumped up from the chaise despite her aching back. "That must be Dean and Sherri, and the baby!" She wanted to be the first to welcome her precious grandson. She trotted toward the driveway.

"Hello baby Todd." She took the little fellow from her son, Dean, standing near the garage and hugged him tight. He cooed as if on cue. It was one of grandmother's favorite sounds in all the world.

"Evening Dean," said Uncle Vic, following his greeting with a warm handshake. His nephew was a handsome young man with hazel eyes who looked like he was going places. His hair was slicked back with oil. His light blue, button down shirt was open at the throat. Sherri trailed in behind all the commotion. She wore her light brown hair in a wavy perm and had a pale green spring sweater draped over her shoulders. She was carrying the diaper bag. Dean had fallen in love with her at Ohio U. She was enrolled in the nursing school, there, and had been working in the dispensary the day they had carried him in to treat his blown out knee. Her skin was fair and her face had a sweet beauty about it. Dean always thought she looked kind of like Grace Kelly.

"Sherri, you look so pretty tonight," said Lucy, kissing her daughter-in-law even as she squeezed Todd in her other arm.

"Hi mom, your yard looks so nice!" she replied. "Isn't he getting big?"

"Such a big boy!" cried Lucy, bouncing him up and down. They slowly made for the patio.

"I see the guest of honor has arrived!" shouted Dick, appearing with a tray full of refreshments. He quickly distributed the martini to Nell, beers to Vic and Dean, a coke to Sherri, and another beer for Lucy and himself. They all settled down in chairs except grandma, who stood monitoring the charcoal fire.

"Here's to the U.P." said Dean, hoisting his bottle of beer patiently until his father was able to clink it with his own brew.

"That's right! It's almost fishing season up there," Vic said, then guzzled some beer. He'd been up to fish camp six or seven times with his brother over the years. The cold beer tasted extra good, and he remembered how refreshing that particular Wisconsin beer tasted around the campfire. "That Leinenkugel's- that beer can't be beat out in the open air."

"Sure you can't make it, Vic?" asked Dick almost playfully. "There's lots of room for you, isn't that right, son?"

"You bet!" said Dean. "Hey Uncle Vic, it'd be just like old times."

"No, I'd like to- really. But we got two closings coming up here in the next couple weeks. I'll just keep the home fires burning while you two boys are up in the north woods." Vic glanced at Nell, who gave him an appreciative nod.

Dick said, "Hey son, why don't you bring out some more beer. My brother's drinkin' like he's sittin' around the campfire without a care in the world, listening to the big ones jump."

"Whoa!" laughed Vic. Dean went on a beer run. "Big brother, remember the night when you and me left old Uncle Jessie snoring in the tent and headed for the Sawmill Bar in that little town where your war buddy lives- Birch?"

"Hell, yes," replied Dick. "We didn't get back to camp til sun up, as I recall." Lucy and Nell rolled their eyes, sipping their drinks.

"We took Jessie out on the lake and ran into a school of walleye second to none," Vic said. Dean returned with the beer.

"You passed out," said Dick. "We just thought you were leaning to starboard, then you hit your head on the goddam anchor." Dean and Vic giggled. The women were talking to Sherri about baby clothes.

"Evening, Chapmans. Sorry if we're late!" The next-door neighbors, Harold and Janie Prescott, strolled toward the patio.

"You're fashionably tardy," said Dick, setting his beer on the picnic table. "Can I offer my favorite neighbors a vodka martini?"

"You bet," said Harold. Janie presented Lucy with a large mixing bowl of coleslaw.

"Honey, while you're pouring the drinks, I'm gonna get the meat on," Lucy informed her husband.

"Nobody noticed you when you came in, Prescott," cracked Vic, his face reddened by the ale. "That dog of yer'in makes one hell of a doorbell."

"And I have to apologize," said Harold.

"Hell no! He's a great watchdog," Vic replied. "He keeps the crooks at bay."

"And the meter reader, and the milkman, and the paperboy," advised Harold somberly. "You know, we think the meter reader whacked our boy dog on top of the head with the back of his clipboard."

"The son-of-a-bitch!" offered Vic.

"Must have hit him with something," added Janie, overhearing the conversation. "Gosh, Roscoe never used to sound so mean and hateful. He's really a gentle animal. He sleeps between Harold's knees."

"I guess Harold doesn't sleep in the fetal position, then," said Vic good-naturedly.

Janie's eyes widened. "Who? Harold? No, you mean Roscoe!"

Dick reappeared with two cocktail glasses and a small lemonade pitcher half filled with martinis. He filled the glasses and plopped an olive into each. He splashed ice cubes from the bucket on the picnic table into the drinks, and then stirred them simultaneously with the tips of his index fingers. These, he handed to the Prescotts.

"Thank you, Dick," said Harold, tinkling his ice cubes deftly.

Dick reached for his beer. Lucy had spread out the white-hot briquettes, and now she distributed hamburgs and hot dogs evenly across the grill. A noisy sizzle mixed with the conversation and laughter on the patio. Dick sat back on the picnic table bench to relax a bit. He looked up into the big elm trees, at their comforting, familiar shapes and sipped from his beer. The sky had basically cleared, save for a wide band of puffy, cumulus clouds painted pink by the sinking sun. Red sky at night- he looked forward to good weather on his day off.

Sherri led baby Todd over to grampa. Dick set the little fellow down on his knee. "Hi big boy! Gitee-up!" Todd's mouth opened wide as he rode the horsy.

"Look at that smile!" cried Nell, admiring her little nephew. She leaned back, tilted her glass, and sucked the olive into her mouth.

"There's more where that came from, sis," said Dick, jerking his head sideways and gesturing toward the lemonade pitcher. "Help yourself."

"Think I'll wait a bit," she said giddily. "I'll have one after dinner."

Dick hugged his little grandson. The baby was bug-eyed and trying his darndest to make the horse go. "Here we go, again!" cheered grandpa, "gitee-up!"

"Dad, I was able to get the whole week off," Dean said, having diplomatically backed away from Uncle Vic in the midst of his obnoxious assessment of Chilicothe's real estate market to anyone within earshot.

"We won't have to rush home, then." Dick handed the smiling baby to Sherri. He thought briefly of the big pine trees standing tall in the campground way up north, there, on Lake Independence. He needed to get away.

"Dad, I was thinking." Dean's soft hazel eyes met those of his father. His youthful face was etched with concern. "Don't you think it would be good to see your friend from St. Ignace, again? If you like, we could spend a night there. It's not that you're old or anything, but someday you might regret breaking off that friendship. It was just a thought." Dean looked sheepish.

"Damn, but you're a good man, you know that?" Dick patted his son on the arm. "Old Toivo, he made it clear that he'd just rather not see the likes of me, anymore. Hell, it's been at least six or seven years since I even stopped there. I got the feeling he didn't even want my business at his fuel pump. There's a story behind Toivo and me. I've let on about it before. It's not a pleasant one."

Dean nodded knowingly. "War experiences. I know there are men who talk about their war stories with anybody who'll listen. Most men bottle them up and take them to their grave. You and Toivo are the type that bury the dark, nasty business deep. Maybe in your friend's case, no matter how deep the hole, it keeps digging itself back up again. That must be why-"

"Honey!" shouted Lucy. "Help me get the meat off. The hot dogs are splitting!"

Dick stepped toward the grill. "Good thought, son." Dean followed him and took the meat platter from his mother.

"I thought that what with the new bridge going up and all, we could spend some time at the Straits. I am an engineer, you know. This bridge project fascinates the hell out of me. It would be a good excuse for you and your buddy to spend some time together while I learn something. Positive experience, Dad. Guaranteed."

Dick flipped the last of the burgers onto the big plate. "Good thought, son," he repeated, "but I'd rather not- at least not this year. Toivo would deserve a letter, first. Then, the necessary time to respond." Dean shrugged.

Roscoe began to bark viciously. He crashed into the picket fence repeatedly, growling wildly. "Bad dog!" screamed Harold Prescott from his lounge chair. He set his martini down and jumped to his feet. Roscoe seemed to become all the more ferocious. Dick handed Dean the spatula.

"Expecting anyone else, honey?" Lucy asked.

Dick replied, "heavens, no!"

Prescott was two-thirds of the way to the garage. "Dick!" he shouted, "it's the police!"

"What the hell?" Dick walked briskly toward the driveway. Everyone else followed in a tight, little pack.

Dick met two officers in front of the garage. Prescott went through his gate, took hold of the snarling dog and led it behind his house. The dog yelped loudly.

Dick recognized the older of the two men. He came into the hardware store all the time. "Henry," said Dick, "is there some kind of trouble?"

"Evening, Mr. Chapman. Sorry about all of this. We don't mean to break up your party." Henry tipped his cap with the end of his big flashlight.

Vic barreled past Dean and stood next to his brother. He had a few beers in him. "We bein' too loud or something, officers? What's this all about?" Dick squeezed Vic's forearm.

"Take it easy, Vic. Now, Henry, what's this all about? We're ready to sit down to dinner."

"I'm sorry to say that a young woman was murdered sometime this afternoon, downtown." Dick became light-headed. "An attractive young woman. A Mrs. Thomas. Her husband told us that he had sent her to your hardware store, to pick up a wax ring for their new toilet."

"She came in late this afternoon," Dick said in a monotone, his voice distant and strange. "It was during the storm. Our lights went out. My God, who did it?"

"No one in custody, presently. Believe me, Mr. Chapman, you are not a suspect. We'd like you to come downtown after you finish dinner. The investigators are trying to ascertain the time of death. You apparently are the last person to see Mrs. Thomas alive."

"Of course I'll come down- at once," said Dick, clearly shaken. "Hold dinner for me, Lucy. The rest of you- please go ahead and eat. I'll return shortly."

"Please let us drive you," said Henry, tipping his cap to the picnickers. "We'll bring you right home, just as soon as you're done."

"Fine," said Dick, and then he walked to the back of the black and white patrol car and climbed in.

Late in the evening, Lucy sat nervously in the living room with Dean and Sherri when a flash of bright headlights played on the front draperies and then a car door slammed shut. Little Todd was sleeping soundly on one end of the colonial style, chocolate brown davenport.

When his Lucy met him at the door, Dick looked tired and much older than his fifty-six years. To Lucy, her husband's face had died that night. He looked stricken.

"What a God awful night," he said, walking past his wife and briefly surveying the comfortable room. "What, did everybody go home?"

"The party ended shortly after you left," Lucy said. "Everyone managed to eat, save for Mrs. Prescott. Vic was very concerned. I think you'd better call him."

Dean stood up and laid his arm on his father's shoulder. "You okay, Dad?"

"She was my last customer- a very pretty young lady. God, she was hit over the head and raped. Apparently, she wasn't raped- in the usual sense." Dick made a gurgling noise in his throat. He was glad his stomach was empty.

"Not raped? What do you mean?" Lucy blurted.

"Her attacker used some kind of weapon on her. She- she bled to death."

Silence gripped the living room. Dean looked at his father. There were crocodile tears on his weary cheeks. "Dean," he began haltingly, "the fishing trip will have to be cancelled. I feel just sick about all of this. I don't want us leaving our family alone if there's a killer out there- somewhere."

"They'll nab the guy, and they'll be quick about it, too," said Dean.

"Probably a drifter- some nut just passing through," added Sherri. She folded her arms and took hold of her shoulders. "The whole thing just gives me the shivers. Right in downtown Chilicothe; Cripes!" Her brown curls shook softly.

"I may as well make some more coffee," Lucy said. "I don't expect we'll be getting much sleep tonight."

Dick looked down at his grandson, spread eagled at the end of the davenport. "At least the little fellow, here, is out like a light. He's gonna leave all the worrying to the adults."

Dean took Sherri into his arms and hugged her tightly. "Mom, I think we'll have to pass on the coffee. It's about time we headed home. It's getting late."

"Leave the baby here, dear," said Lucy with some urgency, "he's sleeping so soundly. Your father can roll the crib into our room-we'll make sure he gets a good sleep."

"Appreciate the offer, mom," said Sherri.

"We insist!" cried Dick. "I think it would help to have Todd around

tonight. It- it would, you know, take my mind off things somewhat-"
"That will work- but I'll swing by early in the morning to get him," Dean said. His mother helped Sherri with her sweater.
"We'll meet you at church in the morning. That's a good way to work it," suggested Dick. He managed a faint smile. His daughter-in-law glanced at her husband and nodded.
"You kids just run along, then," added Lucy. "Let's all forget about what happened. I just wish she had shopped at the drug store instead. We wouldn't have heard about it until church."
"Lucy!" snapped Dick. "Please! I can deal with this. It might take some time to sort out, that's all. The police department will be working night and day until they arrest their suspect. Now if it was a drifter, they may never solve the case. I don't know."
Dean ushered Sherri to the door. "Good night, folks! See you in the morning." Dick trotted after them and gave his daughter-in-law a royal hug.
"If you sleep in late, we'll bring Todd over after the service."
"Thanks, dad," said Sherri. "We love you. Hope you sleep well."
Late that night, Dick tossed and turned in the double bed, next to Lucy. Todd slept soundly in the crib at the foot of their bed. Dick kept playing the afternoon scene in the hardware over and over again in his mind. She was such a pretty, vibrant young woman. She was so sexy. He had been so attracted to her, in a safe, innocent sort of way. When he imagined her in his store, bending over, the front of her dress open; God, what was her young husband going through tonight? How totally devastating; Unbelievable. Dick would never forget her. The obituary would probably show up in Monday's paper. They had better find the monster responsible for this. They had better find him.

CHAPTER THREE

"The Straits"
St. Ignace, Michigan
June 1955

The barometer, which predicts the weather with relative accuracy, fair or foul, is also a reliable indicator in foretelling the number of tourists vacationing at the Straits of Mackinac during the month of June. High pressure, translating into mild, sunny weather, causes a swarm of visitors to descend upon Mackinaw City to the south, St. Ignace to the north, and to world famous Mackinac Island without fail. If the same needle moves toward foul and the ever-changing Straits clime turns cool and cloudy, then cold and rainy, the same tourists scatter to the four winds, leaving grocery store shelves and restaurant kitchens overstocked, motels and resorts vacant, and souvenir stands and gift shops empty in their collective wake. The Straits become a desolate place.

June is the month that makes or breaks the fiscal year for the Straits area businessman dependent upon tourism. He knows that from July 4th through Labor Day, his cash register will overflow, even in a warm rain. But the visitors of June are a persnickety lot, and it takes an extended run of favorable weather that month to get a jump start on brimming the coffers for the season, thereby chasing away the red ink from the books for another year when the climate might prove less cooperative.

Toivo Ahonen, a longtime resident of St. Ignace had, for many years, witnessed the ebb and flow of tourists and travelers in that Upper Peninsula town. He owned Toivo's Marathon service station on State Street, which was located directly between the main docks of the North Star and the Hiawatha, the town's two competing ferry lines offering daily passenger service to Mackinac Island.

Toivo was a rather plump man, pleasantly rounded at the shoulders, elbows, and hips. The top of his big oval head was void of hair, and it often shone brightly with skin oil, particularly after several hours at work around his shop. His nose was wide and flat, his dark eyes darted about and his thin lips exposed a yellowed set of dentures whenever he cackled and laughed, which was often. He always wore dark blue overalls with 'Toivo' embroidered in red letters in a little white circle over his heart.

Upon Toivo's return from Europe following World War I, he had hired on as a mechanic on the Chief Wawatam, the giant railroad car ferry owned by the Mackinac Transportation Company that ran back and forth through the Straits between Michigan's two peninsulas. He had moved back into his mother's house and never thought seriously of taking a wife. He was content to save his money, survive the Great Depression, pick up extra work repairing automobiles on the side, and finally, in the spring of 1946 realized his lifelong ambition by opening his own service station.

In winter, St. Ignace pretty much shut down and emptied out. Besides another gas station on the westerly outskirts of town, the only other businesses that remained open were the bank, a doctor's office, two grocery stores, two restaurants, and two taverns. Right after deer season, Toivo cut back on his own operating hours and reduced his work force from five to two, including himself. The slower pace of life allowed him time to ice fish for whitefish and lake trout in the Straits, and to cut and split the following winter's supply of firewood, which was used as the main source of heat in his mother's house, and at the service station as well.

It wasn't until early May that there would be a noticeable influx of summer residents and seasonal employees. Out in the Straits, the work crews were laying in the underwater foundations for the new Mackinac Bridge, a span of wire, concrete and steel that would surpass the famous Golden Gate in San Francisco. Toivo preferred to reserve judgement on the project until the day came when he could hop into his three-quarter ton pickup truck and drive over to Mackinaw City with his elderly mother for breakfast. In the meantime, some of those talented construction workers were in need of repairs and maintenance on their vehicles and with all the overtime they were putting in, they had plenty of money to pay for Toivo's good work.

Business was so brisk that, even before the Florida snowbirds began to pour back into town, Toivo was forced to slip right into his summer schedule. Traditionally, he worked from seven in the morning until close to midnight when the weather finally warmed. This was due to the fact that, except for oil changes and tire repairs, he insisted on doing all of the mechanical work himself. Through the years, Toivo had established a reputation far and wide for fair dealing and quality work and being a stubborn old Finn, he was just too much of a perfectionist to allow a less experienced mechanic to tear a customer's car apart in his shop.

One Wednesday evening in the middle of June, Toivo found himself with two jobs on his hands- both promised by the next morning. He expected to be laboring feverishly until well past eleven o'clock. He employed two local boys to operate the gas pumps and the cash register from five until closing, and at nine o'clock, he shut off the outside lights for the night and sent his charges on their merry way.

"Now Stevie," he said to the more reliable of the two, "you do remember that you're supposed to fill in for Gus in the morning, eh?"

"Right, Mr. Ahonen. I plan to be here at seven. Make sure you've got some hot coffee for me 'cause I'll sure as heck be needing it." Stevie was a new 1955 graduate of St. Ignace High, and he'd only just become addicted to coffee drinking during the winter of his senior year.

Toivo smiled. "I'll make sure it's good and strong, just for you, guy."

"Good. And hey, Mr. Ahonen, we've got the register all totaled out and everything so if you wouldn't mind putting the money in the safe, we could, you know," and Stevie of the pimply face threw his head in the direction of the street, "get going, if you know what I mean?"

Toivo nodded, set down the ratchet which he was holding, and walked into what he liked to refer to as the customer lounge, where a cheap, grease stained orange vinyl couch was pushed up against one wall next to a candy machine on one side and a cigarette machine on the other. The cash register sat on a plywood table opposite the couch, facing the fuel pumps outside. Toivo opened the cash register.

"Okay boys, have a good night," he said, folding the register tape and stuffing it into a blue bank bag along with the money from the till. He slid open the cupboard beneath the register and spun the dial on the combination safe. Upon opening the safe, he placed the purse inside, listening as Stevie revved up his father's new Chevy and peeled into the street, leaving a good quantity of rubber on the pavement from the sound of it. Toivo locked the little safe, and then bolted the outer door before making his way back into the bay.

He turned up the volume of the Philco radio on the shelf above the door and then turned his attention to the spark plugs and points of a 1946 Kaiser. Country-western music strummed throughout the garage. He had to finish the tune up and then replace the tail pipe before moving the Kaiser back out into the lot. That would allow him to bring in the Ford sedan belonging to Darryl Brewster, the President of the Chamber of Commerce, who was heading out of town on business early the next morning and needed a linkage repaired in his gearbox before he could even depart.

Toivo liked young Stevie. If he had ever gotten around to taking a wife and having a family, a boy like Stevie would have made a fine son. Toivo had never given much thought as to whom he would leave the business to when his productive days were behind him, but a son like Stevie would have made his decision academic.

It was during these solitary times, particularly when laboring into the late evening hours, that he sometimes fantasized about owning a big house on the hill next to Doc Ramsay, and being married to Colleen Stapleton, the attractive, raven haired owner of the coffee shop in the next block. They could have had a whole houseful of kids together. An Ahonen tribe, at that; Too bad Colleen had rejected his initial attempts at flirtation. Maybe he should have spent an extra hour scrubbing his thumbnails....

He removed the six spark plugs on the Kaiser, then opened up a fresh box of AC's and began adjusting the gaps, one by one. He thought he detected a tapping noise, which he first attributed to the background beat of that country song twanging over the radio. He listened more intently, and then realized that someone was rapping on the glass door that he had just bolted, out front. He ignored the disturbance, continuing to check the gaps on the rest of the plugs. If someone out there wanted gas, they'd just have to go out to the highway. His pumps were locked up, and, with the work still left to do on Darryl Brewster's Ford, he just didn't have time to stop what he was doing. 'The sign on the door reads, closed,' Toivo thought. Then, there was a noticeable increase in the intensity of the rapping.

Toivo set the plugs on the engine block, wiped his hands on his overalls and grudgingly headed for the front door. The lights in the lounge reflected off of the glass door so that he couldn't really tell just who it was knocking so insistently, whether man or woman, acquaintance or stranger. When he appeared at the entrance, the rapping subsided. Toivo unbolted the door and leaned out into the deep summer twilight.

A thin, wiry man of perhaps fifty, his cheeks and eye sockets sunken and his graying hair disheveled, stood before him. He appeared frail and somewhat confused, and adding to his odd condition was an elongated black instrument case that he carried in his left hand. The case was disproportionately large for a man of his stature, though he didn't seem to be compensating for its bulk and weight with any appreciable lean to the right.

"May I help you?" Toivo asked, eyeing the rounded, silver rimmed glasses that the stranger wore.

"Yes, please." The voice carried a definite accent that Toivo couldn't quite place for a moment. "My car broke down up the road. I was told at the restaurant that you make repairs and that you are the best." The tone was firm and confident, belying the unruly countenance.

"I'm quite busy here," replied Toivo, trying his best not to sound irritated. "But if you don't mind a short wait inside, I'll be able to take you over to your car and have a look- just give me a few minutes." He pulled the door open and the stranger walked through, banging the instrument case on the edge of the doorframe. The contents collided inside- there was the muffled clanking of metal against metal.

"Careful there," instructed Toivo. "You a musician? That's a pretty big case to be carrying down the road, eh?"

"I never go anywhere without my trombone. You are Mr. Ahonen?"

Toivo's eyes met those of the stranger's. He recognized a German accent. The eyes behind the spectacles were a cold, piercing blue. "Yes. I am Toivo Ahonen. You know me?"

"The owner's name is listed above your door."

"Yes, of course." Toivo held out his hand. "And who do I have the pleasure of doing business with?" The handshake was firm and strong.

"I am Vladimir- Vladimir Tepesh."

"Yugoslav?"

"Romanian. I was born in Germany. My father- he was Romanian."

Toivo turned on his heel, his ample behind swiveling. "I've got about ten minutes left on this tune up, here. Your car, did she overheat?" he asked over his shoulder.

"Just went dead. I waited and tried it many times. Then, the battery seemed to go dead."

"It's probably not vapor lock, then. Be with you in a few minutes. Have a seat. I like trombone. If you're in the mood to play, let me know and I can turn down this radio."

"I may get out my instrument, Mr. Ahonen."

Toivo returned to his work. He screwed the new spark plugs into the cylinders, using both hands. He then ratcheted each plug, tightening them carefully. He crossed the front of the vehicle and began to install the three plugs on the passenger side. He did not pay much attention to the footsteps that came up behind him. As he reached down with both hands to fit the socket over the last plug, he heard a sickening thud, all at once felt a terrific pain along the base of his skull, and then everything went black.

Stevie Smith dropped his co-worker Alfie off at home first, and then drove straight to his parent's house where he showered and changed clothes. He had yet another graduation party to attend. A friend from homeroom was throwing a beer bash on short notice- his parents had left town unexpectedly due to a death in the family, unwittingly making their home available for such a noxious celebration.

Stevie wasn't overly thrilled by the prospect of reporting to the gas station so early the next morning. He had grown accustomed to the fun and excitement inherent in guzzling large amounts of beer with his fellow graduates and the thought of moderating his intake to meet a responsibility suddenly thrust upon him by his employer, as nice as Mr. Ahonen was, made him rebellious enough to plan on drinking even more beer than he could otherwise hold. Yes, he'd just get stinking drunk and horrendously hung over and blame it all on Toivo.

Before disappearing into the night with his father's new car, Stevie made the obligatory trip into the living room to visit with his parents, his hair dripping wet from the shower. This move kept him in good stead with the owner of the new Chevy, if nothing else.

"I'm gonna be takin' off, now," said Stevie, massaging a blackhead on the cleft of his chin.

"Be careful with the car, son," said the father. "And, be home before sunrise this time."

"I got to be at work in the morning, seven A.M."

"That's tough," said the father with a wry smile.

"And I ain't too happy about it, neither."

"And take the garbage to the garage on your way out. Good night Steve."

"Good night, Dad."

"Now no beer tonight, Stevie. You don't want to become another Uncle Alex," added his mother, peering over her cross-stitch. The side door banged shut.

Toivo Ahonen regained consciousness in a heavy fog. His whole head throbbed. It hurt just to blink his eyes. He was having difficulty breathing through his nose. He suffered from allergies in the spring and his sinuses were often swollen, causing him to snort, or breath through his mouth. It suddenly occurred to Toivo that his mouth was sealed shut. Something had been tightly wound around his head and over his lips in such a fashion as to impede any air flow through his mouth. As his wits were restored, a sense of alarm gave way to full blown panic. His heart raced and his breathing became rapid and shallow and his swollen nasal passages barely permitted enough respiration to sustain him in his extreme state.

He was now looking up at the rafters in the bay. His arms were bound behind him and he shifted his weight from his right shoulder to his left because his entire right arm was numb and prickly feeling. He also became aware that his overalls were down around his ankles and when he lifted his head slightly he could see the strong gray duct tape which had been wound around and around at his ankles and assumed the same material must also be wound around his head. Toivo's legs were spread and his knees were bent, and tied at the kneecaps with separate lengths of cord. His left leg was held wide by a rope that was stretched tight and knotted securely to the driver's side door handle of the Kaiser. His right knee was pointing toward the opposite wall of the shop, anchored in similar fashion to a bolted leg on his big workbench. When Toivo had shifted on the floor from his right to his left, he confirmed that his underwear had also been removed, for he felt a film of cold oil coat a section of his left buttock.

Then, Toivo focused in on the shifty little man who had engineered this whole scene. He appeared in the garage area, carrying his instrument case. He was wearing a rhinestone band about his head mounted with a silver pentagram star right over the center of his forehead. He had also glued a preposterous, phony, black handlebar moustache to his upper lip, the drooping ends of which shook with his mearest movement. He set his case down on the concrete and opened it slowly.

"Mr. Ahonen, I'll bet you have never heard of me before! You have never heard of Vlad Tepesh? Vlad the Impaler? Surely, you never have?" He lifted three metal tubes from the case. They were uniform in length and diameter. He laid them out and began connecting them at the ends. Toivo looked at them in wonderment and concluded that they were just like the portable flag poles which people assembled around Memorial Day and the Fourth of July. Screwed together end to end and mounted out on the front lawn, they allowed for a first class display of Old Glory.

This pole was unlike a flag pole, however, and Toivo was greatly distressed by the sight of the little man as he twisted the sections until they were tight and formed a formidable steel pole approximately nine feet in length, topped off by a tapered, razor sharp point- like the arrowheads used by serious bow hunters. Vladimir now picked up the shiny pole and swung it around slowly, being careful not to come into contact with the ropes or the double bay doors and then Toivo let out a muffled cry and his eyes bulged in unspeakable terror as the little man brought the razor sharp point to rest less than an inch away from his rectum.

"You see, Mr. Ahonen," and there was unmistakable menace in his voice as he said, "you have been found guilty of committing a war crime- a crime for which I fear you must now pay with your very life."

Toivo struggled gamely in the web of ropes and tape but only succeeded, in all of his gyrations, in moving a few short inches along the floor. The little man walked over and knelt before him, smiling through that ridiculous moustache, making the evening seem all the more unreal and dreamlike to Toivo.

"Come, come now, Mr. Ahonen, you really must remember that night long ago- yes, in Germany. Your kindly visit with your friends, to the doctor's house in Koblenz?" Toivo squinted. "Yes! You do remember! And of critical importance to you is that I remember very well your prostitute girlfriend and her bloody head. You bastards!" Vladimir then lowered his voice to a thick whisper.

"Vlad the Impaler drives angry stakes into the loins of wanton criminals such as yourself, Mr. Ahonen. You are then to be displayed! Your suffering must serve as a deterrent to any red-blooded American boy who desires sex at whatever the cost. You are to be mounted in your greasy gas station and allowed to serve this final, useful aim!"

The little man moved back to the instrument case again and brought out a good strong rope that had already been strung through a double pulley, and along with it, a separate length of rope. He set the pulley on the floor, took the other heavy cord and, looking up to the rafters, flipped the rope over a metal beam twelve feet above the floor and then grasped the two ends, as though he were testing the beam for strength. He tied the pulley system to one end, and when he was fully satisfied with the strength of his knot, he pulled the opposite end of rope until the pulley hung at the bottom of the beam. He lashed the end of the rope to the rear bumper of the Kaiser and pulled that knot tight with all of his might.

Toivo shook his head in disbelief, unable to accept his apparently hideous fate. He had blocked out that old incident from back in his youth. All was fair in love and war, without repercussions. Yes, it was true that the girl had died, but it was certainly no fault of his. He looked out through the dirty little row of windows along the top of the service doors, wishing that he had kept them a bit cleaner. If somebody would just stop in- he could clearly see the beams of light given off by the headlamps of the passing traffic and he was using every ounce of will to direct just one of those cars to turn into his station. He now believed that this was all that it would take to save him- a radiator hose leak, a rear tire in need of air, a broken fan belt; Any of the dozens of incidental little mechanical failures he had dealt with each and every day.

Vladimir made a slipknot on one of the ends of rope running through the pulley system and he eased it over Toivo's head and torso, down beneath his bound up wrists, and then he pulled firmly in order to eliminate any slack. He walked back around his victim and lighted upon both of his knees, aiming the lance gleefully.

"Impalement, Mr. Ahonen, will allow you time to reflect on any past misdeeds and make the necessary amends with your maker before you expire. May your pain serve as recompense to those whose very lives you chose to destroy. To me, I must admit, you will be little more than a stuck pig!" And he concluded this brief discourse with a lurch and a thrust of such effectiveness as to bury the terrible point of the death instrument deep within the abdomen of the condemned.

Toivo was overcome by the ghastly, searing heat caused by the sudden introduction of the stake. As his executioner cut the clothesline running to the car door handle and to the workbench, the pain was deadened. Toivo was in shock, gratefully slipping in and out of consciousness and was barely aware of the sensation of being hoisted high above the floor in short, jerking bursts of motion. The pole was now nearly vertical, with the tops of the big Finn's shoulders jammed against the beam above.

The Impaler gave the base of the pole a series of kicks, wedging it upright against the surface of the concrete and holding Toivo securely aloft. Blood began to run down the sides of the pole in small streams and Vladimir eyed his victim contentedly.

"Mr. Ahonen, the night you left the girl dead, your associate beat the old doctor severely. The three of you just left him lying there in his own home, clutching his stomach, moaning. He moaned and he moaned, and then he died the next afternoon. Internal hemorrhaging; Dr. Von Himmler was my father."

Toivo's gaze became less translucent. "Yes, Mr. Ahonen! I was the boy who leapt upon your back from the staircase. You almost killed me, too, the way you threw me back head first into the wall. You should have finished me off when you had the chance, you really should have, you know?"

Toivo's eyes were slowly closing. Vlad held the lengths of cord that were bound to his knees above, one cord in either hand, and then he pulled down cruelly with a brutal jerk. The eyes opened wide, contorting in renewed agony and with it, the fresh hemorrhaging.

"You will soon be finished, Mr. Ahonen. Mr. Rutledge will be next to pay his price. I have already paid a visit to Mr. Chapman. I will finish with him later. In case it crossed your mind, your names were recorded at the American Military hearing the very day my father died. They put you on the next ship to New York, I believe.

"For many, many years, my mother made me vow not to take up the sword of vengeance to right the terrible wrong which you Americans inflicted upon my family. I always honored her wishes. She was a kind, forgiving woman. She counted my father's death along with the millions of others who gave their lives up in the Great War. My father was a soldier of mercy who did his best to heal the afflicted, who ministered faithfully over the grievously wounded, giving of himself without reservation, without any expectation of reward. I was chosen to follow his saintly path to the higher ground of self-sacrifice for my fellow man, but alas, I failed miserably in this undertaking. My bitterness and hatred have consumed me, leading me on another path more in keeping with the blatant savagery so inherent in my kind."

Toivo was delirious and ghostly pale from the great loss of blood. This Vladimir, then, was the grown child whom he had rendered unconscious in that German tenement dwelling on that awful evening almost forty years before. Delivering such a heavy blow to so young a child had eaten away at him for the many years afterward. Often, late at night, while lying in bed, having awakened suddenly from a deep sleep, Toivo would play the incident over and over in his mind. He recalled how the boy had landed on his shoulders from above, knocking them both to the floor, and then how the boy had driven those sharp fingernails deep into his neck, gouging and pinching with the wild fury of desperation. Toivo had always justified his actions as a reflexive response triggered by the painful assault perpetrated by the youth. The prostitute's and old physician's deaths, on the other hand, were solely at the hands of Rutledge, that filthy, mindless bastard! Rutledge had gotten away with murder, literally, having been hustled out of that God forsaken locality before full knowledge of his atrocity could spread throughout Koblenz.

Vladimir Tepesh, alias Wolfgang Von Himmler, once again gave a tug on the ropes dangling from Toivo's knees. "You have brought this miserable end upon yourself, Mr. Ahonen. Your execution is at the hands of one of the darkest rogues in recorded history. Vlad the Impaler staked thousands of his enemies in a like manner in the countryside surrounding the villages and towns that he conquered. This is, I think, your final lesson in history."

Von Himmler smiled. He knew full well that his own father had been escorted into the afterlife by a great band of cherubic Valkyries. At that dark, shadowy time, Wolfgang had laid in a coma at the hospital and was not even able to attend his father's funeral. In the years since he had come to realize that during that long, dreamless sleep he had indeed sprouted wings and joined in his hero's heavenly procession into Valhalla. Von Himmler looked up into the dark rafters. There would be no ceremonial march into the afterlife for this scum of a man. Of that, he was certain. Toivo was in shock. He could feel his very life draining away, forming a gleaming puddle at the base of the stake. He looked down and watched the little man gingerly touching the tips of his shoes in the ever-widening pool of blood. He knew then that he should have remained on good terms with old Dick Chapman. Shouldn't have given him the cold shoulder. Maybe the two of them together would have seen this coming-

Vlad looked up at him, the ends of his drooping moustache vibrating anew with each insidious movement. "Mr. Ahonen? I will have the decency which you and your cronies did not possess. You left my father, holding his ruptured abdomen. But I shall remain with you until you expire. As a matter-of-fact, I packed a supper for just such an occasion." The Impaler went into his instrument case again and moments later, he was munching voraciously on a chicken wing. Toivo blacked out.

It was nearly four in the morning when Stevie Smith finally left the graduation party. He was thoroughly intoxicated. He had had his hands up Sylvia Warner's dress and, looking back now, was pretty sure that she would have gone all the way with him if there had been a place for them to go. He didn't want to risk staining the upholstery on the backseat of his parent's car. On top of it, he had been drunk as hell. Alfie from the gas station and Marie his girlfriend had soaked the seats in his old man's car right around Easter and she had gotten knocked up to boot. It looked more and more like poor Alfie was headed for the altar pretty quick. Stevie was stopping in at the drug store for a fistful of rubbers before the next party Friday night. The erection in his pants wouldn't let him forget.

The night had been great fun as he had anticipated. Most of the Class of '55 was there to share in the barrels of Miller High Life. The comradeship among the new graduates had been further strengthened by the carefree raucousness that characterized the evening. It was one of those magical times in youth when alcohol mixes with good memories and the permeating emotion that something wonderful is over and done with and no one can ever go back. Stevie had wanted the night to last forever.

He drove his father's car with great care. A stop at Colleen's coffee shop on State Street was certainly called for under the circumstances. Stevie could barely see past the front hood.

The coffee shop housed a long counter with twelve stools and a row of tables along the window wall facing the street. Stevie wheeled over along the curb, bounced off of it, and shut off the engine. He got out of the car and stretched his arms high in the air over his head. His dick was aching. Sylvia Warner had blue-balled him.

Stevie looked up the street at the gas station and whimpered. Within three hours he would be dispensing gasoline, cleaning windshields, and checking dipsticks. 'Better get some coffee,' he said to himself.

The little restaurant was practically empty. Stevie took a seat at the counter, trying his best to look sober. "Hi there, Stevie!" greeted the gray-haired lady holding a glass carafe brimming with fresh, black coffee. "You sure are up early- or from the looks of it you're out awfully late, hey?" She chuckled, filling his cup.

"Good morning, Mrs. Beauchamp." Stevie raised the cup to his mouth and gulped. The coffee was boiling hot and he smacked his lips in order to cool the affected parts. "Whuh! Hot stuff!"

Mrs. Beauchamp handed him an ice water. Her face was round and jolly and had too much rouge smudged in half circles at the top of her cheeks. "How about a donut, Stevie? They're fresh made. Still warm, in fact."

"Sure. Thanks."

Two other men, fishermen from the looks of them, were seated three stools down from Stevie and one of them spoke up. "I hear they arrested some crazy Canuck in the Soo yesterday mornin'. He'd been on the loose all over Ontario, stranglin' and killin' counter help in bakeries and donut places. They say he went right into old man Perdie's Donut Shop right near the river and just about kilt old man Perdie his self! Took four strong men to pry him off 'is throat. I'm willing to bet they lock that lunatic up in one of them towers in Newberry Joy mental ward. Autta hang him by the ankles an' whip him till they can see his bones. Christ almighty!"

Mrs Beauchamp placed her hands to her throat and, for a moment, clearly had some difficulty swallowing. "Imagine that!" she said. "What will they think of next?"

Stevie finished the cake donut and asked for another. The coffee and the sugary food were helping to improve his vision, but it was going to be a slow process. He made a wobbly trip to the rest room and relieved himself for the umpteenth time that night. While rinsing his hands, he determined that, owing to the lateness of the hour, it would make considerably more sense to park over at the gas station and sleep in the car until it was time for work, rather than driving all the way back home just to crawl into bed for two hours. When he did report for work, he would just call home and explain to his father that he'd spent the night at his friend's place. His old man would just be getting up for work then, anyway. Good timing. He dried his hands and walked back past the counter, heading for the door.

"You sure you're not too tired to drive, Stevie?" asked Mrs. Beauchamp softly, so that the others couldn't hear.

"I'm fine. Thanks for asking. I'm s'posed to be at work at seven so I'm just gonna sleep in my car over at the station until we open up."

"You young folk!" wheezed the lady. "I'd have to stay in bed for a whole week if I came to work on two hours sleep- after raising Cain all night. Don't know how you can tolerate it."

"Must be the donuts," he said, waving at the fishermen. "Good morning." He walked out into the night.

Stevie pulled the Chevy up near the double doors leading into the service garage and killed the engine. He'd be lucky to get two hours of sleep. The eastern horizon was already streaked with light so between the coffee and donuts and the first rays of morning he was feeling unusually wide awake and alert. 'Sure beats throwing my guts up,' he thought. He nestled his head back against the driver's side door and propped his feet up on the passenger side of the big bench seat and closed his eyes.

The freight trucks that had crossed the Straits on the auto ferry from the Lower Peninsula during the night began to rumble slowly past. As each truck approached, its diesel engine roaring, the pavement trembled and the Chevy shook. The atmosphere was just not conducive to falling asleep and Stevie tossed and turned and burped up the taste of half-digested donuts and his eyes opened briefly and he found himself looking directly into the gas station through one of the dirty little windows in the service bay doors. There was something there- something that was not at all normal- something that was not at all right, and Stevie threw open the car door and approached the window.

The scene, surreal as it was, provoked him to feel at once nauseous and he vomited. There was a man, all bound and gagged, hunched up just below the rafters, held there by a shiny, vertical metal shaft which protruded from between his bare legs. At the base of the pole, a very large pool of blood had collected. Close by, in the center of the floor, there lay a man, either asleep or dead, Stevie couldn't quite tell which, all curled up the way he was, in the fetal position. Stevie was positively sure that the man all taped up and gagged and dead near the ceiling was Toivo Ahonen. He ran back to the car and drove directly to the St. Ignace police station.

The authorities had Wolfgang Von Himmler cuffed and in custody sometime before six o'clock. Stevie had returned to the gas station in the rear seat of one of the two patrol cars that had been hurriedly dispatched. The two officers on night patrol had jimmied the door near the cash register and had entered stealthily with their pistols drawn and, Stevie would add to later versions of his story, thoroughly shrunken testes, owing to the few times that they had ever drawn their weapons in that Upper Peninsula town.

Within a minute, though it had seemed like an hour to Stevie, the officers had emerged from the darkened station, dragging a little man who was very much alive, Stevie could see, towards the other patrol car. One of the officers pushed him into the rear seat and then slid in beside him with a clipboard that he had lifted off of the front dash. The other officer reached into the rolled down driver's side window and pulled the radio handset out, stretching the spring cord as far as it would go.

It was now daybreak and the officer, while speaking into the radio, began waving customers away from the gas pumps. He soon turned and hung the handset back up inside the car. Stevie had discovered that there were no door handles in the back seat and so he began knocking loudly on the window glass, gesturing wildly at the officer, afraid that he might venture back into the station and leave him there in his own private prison. The officer trotted over and let him out.

"He did it?" asked Stevie.

"Looks that way, kid," replied the officer. The two of them walked slowly toward the front of the station together. Stevie found himself staring at the black lettering directly above the customer entrance- 'Toivo Ahonen, Independent Owner.'

"I called for the ambulance. They have to get Mr. Ahonen out of there."

"This is so sick," said Stevie, sniffing the vomit taste up his nose. "Tell me I'm asleep in my old man's car." He looked at the patrolman for the first time. He was about thirty, with plenty of pitted old acne scars on his cheeks and chin- enough to give him that tough, cold look. He had a five o'clock shadow, and brown eyes that failed to generate any warmth. He must have written five thousand tickets and heard ten thousand stories, and his face showed it.

Another car pulled up and the officer began waving it away. Instead, a well-dressed man in a blue suit stepped out from the passenger side door and adjusted his cravat. "What gives here, Herb?" he asked the officer. It was Darryl Brewster, President of the Straits Area Chamber of Commerce. The woman driving the car, undoubtedly his wife, kept her foot on the brake, a look of puzzlement etched on her face. "Did we have a hold up or something?"

"Not exactly. It's a little more serious than an armed robbery. Old fashioned murder is more like it." The officer had measured his words carefully. Stevie thought he sounded kind of goofy for a cop.

Mr. Brewster waved to the woman who had brought him and blew her a goodbye kiss. She smiled cheerily and drove off. A slight breeze fanned in off of Lake Huron and ruffled his wavy brown hair as he turned once again toward the policeman.

"I had the wife swing me by on the way to her breakfast club so that I could pick up my car. Had some work done. Toivo promised it for this morning. I have to be in Escanaba by eleven." Apparently he had paid no attention to Herb's last statement.

"I don't expect your car is finished, sir," said Stevie.

"What is going on, Herb?" The officer motioned him toward the front of the station.

"Now Mr. Brewster," he said with a shrug of his shoulder, "it ain't a very pretty sight in there. Mr. Ahonen was, er, was murdered in a way I ain't never seen or heard of before."

"Murdered!" cried Brewster. Stevie had seen the man around town almost every day, especially since late April, when he had started working at the gas station. This Mr. Brewster was in for a fill up every other day. He was intimidating to Stevie, all dressed up and darkly handsome-like some hot shot lawyer.

Herb continued: "I got a subscription to one of those detective magazines and I seen a lot of ropes and chains and ballpeen hammers and such but they never had anything like what's in there. When word of this gets out, we're all gonna make it into the Chicago Tribune!"

Brewster frowned and then he charged right into the station with the officer while Stevie lagged out front. The young man had seen all that he wanted to from that little window in the bay door. He kicked a stone across the pavement until Brewster and the policeman were well inside. The door closed behind them and as Stevie approached it, he kept his eyes fixed on the front of the candy machine next to that cheap couch. He was afraid to focus on anything else in there. With his luck there'd be fingers on top of the cash register. He whirled and looked into the back of the other patrol car, at the second officer in there as he continued questioning the little man that did it and then he looked back at the front of the station again and suddenly there was Brewster, hurtling back outside for fresh air, white as a bleached sheet, beads of perspiration forming at his brow. 'That sure knocked him down a couple notches,' thought Stevie.

"And you've obviously got the man who did this, Herb?" Brewster was able to ask, rubbing his eyebrows with his thumb and forefinger.

"He's a nut, plain and simple. He admitted it right off. He's got some kind of a funny accent. He was just in there layin' on the floor when we busted in on him."

"We're keeping this out of the newspapers, Herb. I want to talk to the chief. We just can't let word leak out." Brewster peered over at Stevie. "Okay? We all have got to keep this under our hats. We can say there was a robbery and a stabbing- something to that effect." Herb frowned at the thought and then decided to give it one last try.

"But Mr. Brewster, this would get us in the news from coast to coast! I mean, we would be in one of the detective magazines and everything! They got a he-nee-us crime of the year contest. I see St. Ignace right on the damn cover!"

"No way in hell, Herb," replied Brewster firmly. "With our summer season in full swing," and then he thumbed back in the direction of the station with a look of revulsion on his features, "if word of that gets around town, our business could drop as much as fifty percent. No, as far as I'm concerned, this is cut and dried. I have got to look out for the business interests in this community, and, I'm positive the chief will concur. Judge Thompson will be handling this ultimately- he's a personal friend of mine, and part owner of the Northern Lights Motel."

Yet another vehicle rolled up toward the gas pumps. The motorist and his passengers were craning their necks, gawking at the police cars curiously. Brewster gave them a stern look and motioned toward the 'closed' sign next to the front door. They pulled ever so slowly back out onto the street. "Herb, why don't you radio for some of those barricades to block this area off?"

"Sure Mr. Brewster, right away."

Stevie thought the officer looked very disappointed as he turned heel and trotted back to his patrol car. Stevie found himself standing next to Brewster, watching Herb get on the radio again.

"Well, I'm so terribly sorry you had to find your boss like this, son," Brewster said, having regained some of the color in his face. "That was quick thinking- going right to the police like that. Let's see, what's your name, again?"

"Stevie. Stevie Smith."

"So you must be Martin Smith's boy?"

"That's right."

"I'm sure you realize, Stevie, just how important it is to keep the details of this crime to ourselves. There's been a murder here. A stabbing, I guess you'd say. Let's give Mr. Ahonen the respect he deserves. None of us would want to make this into some kind of spectacle. Look! Chief Crimmin is here! Thank God!"

A Chippewa County ambulance pulled into the station, followed by a car driven by the Chief of Police, Scott Crimmin. Stevie watched as Herb and Mr. Brewster both walked over and joined the chief and the ambulance attendants at the rear of the wagon. They conferred for a few moments and Herb pointed to the back of the other patrol car and they all turned and stared for a moment. Then Crimmin took a camera from the front seat of his car and went into the station. The ambulance crew finished their cigarettes, then wheeled out the stretcher and rolled it slowly toward the building. Stevie decided all of the tea in China wouldn't convince him to trade places with either one of them right now. Brewster came over and rejoined him.

"Stevie, they told me you could ride back to the police station to make your statement. That all right by you?"

"Sure. Whatever you want. I just got to give my folks a quick phone call- but not from in there."

"I can certainly understand. By the way, the chief wants all the details kept secret for now. If anybody happens to ask you about it, and I'm sure you'll be asked plenty, just tell 'em you saw Mr. Ahonen through the window like you did- but, you know, stabbed to death." Stevie nodded.

Herb came over and handed Brewster a car key. "Here, Mr. Brewster. I'm gonna be driving Hal and the killer to the jail in Hal's car. If you wouldn't mind, you and the boy could follow in my car. Just make sure the kid doesn't go playin' with the lights." They managed a smile together.

"No sweat Herb. I haven't got my car in working order anyway, apparently. C'mon Stevie, let's go!"

CHAPTER FOUR

UPPER PENINSULA OF MICHIGAN
MAY 1965

Dick Chapman breathed in deeply. He couldn't seem to get enough of the fresh, spring air roaring in through his car window as he sped along the south shore of Lake Superior on Highway 28. The weather was unusually warm for the middle of May in Upper Michigan. Over the years, Dick had driven this particular stretch of highway in every type of weather imaginable, all within a day or so of the exact same calendar date. On the warm days, such as this one, he needed only to open the car window a crack for a free blast of Mother Nature's air conditioning off this largest of all the freshwater lakes.

Dick peered over at his grandson, Todd, lying at an awkward angle across the front passenger seat of his "62 Ford Falcon. The eleven year old's mouth was propped open wide- the boy was in a deep sleep. He had been sucking air for a good seventy-five miles and his grampa decided that he'd have just a horrible taste in his arid mouth when he finally came to. Dick, therefore, was determined to stop along the road at the next picnic sight in order to grab a cold bottle of coke from the Coleman cooler in the trunk. This way, the boy would only suffer from serious cottonmouth for a very short time. 'What a great grandpaw I am,' Dick thought. And indeed he was.

He had originally begun this yearly trek north from his Chilicothe, Ohio home back in the spring of 1940 at the suggestion of his old army buddy, Rutledge. The first trip was with his then fifteen-year old son, Dean. Lucy, his wife, never did like fishing or camping, and those were the primary reasons she gave for never coming along. And that was just fine by Dick. This annual trip to Lake Independence for the Northern Pike and Walleye season opener had allowed him a week of elbow rubbing with, at first son Dean and his own dear Uncle Jessie, God rest his wonderful, old soul; And then in later years, he'd managed to drag along his brother Vic a number of times, when he could pry him away from that real estate office, and finally, this spring, his only grandson was making his first trip.

For Dick, this was also his first trip away from home since he had more or less retired and turned the day-to-day operation of his successful hardware business over to a full time manager. This, he had accomplished on St. Patrick's Day. In the two months since, he had made every repair and improvement imaginable in and around his own home. Some of the projects, like the re-grouting of the bathroom tile, had been put off for years. But with all the free time, he had entered into each chore with extra gusto. Not unexpectedly, with all of his enthusiasm, he had been driving Lucy bonkers, and knew that she was probably glad to see him take off for a while. After all, he only planned on being gone for a week.

The campground was less than ten miles from Rutledge's hometown of Birch, and Dick made a point of getting together with him at least once during his visit. Rutledge had mellowed over the years. He had been running his big logging business up there, and was a respected member of the community. Dick usually met him at the local Sawmill Bar, a rough pine structure that had been constructed on the historic site of a lumber mill that was once the largest in the Upper Peninsula. They generally had a few beers, then retired to the living room of Rutledge's big, sprawling green-framed house. There they would get into a bottle of brandy, and discuss old times. Rutledge's wife had died a few years back, and he now lived alone.

The camping experience was worth more to Dick than anything else. He still loved to rough it, just as long as it was for not more than a five or six night stretch. In addition, the fishing was generally excellent, even in the occasional snow squall. And what could possibly ever taste better than a pan-fried walleye fillet cooked over the campfire and washed down with an icy cold Leinenkugel?

Dick's grandson rolled over onto his back next to him, still sleeping. He wedged the top of his head between Dick's ribs and the car seat. His mouth was still open. His lips and gums were looking dry. Keeping one eye on the road, Dick reached back and searched through the pockets of his overcoat on the backseat and found his little tube of chapstick balm. It was then that he sighted a picnic area looming just ahead along the lakeshore.

Dick pulled off the highway and stopped the car. He removed his dark brown-framed glasses and rubbed his eyes. The little rest area was otherwise deserted. The first real wave of tourists wasn't expected in the 'U.P.' until the end of the month at the earliest. Dick got out of the car, leaving his door open, moving about gingerly in order to combat his stiffness. Two days spent in a car was more than enough of a reminder that his sixty-sixth birthday was barely two months hence. He opened the trunk and released the latch on his bright red Coleman cooler. He pulled out the coke and pried off the cap. He was at once aware of his grandson's voice scarcely discernable above the steady din of the lake waves crashing up on the beach nearby.

"Hey! We almost there, gramps?"

Dick shut the trunk and returned to the driver's side of the Ford. He could see that the boy was sitting up, squinting in the daylight, winking sweetly until he could manage to keep both eyes open. Dick sure could see plenty of Dean in him. "No Todd, not quite yet. We should be pulling into Marquette in about forty minutes. Patience, my boy, patience."

"Shucks!" Todd's tired eyes brightened noticeably. "Hey! Is that a coke? My mouth feels like it's full of sand."

"I got it out just for you, young man. I knew you'd be wakin' up as soon as the car stopped rolling." Todd grabbed the bottle and took a big swig.

Dick held out the chapstick balm. "When you've finished, you better coat your lips good with this stuff. I'll be in the rest room over there." Dick pointed at the wood-sided privy. "Might be a good idea if you use it, too, before we get back on the road again." He strolled onto the sandy path that wound through some straggly jack pines to the men's bathroom. The leaves on most of the surrounding trees were just peeking out from their buds. At least there was no snow left on the ground this year. Dick could recall many an early May when the snow was still collected in big, dirty drifts, having much the same consistency as wet cement.

When Dick opened the door to the outdoor toilet, he wondered if he was going to give the place its summer christening. It sure didn't seem like anybody had been in there, yet. The air was as fresh as outside, and not a fly could be found. It would be a welcome surprise for Todd, especially after his piss poor experience in the john of that donut shop in Gaylord.

Somebody had vomited in the giant plastic wastebasket in the place- but not before they'd filled the toilet with diarrhea and the air with sick farts. They didn't even have the decency to flush it. What pigs! Poor Todd. He hadn't been able to touch the big brownie that they'd bought him until they were in sight of the Mackinac Bridge.

Dick now stood, urinating. He had always been known to house an unusually large, efficient bladder- had quite a reputation for it, in fact, dating back to his stay in Germany while in the Expeditionary Forces at the close of World War I. He wondered how Rutledge was getting along; Rutledge, the one who had introduced him to fishing in Northern Michigan. Rutledge was the one who used to say that Dick could drink that good German brew all night, and then take until at least noon to piss it all out the next day. And then Rutledge would tell everybody within earshot that he was proud to know Dick, just for that reason alone. Dick smiled, shook himself, and then tugged up his zipper. There was a polite tap on the door.

"You 'bout done, gramps?" Dick opened the door.

"I sure am, Todd. It's all yours."

"That's alright," replied the grandson, "I peed behind them trees above the beach. There's no cars that coulda seen me."

Dick smiled. He sure loved this kid. He was just under five feet tall with a Princeton haircut- buzzed on the sides and back with a shock of longer hair spilling down onto his forehead. His blue eyes were still innocent looking, though Dick expected that to change shortly. His little nose was turned up slightly and his lips were full and fleshy, like those of his father's, and grandfather's before him. Dick gave him a quick hug.

They resumed their travels. This was not only Todd's first fishing trip with gramps, but his first real drive into the North Country, as well. The view from the middle of the Mackinac Bridge, linking Michigan's two peninsulas, had been spectacular. They had crossed the bridge earlier that same morning. The bright sun had gleamed off the sparkling, blue waters, hundreds of feet below. Gramps had told him about the car ferry- the only means of crossing the five-mile wide waterway in all those years prior to 1957. He told him about the Chief Wawatam, the old railroad car ferry which his dead war buddy, Toivo Ahonen, had used to work on back before the Depression.

"How did he die?" Todd had asked.

"He owned a gas station. One night, he was robbed and stabbed to death. Just terrible; It's been close to ten years since it happened."

"Did you talk to him much before he died? You must've seen him when you come up this way?"

"Used to stop in every year- fill up the gas tank, maybe have some lunch. But old Toivo, he wasn't one for visitors. I think I just reminded him of some bad times- back during the war. We just went our separate ways, I guess, him and me."

As they had approached the tollbooths at the north end of the span, Dick told Todd how easy it was to forget about the workers who had plunged to their deaths during the construction of the bridge.

"It's the same as with Toivo Ahonen," he said, "ten years dead and I don't think of him but once a year."

"When's that?" Todd asked.

"Couple weeks before Christmas," gramps found himself answering.

Dick remembered that look of pure excitement in Todd's blue eyes, back when they had first pulled onto the bridge. It made him feel so good to provide this experience for his grandson. Now he saw that look again. Fresh from his midday nap, Todd was looking off toward the horizon, following the lakeshore as it curved north. He could see smokestacks and the hint of a settlement in the far off haze.

"That's Marquette," said Dick, "largest city in the U.P."

"How much farther is it past Marquette?" asked the boy impatiently. "We gotta get to where we're goin' in time to set up our tent! D'ya think we're goin' fishin' before dark, gramps?"

"Don't worry, Todd. Once we get going north out of town, it's only about another thirty-five miles and then we'll be at the lake. We'll have plenty of time to wet our lines and cook some fish up for dinner."

"That friend of yours- the one you always visit when you're up here- d'ya think he'll be meetin' us up there? At the camp, I mean?"

"Not likely, kiddo. Mr. Rutledge is generally real busy with his logging operation. He's one of his town's leading citizens. Owns a great big house up there in Birch."

"That's a funny name for a town- Birch!" said little Todd.

"Mr. Rutledge told me one time that on Devil's Night, the local kids used to go out to the village limits and change the R to a T on the town sign."

"Bitch!" Todd guffawed. "That's funny, gramps! Welcome to the town of Bitch!"

"Okay," Dick said with a mock frown. "Now I'm not at all sure your grandma would approve of me tellin' you about that. And I know she wouldn't approve of your reaction. Anyhow, Birch, at one time, was quite a booming town. They had a great big lumber mill, and Ford Motor manufactured some of the wooden parts for the Model A in a great big brick building that's still standing. I was told they even had a bowling pin factory up there somewhere. All of those enterprises kept Rutledge Logging mighty busy. You know, back during the Great War, Mr. Rutledge was always saying his family had the biggest logging operation east of the Mississippi."

"They still make bowling pins?" Todd asked with wide eyes.

"No. Sorry Todd, the bowling pin factory has been closed. The only industry left of any note is Rutledge Logging."

It was two o'clock by the time they drove by the gothic gate of the Marquette Branch Prison, a dark, sinister complex hidden in the hills three miles south of town. Michigan's most notorious felons were housed there. Todd kept staring at the ivy choked walls and the castle like towers of the administration building beyond until they had climbed to the top of a large hill and the panorama of Marquette appeared before them.

"It's a pretty town, ain't it, gramps?"

"This town's got character. I've always liked those old buildings."

The old city was built on a steep hillside. Directly ahead, the center of downtown was comprised of a number of five to eight story turn of the century sandstone buildings. Off to their right, An old iron ore pellet docks that serviced the nearby mines jutted well out into the harbor. Todd took it all in for the first time.

"This sure is a big town for bein' up north."

"You're right about that, young man. Hey, I don't know about you, but I'm famished. Think you could eat a hamburger?"

"I think I could eat three," replied Todd, his eyes widening at the prospect.

They ate a hurried lunch in a downtown bar. Afterwards, Dick led them into an adjoining storefront- a fish and hunt shop, to register for his

non-resident fishing license and pick up a few extra crawler harnesses.
   A lone employee stood behind a counter in front of a long gun rack that was mounted to the right side wall, polishing the barrel of a center fire rifle. He had a salt and pepper beard, uncombed hair, and a long, green and black flannel shirt with the shirttail out.
   Gramps shopped unhurriedly, comparing prices on 250 yard spools of twelve pound test line. He eventually picked up several night crawler harnesses, after spending half again as much time considering red and white daredevil spoons.
   All of the anticipation was getting to be too much for Todd to handle. He tugged gently at his gramps' sleeve as he chatted with the store clerk after finally making it as far as the cash register. They talked about recent weather conditions and the resultant fishing prospects.
   The clerk voiced this opinion: "The sunshine'll warm that water right up. The big ones, they'll be on the move, eh?" He folded the top of the bag filled with crawler harnesses and handed it to Dick.
   "And a little rain wouldn't hurt anything, either, if it comes," said Dick, covering his bets.
   "Where you goin' out? Teal Lake? That's sure a hotspot in the early season."
   "I go up to Lake Independence every year," Dick said proudly. "Every year but one, since 1940. Always here for opening day."
   The clerk pursed his lips at the mere mention of Lake Independence. He stroked his beard thoughtfully. "Well," he said after a pause, "they did just re-open the road up there after the snow melt. There's been some major changes up there- don't reckon you've heard too much about 'em, heh?"
   "Sounds like progress," said Dick uneasily.
   "I wish I could call it progress," replied the clerk uneasily. "The Federal Government went in and evacuated the town of Birch- that's the God's truth. The official story they're givin' everybody is that the multimillionaire who owned the land near Birch bought up what was left of the town- wanting to enlarge his hunting preserve and all- wanting all the privacy his money could buy- supposedly paid unheard of prices to buy everybody out. He has holdings outside Reno somewheres- he traded some of his prime property there for some of the Birch property."

"I don't believe it!" cried Dick. "I've got an old war buddy up there- Rutledge, Sam Rutledge! Everybody knows him! Sam wouldn't sell out to anybody- for any price!"

"I seen Sam around. Sam made out real good on the deal, from what I understand. He doesn't answer any questions about the why's and wherefore's. The rumor about the real story up there that's been goin' around- I s'pose I better come out with it, eh?"

Dick's stomach was churning. "What's this real story?" he asked, his voice going flat.

The clerk pushed his moustache away from his top lip. "The government was using the old Ford factory for a chemical weapons experiment. Something happened up there, and next thing you know a bunch of MP's from the Sawyer air base south of here were sealing off the area. They even brought reinforcements in by helicopter so the locals here in town wouldn't notice any troop movements along the roads- and that's the honest-to-God truth. You know, you can't get into Birch no more. Everything's no trespass up there now. That millionaire made his fortune off of defense contracts, so they say. Folks think he covered up the accident. Wouldn't be surprised if he's not making a fortune off this deal, too."

"Wh-what about the campgrounds up there?"

"No problem. The campground's open. Lake Independence must be, I don't know, ten miles north of there. Then again, I'm sure I don't have to tell you that." Another customer entered the store. "I sure am glad you stopped by," said the merchant with a wink. "At least this way, it'll spare you any shock."

"I appreciate that," said Dick hollowly, aware that his grandson was no longer tugging at his arm so eagerly. "Do you know where I might find Sam Rutledge? I'm sure he'd want to see me-"

"He came in here last fall- right before deer season," said the clerk. He gestured towards the other customer, who just then was getting together some fly tying materials. "Hey Kelly, you seen Sam Rutledge from Rutledge Logging anywhere lately?"

"He doesn't hang around Marquette, never has," he answered icily. "He tried to run me off a stretch of the Yellow Dog a couple years ago near his clear cut. I got no use for the man."

"Well, I guess the boy and I'll make the best of it- this is his first fishing trip to the U.P." Dick patted Todd on the shoulder. The eyes of the other man shone more warmly.

"I'm sure you'll catch some big ones," said the clerk with a whiskery smile.

"I might see you on the lake this weekend," said the man called Kelly.

"Now make sure you leave a couple big ones in the lake for me, okay?" Dick led Todd back out to the car. He had no intention of ruining his grandson's fishing trip. He could see that the little fellow wore a long face already.

"Hey Todd!" said gramps with renewed enthusiasm, "if I don't see my friend on this trip, it's no loss, okay? Let's go get the tent set up and hook a walleye for dinner- whatdayasay?" The boy's eyes brightened considerably.

"Yea! Let's go!"

It wasn't quite three o'clock when Dick turned onto the winding, paved county road that ran north to Birch and Lake Independence. Under normal conditions, this was Dick's favorite stretch of roadway. The ancient Huron Mountain range had forced road construction through outcroppings, along streams, by cliff-like formations, and past glacial meadows. The top of the steepest hill provided a spectacular view of a rocky, aquamarine lagoon way down below on the Lake Superior shoreline. Admiring the view from the passenger side window, Todd decided that this was the ultimate pirate cove- a hideout worthy of Long John Silver.

"Hey gramps, this must have been Indian country back in the old days, huh? Just like Great Uncle Ned's farm back in Chilicothe. Think there are arrowheads in these woods? Could we go lookin'?"

Dick was totally focused on the story that was told to him in the tackle shop. He couldn't even begin digesting the possibility that an era in his life had come to an abrupt end- at least not until he had ingested all the facts. Imagine! A town of over six hundred people- admittedly a dying one- disappearing from the official state map- Dick was dumbfounded.

"Yer worried about your friend, Mr. Rutledge, aren't ya?"

Dick forced a smile. "I'm concerned, Todd. I've been coming up here for twenty-five years. I've drunk many beers in the Sawmill Bar- and that's right in downtown Birch. It's inconceivable- I don't understand, how or what has happened." Dick shrugged at his grandson.

"They talked about Mr. Rutledge like he's okay. He's still around, right? I don't think that one fishing guy likes him. Sounded like Mr. Rutledge was mean to him."

"I would think he's up in this area somewhere, Todd. Except, knowing Sam, he must have gotten a good settlement out of this. He may have just high-tailed it to Reno, Nevada, like most of his neighbors."

"Maybe you'll feel better after you catch a big fish, huh gramps?"

Dick placed his arm around the boy's shoulders and squeezed him with great affection. "Damn right, Todd! After we get camp set up, while we're breathin' some of that fresh northern air, heck- life'll be orderly in a big hurry." Dick glanced over at the boy, who seemed to sigh imperceptibly, a wave of relief sweeping over him ever so gently. All must be fine with gramps, again. The camping trip would go on as planned and they would have the time of their lives together.

Dick was easily able to mask the overwhelming realization that something was terribly wrong. At least he would be spared the experience of actually passing through the little town. The county road wound past the outskirts, on the fringes, within view of some of the cracker box houses put up hurriedly all in a row during the height of the boom times, at the beginning of the century.

There was very little in the way of traffic heading south. Only a handful of oncoming cars passed them by. Virtually every one of them was either pulling a boat trailer, or had a small boat or canoe lashed to the roof. In other years, logging trucks loaded with huge pine logs, southbound for the pulp mill in Escanaba, would rumble past him somewhere between Marquette and Birch.

Todd was enjoying the drive. Normally, nearing the end of a long car ride found him miserably impatient (his father considered him an impossible passenger even on the ride from Chilicothe to Columbus to attend the Ohio State Fair). But now he and his gramps were entering a densely forested, rolling land. The tree leaves had not popped out as yet so Todd could look deep into the forest, taking in the freshness of the full-blown, northern spring. The trees were heavily budded, and the sugar maples were tinged with red and orange hues and, illuminated as they were in the late-afternoon sunlight, gave off a surging sensation of lushness and renewed life.

It wasn't long before they had neared the ghost town of Birch. Dick had noticed that all commercial and directional signs relating to the town had been uprooted and removed. The Sawmill Bar's faded old sign was gone, as was that of the local IGA grocery. Dick slowed to a crawl and found that he was taking the old turnoff toward the village, in spite of himself. It was no surprise to him that within one hundred yards of the main road, a ten foot, barb wire topped cyclone fence blocked the way. Dick pulled his Ford right up to the barricade and stopped. He felt an emptiness in his chest which gave way to a wave of nausea and a bout of light headedness and for a moment, he thought he might actually faint. He shook his head and, not wanting to scare Todd, threw open the car door, climbed out and stood next to the fence, taking in air in measured inhalations. That was better. He looked up at the top of the fence, at a small white sign painted with bold, red lettering:

PRIVATE PROPERTY-TRESPASSERS WILL BE PROSECUTED

He looked along the whole length of fence, first to the north, then back toward the south. To have a town, or a significant portion of it fenced off from the general population elsewhere in the Upper Peninsula was not all that uncommon. Frighteningly deep mine shafts, too numerous to count, blasted out in the days of the famous copper and iron ore strikes, dotted the landscape, waiting to literally undermine the surface above. The iron town of Negaunee, in fact, has a number of residential areas where children are banned to this day from so much as playing in their own backyards, lest they be swallowed into the very bowels of the earth.

The boarding up of Birch, then, looked to Dick like an accepted fact by the locals. They simply had added this little town of wood framed houses to the long list of other towns and hamlets that had gone bust in the U.P. during the preceding hundred years.

"C'mon gramps! We better go!"

Dick had come to his senses enough to hear his little grandson shouting from the car. He turned away from the fence and eased back behind the steering wheel. As he notched the car into reverse, he concluded then and there that this matter simply could not rest. He would be compelled to see firsthand what hard evidence, if any, remained behind which would indicate the reasons for the town's abrupt abandonment. If he were on foot, walking along the parameter of the barricade, he knew he would find an opening, a soft spot in the armor through which he could enter in order to personally investigate. Most of all, he had to see Sam Rutledge, wherever he was keeping himself.

"Hey gramps, this is weird," said Todd almost reverently, observing a portion of the wood framed skyline of the empty town. He had been quiet for several minutes, out of respect for his grandfather. He had watched the pain flash across the old man's wrinkled face. "I ain't never seen a place like this, before; No people. It's pretty neat! I was wonderin' if we could get in there someway?"

Dick wheeled the car around and headed back out to the open road. "Todd, the 'no trespassing' sign means just what it says," he answered firmly. "I didn't bring you up to the North Country to wind up in jail- grandma would kill me, sure as shootin'!"

Perkins Park on Lake Independence was another ten minutes north of there. Dick had always reserved the same campsite each year- number nine, the site closest to the boat landing, so it was not necessary for him to stop and check in with Ned Baker, the longtime park ranger, prior to setting up the tent.

When Dick finally pulled off the county road and onto the campgrounds gravel drive, Todd was so impatient all he could do was sit on his hands and bounce. The drive was lined by maples, pines and white birches and after easing down an incline and around a curve, the five-hundred acre lake sprawled out before them. The water sparkled.

"Wow! What a big lake!" cried Todd.

They drove past the park store and Dick pulled up to their campsite beside the lake.

"Hey! This is really great, gramps! Just like dad said! Is this our campsite?"

"It certainly is," replied Dick, mesmerized momentarily by the intriguing sight of a large fish breaking the surface not fifty feet from shore. They got out of the car and Dick went ahead and opened the trunk. He lifted a brown, bulky canvas bag out and carried it over to the picnic table. "Okay Todd! We'll be setting up the tent right in this area. I want you to pick out any sharp sticks or stones from the dirt. And be thorough- your old gramps needs a soft bed."

The boy sprang to the spot and worked diligently to smooth the ground out. Dick, in the meantime, unloaded the cooler, the gas cook stove and lantern, and the crate of pans and dishes and stacked everything on the picnic table. He returned to the trunk, took a deep breath, and hefted his seven horsepower Mercury outboard motor up and away from its nicely cushioned resting place.

"Todd!" he shouted, his face beet red with effort, "let's go mount our motor on the boat!"

The boy tossed the last pebble from the tent site and scurried over and took hold midway along the drive shaft of the old motor. Even at eleven years old, he managed to ease Dick's burden considerably.

"There's a boat down here with our campsite number on it," said Dick, huffing and puffing in the soft beach sand. "Look for number nine. Christ!"

"There she is!" Todd announced. There were a dozen wooden boats all freshly painted dark green, pulled half up along the water's edge, their anchors digging firmly into the sand. Todd led Dick by the small end of the motor that he held so firmly in his arms, and now steered him in a relatively straight line through the sand to the boat with the little 'nine' painted on it.

"Whew!" Dick gasped upon placing the motor mount on the stern of the boat. He pulled a white hankie from his pants pocket and wiped away at the beads of sweat freshly popped out all over his forehead and face. "This is the most tiresome chore," he said aloud.

"I'm gettin' the fishin' gear!" cried Todd, breaking into a dead run for the car.

"Don't forget the bag of crawler harnesses and the net!" Dick shouted after him. He sat down in the rear of the boat, tightening down the bolts on the motor mount. He was finding such a young, eager pair of legs to be a real bonus in this situation. Invariably, two to three trips from car to boat were necessary in order to be fully prepared to embark upon the waters. Dick remembered all too well that for many years, his own legs provided most of the power, his Uncle Jessie having had such frequent run-ins with gout as to make him ineffectual as a camping partner, capable of only eating, sleeping, and evacuating his bladder and bowels with any modicum of consistency.

Todd now returned to the boat in high gear, despite being handicapped by an adult sized load of tackle boxes, fishing poles, seat cushions, and net. "Here you go, gramps!" he said, distributing his burden haphazardly in their boat. "Think we can git out there, now?"

"It's still the highlight of our agenda," replied Dick, standing in the boat and then carefully stepping back out onto the bank. "First, we have to get that tent up. Then, we have to check in at the park store. Need some beer, and some night crawlers."

Todd looked doubtful. "You sure we gotta do all that?"

Dick smiled and rubbed his knuckles on his grandson's scalp exuberantly. "C'mon Todd! We'll be back in the boat before you can say, Jiminy Cricket!"

After setting up camp, Dick drove them to the park store to pick up the last minute provisions and check-in to their campsite. As usual, the campground was practically deserted. There were half a dozen trailers scattered throughout the section of the park that provided electrical hook-ups and water, but Dick knew that at least three of those had been brought in for the season because he had seen them in previous years. Only two of the remaining trailers looked like they were getting any use. Dick also counted four other tents besides his own, so until the weekend, at least, things would be very quiet.

To young Todd, the camp store, a smartly constructed log cabin with cedar shake shingles and a field stone chimney was an irresistible place to spend what little money he had earned from chores and brought with him. He emptied his pockets in order to buy picture postcards featuring bear and deer, a bow and arrow set (Dick later peeled off the 'Made in Taiwan' label), and a fistful of bubblegum.

For his part, Dick ordered up two-dozen night crawlers, a case of Leinenkugels beer, a quart of milk, and marshmallows, graham crackers and Hershey bars in order to manufacture s'mores, the universal late night snack of the campfire crowd. He filled out the campsite permit and handed it to the pleasant, young red-haired girl working the counter.

"Is ol' Ned around today?" Dick asked, setting the pencil on the counter.

"I'm sorry to say we lost Ned last year. He passed away." She looked dolefully down at the maple floorboards.

"That's so sad- I'm so sorry," Dick managed awkwardly. "Gee, he was getting pretty near retirement age, wasn't he?"

"I don't think Ned would have ever retired," she replied, and then she came up with a soft smile. "He really loved his job."

"He'll always be here in spirit," Dick said, gesturing around with his right hand. "Heck, Ned always knew where the walleyes were. He helped my catch considerably over the years. I would have liked for him to meet my grandson, here. This is his first visit. Ranger Baker was sort of an institution."

"It will never be the same around here as it was with Ned. Thanks for your kind words." She smiled again and got busy with something behind the counter.

Back at camp, Dick put the milk and six of the beers on ice, and then got hold of the five gallons of pre-mixed fuel that he had brought for the outboard. "Todd, my boy," he said, hefting yet another heavy load through the sand, "high time to catch some big ones."

After only two hours on the lake, all of Todd's expectations were met. He had caught and grampa had netted the biggest fish in his life, a six pound, thirty inch Northern pike. As for grampa, he had reeled in two nice walleyes in the twenty-inch range. They had remained out on the lake until the sun had dropped low enough into the western sky to allow the air to cool rapidly, at which time it occurred to Dick that his rag wool sweater was still in the car, and his light windbreaker was no longer doing the job.

"It's getting chilly in a hurry," he said. "Besides, I'll need some time to clean these beautiful fish."

Todd was warmed by their noteworthy success. He had planned to eat beans the first night, just like the cowboys on the cattle drives, but instead was in awe of the number of nasty teeth belonging to the giant fish which he'd caught, and couldn't even imagine how much flesh gramps could so skillfully cut away with that funny looking knife of his. "Can I help you clean 'em, gramps?"

Dick pulled on the starter rope and throttled up the engine. He turned back towards his grandson. "You most certainly can!" he yelled above the din. "I'll show you how to cut a fishes' heart out and hold it beating in your hand!"

"Naw!" bellowed the boy. "Can you really!?" Dick just nodded and pointed the bow of the boat towards their shore.

As dusk gradually descended upon Lake Independence, the much cooler air settled over the sun-warmed waters, creating an eerie mist which formed wispy fingers on the surface of the lake. Propelled by the light, swirling air currents, the wraith-like fog patches danced, drifted and curled in constant motion, as if celebrating on the first beams of the newly risen moon, its bright, full face having just then cleared the tops of the distant, eastern hills.

Dick scraped the remaining fish fillets and overly done potatoes out of the cast iron fry pan and onto his plate. Todd was nearby, searching for a suitable marshmallow stick in the gloaming, having stuffed himself with walleye and American fries until he could eat no more. Courteously, Dick asked, "Todd, sure you don't want some more fish?"

"No thanks gramps, I'm full."

Dick realized that he, himself, had eaten more than enough, as well. But the well done potatoes, delightfully crispy and full of flavor, mixed with the lightly battered fish was a treat that could not be passed up, especially since he was using an icy cold bottle of Leinenkugels beer with which to wash it down. Dick chewed on the final couple of mouthfuls while Todd whittled at the end of a maple switch, then skewered a marshmallow and directed it over the hot embers of their campfire.

Dick took a final guzzle of beer. "You just can't beat a meal cooked in the outdoors like this- the fish doesn't get any fresher. For breakfast, I'll cook us up some peas and your pike."

"I'm hungry for some of them s'mores," said Todd, turning the marshmallow carefully until it was a toasty brown.

"Just a minute," replied Dick, leaning over the picnic table and frantically pumping the pressurized tank on the gas lantern. "I have to throw a little light here, first."

The lantern soon burned bright, centered on the picnic table. Dick opened up one of the chocolate bars and the graham cracker box and Todd was in business. "I bet you want some milk to go with this?"

"Yea, thanks gramps," replied the grandson. By the time Dick had lifted the carton of milk from the ice chest and filled a dixie cup for the boy, a sticky mess of cracker crumbs, melted chocolate, and dried marshmallow had been glued to the youngster's lips and chin. Gramps handed him the cup. Todd took a hefty swallow and let out a sigh of absolute satisfaction. "Hey! That moon sure is pretty, ain't it?"

Dick sat back, lounging as best he could on the picnic table bench, his feet propped up on the big rocks surrounding the campfire. He looked out over the lake. What a generous bonus from Mother Nature this was. The moon was full, or close enough to it. The clear, northern air made it seem all the brighter, and the fact that the leaves were still not fully out on the trees reduced the shadows in the woods surrounding their campsite and beyond. "Gorgeous view! Just beautiful." The fire popped and crackled, sending a shower of sparks onto the edge of the pit. "Todd, I think this is what they call being in perfect harmony with nature." Dick belched loudly.

The boy ignored him, packing another marshmallow and chocolate sandwich into his mouth. He no longer was taking the time to roast the marshmallows carefully to a golden brown, but instead was holding each one in the actual flames of the fire until a miniature blaze would engulf it, then, turning it until all surfaces were a uniform shiny black, he would blow out the flame and squeeze it off the end of his stick into a waiting pair of graham cracker sections which had been stacked up assembly-line style on top of the picnic table. In this manner, Todd could eat a tremendous number of treats in minutes. Todd swallowed and gulped from his milk cup. "Here gramps, I made this one for you."

Dick smiled, taking the treat and biting off a corner. "M-m-m Todd, you make a mean s'more!"

Todd was not able to reply. His mouth was crammed to the gills again.

Off in the distance, an owl hooted from the depths of the forest, giving fair warning to the local hares and rodents that the evening's menu was beyond the planning stage. "Bright enough to go night fishin', huh gramps?"

"A little cool out on the lake, but there's more than enough light, that's for sure." Dick picked up a stick from the kindling pile and stirred the hot coals of their fire into the dirt. He usually felt a touch of sadness when the time came to extinguish a campfire- it being the source of such warmth and good cheer. But not tonight; Dick had other things on his mind.

"I'm gettin' sleepy, gramps. Can I lay out the sleeping bags, now?"

"You bet. They're keeping warm and dry in the backseat. And don't forget my fluffy feather pillow!"

While Todd was preparing their beds, Dick sat quietly on the edge of the picnic bench, slowly stirring out the fire. In the cool night air, he was certain that Todd would be fast asleep just as soon as his adolescent head contacted his pillow. Dick made the decision then that when he was sure the boy was fast asleep, he himself would take advantage of the moonlit night and drive back to Birch in order to do a little poking around- to look for any remaining evidence of the town's sudden demise. He was startled by a shout from within the tent.

"Okay gramps! Sleeping bags are ready!"

Dick rose to his feet, still feeling the effects of the Leinenkugels, and headed toward the tent flap. He threw it back and found Todd maneuvering around inside with his boy-scout flashlight. The grandfather was pleased. The child showed every sign of having inherited the Chapman work ethic. "That was quick work, young man. Now, I've got some soap, towels, toothpaste, and toothbrushes all packed in that duffle just inside there, on the floor. We'll head right over to the bathhouse and get cleaned up for bed."

"I promise to brush first thing in the mornin'," Todd bargained hopefully.

"Sorry my boy. You sound just like your father. No, we need to brush the chocolate out of our teeth- and you've got to wash that face of yours- by golly, you're almost old enough to get pimples! Better keep those pores clean." Todd rolled his eyes, but offered no further resistance.

Later, as they lay side-by-side in their sleeping bags, Dick reached for his own flashlight and briefly illuminated Todd's face. The boy stirred slightly and mumbled something unintelligibly. "Todd," Dick said softly, "I'm going to drive out to the pay phone at the park entrance and give your grandma a call before it gets too late." The grandson licked his lips, then rolled over and fell into a deeper sleep.

Dick eased out of his sleeping bag and slipped into his hiking boots. He pulled on his rag wool sweater and his windbreaker, then slowly unzipped the canvas flap and stepped out of the tent. He zipped the door closed again, then secured the tie downs, listening for any sign of a wide-awake boy within. Satisfied, he arched his back and looked up at the moonlit sky, and then he involuntarily shivered. A rush of cold and clammy shot along his spine; Obviously, his subconscious knew what he had in mind.

He reached into his jacket pocket and pulled out his key chain, then walked to the back of the car and opened the trunk. Using the flashlight again, he located a small toolbox beneath the fishing poles, and working quickly, opened it up and took out a pair of good pliers and a screwdriver. He pushed the trunk closed, stuffing the pliers, screwdriver, and flashlight into the jacket pocket, then walked around to the side of the car and climbed in behind the wheel.

Dick drove slowly through the campground using his parking lights. The whole area was dead quiet. At only one other campsite was there a sign of any activity- two men could be seen seated in fold up chairs near their campfire, drinking beer. Dick continued on out to the county road, lit up his brights, and turned towards Birch.

The eight-mile drive was uneventful. Not one car passed him along the way. The highway was in good condition and Dick was able to cruise along at top speed. It wasn't long before he approached the old Birch turnoff.

He slowed to a crawl and turned off his car lights. In the sudden darkness, he scanned for headlights out ahead, and then back to the road behind him. There being no sign of any other vehicles advancing upon the old intersection, Dick turned his lights back on and took the unmarked road to the right, toward the chained and bolted gate which he and Todd had encountered earlier in the day. Remembering how clearly the area near the gate could be seen from the main road, he decided to turn south and follow the fence line. He drove slowly through the grass and brush, along the edge of the chain link fence. Far ahead, two pairs of eyes reflected in the glare of his headlights, high off the ground. 'Whitetail deer, is all,' Dick thought. He looked at the terrain just ahead of the car and when he glanced up again, the eyes had vanished. He crawled along for another hundred yards or so, until the area immediately ahead of him became increasingly soft and mushy from the spring thaw. He stopped the car.

Dick turned off the engine, glancing at his watch. Ten minutes to midnight; He felt for the tools and flashlight in his coat, then opened the car door slowly. Having stopped on the edge of a bog, a loud chorus from the large population of spring peepers inhabiting the swamp overwhelmed the area. It sounded to Dick like there were thousands and thousands of the little creatures all in synch with that high-pitched chirp that had given them their popular name.

Dick's plan was to continue on foot to the south and then turn to the west along the back side of the fence line, if necessary, searching for a likely spot where a minimum of snips of the aluminum wire would enable him to access the inner confines. Cutting a big hole in the chain link at this point would not only be terribly time consuming, but would constitute destruction of property, and Dick was not quite ready to cross that line. If it became necessary, he would re-evaluate his thinking. He closed the car door as noiselessly as he could, then taking one last look back toward the gate, turned and began his trek.

As he walked along, brushing the chain link fence at intervals with his right hand, he became aware that an inner feeling of intense excitement was spawning a surge of adrenaline through his rusty loins, the likes of which he hadn't felt in many years. He picked up his pace and at the same time, felt that his vision had become much more acute. This latter sensation may have only been caused by the adjustment his retinas had made to the low level of available light. But Dick felt more aware than before- more alive.

A light breeze was freshening from the west and the woods surrounding him, already alive with the sounds of spring, now rustled and creaked softly in the moonlight. A pack of coyotes, preparing for their hunt, let out their shrill-pitched wailing cry somewhere off in the night, curling the hairs on the back of Dick's neck as he strode along.

The fencing itself remained tall and impregnable- especially for Dick, who had lost much of his climbing ability over the years and now, only as a last resort, would he consider straddling the top of the fence and clipping away at the barbed wire strands in order to enter the forbidden area. He could see out ahead that the terrain dipped down and then rose up along the slope of a grassy hill. It looked as though at the top of that rise, the fencing cornered and then headed west.

When Dick reached the base of the hill, he found the ground to be wet and soggy. His boots made gurgling, suctioning noises and he slowed his pace to keep from losing his balance. It was bright enough out to allow him to see that the bottom of the fence in that area was raised up off the ground several inches but he ruled out the possibility of trying to squeeze underneath- he would become a water soaked, mud coated mess. Hell, he'd probably drown! After a few more paces through the muck he began the gentle climb up the hill and found firm ground within the first five yards. He advanced toward the corner post and when he finally had reached it, he had to stop to catch his breath.

He turned and looked back along his path and discovered that from his vantage point upon the crest of the hill, he had a commanding view of the whole area. He could see the chrome on the rear bumper of his car, reflecting the light of the moon. He could see the tops of the surrounding hills, and he could make out the central core of the abandoned town in great detail. It was a haunting sight, indeed, to see the rooftops, the chimneys, and the two church steeples all bathed in the stark, white light.

Dick took several deep breaths because he was conscious of his heart as it motored in his chest and he wished to settle it down before pressing on. The way the town loomed before him sent another shiver through him. This one started in his toes, coursing up his legs, through his vitals, and into his neck; He touched his wrist and felt his racing pulse, continued with his deep breathing, all the while wondering how much excitement his heart could take in one evening. After a minute or two, his heartbeat slowed. At no time did Dick consider turning back. As uneasy and nervous as he was, he had committed himself to the task at hand, intent upon investigating this matter as best he could.

When Dick felt sufficiently rested, he turned to the west and continued on his route. At the top of the rise, the night breeze was more pronounced and the air had chilled noticeably. Dick turned up the collar on his jacket and was grateful for the rag wool sweater underneath. The fence line led him along the backside of the slope and into a thicket of brush and cover. The fence had been installed right on the edge of the forest and Dick had to carefully step around deadfalls and protect his face from the whip-like sting of the brambles and switches overgrowing his way.

While receiving a sharp sting from one particular springy switch in the dark, Dick stepped sideways, and his left boot almost slid out from under him. He trained the flashlight onto the ground and then jumped reflexively. He had trod on a dead porcupine lying in the brush, half skinned and disemboweled. The meat on the hindquarters had been cleaned right to the bone. Whatever it was had also gnawed away one of the shoulders. Most likely the work of a coyote, he decided.

He walked on for several more minutes until he found a spot such as he was searching for- a weak link in the barricade, an unmistakable point of entry. A large, dead white pine had blown over in a strong wind and had come crashing down with its great weight onto the top of the fence. The aluminum posts and poles had given way underneath and the entire fence had been pushed over onto a forty-five degree pitch, angling sharply inward toward the prohibited ground. Dick paused and then walked right up onto the face of the fence. When he neared the top, he knelt down and pulled out the pliers from his jacket pocket. He began working at the barbed wire strands, four of which ran across the top of the fence. Patiently, he squeezed on the pliers and moved them back and forth, and up and down until he heard a 'pop,' and felt the tension in the wire release. He attacked each strand patiently. When he had clipped through the fourth strand, he used the pliers to bend back the wires at each end, prying them back out of the way, creating a three foot wide space through which even a man of retirement age might enter safely.

That being accomplished, Dick sat on the edge of the opening, scooted awkwardly forward on his butt until his feet dangled freely over the edge, then jumped the five feet to the ground without complication.

Once inside the fence, he continued west until he intersected a trail that broke off toward the north. He followed it without delay. Dick felt reinvigorated by the ease with which he had been able to get past that tall, intimidating fence and his mind began to swell with the ideas and options from which he would have only a short time to choose a plan of action.

He made his way along the narrow path- a path, he imagined, that had seen its share of children passing both upon bicycles, as well as on foot. Dick was trudging along on the packed down dirt that had been sculpted and smoothed by the tread of innumerable sneaker soles through the years, and it occurred to him that this poor, unfortunate, time tested path would never again echo with the teasing, the crying, the laughter, and the playing of children. This path, which had existed solely for the pleasure of each succeeding generation of Birch children had seen its heyday and now, before another summer was to pass, it would be weed choked, overgrown, and forgotten by all who had ever used it.

A hundred yards further on, the path suddenly widened, the trees thinned, and Dick found himself on an alley running behind a loosely arranged grouping of old, wood framed houses. The alley had been topped with crushed cinders and gravel, and he found good footing in the shadows. Several of the back yards were surrounded by picket fences of an identical design, and they were in a sturdy condition, creating the impression that the owners of most of these homes had taken great pride in their outward appearance. If Dick had the time and the inclination, he was sure that upon close inspection, the dwellings themselves would be found to be in excellent condition, with well applied coats of paint or stain, sealing them from the vicious winters and powerful summer storms which were forever blowing in off Lake Superior.

The alley soon intersected a side street and Dick turned to the right and walked along into an ever-thickening jumble of houses and garages. The night breeze came and went, and as it blew between the structures and down the streets and alleys, the town came eerily to life. Loose shutters and unlatched shed doors opened and closed. Wood clapboard siding, swollen with the moisture of springtime, creaked softly, rubbing in certain spots in the same way that old, hardwood flooring tends to squeak underfoot. Dick was prepared for all of these sounds, and he turned a deaf ear to them without much trouble.

Dick wasn't above whistling in the dark, to quiet his jangled nerves, but he thought it somewhat disrespectful in this circumstance. He likened the idea to singing gay ballads in a cemetery, or dancing down the corridor of a cancer ward. He just wasn't one to press his luck with the forces of good, and neither was he about to snicker in the face of the dynamism which he was more likely to come into contact with on this night- the forces of unbridled evil.

Dick turned onto Birch Avenue- the street sign was as plain as day, and he found himself nearing the center of town sooner than he had anticipated. Birch Avenue was lined with the largest homes, including, of course, Sam Rutledge's place. There were also two churches, and further down, a short block of storefronts and the Sawmill Bar.

He passed by the Rutledge place, a big green, three-story clapboard house. It sure didn't appear that anybody had been doing any yard work recently. He trained his light on the untrimmed lawn. The house itself had a face in the dark, as plain to Dick as the man in the moon. It had a definite human-like countenance in its blackened windows and door, reminding him of a contorted face on some half-scorched Halloween jack-o-lantern whose candle had long since gone out in the night. 'Where the hell are you, Sam?'

He walked by the next stately, whitewashed home with a wrought iron fence running the full width of the property. Dick saw the outline of a white painted sign in the shadows, standing out fairly close to the street. He trained the beam of his flashlight on the glossy, black lettering and remembered well that this was, 'Herman Bancroft & Son's Funeral Home.'

'Ned, the park ranger must've been laid out here,' thought Dick. He made his way down the middle of the blacktop into the central business core of Birch. He slowly approached the two picture windows fronting the Sawmill Bar and held up the flashlight against the glass. He was pleasantly surprised to note that every table, chair and stool had been left in its proper place. The bottles of hard liquor had been taken from the shelves but every other piece of equipment had been abandoned in its everyday location.

Dick had decided to go to the old Ford parts factory first. He just wanted to see for himself if there was any shard of evidence that there had been a secret chemical weapons operation there. He would put the theory repeated by the Marquette tackle shop clerk to an immediate test. Personally, Dick was very pessimistic of finding a small-scale operation in a place like Birch. Such a minuscule set up could be much more securely controlled right on a military base and if chemical or biological weapons were involved, Dick figured from what he had read on the subject that Fort Detrick, Maryland, would be the most appropriate choice.

The old, red brick factory building was at the extreme north end of town. Dick easily recognized its large smokestack in the moonlight still well out ahead. He walked on, in the direction of that factory. He began to pass by the Birch Community School.

He had paid little attention to the school during his previous visits to the area, having been most preoccupied with the goings on inside the Sawmill, and he was surprised by the size of the building. It was built with the same red brick as the factory and housed what Dick guessed was either a sizable gymnasium or auditorium that had been clearly erected during the final phase of the school's construction, for the planners had no other alternative than to locate it out near the edge of the street.

It was at that precise moment that a feeling of melancholy took hold of Dick, dampening his agitated and aggressive state. He knew in his heart then that this school had been the focal point of community life in this small, isolated town. The American dream of a brighter future for each succeeding generation was the central theme of life in the U.S. since the Industrial Revolution and nothing was more representative of that ideal than the supreme importance of offering the best possible education in the local school. The people of Birch would clearly have clung to this notion with fierce determination, for in the face of spiraling unemployment and a dying local economy, they would have naturally pinpointed their only hopes for a future of prosperity for their sons and daughters by providing the best educational opportunity that they could muster.

Dick was picking up this magnetism as if a set of Martian antennae had magically sprouted from his forehead. All those people whom he had ever seen in the store, the streets, and the Sawmill Bar were gone forever. But their collective, energetic vision of a better tomorrow remained suspended in the air around the school and Dick was honing in on it like a short wave ham with a high-powered receiver.

All at once, the finality of the whole situation had hit him with the delicacy of a speeding mack truck. Here he was, strolling through a newly minted ghost town, with the bright full moon his blazing cresset, and he was attempting in some small way to grasp, to understand, this manifestation that was so unmistakably present in the form of this existential energy capable of crying out in a tumultuous, bewildered, collective scream due to the loss of everything orderly and purposeful on this small bit of planet earth. This loss, brought on by a premature, untimely end to a way of life as dependent upon the future as an addict dependent upon opiates, and now there was no future and the scream was like that of the chaotic cry of Poe's burial victim. This field of energy, whirling about Dick at the front of the school, and consisting of the rhythms of organic human existence- of births, deaths, inspirational enlightenment and faith, and miserable human and moral failure; Rhythmic waves, that once set in a state of motion, continue across the infinite surface until finally, the energy is spent, and the waters calm and quiet. But for Dick, at that point in time, the waves were rolling with storm like intensity, and he was the watery plain across which they were crashing, and only he was there to absorb their power and might that the storm's eye might be calmed.

Dick tried to clear his head, to blank out his thoughts. He rationalized: if his senses were much more acute than usual, due to the great rushes of adrenaline through his body, a body far more used to watching the weekly adventures of Wally and the Beaver, he would be far more susceptible to spiritual forces broadcasting their final end, the way scientists hope to one day pick up a distant mayday on their radio telescopes from some far-flung galaxy.

Dick tried to convince himself that his imagination was running wild, indeed. He was downright frightened. He took a deep breath and started to walk towards the factory, trying to just put this out of his mind. He did have a final thought in passing: 'Did Hiroshima's clean up crews share a like experience? Never mind all of that, Dick. Just concentrate on your surroundings.'

Ahead, along the left, he could now see part of the old, iron fence that enclosed the town's cemetery. That was more food for thought. How could a private owner close off a public cemetery like this? People had a legal right to access their loved ones' remains. At least in Ohio they did. Dick was sure that that was a universal right. After a few more steps, he could distinctly see the outlines of the markers and monuments that were sectioned off by a network of narrow, gravel roadways running through the expansive clearing. When he passed by the open gate of the cemetery, he suddenly stumbled and fell. He broke his fall with his forearms, and his left elbow took the brunt of his crash. He pulled himself up, and felt a tinge of pain in his right knee. He rubbed his elbow and decided that he was all right. 'You had better be more careful, old man, 'cause there's nobody around to save you.'

He looked down and saw the pattern of deep ruts that stretched out from the gate itself, imbedded in the short, gravel drive until it intersected with the asphalt on Birch Avenue. While peering into the cemetery, Dick had wandered from the center of the blacktop over to the edge of the road and his left boot had caught on one of the deep, dried mud ridges. He was thankful that the palms of his hands hadn't gotten all skinned.

He gratefully took the first of his remaining steps toward the factory. He angled back to the center of the roadway and remained there, concentrating on the smooth pavement ahead of him. Within two minutes he had entered the parking area that surrounded the factory.

The height of the building was equivalent to three or four stories and Dick could see that the roof was in a state of severe disrepair. The rolled asphalt roofing was torn away in many areas, exposing bare wood boards beneath. These old slats appeared moist and rotten- they glistened in the moonlight. This was convincing enough evidence to Dick to immediately conclude that the military would never have run an operation of any kind in such a dilapidated structure. Somebody was sure dreaming.

Dick walked up to a wooden door on the right hand corner of the building. He grasped the doorknob firmly, and then gave it a good hard turn as he hit the door with his right shoulder. To his surprise, the door swung back easily on its hinges, the knob leaping from his grasp. There was a grating noise- the bottom of the door had wedged tightly against the old, concrete floor. Dick left it wide open because it brought a good deal of moonlight into the dank, dark structure. A musty smell indicated to him that the roof must have been leaking for a long time.

He turned on the flashlight again and slowly began scouting the building. All of the old machinery had been auctioned off years before, so he didn't really expect to come across anything of real value. What he did discover right off the bat was the fact that the old building had served, apparently for decades, as an enclosed salvage yard for old automobile engines.

The engines were scattered about the floor, in various stages of disassembly, throughout the main work area. Dick sidestepped through the maze of cylinder heads, piston rods, and other engine parts of all kinds. He had instantly put a lid on the chemical weapons spill theory. This building was little more than a junkyard. Dick picked his way over to the inner door and window of what had served as the business office during more prosperous times.

There was a rectangular window about three feet wide that looked out from the office into the outer shop, and next to it was a door with a much smaller window mounted into it. The door was closed. Dick tried the door but it was locked. He aimed the flashlight into the office and saw two large, dust covered tables, some gray metal filing cabinets, a desk in the corner heaped with rusty engine parts, and, back against the outside wall, a row of six old lockers. He tried to push the window open, hoping it was on hinges, and then tried to slide it both ways but it wouldn't budge. He looked around in the adjacent area and spotted a five-foot length of metal pipe which he carried back over to the office and wielded baseball bat style, swinging it at the window a half dozen times until he had cleaned all the glass shards from the frame.

Breaking out that window had created such a burst of sustained noise in the quiet night that Dick leaned the pipe up against the wall, then tiptoed back to the door where he'd first entered the building and slowly stuck his head out into the moonlight, like a wary turtle stretching its head out of its shell. He stood that way for quite a long time, listening to the excited beating in his chest, reassuring himself that everything remained tranquil beyond that door- that there were no prying eyes whose ears had been alerted to the loud breakage of glass and who might, at that moment, be coming for him. Dick waited at least another full minute. No, the dead town had not been awakened by his act of vandalism. There were no footsteps, no muffled voices from the shadows, no flashlights; He returned to the task at hand.

Back at the smashed out office window, he was now able to reach in and unlock the door with ease. He then stepped back around to the front of the doorjamb and walked into the office. He methodically rifled through the desk drawers and file cabinets, not sure of what he should be looking for. As each drawer in its turn proved to be void of any perplexing contents, he began to debate what the next logical step was on this nocturnal mission of his. What other theories could he dispel on this night? He was learning that perhaps he had already satisfied his curiosity.

The next thing he would have to do was to locate Sam Rutledge and hear his story. If he couldn't find Sam, maybe he could set up an appointment with this mysterious land baron who had reportedly bought up all of the Birch property with the government's full cooperation. Dick would carefully pre-plan his line of questioning to the man and then record his ensuing responses. He would look for any statement that seemed vague, misleading, or inordinary- any weakness that he might then be able to pounce upon.

Dick opened the middle drawer of the third file cabinet, lifted away a dirty, old towel, and his lower jaw dropped onto his chest. Lying in the bottom of the drawer, atop a bed of several other old rags, were five long, green metal canisters, their seams ripped open as if by gunfire. They were marked with the international warning sign- the skull and crossbones, signifying poisonous contents.

Dick just stared at his sinister find- five cylinders that had contained some type of lethal gas. These canisters were undoubtedly the basis for the rumor repeated in the Marquette tackle shop regarding the probability of a chemical weapons spill. That, at least, was a logical assumption on which to base further inquiry. He bent down and took hold of one of the cylinders, wrapping it first in one of the old rags, and lifted it up carefully, holding it with both hands at arm's reach. It was cool to the touch, and he could feel the chill right through the rag. He brought it slowly up next to his abdomen and cradled it in his left hand so that he could train the flashlight on it with his right. The size of the cylinder reminded him of the spent mustard gas containers that he had encountered behind the fractured German line during the last days of the Great War. What were these five canisters doing in this office, and just who had put them here? Filled with poison gas, they would obviously have posed a considerable hazard. But even if the gas in the five cylinders had been released simultaneously, Dick just didn't see how there could be a risk of contamination to the degree that would have necessitated a permanent evacuation of all the citizens of Birch.

He laid the cylinder back into the drawer and closed it. He made his way over to the line of lockers along the rear wall and opened them. Nothing but a ratty, old change of clothes in one of the lockers with the pockets turned inside out; Dick figured that he was not the first to ransack the office, only to discover that there wasn't a whole hell of a lot to turn upside down or inside out- besides the pockets in those moth eaten pants, and the empty poison canisters in the file.

Dick flashed the light on his watch. It was one A.M. He pictured little Todd, sleeping soundly back in their tent, he hoped! His grandson would be wrapped up in that sleeping bag like a mummy, and he was probably grinding his teeth, just like Dean had when he was a boy. Habits like that tended to run through the generations. Why, Dick's own mother used to shake him awake deep in the night when he, himself was young, warning him to stop grating his teeth. She maintained that any child who cracked and snapped his or her teeth in the dark most likely was reacting to the presence of worms. She explained one time to Dick that if she was to pull his nightshirt up without waking him while he was in the midst of grinding, and then if she was to hold a light to his behind, she would surely spot those worms of his, pausing in their destructive work to take in a little air at his anus. Dick now involuntarily squeezed his buttocks. This, he had done all of his life, whenever he pictured his own mother actually holding a candle to his bare ass.

Dick was more than ready to call it a night. He stepped out of the office, then made his way back through the shop to the entrance for the last time. Once outside again, he turned and gave that door a good, stiff pull to free it from the concrete floor and then he closed it firmly behind him.

The moon had now climbed high into the night sky, further shrinking the length of the dark shadows. Dick was relieved to be heading back to the car. His soiree had been somewhat of a success. He had satisfied his burning need to investigate firsthand the terrible news that he had heard only eleven hours or so before. He still didn't have any answers, but he did have a starting point. And, more importantly, he knew that this visit would help him accept, in time, the dramatic changes that had taken place here. To walk the empty, desolate streets of this little village at the witching hour was an experience he would truly never forget.

The Kennedy funeral had done that for him. He and Lucy had been glued to the television during that entire fateful weekend two Novembers past, and he had spent the first three days in shock and disbelief. He had voted for this young man, and then had watched his country come to life again. One burst of gunfire, and he was gone. It wasn't until he saw De Gaulle take that funny hat off for the twenty-one gun salute in Arlington Cemetery that Dick was able to accept the vibrant, young President's death and the changing of the guard in Washington. Maybe the deserted inside of the Sawmill Bar had really been De Gaulle's bald head revisited.

When Dick drew near to the cemetery gate, he paused, and then a strange impulse overtook him. He decided that, due to the brightness of the full moon, he might take just a few minutes to locate the final resting place of Ned Baker, the Lake Independence park ranger who had passed on, Dick had learned, sometime the previous year. He had thought much of old Ned, and if nothing else, this might be his only opportunity to say a little prayer over the grave and pay his final respects.

Remembering his fall on the way to the factory earlier, he paid extra attention to the deep ruts on the dirt road leading through the cemetery gate. Long, thin lines of shadow out ahead indicated that the ruts extended down the service road as far as Dick could see. He couldn't imagine what had caused the damage to the road. He surmised that to begin with, there must have been a considerable amount of rain to soften the ground, and then some kind of heavy equipment had been brought through, digging into the roadbed.

Walking by the markers and monuments, Dick began to pass the flashlight across the faces of the stones, looking for the 'Baker' plot. He was intrigued by the sheer size of the Birch cemetery. The old boom times had resulted in a population explosion- an explosion with a delayed reaction- a cemetery overflowing with its dead.

Dick had never been particularly uncomfortable in graveyards. In fact, the experience had always soothed his soul in some unexplainable way, which was one reason why he hadn't hesitated to enter this one in the middle of the night. He was becoming weary from all of the walking, however, and was to the point where he was about to cut short his search. It was then that he discovered something truly out of the ordinary.

About a quarter mile from the main gate, the deep ruts that he was so careful to avoid had abruptly angled off of the service road to the right, and a good-sized area of freshly tilled bare dirt lay there, approximately fifty feet off the road. Dick just stood there for a moment, perplexed. He shuffled across the grass and came to a halt at the edge of the turned up earth. He illuminated the dirt at his feet and realized that someone had spread a generous amount of seed across the top of the soil and that the new grass had sprouted. The seed had been planted very recently, owing to the diminutive size of the grass blades poking up from the dirt. Dick could see that the area had not entirely settled. There was a definite mound in the center. He stepped onto the dirt and his boots sunk a good three inches. 'Whatever could be buried here?' he asked himself. He trod across the area, the soft earth collapsing beneath each step.

Dick now stood in the center of the mound. He slowly made a complete rotation, trying to fathom what this was and if it was one of many pieces in the complicated puzzle he was trying to put together. He walked back over to the edge and then paced the full length and breadth and concluded that the area was roughly thirty by sixty feet. He knelt over on the sod, now dampened with dew, and tried to keep from thinking the unthinkable- that there indeed were victims of some unexplained accident and that their bodies were contaminated in such a way as to compel a higher authority to rule that they be buried together, beneath this mound on which Dick had trod.

Or, had something altogether different been shoveled under at this sight? Leaking barrels of hazardous waste, or containers of highly toxic agents? The definitive answer was available, Dick knew, to anyone with a strong back and a handy spade. But that was a chore fit for a different night, however, and at his age, it would be wise to recruit younger, stronger backs to provide the earthmoving.

Dick remained on his knees, and as he faced the dark earth, he felt the need to pray- to pray for the poor souls whose bodies might rest just beneath the surface. "Oh Heavenly Father," he began, and with his eyes closed tight, those words from his lips had provoked an ache from deep within him, and the ache was caused by a kind of groan from below the very ground upon which he so piously knelt. "Dear God, bless those who have given up their lives lived so fully in this pure country of Yours. Oh Lord, keep them close to You, recruit them into Your Heavenly Army. In Your power and everlasting glory! Amen!"

Dick began to shiver involuntarily, from the cool, damp air as well as his emotion. He was overcome by this experience. And the groan and the hurt did not subside. It thrust right up through his soul, feeding voraciously upon his love for his fellow man. Innocent victims, a hundred fold, perhaps, were crying out for justice- or at least for peace, that their story be told and known. Dick's legs and knees were stiffened, and he felt it quite impossible to rise. He was so entranced for a timeless interval.

But when the big, cold hand lighted upon his left shoulder, he found himself floundering in a wild, quavering terror such as he had never before experienced.

"Dick Chapman? You goddam son-of-a-bitch!!"

Dick recognized that big, booming voice right off. His heart, which had taken off like a hobby rocket high into the night sky, came back down again and managed to land in the same old spot in his chest. He opened his mouth to speak, but the words would not yet come. His old friend, Sam Rutledge, was leaning over stiffly with that big hand out, proffering his services in helping him to gain his feet.

"Goddam Sam!" Dick was finally able to crack, "what in tarnation are you trying to do? Put me in the grave? You don't just scare the living hell out of a retired, old man without just cause!" Dick was helped back up to his feet by his friend.

"Sorry, buddy. I wasn't sure just who the hell was flittin' about town. I been stayin' in my house these past two nights. I stepped out for a cigarette and I heard this glass breakin', eh?" Dick took a good look at Rutledge in the moonlight. He looked the same. He had that same barrel-like upper body and the thick shock of hair on his head that, like his full bushy eyebrows, had remained jet black through the long years.

"I just pulled in this afternoon," Dick explained. "I was picking up my fishing license in the tackle shop there in town and the fellow told me what had happened up this way."

"And just what did that jackass tell you?"

"Well," Dick was searching for the right words carefully, "he really didn't know the details. He told me that the millionaire from the club bought everybody out. Is that accurate?"

Rutledge was about to speak but instead he began to cough, and cough violently. It was a dry, hacking, laborous cough, and Dick was sure it would never end. It was the kind of cough that racks the body with painful spasms, and it caused Rutledge to hold his rib cage by crossing his forearms beneath his armpits in order to ease what must have been side-splitting agony. Finally, he cleared his throat with a terrific grumble and spat a glob of thick phlegm a good ten feet into the darkness.

"Sounds like you're getting over the flu, Sam. That's nasty."

"Motherfuck!" Rutledge tapped a Marlboro from his soft pack, held it between his teeth, struck a match and cupped it in his hands in front of his face. He took a hearty first puff from the freshly lit cigarette, and then directed its bright orange end toward the ground. "I see you been tearing up my grass," he said, a mass of smoke oozing from his lips with each spoken word.

"Sam, what in God's name happened here?" Dick asked. Sam's expression went sort of blank and a part of Dick wanted to pack up and head back to Chilicothe without pressing the issue any further. "Sam, I'm so- so very sorry. I don't know what to say- I have to know what went on here."

Rutledge began to laugh, the kind of big, empty laugh that comes out of a carnival spook house to attract business, but his merriment was brief, cut short by another round of coughing. Dick placed his hand on Rutledge's back, trying in some small way to quiet the convulsive attack, to lessen the painful jerks and bobs. "I got a bottle of brandy back at my place," he was finally able to say, pulling at Dick's arm firmly. "Let's have a drink- just like old times."

The Rutledge place was the second largest house in town, after the funeral parlour. It was a green coated, New England style clapboard home of three stories with black shutters and it was built on a native granite foundation. Sam's father, Eldred, had constructed the place just before his only son left for Europe during World War I.

Sam had three sisters, two of them younger, and they had all married local boys while still in their teens. The two younger girls had moved with their husbands out to the Pacific Northwest. The two brothers-in-law had decided to try their hand at lumbering the great redwoods of northern California and had become so successful that they never again gave a thought to returning to Northern Michigan.

Sam's older sister, Ruth Ann, had married the foreman of the Ford factory and together they had remained lifelong residents of the area. He had died of a heart attack five years before, at age seventy-four. Ruth Ann had gone down hill after that, ended up suffering a nervous collapse, and Sam had finally signed the papers of commitment to Newberry Joy Regional Mental Hospital. He had never driven over to Newberry to see her in the two years that she had been confined.

The golden years of Sam's life had really begun following his return from Europe at the close of the war. He married June Huxtley, the prettiest girl in town and the daughter of the Lutheran minister, and together they lived right with Sam's parents in the big green house on Birch Avenue. Sam, ever the tireless worker, helped his father build the family logging business to the highest level of efficiency and prosperity. They had always liked to refer to their operation as the largest of its kind east of the Mississippi, in deference to Sam's two brothers-in-law, who had built up their own operation in California and Oregon into an empire.

When Sam's father and mother passed away, having died only seven months apart in 1949, they left their home and their business to their only son, his wife June, and Sam Jr.

Sam went on periodic drinking binges, and it was said that he struck his wife more than once. June finally succumbed to cancer, after a long battle with the illness, in the summer of 1960. Their only son, Sam Jr., had gone away to school and eventually had gotten a job with the city of San Francisco's water department and only returned home each year to visit his parents at Thanksgiving, primarily because his black bear of a father remained so domineering and abusive. Young Sam hadn't been seen in Birch since his mother's funeral. That was the extent of the negative rumors about big Sam. Conversely, he was known as a dependable employer who would go out of his way to help a worker deal with a personal problem, and a good neighbor who was always there to lend a hand when it was needed.

Dick had always felt thoroughly at home in Sam's house. They had made their walk from the cemetery in silence. Dick had been concerned with the effort that Sam had expended in simply breathing, and so refused to tax him further by asking him questions along the way. As they neared the residence, Dick was surprised to see several lights, including the yellow bulb over the front porch, burning bright. They climbed the cement steps together, one at a time, and then Dick wiped his boots on the outdoor mat.

"I got the only electricity in town," Sam said, holding open his front door for Dick. "Damn, could we use a stiff drink, eh?"

Once inside the house, while Sam rounded up the bottle and two snifters, Dick removed the tools from his jacket and set them on the entryway table (so they wouldn't wear any holes in the fabric), checked the other pocket to be sure the flashlight was safe, and removed the jacket and slung it over his arm. For the moment, at least, everything felt perfectly normal. Dick could hear the warm tick tock of the grandfather clock in the living room next to the hallway to the kitchen. He knew that if he flicked on the big, console television in the opposite corner of the living room, it would pull in the Marquette channel like always. And then Sam was motioning Dick to join him on the couch with the bottle of brandy in his hand, the way he always did.

Dick tossed his jacket on an overstuffed chair, then walked over and plopped himself down on the big, soft, red velvet couch, put his feet up on the coffee table, took a full glass of brandy from Rutledge and began to warm it in his hands. His legs were dead tired. Sam sat close to him, on the next set of cushions over, and now held his glass up to his lips, which Dick noted was exceedingly full, tilted back his head, and emptied the snifter with three huge swallows.

"Who you come up with this year?" Sam asked, one of the first questions he always asked Dick each May when they met.

"My grandson, Todd. He's eleven this year, and his mother agreed he was old enough to hook some monster walleye." Dick looked Sam in the eye and smiled.

"Goddam it, Dick! I think- I mean I know I remember the year when you told me he was born. Seems like yesterday, heh?" Rutledge pawed the brandy bottle off of the coffee table and reloaded. "Where's he now, Dick? Not sleepin' in the tent alone, I hope?"

Dick felt a pang of guilt, which he washed away with his first slurp of brandy. "Yes Sam, he's sleeping in the tent, alone."

"And just what's gonna happen if the boy wakes up?" asked Sam, a twinkle in his eye.

"He's not gonna wake up! Goddam it, Rutledge! I want the whole story! And I know it's gonna hurt!"

Rutledge rolled his eyes and shook his head, then brought the glass up again and drained it. "Hurt," he said softly, almost coolly. "Hurt, it did. Hurt, it does. Hurt, it always will." He looked over at Dick, his eyes mournful. "It's gonna hurt to tell it, and God knows, I don't need anymore pain, Dick. So, fuck you."

Dick had a hold of the brandy this time, and quickly refilled both glasses. There was dead silence for a minute. He thought he heard a little creak on the stairs. Old houses always made their own distinctive sounds. Then, Dick said, "Sam, your world is gone, and a big piece of mine is, too. Let me try to help you. I'm your friend, goin' on fifty years."

Rutledge coated the inside of his mouth with booze. "You're not takin' a piss til I'm through tellin'," he said, and turned full towards him, wearing that look of sheer despair that would haunt Dick for the rest of his days.

PART 2

LAST FLIGHT OF THE FALLEN VALKYRIE

CHAPTER FIVE

NEWBERRY, MICHIGAN
OCTOBER 1964

'Doctor Katz, Doctor Katz, Dr. Julian Katz- Please report to the reception area, Doctor Katz.'

"You have been improving month after month, Josef. You carry out your duties just as you're told. This is very encouraging to me- and to you, too, I trust?" Julian Katz placed a warm hand on the great shoulder of Josef Brahms.

"Yes, doctor. I can leave hospital soon? Go home? Go home to Canada? I better now."

"I am afraid that isn't possible quite yet, Josef. Not just yet. Perhaps next month we'll take a long look at you, again. By the way, Mrs. Piggins asked me for a glass of fresh water. Would you please go and fill your pitcher with water and take it to Mrs. Piggins? She's in her bed, again. She's not feeling too well today."

"Yes, Doctor Katz," Brahms said eagerly. Katz smiled at the large hulk of a figure, the stringy hair in disarray, the face, big and round and still youthful.

"I have been paged downstairs, Josef. I would like to visit with you again, later, if I may. Doctor Von Himmler would also like water, by the way."

Katz made his way to the locked door of Ward C. Josef Brahms had seemed to have stabilized these past two years, there was no question. His loud, unintelligible outbursts were being controlled very well with drugs. It was certainly an irony that the fabled killer who had single handedly terrorized Northern Ontario, hunted for months by the Royal Canadian Mounted Police in the course of brutally murdering a dozen bakery workers in the remote, far flung communities of that province, in reality was but a massive, clumsy, mentally retarded lumberjack.

Brahms plodded into a stuffy cubicle through a doorway off of the main hall. He glowed with self-satisfaction, leaning down over a deep, rust-stained porcelain sink to fill an old metal pitcher.

Mrs. Piggins was a silver-haired woman now in her late eighties who had killed her husband by mixing rat poison into his hot oatmeal for several weeks during the Lenten season some thirty years before. For the past year, she had been confined to bed in room 419, across the hall from the janitor's closet.

"Mrs. Piggins, Mrs. Piggins, Pig-gins, Pig-gins, Mrs. Piggins," chanted Brahms, carrying the plastic tumbler full of water carefully. The old lady's head and shoulders were propped up at the head of the bed by three pillows.

"Are you from Cedar River?" she asked. "The bridge is washed out! You'll just have to stay, if you're from Cedar River."

"Water for Pig-gins, Mrs. Piggins."

"I don't need water now! Not that water! That water washed out the bridge. I didn't hear you. Are you from Cedar River proper?" Mrs. Piggins rubbed the bluish, pink tops of her hands. The door closed quietly.

Julian Katz lit a cigarette, adjusted his black horn-rimmed glasses, and rubbed his balding head, stroking backward as though he was smoothing an imaginary shock of hair. He walked into Newberry Joy Hospital's reception lobby.

"Doctor Katz?" A tall young woman came forth. The lobby was otherwise deserted, aside from a man in a white uniform mopping the old, heavily traveled tile floor.

"Hello," he answered, taking her hand firmly.

"My name is Nancy Palmer, from Western Mutual Insurance. Doctor Drake told me that you are the man to see in regard to the damage claim." She wore a smart, navy blue business suit with a white silk blouse ruffling at her throat, and high-heels to match. Her brown hair was tied back in a bun. She carried a leather folder under her arm. She looked to be twenty-five or so. She possessed striking blue eyes. Her cheekbones were high, and her complexion was flawless. Katz's heart fluttered when they made eye contact.

"Yes, that's right," said Katz. "I discussed the matter with Doctor Drake. He told me I could expect a claims adjuster. I can take you up there right now, to the fourth floor nurse's station, I mean. That's where the vandalism occurred. One of the patients gained access, somehow, to a restricted area. I would imagine that you will want to inspect the damage personally." Katz blushed. "It isn't often that we have such attractive visitors, here." He led her toward the elevator.

"Thank you, doctor. It will only take a couple of minutes, really. Doctor Drake has gone over the itemization list. Everything appears to be in order. I have only one form to complete." Katz pushed the four button inside the elevator and the door closed with a screech.

"Did Doctor Drake tell you? Probably not; It was an oddball thing, really, Miss Palmer. Nurse Krathkirk has been on the night shift for almost three years. She left for the cafeteria on her two o'clock coffee break and when she returned to the station, not twenty minutes later, she found the drawers on the cabinets and desks forced open, and many of our patient files were torn to shreds. And," he continued, waving his index finger, "the orderlies claim they didn't hear a doggone thing!" Katz winced with abdominal pain. The elevator had halted, slightly pressuring his stomach ulcer.

"I'm not here to investigate the incident, doctor," replied the woman as the elevator door flew open. "I am only here to make sure that your institution is properly reimbursed."

The nurse's station reflected the lingering effects of the attack that Katz had described. Two steel file cabinets were dented and mangled and the drawers would not close. Both desks leaned precipitously due to leg damage. Matching office chairs were shoved off into a corner- their casters broken. An oversized typewriter had taken a serious beating, as well. Nancy placed a hand beneath her chin.

"So!! You have come to see it, too, have you?!" screamed a high pitched voice. Nancy gasped, startled. Julian Katz felt the warm softness of her body as she brushed against him.

"Bryan! I have discussed this with you many times- you must not approach people so suddenly. You are being very rude!" A compact little man in his sixties, dressed in a green hospital smock and penny loafers, his face red and chapped, and his nose burnished with acne scars, the result of years of excessive alcohol abuse, observed them suspiciously.

"I heard this happen, and you know it! I told you about it, too. Krathkirk did it! I saw some of it!" Katz grabbed the little man by the shoulders and shook him several times, the black, horn-rimmed glasses bouncing halfway down his nose. The insurance adjuster was appalled.

"Stop this, Bryan! We have a visitor, a very pretty one. Now settle down. Settle down, now."

"Von Himmler gave Krathkirk a shot! I told you he is dangerous!"

"That will be all, Bryan. I just may have Josef Brahms come sit with you."

"No! Please, no!" pleaded little Bryan. "He pinches and he's mean! Stupid, too! I'll go and draw- I'll draw a picture of her, naked." His quick, jerky eyes roamed over Nancy Palmer's shapely legs.

"That will do it," announced Nancy, jotting in a notebook. "You will receive a check to cover everything in about four weeks." Katz nodded approvingly.

"Here, I insist on escorting you out to your car," he said, pushing his glasses back up to the top of his hawk nose. Bryan scurried around the corner and back down the hallway to the lounge.

"I was under the impression that this is a restricted area, doctor."

"At night, all hallway doors are locked. The orderlies keep a watchful eye on those patients whom we consider potentially dangerous to themselves or to those around them. The day nurses are on their rounds at the moment, dispensing the mid-day meds."

"Escort me to the elevator if you will," she said. "But I will have no trouble finding the parking lot myself. I think you should stay right here."

Katz smiled warmly. He would undress her with his teeth, if she wanted him to. He had all of twenty seconds, the time it would take them to reach the elevator shaft, to figure out how to ask her to dinner.

Nancy beat him to the elevator and touched the down arrow. Newberry Joy was a raunchy place. Ugly, dark gray tile floors, splotched, creamy yellow plaster walls with dusty corners, ceiling cracks and glass partitions that needed Windex; On the job, she had been in dozens of hospitals, rest homes, and health clinics. Nothing was quite so awful as Newberry Joy.

"Miss Palmer, I was wondering if you would like to join me for dinner tonight. I know a place that has some terrific home cooking. You look like you could use a good meal." Katz looked at her hopefully through the glasses, which were somehow off center, riding high on the bridge of his nose.

"I'm sorry doctor, I'll have to take a rain check. I have a previous commitment this evening." He looked to her like the Nutty Professor. This guy was a real spaz. The elevator door opened with it's familiar screech.

"Nice meeting you, miss."

Nancy shook his moist hand, smiled, and after the elevator door had closed, wiped her right hand on her hip with disdain.

Wolfgang Von Himmler, his puffy, gray hair glistening in the afternoon October sunshine, was sitting on the edge of his bed near the window when Brahms walked in. "Hello, Josef! You've brought the water, and I am glad." Von Himmler checked the big room and saw that only two of the twelve other beds were occupied. He lowered his voice substantially. "We can take this opportunity to talk."

Brahms set his pitcher on the windowsill and leaned down before him. "D-Doctor Katz say I better," he undulated. "Can go home soon." Von Himmler smiled whimsically, taking a handful of salt and pepper beard and twisting it to his lips. He had put on weight during his long stay in the psychiatric ward. The professional staff was convinced that he believed in his delusion of being an old country physician. He was always available to his fellow patients if they needed counseling or healing. 'Doctor' Von Himmler is what everyone called him.

"Brahms, I am surprised at you! You have murdered, what was it? Twelve people, if I am not mistaken. The Canadians wanted to extradite you for trial. But the state wouldn't allow you to go, unless they judged you to be sane. You're lucky to be here, in this country. They will never release you, never!" A slobbery drool eddied down the lumberjack's chin.

"But Doctor Katz! He p-p-p-promise me!" The dumb tone was choked with emotion.

"My own father was a doctor in my native Germany. I understand, now, that a physician has no political power. Pfanmuller was the exception, of course." Brahms grew silent. He filled another plastic cup with water. His jaw clung to his chest in despair.

"Do not give up all hope, Brahms. I have a plan."

"A plan?"

Von Himmler picked up some type of paperwork that had been setting out on the bed and crammed it into a manila folder. "You must not say anything about this to Doctor Katz, do you understand?"

"I say nothing."

"Good." Von Himmler's voice, tainted with the German accent, had a hypnotic effect on the troubled giant standing before him. He pulled off his glasses and cupped his eyes with his hand. "I will need a strong boy like you to carry my trunk when I go."

"What trunk?" asked Brahms, looking beneath the bed.

"It's not here, you imbecile. It is in a storage room, down in the basement. It is very heavy."

"I strong. A strong boy."

"Yes Josef, you are very strong. I may wake you up tonight. Remember, not a word of this to Doctor Katz, nor even to your Mrs. Piggins."

"I will miss the Piggins."

"Remember Josef, if you keep our secret, you will be going home, and soon. You have to trust me."

Brahms raised his eyebrows at the thought and smiled a cheesy grin.

Friday, October third dawned bright and clear. For Herman Bancroft and Gloria Shutz, the day would prove to be a very busy one, indeed. Herman stood out front on the carpeted expanse of still dewy lawn, trimming the hedge for the last time before winter set in. These chores always needed tending, and on a consistent basis. A funeral home had to look spic and span. He was beginning to feel too old to keep up with all of this, especially on these cold mornings. He needed his strong, young son.

Herman had just turned sixty in August. Back when he'd reached fifty, he remembered looking at himself in the bedroom mirror and quietly praising himself for looking so young and trim. He had a photograph of himself snapped that day by one of the workers, and he had popped it into a pewter frame and stuck it on his dresser. In the decade since, his body had slowly become lumpy around his midsection, he had developed bursitis in both shoulders, and his hairline had receded to the point that he had actually purchased a toupee through a mail order catalog. When he looked into the mirror now, his salt and pepper hairpiece appeared much darker than the natural hair at his temples and, by comparison to himself in that photograph, it appeared his whole face had sort of sagged forward, creating deep ruts between the ruddy globs of flesh beneath his bloodshot, brown eyes. He glanced up at the familiar black lettering on the whitewashed sign as he toiled:

HERMAN BANCROFT & SON
FUNERAL HOME
since 1915

Herman had just recently added the words, '& son' to the sign. Twenty-six year old Hector was in his final year of mortuary school at Wayne State University down at Detroit. Herman was proud of him, as he was sure his own father was when he had finished school and was ready to return to the Upper Peninsula to take his place in the family venture.

The village of Birch had been good to him and his family, there was no doubt about it. The Bancroft family business was the only such establishment of its kind in northern Marquette County. Despite the fact that the 1960 census had indicated an alarming 25% population decline in Powell Township, the demographics reflected a community that was aging much more quickly than the state average. As a direct result, the funeral business was booming.

The large, white front door opened. It was Gloria, of course. "Herman," she said, "Mrs. Greeley at the hospital is on the phone."

"I'm coming," sighed Herman, dropping the hedge shears. Gloria was such an attractive girl. Only God knew why she chose to be such a faithful employee to him here in the boondocks of the Upper Peninsula.

Entering the home, things looked to be in tip top shape. Gloria had watered the flowers and plants, vacuumed the beautiful rouge woolen carpeting in the foyer, and even adjusted the bright purple tie that Mrs. Hintimaki had insisted that her husband wear. This was to be his final day at Bancroft's- the funeral was scheduled for that afternoon at the Lutheran church. Herman walked down the hallway and into his office and picked up the plain white telephone receiver off of his desk. He cradled the phone on his shoulder, "is that you, Marilyn?"

"Good morning, Herman," greeted a pleasant voice. Bancroft picked at a fingernail that he'd torn while doing the yard work and flicked it across the room and onto the floor. "How's business?"

"Well, we have a funeral this afternoon. Looks like a fine day for it, too. Sunshine, warm temperatures- expecting a good sized crowd; How is it at your end, Marilyn? I know you didn't call just to ask how business is."

"You were never one to waste words, Herman. There was an accident on County Road 550 last night. A boy and girl from Birch, Jerry Higby and Julie Marcotte, ran off the road and hit a tree. They were brought in by ambulance D.O.A. Both of them; Their parents, as you might imagine, are just sick. We've been instructed to deliver the remains to your funeral home this morning."

"A loss of two young people is something our town can never afford. I'll be expecting the delivery."

"Within the hour," announced the woman.

"Fine." Herman hung up the phone, puffing out his cheeks. "Gloria, could you come here for a moment?"

The pretty cosmetologist poked her head into the office doorway, her blonde hair waving, her thin brows above her attractive, blue eyes raised in question. "Yes, Herman?"

"Dear, I know I guaranteed that you'd be able to leave for the convention this morning, but, s-something's come up. Something unexpected."

"How many?" snapped Gloria caustically. Herman held up two fingers.

Josef Brahms rolled over on the wet, half-frosty leaves that had served him as a bed for the preceding two hours. Von Himmler had chosen a level space near the bottom of a deep ravine on which to camp. Brahms could see him, now, down below, splashing brownish red water on his face and beard. Von Himmler was wearing a green janitor's uniform and had a brown leather tool belt slung around his waist. The lumberjack hungered and thirsted. "Do-nuts, do-nuts, do-nuts," he chanted.

Von Himmler looked up from the brackish creek bed, drying himself with a gray hospital blanket. Up above him on the ledge hovered Brahms, his round head silhouetted against a deep blue sky filled with tree branches glowing in fall foliage and singing chickadees. "You will get your breakfast!" he shouted. "We are leaving here. Come down to me."

Josef loaded his arms with the heavy brown and black-strapped trunk that they had taken from a storage area in the hospital's basement, and slipped down through the mud and moss to his master's side.

They began their hike in silence. The footing in the ravine bottom was firm. Every so often the two travelers had to cross the little creek. This was not a problem because in most places it was only about a yard wide. Fifteen minutes passed. The sound of traffic above them became unmistakable. Von Himmler stopped. "Brahms, we will be well out of the area by nightfall." He looked at the gold plated pocket watch that had once belonged to his father. "It has been six hours since the escape. I doubt that those in the asylum have missed us. They are slow at the hospital. Word of our absence will take time to reach the authorities."

Brahms set down his heavy burden and rubbed his face, spreading a coating of mud and slime over a stubbly growth of whiskers. In just the last few hundred yards, the ravine had twisted and turned through dense brush at times, and prickly briars were beginning to take their painful toll on both men. Von Himmler knew it was time to lead Brahms up the steep slope of the wall of the ravine.

"Before we leave, we are going to steer the police to the east. They're easy enough to fool."

They surfaced from the depths of the gully and into the parking lot of the Red Roof Motel. Von Himmler surveyed the immediate area carefully. The Red Roof was a ten unit, single story motel built in an 'L' shape, with the office facing a two lane highway, which, as he looked, was to his extreme right. The long row of guest units was perpendicular to the roadway. The motel was three miles west of the city of Newberry limits, so the escapees had covered a fair amount of ground, much of it in pitch darkness, curving back and forth as they had, along the bottom of the ravine. There were three cars parked in front of the guest rooms of their respective owners, and Von Himmler took note of the thick dew that coated each of the rear windows. The motel would fill up later that day because it was Friday, and the weekends during the autumn color season were always busy.

Von Himmler instructed Brahms to remain still, at the edge of the lot, and within minutes, a young woman wearing a red sweater and gray slacks bounded out of her room with a suitcase in hand and opened the trunk to her car, a blue and white Chevrolet Biscayne. Von Himmler saw that she'd left her keys dangling in the trunk lid, and as she walked back into her room for another load, he tugged on the sleeve of Brahms' hospital smock, leading him along the edge of the lot, making a semi-circle around her car. As he anticipated, she carried a larger suitcase this time, out to the car, and as she lifted up its full weight and maneuvered it into the trunk, they ran over and grabbed her, with Brahms dragging her struggling to the passenger side door, her cries for help muffled by the huge hand which he'd clamped tightly over her mouth. Von Himmler helped the lumberjack load her into the car quickly, and then he walked over and took hold of his brown and black trunk and pulled it across the blacktop and into the motel room. He picked her room key up off of the nightstand, hung the 'DO NOT DISTURB ' sign on the outer doorknob and locked the door behind him. He pulled the car keys from the trunk lock and slammed the lid closed, and then hopped around like a geriatric hare and got behind the steering wheel of the car. It had been ten years since he had last even driven a motor vehicle, and he was pleasantly surprised with the ease with which the engine started up, and the fact that the car was equipped with an automatic transmission. He pulled out onto the two-lane highway and headed east, towards the now risen sun.

Von Himmler eased Brahms' hand from the woman's face. She was crammed between the two men, and had stopped fighting. "Good morning. I am sorry if we have unnerved you. You won't be hurt, I promise you."

Nancy Palmer, the Western Mutual Insurance claims adjuster, eyed the ill-fitting dark green jumpsuit which the old man wore, as well as the hospital smock imprinted with 'Newberry Joy Hospital' on the chest of the giant who had taken hold of her, in sheer terror. She tried to catch her breath. Her young heart was drumming and her hands were cold and wet and she started to cry but managed to catch herself. "Do you work at the hospital?" she asked, doing her absolute best to keep her teeth from chattering.

"We're from the hospital, yes," replied Von Himmler, toying with his silver rimmed glasses. A sign over the road indicated the turnoff into the city of Newberry, but Von Himmler kept them on the highway, heading east, and a mileage sign indicated that Sault Ste Marie was sixty-two miles, and Eckerman was eleven.

"Where are we going?" asked Nancy, trying to swallow the big ball that had rolled into her throat. "Where are you taking me?"

"Just for a drive," Von Himmler answered. "We have business in Eckerman."

"Then you'll let me out of the car?" asked Nancy, gaining strength from the fact that she was able to converse with her abductor.

"You're much too beautiful to keep in a cage," replied the gray beard. "The most beautiful birds must be allowed freedom to fly."

Nancy tried to reassure herself. These two lunatics simply had needed a car, and she had been in the wrong place at the wrong time. She would just have to keep her composure. She had read about situations like this- there had been a first person article in last months Reader's Digest. Losing her head could mean the death of her. She closed her eyes and tried with all of her might to settle herself down.

With her eyes closed, her other senses seemed to become all the more acute. She heard the roar of her car engine as they rolled down the road. It didn't even sound like her car. She smelled something non-to-pleasant so she opened her eyes just a crack and she turned her head just enough so that she could see the monstrous creature muscling up to her right out of the corner of her eye. The bad odor, she now surmised, was a mixture of body odor and stale breath and then she turned full towards the big fellow in spite of her better instincts and was aghast with his overall appearance.

First, she focused on the open mouth, with all its dark gaps here and there where she had expected to see teeth. The teeth that remained, all twisted and angled oddly in the gums, were coated with a dull, yellow cheese. Apparently, this man had been taught that brushing one's teeth was an occupation for the idle rich. His tongue was in constant motion, flicking out through the aforementioned gaps and moving across the cracks and sores on his severely chapped lips. The nose was long and blunted at the end and looked as though it had been broken on more than one occasion. It was surrounded on three sides by a dried coating of dirt and mud which had been plastered to the face and held fast by a crop of blonde whiskers which were present in thickets on some areas of the cheeks and neck and almost entirely absent in others. The dumb eyes were what caused Nancy the most concern. The unwashed face and the odor could be successfully dealt with- some soap and water, a razor, a toothbrush and some mouthwash would suffice- but the look in his eyes- or the absence of a look in his eyes- how could that be corrected? Nancy likened the experience to making eye contact with a milk cow on her Uncle Hank's dairy farm.

Brahms' eyelids were half closed, due to the bright morning sun. The brown eyes displayed no emotion, no sense of knowing or being. Then, Nancy hurriedly looked away because a soft smile had formed on the outside edges of the chapped lips.

"Pretty, pretty, pretty girl," said Brahms.

"Yes Josef," and then Von Himmler echoed, "a very pretty girl. Very pretty."

Nancy was extremely frightened, again. She wished that her red sweater wasn't quite so clingy. She could just feel the giant looking at her, staring at her, wanting her. She glanced over at the driver, hoping to settle her nerves. At least he looked normal enough. The bearded old man was smiling and humming softly, keeping his eyes glued to the road.

"I-I w-work in the insurance business," she said, her voice cracking. She cleared her throat. "I was over at the hospital, yesterday. Were you the fellow mopping the floor in the lobby? That was you, wasn't- OUCH!!"

Brahms suddenly leaned way over, took hold of Nancy's chin in his right palm, and all at once buried his tongue deep into her right ear. She cried out, shocked at the intensity of the violation. She could hear the slurping, sucking, and licking greatly magnified in her inner ear, and she tilted way over against the shoulder of the old man. "Stop!" she cried loudly, "stop that!!"

"He thinks that he's having sex," explained Von Himmler with a wry smile. "He asked me about kissing and loving once. I taught him that when boys and girls neck, they try to stick their tongues in each other's ears. I suppose this is his way of making love to you."

The fervor of Brahms' passion intensified. He was cleaning out her ear so thoroughly, vacuuming dainty bits of ear wax with each suck, lathering her lobe in retarded, exalted splendor. Nancy just had to make him stop it, somehow. "Stop! Stop- hurting me!" she ordered, her eyes closed tight in a grimace. The big brown-eyed cow had transformed himself into a slobbering St. Bernard. "You're hurting me! Stop it!"

The tongue slowed to a barely detectable slither. Nancy lay very still, praying that the attack had ended. Then, Brahms kicked his lovemaking into overdrive. Nancy's ear canal seared with each new flutter of his tongue. "My God!" she screamed. "My God! Leave me alone! You're killing me!" She cowered against the old man, her blue eyes overflowing with tears.

"Pretend you like it," he advised. "Pretend you're satisfied."

It took all of Nancy's available self-discipline to ignore the discomfort and begin to pant, but pant she did, her breath quickening, her young form quivering in fulfillment. She knew that sometimes, a rape victim had to pretend to like it just to get the fucking bastard to stop. "Ohhhhhh! Shit!! Ohhhhh!" and she went limp and Brahms' great tongue was stilled. "Please stop," she murmured, her eyes tightly closed, her body displaying a newfound tranquility. The tongue was withdrawn and she could feel the giant sit up, back away from her. She opened her eyes and eased off of the driver's shoulder, being careful not to rekindle any further passions.

"We're almost to Eckerman," said Von Himmler. Nancy glanced over at the huge bulge in her lover's green, string drawn overalls.

Buddy's Cafe was located at the corner of Highway M-28 and County Line Road in the hamlet of Eckerman, just east of Newberry. Buddy's was known for their famous sweet roll, which was made from a secret bread dough rolled with apple slices, cinnamon and brown sugar and topped with a thick, glazed frosting. The famous roll was sold throughout the day to passersby, and had become such an important element of the business that the owners of Buddy's had built on a separate addition at one end of the building, away from the restaurant, to fully exploit the roll as a carry-out item.

On this bright morning, the carry-out counter was being worked by a young man with a dark complexion and strong, dark eyes by the name of Jeffrey Gobles. He'd planned on keeping his job at Buddy's until the beginning of November, when he was scheduled to begin basic training with the U.S. Navy.

Tony Accosta, the creator of the sweet rolls and other donuts, came from the kitchen, having just frosted two more batches of rolls, and eager to take his coffee break. "I'm goin' next door for some eggs and bacon, Jeff," he said. "Did you get a chance to eat yet?"

"Had some cereal at home," replied the young man. Like most of the employees at the restaurant, when Jeff had first hired on in June, during his first three weeks he must have devoured three of Tony's big rolls each day until he completely lost the taste for them. He had probably eaten only one or two per month since.

Tony removed his pastry hat and fit it playfully over Jeff's temples. "Here," he said with a smile, "this makes you look more professional."

"Oui-oui, monsieur," laughed Jeff. "And take your time having your breakfast, it's been pretty slow this morning."

"The fall tourists will be lining up by mid-afternoon," said Tony, noting the pile of unsold rolls overflowing the shelves in the glass case. "Enjoy the break in the action while you can."

"You know me, I don't move unless somebody makes me," joked Jeff.

"I'm sure you'll enjoy all the comforts of basic training, then. I hear they don't make you move hardly at all!" Tony smiled deviously and headed for the restaurant, closing the door behind him. Jeff looked at his own reflection in the glass countertop. The puffy, bloated white hat clung snugly to his head. The top rose nearly a foot above his scalp. He looked professional, all right. Jeff saw the image of the outside door opening. He looked up quickly.

Josef Brahms walked through the customer entrance and stepped to the counter.

"May I help you, sir?" The lumberjack eyed him speechlessly. "What can I getcha?" Brahms widened the narrow slits that were his eyes.

"Are you baker?"

Jeff smiled nervously, toying with the hat. "No, no- not me," he stammered, "Tony's the baker, I just come in-in-"

"You baker!" Brahms said, beaming. The boy managed to smile.

"Do-nuts, do-nuts, glazed do-nuts!"

Jeffrey shook a white wax bag open, and then he began to cram a dozen glazed into it. That is what this thing had said that it wanted, didn't it? His hands were shaking. He dropped the twelfth one onto the black rubber mat behind the counter. "Just a second, let me get you another one of these."

Brahms reached into the bag with lightning speed and then began to stuff the unpaid for pastry into his mouth. He was an offensive sight, his mouth half-open, drooling onto his dirty green hospital uniform. Jeffrey jumped spontaneously upon regaining his feet. "That'll be a dollar nine, sir."

Brahms first managed to swallow the enormous mouthful, then grabbed poor Jeffrey by the throat. His grip was so powerful, the result of years of toil in the pine forests of Ontario. A blood vessel in Jeffrey's left eye popped from the tremendous pressure that Brahms' six-foot-seven inch frame generated. In little more than one minute, it was all over. Bag in hand, Brahms lumbered out the door. Buddy's sweet roll counter was very still.

Brahms walked to the car and got right in next to Nancy. Von Himmler, holding a big screwdriver in his right hand, had kept the engine idling, and he pulled out onto the highway as soon as the passenger door slammed. He headed west, back towards Newberry. He took a careful look into the rear view mirror and was satisfied that no one had been observing them at that critical juncture when they pulled away from the restaurant. Besides, he had angled the car sharply away from the front windows of the establishment, passed through the gravel shoulder, and floored it when he had felt the blacktop beneath them.

Brahms offered the bag of donuts to his fellow travelers. "No thank you," said Nancy. Von Himmler reached across her chest for a donut and began to eat it hungrily.

"Where are we going now?" Nancy asked the driver. She noticed that he had jammed the screwdriver between his legs. "I think I have the right to know." Von Himmler nodded, swallowing his bite of food.

"Yes, of course you do. It is really very simple, our plans, I mean. We are taking you back to your room."

"That's- that's nice of you," she replied in as relaxed a tone as she could manage. "I've really got to get back to my office in Frankenmuth by this afternoon." These men were indeed crazy. When their backs were turned, she'd have the police at that cheap motel within three minutes.

They continued their drive in silence. If Nancy could have gotten access to a chastity belt for her swollen right ear, she would gladly have worn it, no matter how unsightly it might happen to be. As it was, she sat nervously with a hand on the side of her head and watched the big hulk inhale one donut after another until at last, he turned the white bag upside down, shaking the final flakes of frosting onto his lap. These, he meticulously picked off the fabric of his pants by gently wetting an oily finger and touching it to each morsel. He licked the finger in a final gesture of compulsion.

At about that same moment in time, Julian Katz trotted into Doctor Drake's office with great urgency and reported the bad news. Drake was the head administrator of the Newberry Joy Regional Mental Hospital.

"Are you absolutely certain, doctor?" asked Drake gravely. He wore a gray suit and tie. His hair had that bluish white cast to it of an elderly man, though he was only fifty-two. Katz thought he looked like his namesake, Investigator Paul Drake, from the Perry Mason Show. That was stretching it a bit. He wasn't nearly as handsome, for one.

"We've conducted a search of the entire premises. Every room, every closet, every storage area has been combed and I tell you, they're nowhere to be found. We haven't found so much as a clue. They've escaped!"

"Impossible!" retorted Drake. "God damn it! Do you have any idea of the furor that this will cause? A mass murderer on the loose? My God, Katz! We'll have every paper in the country explaining how inept we are- to let such a monster out of his cell! They'll have questions, questions, questions! God damn it! And this Von Himmler fellow- what of him? He is obviously the brains behind this outrage!"

"The only brain. I'm so sorry, Doctor Drake. I know that in being head of this institution- the ultimate responsibility is yours- I'm very sorry, genuinely."

"Go to hell, Katz! Now I want you to figure out how and where they got out of here! You're job is on the line, doctor. I want the answer by two o'clock!"

Katz could feel his ulcer kicking up. "You can count on me, Doctor Drake. I'll find out for you, right away." Katz left the office hurriedly.

"Vickie!" hollered the infuriated Drake to his secretary, who, dressed in a red and white knee length jumper, was busy stirring sugar and creamer into her coffee. "Get me the state police post on the line, now!"

Tony Accosta bent down behind the glass counter in horror. Tears gushed down his cheeks. Jeffrey lay before him with his mouth and eyes open, next to a glazed donut that had a shoe mark along its rim. Tony's confectioner's hat lay crushed beneath one shoulder. There was a bruised, reddish area across Jeffrey's throat. The young man was bright blue.

"Help!! God Almighty!! Help!!" he screamed, running back into the restaurant. "Murder! A Murder! Somebody murdered Jeffrey!!"

There were close to a dozen truckers and tourists seated in the dining room, enjoying breakfast. Within moments, they had all assembled near the sweet roll counter in a hushed group, looking at the body in disbelief. One of the waitresses bounded back into the cafe and picked the black telephone up off the register counter. Her hand shook so severely that even dialing the operator was a struggle. "Get me the state police!"

Tony got his wits and led two burly truck drivers out into the parking lot. There was no one there. The highway was void of traffic.

"You know," said one of the truckers, "a car went by a couple minutes ago- seemed like it was speedin' up, too. Now, I wasn't payin' no heed to it, understand. Just sippin' my coffee and eatin' my roll. What was we talkin' about, Pete? Goldwater- that's right, we was talkin' about that right wing son-of-a-bitch when I seen that car go by."

"Which way was the car headed?" asked Tony. The trucker pointed east, in the direction of the Soo.

Von Himmler, with Nancy Palmer sandwiched between he and Brahms, had obeyed the posted speed limits and had driven Nancy's car within three miles of the Red Roof motel when two dark blue state police cars, their sirens wailing and roof lights pulsating, suddenly appeared in the oncoming lane, speeding towards them. Von Himmler slowed the car and gave up the roadway, pulling halfway onto the soft, gravel shoulder. He didn't so much as flinch when he saw those flashing lights coming at them. For her part, Nancy was most hopeful of being rescued by the officers until she watched them pass and, as she turned her head and peered back through the rear window of her sedan, they disappeared in a blue blur over the horizon.

Brahms, still licking at the remnants of the glazed frosting on his chapped lips, was entertained by the sight of the patrol cars as they whizzed by in all of their glory, but wasn't able to connect his own work in the donut shop with this sudden emergence of the police and their hasty trip toward Eckerman.

After the police cars had gone, Nancy's spirits plunged and she resigned herself to the fact that she was facing a potentially prolonged period of confinement at the hands of the maniacs seated on either side of her. It further occurred to her that the only way out of this predicament might be to talk to the old man, gain his trust, reason with him, and convince him that if released, she would go about her business as if nothing had happened, and she would certainly harbor no intention of going to the authorities or assist in any other way in their recapture.

"A fine donut. As fine as I have ever tasted," said the driver.

"M-m-m-m-m-m! Donuts!" mustered Brahms.

"Thank you for taking me to breakfast," said Nancy. She knew that within a minute or two, they'd be back at the motel. "Say, why don't you come into my room when we get back? You could get all cleaned up, have a shower or a bath- check out isn't til eleven." Von Himmler nodded.

"You thought that the police might pull us over back there, didn't you?" Nancy would never forget that rich voice, with that accent.

"Oh, no! I would see no reason for them to do something like that! Heaven forbid! After all, we just went for a nice morning drive." Von Himmler smiled softly, touched by her charm.

"Yes, just a morning drive. You'll be rid of us soon enough. And, I promised that no harm would come to you, did I not?"

The motel was looming up ahead, on the right. Von Himmler slowed and turned into the parking lot smoothly. "I agree," said Nancy, breathing more easily. "You did promise."

"Just keep in mind that if you bring added attention to us in any way when we enter your room, I will not be able to keep my word."

"I understand." A tear seeped from her left eye and ran down her cheek.

The parking lot had remained quiet. There was still no one stirring in either of the other two occupied rooms. The blinds on the office window remained shut. Von Himmler drove right past Nancy's room, clearly marked by the 'DO NOT DISTURB' sign, and pulled the car up in an overgrown area along the windowless side of the motel building, out of the sight of passing motorists. "Miss, you get out with me. We'll walk directly to your room and enter, do you understand?" Nancy nodded. "Brahms, follow us closely. Do not hang around outside." Josef nodded, the eyes indifferent.

They climbed from the car, closed the doors softly, walked around to the front of the motel, and, within a matter of seconds, were inside Nancy's room. There were two double beds, and the lumberjack jumped on the undisturbed one. Von Himmler switched on the black and white television in order to keep him occupied and out of the way. Then, the little graybeard kicked into action. "I want you to call the motel office. Tell them that you will be staying here another night. Tell them that you will be in to pay the bill later." He handed Nancy the phone. She saw the big screwdriver still in his hand. He looked at the dialing instructions briefly and then dialed the nine. The girl listened as the phone rang six, seven, then eight times. A sleepy female voice answered.

"Office."

"Good morning, this is Nancy Palmer in room seven. I'll be staying another night, please."

"Hold on." The woman's voice was abrupt and rude.

"Thank you." Von Himmler winked at Nancy. She was still nervous but looking into those blue eyes relaxed her.

"That will be fifteen dollars and eighty-three cents. Our rates go up on Friday nights." The voice sounded less harsh.

"That's fine. I'll be in to pay you this afternoon."

"Or tomorrow, before you go. We have all the billing information right here, Miss Palmer. You're with Western Mutual Insurance. I imagine you're staying over in order to see Taquamenon Falls. The autumn colors are at their peak. You should have a beautiful day for sightseeing."

Nancy set down the phone. "I have to use the bathroom, now."

"Of course, take your time. Your name is Nancy, did you say?"

"Yes." Von Himmler turned towards the brown and black-strapped trunk.

She took her purse with her into the bathroom, and then she locked the door. She really did have to urinate. She noticed that the window behind the shower curtain was small- but she imagined that if the opportunity presented itself later on, if she could move the desk chair into the bathtub, she might be able to stand on it and climb right out. For now, she thought it best not to arouse suspicion and just play along with the old man. She didn't want him wielding that screwdriver at her.

There was the voice of the old man from beyond the locked door. "Everything all right?"

"Everything's fine," she replied. "I'll be out in a minute."

"Take your time, Nancy. I can wait."

She stood at the sink, primping. She could give no rational explanation for running a brush through her brown hair, or blotting on fresh lipstick. To somehow relax herself, she supposed. There could be no other reason for it. She took a deep breath, unlocked the door, and walked out.

Brahms was waiting for her. He manhandled her. This time, sensing the danger, she bit down savagely on the big fat fingers that he'd jammed against her lips and gums. He groaned, cupping his hand over her mouth securely. Von Himmler was ready with the hypodermic and he plunged it into the meat of Nancy's shoulder. She struggled helplessly in the grip of the giant, and then her whole body went limp like a rag doll.

Robert Brooks, the commander of the Newberry post of the Michigan State Police, stood out in the gravel parking lot of Buddy's Cafe, his neck red and handsome face filled with frustration. He had just finished ordering a network of roadblocks throughout the eastern end of the Upper Peninsula.

When the state police had arrived at the cafe, with Brooks in the lead car, they had asked for witnesses, but no one, much to Brook's chagrin, had been able to come forth with a description of the suspect, or, for that matter, the vehicle involved. It wasn't until they received word from the post's dispatcher of the escape of Josef Brahms that Brooks was able to identify the killer. And that word hadn't come until Brooks had interrogated the potential witnesses.

"You mean to tell me that nobody saw a damn thing? Not a car? Not anybody? The food must be damned good here!" he had scoffed. "What do they put in the coffee urn around here?" The patrons had been grouped in a semi-circle around the body. Brooks had clearly been irritated, and his methods were intimidating. Tony Accosta kept staring at his little buddy, lying face up behind the counter.

"Sir," the trucker had said, hesitantly. "There was a car that picked up speed, heading that way," and he'd pointed down the highway toward the east.

"Do you remember the make of the car? The color, maybe?"

"Was green, I think. I'm sorry- I was eatin' my roll and-"

"Anyone else see anything?" interrupted Brooks. The other diners had looked at each other sheepishly and shrugged.

It was then that one of the troopers came running in from his patrol car and informed Brooks of the escape at the hospital, and the peculiar crime that had made Brahms famous throughout Canada.

Brooks got back to his car and got right on the radio. "This is car number one, Brooks speaking. We need roadblocks west of the Soo, east of Seney, north of Engadine and stepped up security at the Big Mac Bridge. Coordinate on the emergency network, and broadcast the descriptions provided by the hospital. Possibly a green sedan driving east on Highway M-28 from Eckerman. Release a bulletin to radio stations, newspapers and television. Over.

"Why in the hell did the hospital take so long to report the escape?" he asked of two troopers who stood alongside the open driver's side door of his patrol car. "All we needed was a little warning. We'd have had the highway blocked in no time."

Brooks looked up at one of the troopers and motioned him into the car. He barked at the other like a junkyard dog. "Fred, secure the area until the ambulance arrives. Dittmeier will be in to lift prints. Stay near your radio."

"Yes, sir."

"We'll get our suspects, men. The Michigan State Police are hot on the heels of a vicious killer. We'll show the taxpayers just what a professional force they employ. Time to kick some ass, men. Oh, and, by the way, Fred-"

"Yes sir?"

"Stay out of the cinnammon rolls."

Brooks sped off back toward Newberry with the other trooper. "You know," he said, "that car that passed us- the one that slowed down and pulled over for us, did you get the make on that, Stan?"

"Blue Chevy sedan, commander," the trooper answered, rubbing his upper lip with the tops of his bottom row of teeth.

"We'll check that out, too."

The Soo Line railroad runs from its starting point in Sault Ste Marie due west across the northern tier of counties bordering Lake Superior in the Upper Peninsula, through the towns of Munising and Marquette, then heads south to Escanaba on the north shore of Lake Michigan, and then westerly, again, into Wisconsin where it makes connections with the Milwaukee Road to points south, terminating at that great hub of railway traffic, Chicago.

Louisiana Pacific Corporation operates a lumber mill and railroad yard just to the south and west of Newberry, along the Soo Line. Raw pulp is railed to the Kimberly Clark paper mill in Munising, and to Mead Paper, in Escanaba. Lumber, plywood, particleboard, wood creosote, and other finished products are also loaded and shipped out, destined for the population centers throughout the Midwest.

Von Himmler and Brahms had left Nancy Palmer lying on her motel bed, having administered to her a dangerously large dosage of a sedative that Von Himmler had plucked, along with various psychotic drugs, from a storage room at the hospital. He had led Brahms stealthily through the parking lot and back down into the gully. They had proceeded along the bottom of the ravine, to the southwest, and within an hour's time, had once again surfaced from the ravine, this time at a double set of the Soo Line railroad tracks.

A long line of freight cars was stopped on the westbound tracks while a dozen or so cars newly loaded with finished wood products were being linked to the train further up the line in the Louisiana yard.

Von Himmler took hold of the sliding door on the side of an old, dull red wooden freight car and opened it up just enough to peer inside. It was empty. He pushed open the door a little farther and motioned for Brahms to climb inside, with the trunk. "This is our ticket, Josef. This is our ride. Destination- Marquette." The trunk made a grating sound as Brahms pushed it across the dirty floor of the car. "Careful Josef! There are certain instruments which must not be damaged."

Von Himmler climbed aboard and then pulled the door closed. It creaked along on its rusted rollers. He left it ajar slightly, hoping to freshen the stale air inside. He looked over at his big assistant, who had carried the heavy trunk for a considerable distance without complaint. He was sweating profusely. Dark lines had appeared down the sides of his face from the streams of perspiration which had run from his hairline down through the dried layer of muck on his cheeks, carrying some of the sediment down his neck to soak into his collar and shirt.

"Josef, you have been of great service to me this morning. Why don't you lie down and sleep? I'll be in need of your great strength again this afternoon." Brahms silently stretched out on the floor of the car. Von Himmler soon lay down beside him and within minutes, the two escaped mental patients were sound asleep in their temporary haven.

Sam Rutledge, having maneuvered the last of the eight foot red pine logs onto the top of the huge pile stacked on the trailer of his logging truck, locked the hydraulic arm on the log loader across the top of the stack and carefully dismounted from the portable seat high above the deisel cab. He tapped a Marlboro from the breast pocket of his brown flannel shirt and lit it, pausing to enjoy the deep blue, late morning sky and the peaking fall colors of the north woods all around him. A day such as this was made for working in the woods. There were no bugs to pester him, the temperature was cool in the shade and warm in the sun, and the forest floor was neither muddy, nor frozen, permitting full usage of all the heavy equipment that made him so much more productive.

Sam headed up Rutledge Logging, and he didn't have to climb up into that little bucket above the truck to work the loader arm- he could have just delegated the job to one of his lumberjacks. But he honestly enjoyed most aspects of the day-to-day grind of his trade, even after all the years of heavy toil. And, the years had certainly slipped by. He was sixty-six, past normal retirement age, but he hadn't given much thought to giving up the business. He had no idea what he'd do with all of his spare time. As it was, when he wanted to fish, he went fishing, and when deer season rolled around the last two weeks of November, he was the first one in camp, stocking up the provisions and readying his blind, and then he was always the last to leave in the deep snows of early December.

The death of his wife, June, five years before to cancer, also had affected his plans. If June had lived, he would probably be spending six months of the year in a retirement community down south with her, because that had always been her dream.

"We'll have Thanksgiving with Sam Jr. (for young Sam always flew in from California to be with them at Thanksgiving or Christmas), and then we'll leave for our place in Florida on December first," she would say. Sam recalled that she'd always planned to stay in the south until at least mid-May. "That way we'll never see a big snowstorm in the springtime, again."

A blue and white Ford pickup drove slowly through the forest towards Rutledge on the two-track logging trail that accessed the highway a mile to the east. He recognized the pickup as his own. It was being driven by Red Tomlinson, an industrious employee of his who regularly drove the big deisel which Sam had just finished loading, to the Mead Paper Mill in Escanaba. Red had been working for the company for five years, and Sam knew that while he, himself, was loading the big pile of logs onto the truck bed, Red had been at another site, operating a skidder and supervising the felling of the huge pine trees which seemed to be in such limitless supply in the north central U.P.

Red pulled up and popped out of the pickup, leaving the engine idling. "I figured you'd have her ready to go," he said.

"Got tired of sittin' around on your butt, eh?" Sam asked with a poker face.

"Right! I plum wore out my back pockets from sittin' on my ass all day. I think I'll go apply for a job at the bank- least off I wouldn't have to put up with this harrassment every time I turn around. When did you say you're retirin'?"

Rutledge took the last drag of his cigarette and shot it at the side of the pickup, flicking the butt with his middle finger. "I retire at deer season. You wanna sight in your gun Sunday, Red?"

"With the Packers playin' the Lions? Hell, no. I'll be at the Sawmill right after church, gettin' primed. We're gonna kick Alex Karras' head in, man."

Rutledge stepped toward the pickup. "Got my lunch bucket in here, and packed enough food for both of us. You want a bologna sandwich?"

"Thanks, but I want to get running with this load. I'm plannin' on one of those big burgers at the Buck Inn. Why don't you ride along? We'd have a good time."

"I've got half-a-mind to join you. But, the other half is thinkin' about headin' up to deer camp later on."

"If you run into Donny," said Red, "tell him he can start loading his rig at the river. Got her piled high already this morning."

Sam nodded, climbing into the cab of the pickup. "Hey Red!" he yelled as he put the vehicle into reverse, "it's so damn nice out, I am going to deer camp this afternoon! See you at the river in the morning!" Red gave him the thumbs up and laughed.

By noon, Bob Brooks and the state police, as well as the members of the various other police agencies in the region who were assisting in manning the roadblocks on the main highways and patrolling the hundreds of miles of secondary roads in the search for Josef Brahms and Wolfgang Von Himmler, were becoming increasingly concerned. A murderous psychopath, albeit a retarded one, was on the loose. He had already struck once. Brooks had personally called the sheriff from each county in the eastern half of the peninsula, asking that any bakeries or donut shops be closed until Brahms was in shackles.

Brooks arose from his desk, sending his padded office chair crashing into the wall behind him. He had quit smoking during the summer, due to a persistent cough, but he reflexively reached into his breast pocket, as he often did when things weren't going smoothly at work. It was high time to take a drive over to the insane asylum. A chat with the attending psychiatrists might yield an unexpected lead. He pulled his blazer off of the coat tree and headed for the car.

CHAPTER SIX

Von Himmler slept deeply, despite the drafty, bumpy ride along the tracks in the empty freight car. From time to time he awoke, but the racket and the jerky movement of the car lulled him back to sleep. He felt confident that a lifelong ambition was soon to be realized. Rutledge, the chief murderer of his father, would finally pay for all that he had done. And, Von Himmler planned to snuff out any 'human ballast' that, along with Rutledge, might be available to him. The plan that he had so carefully laid out, the plan that was hundreds of hours in the perfecting, with all of its variables, would soon reach full fruition.

His mother and Doktor Lange, his psychologist in Vienna who had treated him from the time he had been kicked out of the medical college, there, had both concluded that his father's death was an unavoidable result of war and had time and again impressed their view upon Wolfgang.

"A Christian, son, has to bring himself to forgive all trespasses against him," his mother would always say. He was sure that Doktor Lange and his mother had slept together when Lange had visited Koblenz, offering follow up care.

He had remained with her in the little house in Koblenz, working in the laundry at the hospital for a number of years where his father had once practiced medicine. The frauleins working beside him in that hot, steamy plant asked why such an intelligent, though somewhat aloof young man, had not followed in his father's footsteps and gone on to even loftier heights. Wolfgang found himself making excuses, justifying his failures for his benefit far more than theirs, but never hinted at the real reason for his departure from medical college. The dissections- he had become preoccupied with the dissections in the anatomy pavilion at the University of Vienna.

At the outset, Professor Heinrecht mistook Wolfgang's illness for a level of enthusiasm unmatched by any of his other students. Wolfgang was tireless in his studies of the human body. His hours in the lecture halls and the library were surpassed exponentially by his time at the pavilion, preying upon the cadavers.

Heinrecht secretly kept Vienna's most renowned surgeon, Dr. Henry Richtenstein, apprised of Wolfgang's progress in school. Richtenstein had spent considerable time with the dean of the medical college upon learning from the widow of his old school chum, Horst Von Himmler, that her son, Wolfgang, who possessed an exemplary scholastic record from secondary school, was applying to the University of Vienna, intent upon following in his late father's path.

"The boy deserves every chance which you can give him," he had told the dean during their last conversation together. "His father, an alumnus of this university, was brutally murdered while fulfilling his Hippocratic oath by several drunken American soldiers, as you well know. From what I can gather, the boy went through a very difficult period. But after all, he witnessed his own father's murder- even attempted to physically thwart his father's attackers. He suffered a very serious head injury."

"This matter is of concern to us," replied the dean. "The board has researched Wolfgang's background very carefully, as they would any candidate, and there is a division on this issue. Indubitably, there is a real question of mental and emotional stability, here."

"I would think that any one of us, in being an unwilling participant at such a heinous event, would carry a degree of emotional scarring with us to the end of time," countered Richtenstein.

"And it is the degree of this scarring, Herr Doktor, that is the cloud which palls over young Von Himmler's otherwise impressive credentials."

"My opinion is that this university owes the memory of one of its finest graduates the benefit of the doubt. Young Wolfgang embodies all of the brilliance and character of his respected late father. He must be accepted for the opportunity to study here. I can see no other way."

"I will go back to the board, Henry, and they will concur. You may call Frau Von Himmler and notify her of her son's admission." They shook hands.

"I will make the call at once," Richtenstein had said happily.

From that time on, Richtenstein, through contacts with several faculty members (and Professor Heinrecht in particular), kept a watchful eye on Wolfgang's early progress.

That first semester, which ended in December, 1925, was a major success for Von Himmler. His chemistry, biological study, and anatomy lecture grades were in the top ten percent of his class. He returned home for Christmas holiday triumphantly, into the waiting arms of his loving mother, who, for nine days, stroked him for his productive performance that his father would have been so proud of.

"We knew you could do this, dear son," she said. "All three of us knew you could, didn't we?"

For his own part, Richtenstein, so overly concerned in September, was barely in contact with Heinrecht by December, so confident was he of the boy's academic abilities. At the faculty New Year's dinner, at which Richtenstein was an honored guest, the dean went so far as to take him aside and congratulate him on the progress of their 'prized pupil.'

"Henry, you've done the medical school a service for which I will forever be in your debt. Young Von Himmler's star is shining bright. Let's have a toast to the memory of his father, shall we?"

It was natural, then, that old Professor Heinrecht would keep a particularly close eye on the boy the dean was privately referring to as his 'prized pupil.' The winter semester began, and Heinrecht led his boys into the anatomy lab, where it was said a learned eye could discern a student's degree of skill with the scalpel, or lack thereof, in relation to the abilities displayed by the greatest of talents from out of the past, with Henry Richtenstein representing the true standard by which to measure excellence.

"Von Himmler, in my estimation, was a certain prospect," Heinrecht would explain to Richtenstein sometime later, when he was able to discuss the tragic circumstances of Wolfgang's expulsion without emotion.

The news of Von Himmler's dismissal from the university had reached Dr. Richtenstein in Berlin in the middle of February, where he was treating a high-ranking government official for cancer of the liver. It was upon his subsequent return to Vienna some weeks later, that he'd dropped in on Professor Heinrecht and learned of the startling details in the latter's office.

"His use of instruments, his understanding of anatomical function- Henry, his gift was evident to all. And, he was in the lab whenever he was free. Wolfgang was a student who required little guidance. At every turn, whenever the opportunity arose, he would learn and memorize.

"All was going extremely well, then."

"Yes, until sometime around the first of February. That is when an abrupt change came over him. He no longer had patience. Everyone associated with him- his classmates, his instructors, the laboratory assistants- we all witnessed the frustration, the temper, building within him."

"His studies suffered?"

"He collapsed- he suffered a breakdown. I counseled him, I pleaded with him. I tried to convince him that he was throwing his life away. But, he is a sick young man. My final attempt at saving him was to send him to the dean. And, there was improvement for a week or two afterwards."

"The final straw, Professor Heinrecht, what was this incident which was so appalling?"

"Henry, may I pour you a cognac?"

Richtenstein nodded and Heinrecht opened up a narrow wood cabinet in a cramped corner of the office, bringing out a bottle and two glasses. He dispensed two generous measures and set one of the glasses before his guest, seated as he was at the far end of the desk.

"That Sunday, after taking my wife to church, I stopped in at the pavilion to pick up some papers which I'd decided to go over, and Wolfgang was there. He'd brought three fresh cadavers out of storage and had placed them shoulder-to-shoulder across the width of one of the tables. Needless to say, I was puzzled by this arrangement. The legs and feet, stiff as they were, dangled off one side and the three heads were cocked back over the other- it must have taken a succinct effort to balance them just so. I walked over to examine this configuration and Wolfgang, upon seeing me there, walked way over to the row of windows, to see the sunlight, I suppose.

"Wolfgang had taken the scalpel and the saw and had carved out their three hearts and had carefully laid them on the chests above each incision. What was truly ghastly, Henry, was that he had inlaid some kind of message into the incisions. Without a doubt, when I stood at their toes, I could clearly see a capital 'A' in the first, the letter 'R' in the second, and a 'C' in the third."

The professor took a hard swallow of cognac. Richtenstein could see that his hands were quivering.

"Pardon me, Henry, but this whole thing has given me a case of the shakes," he pronounced with a slight smile. "Naturally, I confronted Wolfgang- lost my head somewhat. I asked him directly, what was I to make of all of this? That he had left me no other alternative but to expel him from his studies, here."

"What was his reaction, professor?"

"He told me that his work at the university was now complete. That he had excised the three hearts with all of the precision of Dr. Richtenstein. He turned away from me at that point, walked out, packed up, and left for home, I believe, on the next train."

"Frau Von Himmler will certainly have a time of it," said Richtenstein. "I suppose we should be glad that Horst isn't alive to hear about this."

"We did refer his case to Doktor Lange."

"Of course."

"Lange brought the boy back to Vienna for a series of treatments in the sanatorium."

"May the boy find peace." The two men emptied their glasses and sat back, savoring the bustling of the packs of students out in the corridor.

Von Himmler had continued, then, to work in the hospital laundry for the next several years, taking many of his meals at a table in the hospital's kitchen, and returning home late in the evening only when it was time for bed. He had also finally shaken Dr. Lange, shortly after Herr Doktor had determined that his overall condition had stabilized, though in Wolfgang's mind, his mother had grown older and her once firm figure was showing signs of sagging and Lange had simply lost his passion for her.

One afternoon, while taking a plate of spatzen and black bread at the table in the hospital kitchen, Frau Fredericka, the respected nursing supervisor, boldly pulled up a chair in order to address the weary Wolfgang. "Wolfgang Von Himmler, I would like a brief word with you, if I may be permitted?"

"Of course, Frau Fredericka, is there a problem in the laundry?"

"No, no, my boy. I have an offer- a job offer for you."

"A job offer?" Wolfgang perked up, and sat tall in his chair.

"We are in need of a nurse, in Ward Six. I knew your father, and I am sure you would do just fine, there. I have recommended you for the job."

"I would be honored. The laundry is a boring, tedious place."

"You shall begin right away, then. Right after you've finished your lunch." Von Himmler bowed, and then scooped up a forkful of the yellow noodles.

"I will be right with you- Ward Six."

"Yes, Wolfgang, you know where it is." He nodded, eating voraciously. "Report to the nursing station. There, you will receive your instructions."

Wolfgang began working, then, in Ward Six, the area of the hospital occupied by the mentally impaired and the physically infirm. The total responsibility for this ward, which had grown considerably in size and scope following the Fatherland's humiliating defeat in the Great War, had been given to Wolfgang's father's old confidant, Dr. Herman Pfanmuller. At first, Pfanmuller had barely acknowledged Wolfgang's presence in the ward. He was involved in implementing the National Socialist's new eugenics policies of racial purification, and was often away for weeks at a time at the new Reich Committee institution at Eglfing-Haar. But over a period of many months, Wolfgang's ceaseless hours in giving the clinical care required in order to keep the patients sanitary and disease free came to Pfanmuller's attention.

It was in April of 1934 that the fat, clean shaven physician with the receding hairline who, at the suggestion of a lady friend, had traded a pair of new eyeglasses for the monocle to better camouflage his shifty eyes led Wolfgang quietly into his new office, which had belonged to the retired Doktor Schmidt, former director of the entire hospital. He walked back behind his desk and plopped gratefully into his softly padded chair. "Nurse Von Himmler, shut the door behind you, please." Wolfgang obeyed the instruction, turned, and Pfanmuller motioned him towards a side chair. "Sit down, please." The doctor produced a colored tin from his desk and offered the contents to Wolfgang. "Would you care for a cigar?"

"No, I do not smoke."

Pfanmuller held one of the small cigars in his chubby fingers and pushed it past his lips and into his mouth, wetting the wrapper, and then he lit it and puffed contentedly. "Your father was a fine man. We did not always see eye to eye politically, but I always held your father in the highest esteem."

"I believe my father spoke of you very fondly, Herr Doktor." Wolfgang was uneasy, having been singled out like this. It reminded him, in some way, of the medical school disaster. When he was separated from his peers, surely nothing good could come of it.

"I have been keeping a careful eye on you, nurse. Your energy level is truly phenomenal. We should all work so hard." Pfanmuller looked into the bright, blue eyes and then studied the round, wire rim glasses and the messy hair, already showing signs of premature gray. "I have something of extreme importance to discuss with you. That is why I have called for you here." He flicked an inch of gray ash into a china cup that he clearly used for that purpose.

"I am appointing you operating head of this ward. You will, in fact, report only to me." Wolfgang nodded slowly. "There is a change in policy which we must be prepared to carry out. It may sound cruel to you at first, but it is a necessary step in order to keep the social organism alive and healthy."

"What is this policy change, Herr Doktor? I am not schooled in medical policy."

"We will begin the willful neglect of the mentally deranged and impaired- specimens like you deal with out in Ward Six. These patients constitute life unworthy of life. The theories of Adolf Jost, my dear young fellow, are finally being taken seriously."

"What of the work of this Jost?" asked Wolfgang. "I have never heard of him."

"His theory in simple terms is that the survival and health of the state is dependent upon the will of society to grant the state the right, or should I say, the responsibility, to kill. In order for the social organism to remain viable, and healthy, the state must be prepared to weed out- to kill in effect, those unworthy of life, and, or, the reproduction of life."

"Euthanasia," said Wolfgang.

"But it is really much more than euthanasia. Do you know of the work of Alfred Hoche?"

"Hoche? No, I do not."

"Hoche wrote of the concept of a 'mental death,' you see. The brain damaged, the severely retarded, the severely emotionally disturbed- Hoche characterized those patients under the heading of human ballast. He pointed out the great economic burden placed upon society by the mere existence of young, healthy, mentally impaired men and women who invariably will live out a full, long life in one of our institutions. There is proven scientific criteria by which it may be determined that a mentally deficient person has no hope of improving his lot in life." Pfanmuller observed Von Himmler's keen interest in the subject. The fellow was hanging on each and every word.

"A new age is on the horizon. In fact, I believe that it is, indeed, here with us now. The gross overestimation of the value of life, and its demands upon the medical field, will capitulate in favor of a policy that selectively scrapes away the bottom of the collective gene pool, namely, eugenics, of which, I am proud to say, I am presently working to help implement."

"I am taken with these ideas, Herr Doktor. Human ballast."

"That is good. For now, the new policy need not be publicized. The foreign press would jump at the chance to tell the rest of the world what they think we are about to do. We are to begin on a small scale. First off, I want you to prepare a list of patients who meet the criteria in your mind's eye. You need not restrict your list to catatonic vegetables. Just be, as Darwin might say, selective."

Von Himmler smiled. "And as for this willful neglect, how shall we begin?"

"No medications, no sponge baths, an absence of preventative hygiene. This will require isolating the chosen ones in their own ward, away from all the others. Perhaps they will, in time, suffocate in their own feces."

"I will draw up this list at once."

"Excellent, Nurse Von Himmler. I knew you were the man for the job. You may rearrange the patients in the ward as you see fit. That is my direct order." Wolfgang rose from his seat and, with a brief salute, slipped out the door and into the hallway.

Over the next several years, Pfanmuller's work was right on the leading edge of Nazi medical theory and practice. The head of the Euthanasia program, Karl Brandt, who also happened to be Adolf Hitler's personal physician, named Pfanmuller the director of the ongoing, experimental research institute at Eglfing-Haar, in the late summer, 1937. So after resigning his post at Koblenz Hospital, it wasn't very long before he summoned his most trusted assistant, Wolfgang Von Himmler, to join him in fully developing what would prove to be the most disturbing program ever put into practice by so learned and skilled a group of men from the field of medicine.

After explaining the general importance of this ongoing medical project to his mother, while shielding her from the actual details of his day to day responsibilities inherent in this new assignment, Hilda and Wolfgang packed his clothing and belongings into the brown and black strapped trunk which had belonged to his father, and that had, for many years, been stored out of the way in a closet beneath the stairs.

"Wolfgang, my son, I worry about you so. You are so sensitive, so unlike the other boys. Promise me that when your work is finished, you will come straight home to me."

"Mother, my work is the most important thing in my life, next to you, of course." He looked at his mother's tired face, at the dark bags beneath her eyes. "When the work is finished, I will return. Our love will grow in my absence."

"Yes, my boy." She gave him a long hug and kiss. A car horn honked rudely from out on the cobblestone lane. "The taxi is here. I will ride to the station with you. I want you to wave to me from the train."

Wolfgang was happy to be leaving her, again. She would never be able to accept the true nature of his work. It was better to leave her in darkness. If she had ever gotten wind of the project in Ward Six at Koblenz Hospital, and her only son's deep involvement in it, the shock probably would have killed her.

At the station, Wolfgang had given his mother a hug and then he had quickly climbed aboard the train without looking back, presenting the conductor with the ticket which Pfanmuller had sent him. When the whistle sounded and the train began to slowly move out, he located his mother leaning over the rail, and as he passed, they blew one another a final kiss.

The Reich facility at Eglfing-Haar was formerly a state mental institution which had become a teaching hospital, of sorts, where courses were held for government administrators and certain rightwing members of the press, courses displaying the most blatant examples of 'life unworthy of life'- patients who exemplified, in the words of Hitler, himself, "the habit of putting their own excrement into their mouths, eating it, and so on."

For the first weeks following Von Himmler's arrival there, some of the old feelings that he had suppressed, feelings that he had previously associated with his extended stay at the sanatorium in Vienna some twelve years before, began to surface. On those frequent occasions when members of the medical staff and various visitors were to gather in a corridor or a nurse's station, Wolfgang felt that he, himself, had become the primary topic of their often animated conversations, even in those rare instances when Dr. Pfanmuller, himself, would join the fray.

In order to deal with this paranoia, Wolfgang would immerse himself totally into his work, which included the strictest measurement of the dwindling portions of food that he would then provide to his patients in quantities relative to their particular stages of emaciation. Sixteen hour work days were the norm for him, and when those patients whom he worked so closely with were finally deceased, he also performed the required autopsies and dissections, and the necessary cataloging and major organ storage which went along with it.

Wolfgang had a fierce interest in his ever-expanding collection of brains. He hoped one day to answer questions such as: why had this man been an imbecile? Why was that one paralyzed? What caused another to slobber when he attempted to talk? And so forth; So, he sliced and cross-sectioned the tissues, and took exhaustive measurements and then he jarred and labeled the specimens and cross-referenced them with a card file detailing the behavioral pattern and condition of each and every patient in the weeks leading up to their deaths.

As a patient approached death, and Wolfgang could always sense when the end was near, he would make his way into the storage room, label an empty jar with the name and number of the patient, and then pare down the often voluminous notes that he had consistently kept, describing in great detail the patient's chronic condition, personality dysfunction, and any other anomalies which he thought particularly noteworthy. Wolfgang was positive that in this manner, he was providing medical science an invaluable service, and Dr. Pfanmuller, another reason to boast.

Von Himmler was convinced that the brain of a mongoloid, for instance, must possess differences and aberrations that were measurable and profound. "Rutledge, and Ahonen, and Chapman," he sometimes said aloud, "I wonder what it would be like to hold their brains in my hands?" He knew that if the opportunity presented itself to him, he might crush their brains, or bounce them on the tabletop, or douse them with lighter fluid and give them a good scorching. He wondered if they would still feel it, somehow, from a detached corner of the room where their damned souls might be in limbo.

In this way, Wolfgang continued on, employing himself, as Pfanmuller put it, in a vocation that continually improved the health of the social organism. He was putting into workable practice the idealism of the National Socialists. This was to be his life's work. The day would come, he knew, when babies born with severe handicaps would be routinely suffocated beside the birthing bed, before a mother could ever bond to her defective infant. Dr Pfanmuller's gene pool, then, would quickly become purer and stronger, and the German Reich would be the genetic envy of all of civilization.

In the spring of 1939, Pfanmuller again came to 'Researcher Von Himmler,' as he liked to call him, with a change in scheme that would stamp Pfanmuller indelibly as a fiendish murderer in the annals of history.

"Eglfing-Haar," he told Wolfgang, beside the shelves of brains, "will no longer house and treat adult patients." Von Himmler reacted with stunned silence. Had he not done everything possible to hold up his end of the bargain? Was his work not extremely useful? Was he not a main cog in the purification of his people? What of his research on brain tissue? Had there been any thought given to the grave consequences inherent in terminating that kind of study? He was, after all, a scientist.

"As of next Wednesday, May one, we are to become a Reich center for the treatment, and disposal, of children with serious hereditary diseases. Idiocy, mongolism, microcephaly, hydrocephaly, malformations of every description, particularly of the limbs, head, and spinal column, as well as paralysis, and spastic conditions." Pfanmuller rubbed his fat hands together, as if he'd just recited some perverted Christmas wish list. "Mr. Von Himmler, you are now officially a member of the Children's Specialty Department."

"Yes, Herr Doktor. And our method of treatment, shall it remain intact?"

"The most simple method," the fat physician replied. "We will continue to follow the nutrient reduction charts. I have drafted a letter to the parents of our prospective patients describing the best and most modern therapies which will be available to their children at this institution."

"What of my work? My work with all the brains?"

"Splendid! And by all means, nothing will change in that regard. Your work must continue." Von Himmler breathed a sigh of relief.

In the days and weeks that followed, the remaining adult patients were removed from Von Himmler's charge, and slowly, the same beds were filled with young children suffering from a variety of congenital abnormalities. Herman Pfanmuller, who enjoyed a fanatical reputation in Nazi medical circles for his grossly enthusiastic campaign championing clinical starvation as the means to accomplish euthanasia killing, now proposed to prescribe this same method in dealing with the poor children who were delivered unto him.

Von Himmler, having been favored with such a loving mother, was astounded that the parents of these children had, in every case, signed release forms, apparently approving this radical treatment for their sons and daughters.

"The entire procedure is the direct result of taking the parents, as well as the rest of society, into account," Pfanmuller explained one day to Wolfgang, standing at the foot of the bed of a whimpering, palsied, four year old boy. "The parents first receive a personal letter from the in charge physician from the local facility which is attempting to care for their child. The letter explains that the best, and most efficacious treatment is now available in dealing with their child's condition. If, initially, there is a hesitation on the part of the parents to act, during the ensuing home visit from a representative of our Children's Specialty Department, it is explained to them that the state is prepared to assume full legal guardianship of the child. In this way, cancellation of the treatment is not a contingency." Pfanmuller grinned broadly.

"Herr Doktor, I have been told that other treatment centers, Gorden at Brandenberg comes to mind, rely on the use of luminal tablets to cause death. This treatment, I think, would take only a matter of a few days." Wolfgang gestured toward the child lying in the bed. His blue eyes were not quite as cold.

"Nurse Von Himmler!" cried out Pfanmuller, reddening at his fat, bulbous neck. "There is a specific reason for relying upon nutritional therapy, not drug therapy, in dealing with these mentally dead. You see," and his manner softened considerably and his neck no longer appeared as red or as swollen as he said, "without the use of drugs, such as luminal, in culling our social organism of life unworthy of life, the newspapers in New York, Paris, and London will have little ammunition with which to spread their false propaganda. The world is envious of Germany for having the courage to improve and purify the Aryan race. They see that we continue to move forward biomedically, to make our Reich impervious to the threats from the western democracies."

Von Himmler nodded. "How do they deal with such cases in America?"

"Herr Researcher, the rest of the world has no such program. Germany is in the lead, and there are no followers." Wolfgang stuck out his skinny chest like a peacock.

"Doktor Pfanmuller, I have never told you, but the day the Americans killed my father was the day my heart turned black with hate. My black heart caused my expulsion from medical school." Pfanmuller placed a fatherly hand on Wolfgang's shoulder. "They have destroyed my life, and that is why I must see our nation rise up and deal the Americans a fatal blow."

"I know of the pains which you have endured, my son. Know now, that your life has not been destroyed. Your hands are caked with the mortar of the Reich builder, caked as heavily as the hands of any other man. You need only stand tall and proud as you carry out my orders and desires. This will be your masterwork!"

"My father was a compassionate, loving servant of mankind. He was selfless and sacrificial in caring for the diseased and feeble. I am none of these things." Wolfgang peered down at the little boy in more of a detached way. This child, he knew, would soon die.

"Compassion," replied Pfanmuller, carefully choosing his words, "is a redeeming quality in he, who can afford to be so. Never forget, that where there is compassion, there must also be misery. The two go hand in hand. To be compassionate is a noble trait in a man, yes. Ernst Mann has taught us that misery can only be removed from this world by the direct extermination of the miserable. Destroy the miserable, you see, and there is no longer the need for compassion. The considerable resources required to keep this child, and the many others like him, alive for a normal life span, may, instead, be earmarked toward government grants engineered to assist the young, healthy Aryan couple just starting out, or go into the development of new centers of higher learning, where the means to improve the quality of all of our lives is perfected, and then handed down from generation to generation. The Nazis speak of a thousand year Reich."

"Zeig Heil!" cried out Von Himmler, his eyes welling with tears. "I see this vision, and know it to be profound. It is a vision, of which, I can play a significant part." Pfanmuller held him by the shoulders and looked into his damp eyes, the madness of the two men merging onto a new plain of practical evil.

"Continue in your work, my son, and this world will one day be yours." Pfanmuller withdrew his hands from Von Himmler's shoulders.

Wolfgang stood over the little boy, his great purpose crying out from the dark depths of his soul. A new, long range idea burst into his brain from the drab, grayish-white walls of the ward. A world controlled by this German Reich would surely have to give up its guilty to be judged for any past crimes or transgressions against the fatherland. The men who murdered his father would be brought to justice and would pay fully for the thing that they had done. Von Himmler began to shake and shudder, as though orchestrated by the same conductor who was directing this small boy to shiver from palsy. Wolfgang gasped at this thought, and he looked up to share it with Pfanmuller. The doktor was gone.

CHAPTER SEVEN

Herman Bancroft wadded up the second of the two plastic body bags into a crunchy ball and stuffed it into a metal trash container in one corner of the preparation room. The two corpses of the young accident victims lay on rollaway carts in an adjacent storage area.

Gloria was off to one side, readying the elongated, hollow needle that fit on the trocar. The trocar was little more than an injection pump used in replacing the deceased's abdominal fluid with several pints of the Champion Chemical Company's all-purpose cavity fluid.

An uncle of Julie Marcotte, one of the victims, had brought suitable clothes from both bereaved homes with which to dress the dead. Herman obtained his highest level of job satisfaction from this aspect of his work. "I've always felt extra good inside when the first visitors come to pay their respects," he had once told Gloria. "Those that lie in view look like they're all ready to pop up and walk to church, attired in their Sunday best."

"Herman," said Gloria softly, aware that her employer was deep in thought, "I talked to Mr. Hintimaki's brother by phone this morning and he promised that the pallbearers will be here at least twenty minutes early." Bancroft looked up with a nod, and then sighed.

"Fine. I suppose it is time to pull the hearse up to the side entrance. Think you can keep on top of things down here?"

"Yep. Just don't forget that I'm here."

Herman rolled his eyes. "Gloria!" he scolded, "how could I ever forget about you?"

"I'm sure you haven't forgotten about my convention trip, have you?" She looked him in the eyes with mock irritation.

"Goodness, no!" he cried, looking sheepish.

"Just remember, I must be on the road by five o'clock. There's a breakfast meeting at seven tomorrow morning."

"They do get started early, don't they? And you'll be so busy! I have the brochure on my desk- what a full schedule! When would you ever have time to play golf?"

"Tomorrow afternoon. I have a one-thirty tee time."

"Well hopefully, we'll have you in your car by four. Gosh, I certainly will be glad when Hector finishes school, this pace is killing me!"

At shortly before quarter of two that afternoon, the pallbearers for Waino Eino Hintimaki gathered before his bier and waited while the cars of his friends and relatives lined up out on Birch Avenue. Herman was busy placing magnetized white flags on each car hood and directing the proper order of the automobiles in the growing line. As always, he would pull out ahead in the big white hearse and lead the line of cars in a procession all around town.

Though the Lutheran Church was roughly the length of a football field from the front of the funeral home, it would take a good twenty minutes to arrive by way of Herman's circuitous route. He would lead them down every back alley and side street. The deceased was taking one final sweep through his neighborhood, and Herman just knew that the shut-ins were most appreciative.

An older man with graying hair, black horn rimmed glasses, and a slight limp made his way up to Herman. "Need any help today, Mr. Bancroft?"

"Charlie, how you doin', heh?"

"Couldn't be better. Would you like me to help get the flowers over to the church?" Herman placed a flag on the last car in line and tucked the extras into the pocket of his trench coat.

"Actually, Reverend Sterling came by and picked up the largest sprays for his altar before lunch. But, there is something that you could do, Charlie, if you'd like?"

Charlie reached around and scratched his butt beneath his sports coat. "Happy to help, Mr. Bancroft."

"Good. The keys are in the station wagon, in the garage, there. Bring it around, behind the hearse. Stay way back. When I drive away with the casket, load the remaining flowers into the back of the wagon and take them over to the tent set up at the cemetery. Dan Carroll should be hanging around there, someplace. I'm sure he'll help you arrange them properly."

"Consider it done, Mr. Bancroft."

"Thanks again, Charlie. I'm sure the whole Hintimaki family appreciates the gesture."

"Glad to help out any way I can."

Charlie stepped up to the sidewalk and walked briskly back toward the funeral home. Herman looked after him, smiling. Ol' Charlie sure could gallop along with that limp when he needed to. Doing chores for the town's funeral director gave him a purpose in life. Herman knew that he was on social security disability. Now and then he handed Charlie a twenty. He was sure it helped him out. More importantly, he knew it made Charlie feel truly useful. 'Just as long as he doesn't ask to drive the hearse,' Herman thought.

Bob Brooks of the Michigan State Police was sealed in Dr. Drake's office at the Newberry Joy Regional Mental Health Center. He tapped his forefinger repeatedly on the arm of the brown leather wingback chair in which he was seated, waiting impatiently. The door opened, and the blue haired Dr. Drake herded Julian Katz into the office and closed the door behind them. Brooks rose to his feet.

"This must be Doctor Katz," said Brooks, shaking the damp, frail hand offered him. "My name is Brooks, doctor, from the state police. Doctor Drake, here, indicated that you've been treating both Brahms and Von Himmler." Brooks noted that he carried a red folder under his left arm.

"Yes, sir. I've been treating them since I accepted my position here. It's been, what? Seven years, hasn't it, Doctor Drake?" Drake just glowered at the horn rimmed glasses and balding head.

"Doctor Katz, do you subscribe to any theories as to their current whereabouts? Any peculiarities or habits that might be of use to us? I imagine that you've been giving this whole matter a good deal of thought."

"That I have, er, trooper."

"Lieutenant. I am the Commander of our Newberry post," Brooks corrected. Katz stretched his facial features and pushed his glasses back up onto the bridge of his hawk-like nose.

"Von Himmler has taken his trunk, and we discovered some medications missing as well. He held the delusion that he was a physician from

Germany. As for Brahms, well, he's always dreamed of returning to his native Canada."

"Just a minute, doctor, if I may. Von Himmler took a trunk, filled with what? Supplies? Clothing?"

"Just some things he has accumulated over the years. Some of our more lucid patients are allowed mail order merchandise, carefully screened, of course."

"What of these drugs which he appears to have gotten his hands on?"

"We've inventoried the storeroom which was broken into last night. There appear to be sedatives and depressants- Nembutal, Seconal, Luminal, Thiopental, syringes, and, some other supplies missing."

"Sounds to me like he's going to play doctor for real, huh?"

Brooks smiled slightly but both psychiatrists ignored his jest. "You must have a list of all his possessions?"

"Clothing, personal items, nothing to worry about, certainly. Believe it or not, he kept up on the Upper Peninsula's economy. He received newsletters from several different trade organizations. Mining, logging, lumber products, that sort of thing. All of it quite harmless, I'm sure."

Brooks looked up at the plaster ceiling. There were cobwebs in the corners. The whole office looked dingy and grimy, for that matter. He had this pet peeve about anything state owned or run and supported with tax dollars. There was no excuse for not keeping everything shipshape. He certainly did not tolerate clutter and filth back at the post. "And what would cause Von Himmler to take an interest in, say, copper mining?"

"I have no idea, commander. Perhaps he wanted to track the job market. No rationale which you or I would be able to relate to. The man was committed to this fine institution. Why he would be interested in the U.P. Logger's Association, for instance, is way beyond me. If I could answer that question, I'd probably have a million dollar practice out in California, somewhere." Katz cackled.

"Let's get back to the items of clothing which he might have in his possession. Did these clothes belong to him, for instance, before he was locked up?"

"The trunk came with him. That's all that I can tell you. It was examined thoroughly, and then stored in our basement. An inventory list was made. He would have legal rights to his possessions if and when he left here."

"A rule he was very aware of, apparently. I would like to see a copy of this inventory list immediately. It could prove crucial to our investigation. What we need right off the bat, Doctor Katz, is a description of these items of clothing. We need color, style, type of jacket, for instance. This man may have changed into civilian dress."

"Unfortunately, this information is unavailable. We had a case of vandalism where records were destroyed. I'm afraid we've scoured the remaining files without success. I'm sorry," Drake replied.

Brooks shook his head in disgust. "What can you tell me about the relationship of these two men? Sounds to me like we have a Svengali directing the actions of a big, stupid dummy- and, a lethal dummy at that."

Katz nodded. "Josef Brahms spent many a day with Wolfgang Von Himmler. He was one of the few persons in Josef's life whom he felt he could trust."

"Good God!" replied Brooks, "our files indicate that this Von Himmler fellow stabbed a gas station owner in St. Ignace to death ten years ago. I've spoken with Scott Crimin, the chief of police over there. He told me that the owner of the gas station was tortured, and that robbery was not the motive."

"A psychopath is capable of the most disturbing of crimes," explained Katz calmly. "That gas station owner was actually impaled, I believe that is the correct term."

"Impaled?"

"On a stake. Mr. Von Himmler told me the details on more than one occasion. It seems he wasn't happy with a repair bill. That ranks right up there with the most hideous crimes that I've ever read about. Here, I'll release his complete file to you. I kept this one at home, for safekeeping." Katz handed the policeman the red folder.

"Why wasn't that case publicized?" asked Brooks. "The news media would have had a field day with that one."

"Everything was kept quiet for a good reason, that's my understanding," answered Katz. "Von Himmler was clearly insane. The county court had him committed. He was ruled unfit to stand trial. It was all hush, hush- they didn't want to scare away the tourists."

Brooks rose to his feet. "Thank you for the information, doctors."

"They can't last too long out there, can they, commander?" asked Dr.

Drake hopefully. "They're certainly suspicious characters. I'd think that they would really stick out in a crowd."

"I'm confident that our roadblocks will hold them," said Brooks firmly. "In the meantime, we can only pray that there will be no more innocent deaths." He glowered at Dr. Katz.

Gloria Shutz stood in the upstairs bathroom of Bancroft's Funeral Home, wrapped in a blue towel while she ratted out her hair. She yawned, grateful that her full day of work had finally drawn to an end. A three-hour drive still lay before her. She wondered if she would have any energy left to enjoy the Northern Michigan Mortician's Convention.

Gloria set down the hairbrush and stepped back away from the sink. She looked at her pretty face. Her complexion was faultless. Her blue eyes were striking, her nose small and pert, her lips fleshy and full. Slowly, she untwisted the top of the towel and let it cascade to the floor, looking all the while into the mirror. She was pleased with her curvaceous figure. Her breasts rounded into pure white globes and she watched as she gave her nipples a quick rub with her index fingers, coaxing them into hard, pink knobs mounted on the ends of the firm girl flesh. She slid her hands down along her smooth waist, her fingers curling briefly into the mat of creamy hair at her crotch. Gloria was a natural blonde. She turned sideways, bringing her forearms up along the sides of her head, slowly undulating her hips and bare behind, feeling the desire again to mount the cold, rock hard young cock downstairs, the need to do so prickling up from her loins and into her stomach and breasts. She felt like a bad girl and it felt good. She knew it was harmless. She was safe and secure.

It had not always been that way. As a young teenager, back in Milwaukee, at the time that she was maturing into a woman seemingly overnight- she had been abused by her older brother. That first time, on that hot summer night, their mother had been sick in bed, their father was long gone, having abandoned the family and gone to live in Florida, and Steven had come right into her room, with no one to stop him. He and his friend from work had been drinking together after putting in a day at the construction site, and Steven had come home from his friend's place, belligerent and mean.

He had pulled the sheet off of her and wrestled her down. She cried out but then he had slapped her. There was no use in fighting him off. He was big and strong and Gloria still winced at the thought of the B.O. smell and beer breath. He had taken hold of her then. First, he had said he just wanted to see her breasts. But then he forced her legs apart and jammed himself into her and in all of two minutes, her innocence was lost. He had lurched away after he was done, mumbling some apology. She cried for two days afterward.

It happened again after that- over and over- maybe two dozen times that summer, until one day Steven was arrested for robbing a gas station in Waukegon, Illinois. Gloria never saw her brother after that. Never went to the sentencing with her mother.

All men were just like Steven, more or less. They looked at her and got erections. Erections were weapons, something that they could use to take control of her.

At University of Wisconsin-Milwaukee, she took courses in mortuary science. The boys in her classes seemed to be a different breed from men like Steven. They were not so threatening to her. Working on the dead bodies also allowed her to face the male animal that she despised, work on him at close quarters. Why had she been given this beautiful body in the first place? Why was it meant that she should be so cruelly deflowered even before reaching full bloom?

Curiously, she had developed an interest in sex- as long as it was safe sex. She could not permit any man to control her- to hold her down with his body, breathing that hot, smelly breath, ever again. The sex had to be on her terms, or not at all.

There was a knock on the door. Gloria reached for the towel and wrapped herself back up. "Come on in, door's open."

Herman Bancroft, dressed in gray suit, white shirt, and black and blue striped tie, entered. He had just returned from the cemetery. "Mr. Bancroft, you look so debonair. I don't mean to be tying up your bathroom."

"Gloria! For heaven's sakes! Actually, I came up to present you with a little bonus for your convention expenses- it's been a trying day and I don't know what I would have done without you." Herman handed her a crisp one-hundred dollar bill. Gloria's eyes lit up radiantly. "By the way, those kids look great downstairs."

"Why thank you, Herman. This will certainly come in handy." She leaned over and gave him a smooch on his cheek. "I don't know where I could possibly find a nicer boss." Her towel unraveled at her bust line, briefly baring her breasts. Herman stared shamelessly at her hard, pink nipples.

"And I couldn't ask for a nicer daughter-in-law, the Lord be willing." Gloria became wide eyed for a moment.

"Hector and I get along real well. We write almost every week. But, we'll just have to wait and see how things go." Gloria hadn't even come close to making it with Hector, yet. She wasn't sure he was her type.

Herman chuckled. "I know, Gloria, and we both know how free spirited the boy is. Reminds me of myself at his age- 'cept I was better, believe me!" he said with a knowing wink. "I was lucky enough to find myself a nice, level headed girl. I'm only wishin' the same for him. You're a beautiful woman, Gloria." Herman licked his loose lips.

Gloria blushed. "That's a real compliment from a true gentleman."

"Now you have a safe drive over to the Soo, and above all, have a great, great time!"

"Thank you, Herman. I'll say goodbye on my way out."

Herman closed the bathroom door tight. Boy, she sure had a nice set of tits. She was built like a brick shithouse. The phone began to ring as he descended the stairs. He trotted into the office and answered the call.

"Bancroft's."

"Hello, this is Herb Marcotte, Julie's father."

"May I convey, on behalf of the house of Bancroft, our deepest sympathy to you and your family, Mr. Marcotte. What a terrible tragedy this is." Herman detected muffled sobs for an instant, then silence. "We will do everything we can to make this dark time manageable for you and your dear wife, Mr. Marcotte."

"Thank you, sir. My reason for calling is that Mr. Higby and I would like to come over this evening to choose the caskets- if there would be a good time?"

"That would be fine. Around eight, or so?"

"Eight o'clock, then. Mr. Bancroft, was- was she cut up real bad? Her face-" The voice sounded strained and cracked.

"No, not at all. Julie looks very beautiful. You can see her and then we'll discuss the arrangements after you arrive." Herman hung up the phone, sat back in his comfortable leather chair, and closed his eyes.

Red Tomlinson had taken the big truckload of pine logs the eighty miles south to the Mead Paper Mill, had them unloaded, then had started back north with his empty rig, stopping off at the Buck Inn for a late afternoon lunch.

The Buck was a busy spot on Friday afternoons, and Red had ordered up two big hamburgers and a small pitcher of Old Style. Red wasn't a particularly big man, but he possessed an immense appetite and could drink beer in great amounts without any apparent outward effects. After quickly downing his hamburgers while seated alone at one of the tables facing several of the well mounted trophy racks of whitetail deer peering from various locations about the dining room, Red bellied up to the bar and had promptly introduced himself to a middle aged man and a woman who also happened to be Green Bay Packer season ticket holders from northern Wisconsin.

"How do you get season tickets?" Red had asked, as though owning a pair of Packer season tickets was akin to having a terminally ill, unmarried rich uncle staying in your spare bedroom while he steadily wasted away.

"My dad was on a waiting list for fifteen years," said the man. "He passed them down to me when he retired to Arizona. Suzette, here, and me haven't ever missed a game. Of course they only play four games at Lambeau." Suzette, her potbelly covered with a white smock top, sipped from her bottle of beer and gave Red a private wink.

"That's bullshit!" cried Red. "What do they got to play in Milwaukee for? I hated it last week when Hornung slipped on that dirt infield. That woulda been a touchdown all the way, heh?"

Their conversation had lasted well into the late afternoon, at which time, Red had looked at the clock above the bar and realized that he'd have to be on his way if he intended to be home by nightfall. He hopped into his rig and followed the road signs he knew so well back toward Marquette.

The stretch of highway running from Rapid River, which was located about fifteen miles east of the Mead plant, to Marquette was surprisingly free of sharp curves and Red always made good time. The one thing he didn't like about traveling this stretch was the dense population of white tail deer and their propensity for feeding along the roadway, particularly in the early morning and late afternoon. At seventy miles per hour, Red could do little more than keep his big rig in the proper lane and if a whitetail wandered out in front of him, he'd have to rely on his big air horn to scare it out of the way. Unfortunately, the deer sometimes froze in their tracks. When this occurred, within two or three seconds they would be flattened by the front bumper of Red's deisel, causing him to writhe uncomfortably behind the wheel at the thought of such a beautiful animal meeting so ugly a demise.

On this trip, however, Red did not so much as see a rabbit, and he made excellent time all the way back to Marquette. He did note that his fuel gauge was reading pretty low and he made a mental note to his slightly inebriated self to stop for a fill before continuing on to Birch.

The old railroad car occupied by Von Himmler and Josef Brahms was pulled into the south Marquette yard and the line of cars slowed to a screeching halt. Von Himmler got right to his feet and carefully stuck his head out into the early evening light. He knew that this was as far as the railroad could take them. He saw that the yard was located down near the Lake Superior shoreline. There were several large storage tanks standing down near the shore, and a massive dock works jutting out into the lake just beyond them. Up on a ridge overlooking the yard, a stream of traffic passed by on what appeared to be a very busy thoroughfare. The graybeard rousted Brahms from a coma like sleep, and led him, with the trunk securely on his shoulder, off the train and over to the base of the steep embankment, below the road.

"This will surely be a tough climb with the trunk, Josef. Take your time. I promise you that we will soon be at our final destination."

When they reached the crest of the hillside, they were met with the thunderous drone of traffic and Von Himmler peered from a thicket of lilac bushes and was shocked and surprised by his good fortune. Expecting to have to somehow hitchhike to the little town of Birch, they would, instead, be able to ride in comparative style on the empty bed of a big logging truck because Von Himmler spied just such a truck parked at a filling station to his immediate right with 'Rutledge Logging, Birch, Michigan,' clearly emblazoned in white lettering on the door of the deisel cab.

Red paid for the fuel, then selected two Mars candy bars from the station's vending machine. "Have a good weekend, eh?"

"You bet, Red."

"Gonna watch them Packers kick butt on Sunday?"

"Gotta work, but the boss brings in a little portable tv. I gotta watch the Packers."

"Good enough," said Red. He walked out the door with a friendly wave and then got into his cab, again, unwrapped one of the chocolate bars and gnawed off a healthy bite. He shifted gears, checked his mirrors, and slowly rolled back onto the road.

The drive back to Birch was an uneventful one. Red had planned to save the second candy bar for a late night snack but instead, found himself ripping open the wrapper and devouring it, as well. Connie, his wife, would not be amused. She was as skinny as a rail and was always accusing her husband of compulsive eating habits.

"I'm not fat," he would tell her when in the midst of one of his binges.

"You'll be a big blimp by the time you're forty," was her patented reply. "I'm keeping after you, Red Tomlinson! 'Cause I don't want you having a heart attack like my father. He was a big man."

Dusk was descending upon the little town just as Red pulled over and parked his rig on Birch Avenue, a half-block down from the Sawmill bar. "Connie babe, you'll just have to keep my dinner warm," he said to himself, as the golden glow from the Sawmill's big front windows beckoned. He hopped out of the cab, and walked up the narrow sidewalk, then disappeared inside the bar.

Von Himmler spied from behind the passenger side of the deisel cab, craning his neck out, standing on tiptoe. The street was still. Across the road, an unkempt hedge sprang up just beyond the end of a long row of houses. "Brahms, quickly!" he lashed hoarsely, Josef opened his eyes, stretching and disinterested. "Follow me over into those bushes! Bring my trunk! Hurry!" They scrambled across the pavement and hid themselves in the brushy thicket. Brahms sat down immediately, exhausted and starving.

"Hungry. I am hungry. Very hungry. Num-num."

"Yes, this I know. You will get food, and soon." Von Himmler's hypnotic eyes, invisible in the shadows, trained on the headlights of a lone sedan that drove slowly by. "No movement, Brahms. Stay low." The car continued on, in the direction of the highway from which the wood truck had just come.

"You come with me, now. I know of the place where we will stay." Brahms reached for the handles on the trunk dutifully. Von Himmler slapped at the big, puffy hands. "Leave the trunk here! We will return for it, later."

Red had walked into the Sawmill and had found it surprisingly empty for a Friday night. He greeted three other townspeople whom he knew to be regulars, but even they appeared to be in an unusually tranquil mood. Bob the bartender cracked open a bottle of Old Style and set it up on the bar in front of Red's usual stool.

"Hey, buddy!" said Red. "Awfully quiet in here. What did you do, raise prices? Cancel happy hour? What's goin' down, eh?"

Bob, a diminutive man in his mid-forties with the typical bartender's reputation for providing common sense advice when presented with a customer's troubles, smiled softly and shrugged.

"I guess you didn't get that radio fixed yet, Red. The town got some bad news, today. Jerry Higby and Julie Marcotte hit a tree on the highway last night. Killed instantly."

"God no! They're such good kids." Red looked down at the wood grain pattern in the bar top. "Poor Herb and Sandy. And Jerry's folks, too."

"Ed and Tina. They were at all of Jerry's basketball games. They usually never set foot in here- unless they were with friends."

"I know who they are," Red said. He took a long swallow of beer. "When's the funeral, Bob?"

"The Mining Journal has the obituaries, already. It says, arrangements incomplete."

"Probably Monday, then."

"Probably so," echoed Bob. Red tilted back on his stool, watching the ceiling fan above the bar slowly whirl.

"I bet Sam Rutledge hasn't heard the news, yet. He was headin' out to deer camp this afternoon."

"You can tell him in the morning." Bob, who rarely was seen taking alcohol, poured himself a shot of Yukon Jack and, hoisting it somberly with Red, took it in one gulp.

Herman Bancroft inhaled the last spoonful of soup from his bowl, and then washed it down with a slurp of cooled coffee. Alone again, for supper on a Friday night; He sure missed the wife. Brenda had been in Iowa for the past three weeks, tending to her mother. The poor, old dear had just undergone exploratory surgery that had successfully cleared away a benign blockage from her colon.

Whatever the wife made for dinner tasted far superior to anything that he could throw together. Well, she was gone, now, and there was nothing that he could do about it. At least his mother-in-law wasn't convalescing under his own roof. 'I'd rather eat canned soup every night for a year,' he thought to himself, managing a half-hearted chuckle.

Herman carried his dishes to the sink and filled his cup and bowl with water. He would wash them later. He rinsed and dried his hands with the towel hanging on the door of the electric oven. "The casket selection room!" he said, snapping his fingers. "Better be sure everything's in order." Herman started down the flight of stairs that led into the basement. There was a loud knock on the front door that stopped him in his tracks. "They're early!"

Von Himmler stood full in front of the funeral home entrance while Brahms hid to one side. He knocked a second time, and the door was promptly opened. Von Himmler walked right into the foyer, past the white shirted funeral director, his large companion following a step or so behind. "Brahms!" he commanded, "seize him!" Herman found himself locked helplessly in a full nelson. Brahms' grip was vise-like.

"What the hell's going on here?!" cried Bancroft. "How dare you! Release me, at once!"

"Shut up, you swine!" roared Von Himmler. "You must be, Mr. Bancroft?" Herman neither uttered a sound nor in any other way acknowledged this question put to him. He was frightened to death. Von Himmler brought the back of his right hand smashing across the undertaker's features. "I say, your name is Bancroft, is it not?"

Herman licked his swelling lip. "Y-y-yes, Herman Bancroft. I am the proprietor of this funeral parlor."

"That is better," said Von Himmler.

"Listen," Bancroft began, eyeing the bearded man in the funny green suit suspiciously, "I'll give you anything you want. You can have money, food, clothing- just don't hurt me, anymore." Von Himmler nodded.

"You are expecting visitors this evening, Mr. Bancroft?"

"Yes," answered Herman. "I have the parents of two young accident victims coming over within the next hour." Of course! There was safety in numbers! How could these two strangers expect to take on a whole town? Herman's strength returned to him. The state police were just a phone call away. "They'll be coming to select the caskets. Now, if you'll turn around and walk back out the way you came, I'll just forget this whole thing." Herman tried to smile. "Maybe this is a big joke?"

Von Himmler ignored him. "Where are these caskets, Mr. Bancroft?"

Herman did not answer him. Brahms applied heavy pressure under the armpits. The bursitis flared uncontrollably. "Down in the cellar, a left at the bottom of the stairs." Herman winced.

"When have you scheduled this funeral? Where is it to be?"

"Monday. N-n-not all of the d-details have been finalized as yet," stuttered Bancroft nervously. This fellow was scaring him, again.

"M-m-m-m-m, where are the corpses, now?"

"In the preparation room, downstairs to the left, and then to the end of the hall. Hey! Maybe you two men could be of some help to me," said Herman hopefully, "m-my wife is away, my son is off to school- I could really use two good men." Von Himmler's blue eyes filled with menace.

"Bring Bancroft downstairs, Brahms. A nice place you have here, Bancroft, very nice." Brahms, still squeezing Herman at the back of the head, now spun him around and all in one motion, leaned forward and balanced the undertaker onto the plane of his massive right shoulder. Herman lurched forward, and then was thrown up and over the huge backside of this creature. Herman's toupee flew off and he found himself staring at it from his precarious perch as it lay on the rouge carpeting directly below him. "You bastards!" he shouted, the blood rushing to his upside down head.

He was carried through the house, into the kitchen, and then down the rear stairway, near the entrance to the garage.

Down in the preparation room, Herman was compelled to lie face up on the operating table, under the bank of blinding, white lights. Von Himmler handed Brahms a long, electric extension cord. "Bind him down to the table, especially at his shoulders and ankles." Bancroft's eyes widened in horror. Von Himmler grinned from ear to ear.

"What the hell is this!? You're mad! Crazy fools! Where are you from, the looney bin!?" Bancroft saw the simple Newberry Joy Hospital logo imprinted on Brahms' filthy, green top. Some of his soup came back up. He swallowed, forcibly.

"My dear Bancroft, you are about to experience that which you, yourself, have practiced upon others time and time again. Think of those who have bequeathed their rigid bodies to you on this very table, perpetuating your despicable calling. Those who have granted your every wish, your every desire; Those who had no other choice but to give in to your sordid appetite. You are a glutton, Mr. Bancroft. You are that gnaws at the good conscience of society." He produced needle and thread from an instrument tray nearby, and held the point steadily three inches above Herman's mouth. "Hold the head still!"

"Goddam you!" screamed Herman, his pupils crossing as he tried to keep his eyes focused on the sharp point of the needle. "You'll never! Ahhhhh!!" The needle was plunged into his inner lip. Von Himmler worked methodically, at a turtle's pace. Four minutes later, the undertaker twisted on the table, moaning, with tears running down his cheeks, his mouth sewn shut.

"Now, we will proceed with your eyes, Mr. Bancroft. I know you must own a glue for this - but we will just have to settle for stitches." He slipped the needle deftly through the upper lid. "And, just how many pairs of eyes have you sealed over the years? This must be quite painful." Herman moaned steadily. The eyes were quickly sutured. Von Himmler examined his labors critically, "Not bad. Brahms, what do you think?" The lumberjack peered down at his master's handiwork.

"Work is good. Hungry now. Food please."

Von Himmler reached for the trocar. "Brahms, release his head. Strip away his shirt." Herman's head rotated in agony. With one powerful pull, the giant tore off much of his clothing. Brahms stared at the old, white scar that had resulted from Herman's gall bladder surgery. Von Himmler placed the great needle at the end of the trocar atop Herman's bare abdomen. It was cold and clammy and the mortician let out a high pitched, terror filled murmur of recognition. "I am going to drain your body fluids, Mr. Bancroft. This should only take a few minutes."

The point was hammered into Herman's torso, just below his belly button. The sensation was horrible. Ghastly. Von Himmler started up the pump. The undertaker mercifully blacked out.

Gloria Shutz had been on the road for a good hour and a half when she reached the state police roadblock just east of the town of Seney. While listening to Munising radio station WMUN, she had heard news reports detailing the escape of two dangerous mental patients from Newberry Joy Hospital, and the grisly murder that they had committed in Eckerman, so the existence of the roadblock had come as no surprise.

A handsome young state trooper, having conversed with the occupants of the two cars preceding her in line now motioned Gloria ahead. "Evening, miss," he said when she'd pulled up beside him, surprised to see such an attractive, young woman out on the highway alone. "Where are you headed, miss?"

"The Soo," was the reply.

"We have a problem, this evening."

"I've heard the radio reports."

"Of course, there's no reason to be alarmed. We're here as a precautionary measure. We don't want you to feel frightened. We're asking that you, and other motorists, take a simple safeguard while you travel through the area just ahead." He reached through her window and attached a yellow sticker to the inside surface of her windshield. "What we're asking, miss, is for you and the two cars just ahead of you, here, to travel ahead in a convoy, with your doors locked, until you've reached the roadblock west of Sault Ste Marie. I'm marking your cars so that the trooper, there, will know you had to pass by us, first. Now, that gentleman up ahead in the big Pontiac will need gas when he gets to Newberry. We'd like you to pull into the gas station with him, wait while he gets his fuel, then continue on, together. Incidently, there's free coffee at the gas station. I hope, miss, that this isn't too inconvenient for you?"

"Oh, no, not in the least. You're so nice about this." Gloria looked into his reassuring, dark eyes. This policeman would respect her. He would have to play by her rules. His occupation would cause even the most private aspects of his life to be held up to glaring public scrutiny if he turned animal on her. "As a taxpayer, I suppose that I should insist that you lead me through this dangerous area ahead personally." She smiled sweetly. This man looked terrific in his uniform. The trooper blushed.

"Do you live in the Soo, miss?"

"No, I'm from Birch, a little town just north of Marquette. I'm headed to the Soo for a business meeting."

"I still keep an apartment in the Soo, but I'm never there, really. I have Sunday off. Maybe we could go for coffee?"

"That would be very nice. I'd like that," said Gloria, batting her eyes. "My name is Gloria Shutz. I'll be staying at the Holiday Inn. Give me a call. Leave a message if I'm out." The trooper pulled a pad and paper from his jacket and hurriedly scrawled a note.

"My name is Jack, by the way." He reached for her hand and squeezed it gently. "I have a feeling we'll be seeing each other, again."

The two cars ahead were now slowly pulling away. Gloria shifted her automatic transmission lever back into 'drive'. "It was very nice to meet you, Jack."

The trooper smiled and watched Gloria's car move on down the road. "Pretty girl," he said to himself, placing his fingers to his nose, hoping to pick up some flowery remnant of her feminine allure. His nostrils flared. "Formaldehyde?" And he winced.

Wolfgang Von Himmler tossed a plastic sack filled with Herman Bancroft's blood into the garbage can, then rubbed his sticky hands on his green uniform. "Follow me, Brahms. Bring Mr. Bancroft upstairs, to his bed." Brahms carried the limp body up the two long flights of stairs to the living quarters on the second floor. Von Himmler led him to the master bedroom, then directed him to ease his burden onto the king size bed. Von Himmler ransacked the dresser drawers and then entered the large, walk-in closet that housed Bancroft's best clothes. He pulled a jacket from the rack. "We are expecting visitors, shortly. Mr. Bancroft's suit coats fit me quite well, do they not?" Von Himmler admired his reflection in the full length mirror mounted on the outside of the closet door.

Brahms was suffering from severe hunger pangs in silence. Von Himmler looked into the mirror at his loyal lumberjack, standing stone still beside the big bed as though he were afraid to move.

"Go down to the kitchen. Find yourself food. Eat quickly. You must stay upstairs this evening, Josef. Be sure you are out of sight. People must not see you." Brahms grunted an affirmation, and then stomped off.

In the bathroom that was connected to the master bedroom, Von Himmler located a pair of shears and a safety razor. He systematically clipped off his gray whiskers. After filling the basin with piping hot tap water, he plunged his face into the steamy water many times, softening the stubble. He lathered his face with soap, and then shaved his face clean, leaving a bushy, white moustache. Then, he wet his hair and combed his gray locks back, and finally, admired his fresh, new look in the bathroom mirror. "I must be convincing," he said to himself. "My name is John Bancroft, Herman's cousin."

Von Himmler dressed hurriedly. The trousers he had chosen were the proper length, but Bancroft was much thicker about the middle, so as a result, the pants began to slide down Wolfgang's hips while he adjusted his cravat. This was easy enough for him to remedy. He skewered a new hole through one of Herman's good leather belts with the sharp point of the scissors, folded the pants in at the pleats, and then tightened the belt about his waist.

Brahms returned by way of the stairs, having first tried the service elevator, which only ran from the basement to the main floor. A bag of wonder bread was tucked beneath his arm. "You look pretty," he said.

"I see you've found something to eat. Excellent, Brahms. In the morning, I will bring you more donuts than you have ever seen before. For now, rest up a bit. We will be retrieving the trunk before bed."

"I love donuts. Nice, fresh donuts." There was a commotion downstairs, originating from the foyer.

"Now, be very quiet, Josef. Remain still until I come for you." Von Himmler trotted excitedly from the room. He walked with confidence down the long staircase. Bancroft's shoes were at least two sizes too big, so his feet shifted back and forth with each step.

Herb Marcotte and Ed Higby found themselves being greeted by an unfamiliar, older man. Von Himmler held out his hand, smiling broadly beneath the bushy moustache. He looked impressive in Herman's tasteful suit of clothes. "Good evening, gentlemen." Herb took his hand and spoke right up.

"We took the liberty to walk right in. Is Herman Bancroft around?"

"I'm sorry, but Herman isn't here just now. My name is John Bancroft, Herman is my first cousin; Our Aunt Lil had passed away this summer and Herman, being the respected family member that he is, was appointed executor of her estate. He regretted leaving so suddenly, under such trying circumstances, gentlemen, but a meeting of the heirs has been scheduled for tomorrow. It slipped his mind completely, in fact, until I arrived from Chicago early this evening."

"Funny Mr. Bancroft never mentioned it," said Herb.

"It actually wasn't until after I had arrived- that Herman even remembered that he'd contacted me a month ago, asking me if I could run the place in his absence. I'm afraid my cousin is becoming absent minded in his old age." Von Himmler grimaced sullenly, and the two men nodded.

"I have worked for many years, for a large funeral parlour in Chicago. Herman told me to expect you. I am greatly sorry if you are inconvenienced by all of this. I know that you've suffered a terrible loss."

"John," said Herb, somewhat puzzled as to the manner in which a Bancroft would come by a faint German accent, "there's no need to explain. I'm sure that the Higbys and the Marcottes are in capable hands." Herb glanced over at Ed, who nodded in agreement. Both man were short and stocky. Herb, the one with the receding black hair, seemed to have more of a gift of gab.

"Fine then, gentlemen. Now that we have cleared the air, we haven't properly introduced ourselves, have we?"

"My name is Herb. Herb Marcotte. This is Ed Higby." They shook hands, again.

"Our casket selection room is right this way, down the stairs, if you will follow me."

Von Himmler worked his way through the ten models that were on display. "I know how difficult this is for you two gentlemen. Any model here would be perfectly suitable." Ed made a motion with his hand in order to attract Wolfgang's attention.

"We was talkin' on the way over, John. We think we'd like something real close- the same model, maybe, what with our kids bein' a couple, and all. They were, well, pre-engaged to be married, I guess you'd say." His voice began to crack with grief.

"Here- these two, here, are almost the same," said Herb. "I can't see any real difference. Why don't we just settle on these?"

"That's alright by me," added Ed with a sniffle.

"Fine, then." Von Himmler led them back up the stairway. "I will draw up the contract. Herman is insistent upon giving you a big break on his normal fees."

"I appreciate that, from the bottom of my heart," said Herb. "We didn't carry any insurance for Julie."

"As far as visitation hours are concerned," said Von Himmler, "I imagine-"

"They're going to be printed in tomorrow's paper," interrupted Herb. "Four until seven, tomorrow and Sunday."

"I betcha the whole town is gonna be here, eh?" added Ed. Von Himmler stroked his moustache thoughtfully.

"Which brings us to another point, gentlemen. Should we plan for a short service here on Monday, followed by another service at your church?" The men looked at one another. "May I suggest," continued Von Himmler, "for the sake of the great many mourners involved, a joint funeral ceremony. Does the local school have a good sized gymnasium?"

"Good idea. Very considerate of you, John, under the circumstances; I think that the children would be very pleased. What do you think, Ed?"

"Let me work on that myself," said Ed. "My neighbor is school board president. I'll tell him about it. He'll do it, hey? Jerry would want this. He was the star of the basketball team," and then burst into tears.

So, the decision was made. Through simple manipulation, Von Himmler had sewn a logical idea firmly into their grief stricken heads. The drunkenness of victory bubbled in Von Himmler's dark being even as he walked them to the door.

Robert Brooks felt into his breast pocket, and then gave the steering wheel of his police car a whack with the guilty fingers. A cigarette would taste good just now. This was the type of case that could drive you crazy. When a mental patient or prisoner walked away, the surrounding communities immediately went into a state of fear and panic, and would remain in that state until the fugitive was recaptured. In the meantime, tremendous pressure was exerted on the local law enforcement agencies.

Usually, these walkaways were apprehended within one to three days following their escape. The commander had begun to get a bad feeling about this Brahms and Von Himmler. Earlier this morning, following the discovery of the Jeffrey Gobles murder, he had thought to himself that by mid-afternoon, surely someone somewhere would report seeing the two men. But as the twilight had fallen and the darkness settled in without any further sign of them, he began to feel uneasy. Brooks wasn't one to believe in premonitions, but the bad feeling in his gut gave even him a cause for alarm.

He certainly didn't need this in his life just now. Things hadn't been going so well at home lately with his attractive, red headed wife, Joanne. They had been married for twenty-three years and had two daughters. Robin, the eldest, was married to a fine young man who was studying to be a veterinarian down at Michigan State University in East Lansing. Robin was now a senior, was herself majoring in marketing, and the two of them were living quite happily, apparently, in married housing on campus. Dawn, their youngest, was a sophomore at Western Michigan, and it was her flight from the nest the previous autumn that was causing her parents some major problems, at least that's how her father saw it.

Joanne had just not adjusted to life after children. For the first few months, she had come down with the blues. The holidays had snapped her out of it, but then in January, she had sunk like a rock. Bob was normally at the post for at least fifty hours per week, but as Joanne repeatedly rejected his pleas to seek some kind of professional counseling, he found himself spending even more time on the job, and even less at home.

Extra-marital sex had never been an issue. There was complete and utter trust on that score. But Bob had become worried about that lately, too. Joanne was in the bedroom so much of the time, sleeping or reading, and one of the symptoms of her depression was that she no longer did the little things to keep herself up. Her hair was usually in a babushka, she no longer bathed regularly, and she had abandoned the household chores. On top of everything else, when her husband did drop in on her during working hours to check up on her, she would complain incessantly about his complete lack of interest in her and her problems, in comparison to the enormous time and energy that he expended on his job. The bottom line result was that in the past fifteen months, Bob had lost his hunger for her, and he could no longer find within himself that caring, tender feeling which he had always had for her.

Some of the women in skirts that he would see as he drove around town were beginning to look mighty appealing to him. There was probably only one idiosyncrasy that was saving him now. He would never make a pass at a woman while fulfilling his duties for the state police. It was damn unprofessional.

He now approached the police roadblock located fifteen miles west of Sault Ste Marie, to visit with the men from the Soo post. Traffic was light and the roadblock was causing the few motorists on the road only minimal delays. Brooks parked his car and sauntered over toward the two troopers who were busy wielding their big flashlights. "Evening, boys."

"Hello, commander, anything new?"

"Nope, all's quiet." Brooks kicked at the gravel coating the shoulder of the road. "My feeling is that they were in a blue sedan heading west this morning, from the murder scene. We've checked everywhere for a blue Chevy. Stan is sure it was a Chevy."

"They're probably off in the woods somewhere. They should be gettin' pretty hungry by now."

"Let's just set up a donut stand down the road, here, a ways," joked the second trooper. "By morning, they'd both be right back in the nut house." Brooks was not particularly amused.

"The tracking dogs came up empty at the restaurant. They left the area by car. This Von Himmler is a complex individual. I had a chance to look over his file at the asylum. He impaled a gas station owner in St. Ignace."

"Impaled?" asked the first trooper.

"Drove a long, metal pole up the guy's ass, then he used ropes and pulleys to lift the poor devil up to the ceiling. I guess they did that sort of thing in Europe during the Dark Ages."

"Hell of a way to go," said the second trooper.

"So you fellas keep your eyes peeled. I think they're crazy enough to try and run a roadblock. They might think even better of the idea in the middle of the night." Brooks looked up to see three cars braking as they approached the blockade's yellow flashing lights from the west.

"They all got stickers," sounded off the first trooper. Brooks watched as his men lit up the front and rear seat areas of each car as the vehicles, in turn, pulled up alongside them. An attractive blonde traveling alone in the last car rolled down her window and winked.

"Hi boys!" said Gloria with a big, friendly smile. "Say hello to Jack for me." Brooks stepped forward and raised his right hand.

"Excuse me, ma'am, but did you say, Jack? You'd like us to say hello to Jack?"

"Yea, you know, the policeman back at that other roadblock. He's cute! He's meeting me for coffee, Sunday."

"Oh, so he is, is he? Meeting you for coffee. We'll be sure and tell him." Brooks waved her on. Gloria waved back and then she disappeared into the night.

"How do you like that shit!?" steamed Brooks in his most berating tone. "So now we're picking up chicks in the course of conducting official state business! At taxpayer expense, I might add!"

"She was a good lookin' gal," said the first trooper.

"I don't care if it was Ursula Andress with bare tits! Jack's gonna hear about this one." Brooks walked back toward his car. "Stay alert out here, fellas."

"Good night, sir."

"I wonder if he'll say anything to Jack."

"He'll put the poor bastard on salt peter for thirty days. Just be glad you don't work out of Newberry!"

"No shit."

Late Friday night, Von Himmler squeezed the rubber plug into the drain of the Victorian style Bancroft bathtub and turned on the faucets. He took a bottle of Mrs. Bancroft's bubble bath solution from the top of the vanity and poured a generous amount into the turbulent waters. As the bath slowly deepened, he checked on Brahms, whom he found to be sleeping soundly in the king sized bed, his burly left arm draped about the shoulder of the late Herman Bancroft, cuddling him like a big teddy bear. Their final, late night trip to retrieve the trunk hidden in the bushes had further exhausted him. Von Himmler pulled the blankets up to the lumberjack's chin.

He slowly removed his borrowed suit of clothes and then climbed into the delightfully hot water topped with lather and foam. He laid back until the soapsuds threatened to overflow onto the floor, at which time, he turned the faucets off.

'This,' he thought, 'is the way life should be lived.' One of the most successful days in his entire life was now drawing to a close, and he was being allowed to savor it fully in this luxurious, bubbly spa. The high point for him, had been at the top of that steep ridge, overlooking the rail yard, when he had sighted that empty logging truck with Rutledge's name painted on the side of the cab. Until that point, he had planned for a high-risk abduction in order to reach their final destination. But then, there it was, a free ride right into the town of Birch. And under a nice dry tarp, no less!

And, how bold he was to storm this funeral home and take it over, like a marauding conqueror of old. Without hesitation, and again, with such good fortune, he had established a beachhead from which to work his dark will.

Von Himmler reached a sudsy hand over to the top of the toilet tank and carefully lifted a copy of the mortician's convention brochure, which he had earlier found on Herman's office desktop, and brought it over so that he might look at it, again, while he lay in the bath. The convention lasted from Saturday morning until Monday morning in Sault Ste Marie, and it was obvious that Bancroft had sent an employee to attend. A note penned on the front of the brochure indicated that, 'Gloria staying at Holiday Inn Friday through Sunday nite.' Von Himmler assumed that this was in Bancroft's own hand.

Von Himmler set the brochure back over atop the toilet and picked up a small, metal file box crammed with three by five inch index cards. The file box was labeled simply, 'Hector.' This, he had also discovered while perusing Herman's office. He slid up against the back of the tub and opened the box with care. There was a piece of notepaper in front, all folded up, and Von Himmler unfolded it deftly one-handed, and read it slowly.

Dear Hector,

Just in case I ever have to leave you, I have assembled this file, which is designed to help you in the day to day operation of the business during my absence. Son, I know how capable you are of upholding our impeccable reputation in carrying out all of our business dealings in our tradition of excellence. The information herein will serve as a guide that you may rely upon whenever a question might come up. Good luck.

Love,

Father

The file was alphabetized and Von Himmler flipped to the letter,'E', and there was a card entitled, 'Employees- Part Time and Temporary.' There listed were the names, social security numbers, addresses and telephone numbers of several Birch residents. "Charlie Beaver," read Von Himmler aloud, "Dan Carroll, cemetery." He smiled and randomly searched through the file. Under, 'P', he found a card with the heading of, 'Pricing.'

'List prices', it read, 'for all product can be found in the notebook titled, 'Product Pricing,' in the bookshelf behind office desk. Prices for all services are commensurate with the service provided and are divided into three tiers. These price guidelines can be found in 'Service Pricing' notebook located in bookshelf behind office desk.'

Von Himmler closed the little metal box and set it out on the bathroom floor. He gazed out through the open doorway, into the bedroom at Brahms, lying peacefully on the bed nuzzling Bancroft. The blanket was pulled up just beneath the undertaker's chin. Von Himmler laughed uproariously. "Thank you, father, for your file!" he cried. And then he laughed some more.

CHAPTER EIGHT

Very early on Saturday morning, just before sunrise, Von Himmler, having slept but little in the big bed beside Brahms, arose, and once again, turned on the bathtub taps. Generally quite tolerant of the body odor of others, he had found the lumberjack to be in need of a thorough cleansing. The foul combination of untreated armpits, horribly bad breath, and giant buttocks in dire need of a good soaping was so profuse as to cause Von Himmler to experience waves of nausea throughout the restless night.

He now approached the well-rested Brahms, slapped him sharply on the cheeks, and then forced open his eyeballs with his thumbs. "Brahms! I have drawn your bath! Get out of this bed!" Josef rolled over the empty shell of Herman Bancroft and off of the mattress, crashing his left knee down onto the birdseye maple flooring with such a thud that it seemed to shake the whole house. Von Himmler chased him into the bath, which he had thoughtfully treated with another big dose of bubble bath, helping to strip away his terrible clothes along the way. Brahms settled into the steaming waters.

"Now soap up completely," ordered Von Himmler. "Wash your hair, your behind, and your feet. When you have finished with all of that, brush those miserable, yellow teeth." Brahms nodded. "I am going over to the grocery store, to buy our breakfast."

Von Himmler entered the garage from a door off of the kitchen. In the dead of night, he had found a cigar box filled with petty cash in one of Herman's drawers, more cash than he would ever need, and he had slipped a thick wad of bills into his trousers pocket on the way out. In the garage, the first thing that caught his eye was the shiny, white Cadillac hearse.

Next to the hearse was parked a black Pontiac Bonneville station wagon, and in the far corner sat a white Dodge Dart, Herman Bancroft's personal auto. Von Himmler walked up to the Dodge and climbed in. The key was in the ignition. He started the engine, then climbed back out and slowly opened the garage door.

The cold morning air refreshed him. It looked like it was going to be another beautiful autumn day. The sun was just then venturing above the tree line.

Nancy Palmer, her head pounding excruciatingly with each beat of her heart, opened her eyes and began to sob. A film seemed to coat her eyeballs, causing her to look through a sort of haze at the surrounding objects in her motel room. She had no idea what time it was- her watch had stopped at 11:25. She became more coherent, and she struggled out of bed and went into the bathroom, where she splashed water on her face. Her head hurt terribly and she reached down to undo her slacks and determined that she had wet the bed in her stupor. Then she realized that she had been drugged. She remembered the needle, forced brutally into the meat of her shoulder. She remembered the two mental patients and her frightening abduction. She stepped out of her soiled pants and panties, and without hesitation, walked back over to the phone located on the desk and she called for the police as she cradled her head.

Robert Brooks turned his car into the parking lot of the Red Roof motel and cruised the length of the modest building, looking for room number seven. He had arrived that morning at the state police post and had just poured himself a cup of coffee when the peculiar call from a distraught woman had been fielded by the dispatcher. Brooks had been notified at once, and he had jogged out to his car, issuing an over the shoulder request that a backup trooper be sent in his wake. The styrofoam cup filled with coffee was left steaming on his desk.

Upon making her call to the police, Nancy Palmer had struggled to dress in her nightgown and turquoise terrycloth robe. Thank goodness these items had been packed away in the dirty clothes hamper that had been left untouched in her room the previous, eventful morning.

She located her night bag, which housed her makeup and personal care supplies, and got hold of her bottle of aspirin, which she opened with difficulty, managing to dispense three tablets which she took with half a glass of water. She then walked over and unlocked the door, laid back down on the bed (after first carefully placing the blanket and bedspread over her soiled sheets), and awaited the arrival of the police.

Brooks knocked on the door of room seven. "Door's open." The voice was faint, and obviously female. Brooks turned the door handle and entered, removing his hat. He tossed the 'DO NOT DISTURB' sign onto the floor. An attractive woman lay on the bed, both hands held tightly to her forehead.

"I'm Commander Brooks, Michigan State Police. You called to report a kidnapping?"

"Yes, I called you here. I've got an awful headache. I- I was drugged. I'm not sure where to begin. What time is it?" Brooks peered at his watch.

"Eight-fifteen, A.M." Nancy tried to sit up, but the shooting pains in her forehead forced her back to the pillow.

"I've been sleeping for twenty-four hours," she moaned. "Today's Saturday?"

"I'm afraid so." Brooks began to write on his clipboard. "Do you have your driver's license handy, miss?"

"In my purse. God! I hope they haven't taken it!"

"No, it's right here," Brooks said, probing for her wallet.

"It's a terrible mess."

"I don't mind. I go through my wife's purse all the time. Hey! A Frankenmuth girl!" He wrote hurriedly.

"There were two men. A big one and an old one; They grabbed me just when I was packing up my car yesterday morning. God, my head hurts!"

"We're going to run you over to the hospital, Nancy. Just a minute, okay?" Brooks picked up the phone and called for an ambulance. Just as he finished, there was a knock at the door.

"Back up, sir."

"Good. Look around outside. Look for tracks, or something. Call in the dogs."

Brooks showed mug shots of the two escaped mental patients to Nancy. "What kind of a car do you own? I didn't see one parked outside." Nancy handed him back the pictures and nodded, grimly.

"A blue Chevy Biscayne."

"That figures. If they still have your car, which is unlikely, then they must be holed up in the woods, someplace. We've been searching the region intensively for these men." Another knock interrupted them. The trooper poked his head in, again.

"Blue Chevrolet parked back in the weeds next to the building."

"Thank God," said Nancy, "at least they didn't trash my car. It's still new."

"Were you with them when they drove to Eckerman?" asked Brooks.

"To get donuts, if you can believe that."

"When did you last see these men?"

"Yesterday morning. They gave me a shot with a needle, that's all I can remember." The trooper entered the room.

"So they didn't take the car," said Brooks. "Of course! The damned train! They hopped a goddam freight train! Must have hiked through the woods to the tracks. You did radio for the dogs, didn't you? I'm calling in a nationwide A.P.B. Von Himmler received all types of literature about business and the economy in the whole region. Damn! He could have traveled a thousand miles by now! Get me a goddam train schedule!"

"Right away, sir."

"Nancy," Brooks said more softly, turning to her, "do you remember if they had anything with them?"

"Some kind of a big box- a big trunk, I guess you'd call it."

"Do you remember what the two men were wearing?"

"Green hospital outfits. The big one, I knew that he was a mental patient." Nancy touched her ear and grimaced with pain. She started crying.

"The ambulance will be here any minute," said Brooks uneasily.

"It's alright, really. I just remembered that big monster stuck his tongue in my ear. God!" She said, grimacing again. "I think he bruised my brain!"

"I'm sorry," Brooks said sincerely, walking to the door. "I've got some more instructions to give to the post, over my radio. Just relax, miss. We won't leave you. You'll feel much better after you're checked by a doctor."

"Thank you."

Brooks made a beeline for his car and picked up the radio handset. "Car number one, this is Brooks. Issue a nationwide A.P.B. with descriptions of the psychos. Copy may have traveled by train or car to Wisconsin and points west or south. And find out what freight trains came through yesterday. By the way, I want those dogs over here and ready to go, pronto. Over."

At the IGA grocery store in Birch, Von Himmler cruised up and down the aisles, filling his grocery cart hurriedly. The bakery display had just been replenished with fresh items, and he took half a dozen boxes of assorted donuts and placed them in the cart. A long, white carton with a clear cellophane window in the top caught his attention, sitting on an adjacent shelf. It was a freshly baked apple streusel coated with powdered sugar frosting and he placed it in his cart as well.

He picked out four half-gallon cartons of milk, ten cans of Dinty Moore beef stew, a big jar of peanut butter, and five loaves of wonder bread and headed for the check-out counter. A woman in her early thirties clad in a blue IGA smock had been watching this unusual shopper with interest.

"Good morning!" Von Himmler simply nodded in response, loading the blacktopped conveyor with his grocery items. "Is this your first visit to the Birch area, sir?"

"Yes, it is, as a matter-of-fact." She looked through the wall of windows out front, and saw the clean, white Dodge Dart parked near the entrance to the store.

"You must be guests of Mr. Bancroft. You helpin' out with the funerals?"

"Yes," he replied, and then held out his hand reluctantly. "My name is John Bancroft. I am Herman's cousin." She shook his hand enthusiastically.

"I'm Jill. Hey! You got kinda an accent, eh? Just a little one," she said with a nervous giggle.

"My father was a great traveler. He was passing through Austria when he met my mother- in Vienna. We didn't settle in Chicago until after the first world war."

"Oh, that's very interesting. So, you're European. We got lotsa Finlanders around here."

"Yes, that's nice. I feel akin to them, I suppose." Von Himmler pulled a twenty from the wad in his pocket. "Now, how much do I owe you?" The lady was staring, and he was becoming edgy.

"I'm sorry!" she said, hiding her reddened face in her hand, "nine-oh-two." She counted out his change, then expertly bagged the groceries. "I'll be stopping by into the funeral home this evening with my husband. Gosh, Mr. Bancroft was just in the day before yesterday. With Mrs. Bancroft away, he buys lots and lots of soup, hey? Least you'll be giving him some stew."

"Actually, Jill, Herman had to go out of town on family business. He flew out yesterday evening." An anguished expression washed across the woman's features. "You see, he is the executor of our aunt's estate." Jill was holding one of the cans of beef stew above the bag, as if her arm had frozen.

"Excuse me. I just can't- can't imagine Mr. Bancroft's leaving us this weekend. Not with the accident and all. Those two kids, they was smashed up pretty bad, I hear." Von Himmler cleared his throat.

"I am afraid it would not be proper for me to divulge the true extent of the injuries in question." Jill became indignant.

"Gracious! You misunderstood me!"

"Excuse me, ma'am. I apologize, wholeheartedly." She finished packing the items. "I did misunderstand, Jill. It must be the European in me. I hope that you can forgive me." Jill's scowl softened.

"Don't worry, Mr. Bancroft. I won't hold it against you." He picked up his groceries, a bag in each arm, and left. "See you tonight," she said, after him.

The grocery store's owner, Doc Morgan, neared the front cash register just as the white Dodge pulled away from the parking lot. "Mr. Bancroft's out early, eh?" he said.

"No, that is Mr. Bancroft's cousin, from Chicago."

"Oh?"

"Mr. Bancroft is tending to his aunt's will this weekend. He had to leave town, flew out, he said."

"Hmmmm, that's not like Herman," replied Doc, " not with the accident, and all. This fellow's filling in for him, then."

"Yea, and he sure loves his donuts. Think he picked up six dozen of 'em."

"Maybe they serve coffee and donuts at the funeral parlors down Chicago way. Who knows? They have queer ways, some of them folks. Harold the pizza man, he always got his meat from Chicago. He was a strange bird, too."

"And this man has a accent- says he was born in Austria." Doc shrugged his shoulders and held out his upturned palms, still bloody from butchering.

"I'm sure this fellow's okay. Least he didn't drive to Marquette for his donuts," he said. Jill snickered.

Having washed himself thoroughly, Josef Brahms had climbed from the bathtub, dripping with water and half-covered with foam. The morning air surrounded his wet skin, and Josef felt cold. He jumped up and down several times, in order to warm himself, then bolted, wet and naked, from the bathroom. This was exciting and new.

He sprang down the stairway, onto the main floor, and ran through the big house like a child, finally coming to a halt in the east wing. The rays of the sun were pouring through the big bay window, and Josef made his way into the light, still seeking a means of warmth. And the sun did feel warm through the clear expanse of glass, and now Josef jumped up and down many times, having the time of his life. In the frivolity and newness in this leaping about in the nude, Josef became excited, and then aroused, and the size of his erection was in keeping, and in accordance with, the size of his great frame, and it bounced off of his thighs and stomach, and Josef took great pleasure in it.

In a front room of the house directly across the street from Bancroft's, the elderly Mrs. Cronin, an invalid suffering from advanced arthritis of the spine, sat, as was her custom most mornings, in her wheelchair, sipping on her tea, with a commanding view of much of Birch Avenue at her disposal. Seated on the table beside her was the brass spyglass that was so useful in identifying the occupants of passing cars, and in observing the outside activities of many of her neighbors.

She took a little bite of the toast that her daughter-in-law had spread with thimbleberry jam, and took another sip of tea, which was now almost too cool to enjoy. She watched as Herman Bancroft pulled up the driveway of the funeral home and then into the garage. Then, she noticed that there was more movement from in front of the funeral home. There it was again! She placed the spyglass on her lap, and wheeled forward, nearer to the window. There was a commotion in the big east window of the funeral home itself. Mrs. Cronin quickly raised the glass in order to get a better idea of just what it was that seemed so out of place to her trained eye. There was a big body! A big, naked body! And it was leaping up and down, as if on a pogo stick, and that penis was so awfully large! And, so hard! Mrs. Cronin's upper denture fell from her pallet and dropped onto the living room carpet like a stone.

Von Himmler, upon entering the kitchen with the groceries, had heard the loud pounding originating in the east wing. He found Josef grinning in ecstasy, an expert in his newfound sport. "Brahms! You fool! You're neeee-uude!! Away from that window! Passersby will see you there!"

Brahms settled his bare feet on the floor and shuffled towards Von Himmler. The old man got a close look at the enormous penis. "Up the stairs you go!" he ordered, "back to the bedroom!" He followed the lumberjack's bouncy bare buns up the winding staircase. They entered the master bedroom, together. Von Himmler proceeded to the edge of the bed, and rolled Bancroft's body onto its stomach. He reached around and unfastened the dress slacks from beneath.

"Brahms, it is time that we tested for your sexual preference." And then he yanked down the pants with a snarl and exposed Herman Bancroft's lily-white ass.

Sam Rutledge had spent a relaxing night at his deer camp, having left his work site in the woods when Red Tomlinson had headed off to Escanaba on Friday afternoon with the load of pine logs. Sam had driven directly to camp, a ten-mile ride on little used dirt truck trails that wound back to the northwest through a wilderness area known as the Yellow Dog plains.

Deer camp was a hand hewn cedar log cabin, built upon a wood stilt foundation by his father, and Rutledge loved to spend his free time there in the fall of the year. The area was incredibly quiet, with the exception of the air force fighter jets which were known to sometimes whiz overhead, and Rutledge could truly find peace. The camp had no power, nor telephone service, and Rutledge would not allow even so much as a portable radio to infringe upon this tranquil world that he maintained. All firewood was cut and split by hand, and this chore alone took up much of his time and most of his energy during the September and October days when he could get away.

Inside the cabin, light was provided by kerosene, and Sam had finally acquiesced to modern convenience when he had reluctantly replaced the old wood cook stove with a propane gas model. The propane, he brought to camp himself in a hundred pound tank. A refill lasted through several deer seasons.

On Friday afternoon, shortly after he had arrived, Sam had cut a large pile of red maple logs with his bucksaw. He always chose small diameters for the ease in cutting. One well placed chop with the splitting maul produced two clean pieces, which he stacked high and dry in an old wood shed on the south side of the camp. Sam was so efficient in meeting the cyclical demands of his existence that the wood he was cutting and splitting this year would not be burned until the next, permitting a full year for the wood to dry, resulting in only scant creosote buildup in the cabin's clay lined chimney flue.

In the late afternoon, Sam had hiked back on the foot trail leading from camp to his deer blind, a good half-mile walk. The blind had been upgraded over the years, and Sam, who had inherited this prime hunting location from his father, had finally assembled a stand out of plywood three seasons previous to protect himself from the often foul weather of late November. Cold and snow, he could deal with like always, but as age had crept up on him, the often fierce northwest winds would chill him right to the bone, no matter how many layers of clothing he wore. And Sam had not allowed himself to move in any way while seated in the old open-air blind, even to warm up. To be successful in hunting from a stand camouflaged with balsam and pine boughs, the hunter was required to sit motionlessly for long periods of time, particularly when targeting a big, old, wary whitetail buck.

Sam had designed his new stand so that the wooden sides came right up to the top of his shoulder. A foot high opening around three sides of the structure allowed for excellent visibility, and sufficient room to get off a shot when the opportunity presented itself. The roof above was also boxed in, creating a dark, shadowy area in which to sit comfortably, undetected by his prey.

Sam sat in the old water stained windsor chair inside the blind. He lit a cigarette. It felt good just to sit in that familiar spot, located at the edge of a small clearing, with the topography of hills and cedar filled pot holes providing the backdrop, as far as the eye could see. This sight had been selected by his father more than fifty years before. What made it such an ideal location was the fact that a major migratory deer trail ran through the woods just the other side of the little meadow. This trail was used by deer late in the fall, when deepening snows forced them from their warm weather feed lots to seek more hospitable locations well to the south, away from the unforgiving Lake Superior snow belt region.

It was also a documented fact that although the firearm deer season lasted for fifteen days, close to half of the total number of animals harvested were taken during the season's first three days. For this reason, the number of hunters in the field dropped off precipitously by the end of the first week, many of them figuring that if they hadn't filled their tags by then, they might as well stay back in camp and play cards, and have a few beers. Sam thrived on this popular notion that thinned the woods of other hunters, while seemingly rewarding him for his patience. His hunting location often saw more deer pass by during the last three days of the season than the rest of the days combined. There was always a heavy dumping of lake snows by the second week of the season and the deepening drifts pushed the deer instinctively along the trail behind the clearing. Sam generally tagged two deer most years, one on his own license, and the second on the 'camp' license, an extra tag that was divvied out by the Department of Natural Resources to finite groups of four or more hunters 'camped' together.

Many of the deer that he had taken over the years were of trophy size, and he rarely pulled the trigger when scoping anything less than a six point with his 30.06 rifle.

Sam remained seated in his blind a while longer, surveying the fall colors around him, which seemed to always increase in their intensity as the sun angled nearer to the horizon. He thought of his father, and how, as the original camp master back in the good, old days, he'd be the first one out of bed in what had to be the absolute middle of the night to his son, Sam, setting up the coffee pot, and then with a tin cup of whisky in one hand, he'd literally roll everybody out of bed and onto the floor with the other.

"Git up! You cockbiters!" he'd shout with the whisky on his breath. Sam smiled at the thought. 'Yep, the old man was one hell of a father,' and, he'd provided a lifetime of wonderful memories.

And then for no logical reason, Sam thought of that old, German doctor, and how he'd laid him out with those punches to the belly. Even after all those years, he would still grit his teeth and feel the surge of adrenaline go through him- the clarity with which he could still recall the feel of his big fist as it penetrated into that old, soft body, the charge of blinding hatred which seared through him, providing the limitless power to deliver blow after horrible blow, until Sam had known that the insides, the guts, were damaged way beyond repair.

'What had it really mattered, that the old man had died? It just meant that there was one less kraut to deal with when World War II rolled around. Never said I weren't no angel,' Sam thought to himself. 'War makes men do strange things. Nasty things. If the Germans weren't dug into France, knee deep in French and Belgian blood, I wouldn't a' been over there in the first place.'

Sam glanced at his cigarette, which had burned down to the filter. He held the dead butt in his left hand. He dropped it onto the dirt floor of his blind. "Time to cook up supper," he said to himself. He got to his feet, and slowly trudged back toward camp.

Saturday morning, Sam was up before dawn. He put the coffee pot on the stove to boil, and then opened the last can of Boston brown bread still left in the cupboard from the previous fall. He cut the sweet bread, then lathered several slices with peanut butter, then diced an apple he had kept in the pocket of his work jacket and distributed the apple chunks evenly over the slices of bread. All in all, it wasn't a bad breakfast. He concluded his repast with several cups of coffee and several cigarettes, skimming through an old outdoor magazine by the light of the kerosene lamp on the dining table.

By the time he had locked up camp and made his way out to his truck, the sky was brightening on the eastern horizon. He started the engine, and then scraped the thick coating of frost that had covered his windshield. The stars above were still bright in the firmament. Leaving the place always made him feel sad, in a way. He could relate to the lonely cabin, off by itself, deep in the north woods. Surely, the cabin was just as sorry to see him go. He began his drive down the two-track trail reluctantly.

Arriving at the logging site near the Yellow Dog River, Sam found Red Tomlinson seated in the big deisel cab, parked alongside another big pile of pine logs ready for loading. Red got out of the truck and waited for Sam to pull on up. Sam rolled down his window.

"Mornin', Red. You shoulda seen the size of the tracks I found out by my blind last night!" Red smiled softly.

"I hear the same old shit, year after year! Hey, I got some news, Sam. Bad news, I'm afraid."

"I'm all ears, Red."

"There was an accident late Thursday night, out on the highway. Jerry Higby and Julie Marcotte were both killed." Sam's face turned pale.

"Man, that's terrible- just terrible! Shit, Red, Herb used to work for me when he was a kid. Julie was like a grandkid when she was knee high. Hell."

"I told the boys to take the day off. I figured that's what you woulda wanted, eh?"

"Sure Red, no work today. Damn." Sam shook his head.

"I came out here this morning to give you the news. I figured you'd headed right for deer camp yesterday. I know there's no radio up there. I figured you couldn't a' heard."

"Nope."

"You can make yourself useful and give me a lift home."

"Hop in, Red. I better get on home and spruce up my front yard a little. There's gonna be a ton of people over to the funeral home." Red climbed into the passenger seat as Sam restarted the engine. His old boss looked like he had seen an apparition. Upon hearing the tragic news, Red was sure every other Birch resident had undergone a similar transformation. Sam looked white and sickly.

"Sam, the wife and I'll come by later. We can all walk over to the funeral home, together, if that would be alright?"

"That'd be a good way to work it. Now, let's get you back home to that wife of yours." Red wanted to reach out to Sam, to comfort him somehow. But that would be like hugging the original Marlboro man. It would probably be a sure fire way to get your balls blown off.

State police trooper Brad Marsh drove his dark blue marked station wagon into the parking lot of the Red Roof motel, and then quickly pulled beside the state police car that was already parked there, waiting for him. Brad had driven over from the Soo post with Lyndon and Lady Bird, the two prized redbone hounds that he utilized throughout northern Michigan whenever tracking dogs were called for. The trooper from the Newberry post got out of his car, holding a white plastic bag at his side, and watched as Brad bounded from his vehicle and unlatched the rear gate on the wagon in order to release the shiny, red coated animals.

"How you been, Brad?"

"Fine, Don, never better, really. How's the family?" He glanced at the little potbelly tucked beneath Don's dark blue uniform.

"Jimmy's last year on the football team. He's starting at halfback, finally."

"Outstanding!" replied the blonde, blue eyed Brad, watching with almost fatherly approval as Lyndon raised his rear leg high and urinated on Don's front tire. "Bet you never miss a play when Newberry has the ball."

"I've got the clothing, here," said Don, holding up the plastic bag.

"Manage to get some underwear?"

"Good and ripe." Brad took the bag from him and emptied its contents out onto the blacktop. Lyndon and Lady Bird went for the pile as if it were a stack of fresh T-bones. Lyndon aarfed eagerly. Brad harnessed them hurriedly.

"Got your radio?" he asked Don as the animals pulled him in concentric circles in the direction of the ravine. Don nodded. Both animals bayed excitedly. "Let's hit it!" cried Brad. "They've picked up the trail! Let's go!"

Don strapped his radio onto his belt, and then re-bagged the dirty underwear that had been provided by the mental hospital. "Fuckin' skid marks," he said to himself, tossing the bag onto the floor of his front seat. He looked back across the parking lot, and watched Brad and his redbone hounds sink down into the ravine and out of sight. Don began to churn after them.

The dogs plowed forward, through the mud, brambles, and raspberry thickets, their noses hovering at ground level. Don was soon out of breath. Brad, it turned out, kept himself in shape for his special assignment by running three miles per day. Don ran on until he was gasping for air and his side hurt. Then, he slowed to a walk.

Lyndon and Lady Bird pushed onward, hot on the scent of the escaped mental patients. Brad's dark blue shirt became soaked through with sweat. His polyester pants were becoming tattered and torn from racing through the wild raspberry thickets, and he was blanketed with annoying burrs, as well.

Don renewed his pursuit of the dog team when his lungs permitted. He easily could follow their path- the beaten down brush and even the little tufts of hair that had tangled in the briars along the bottom of the ravine, clearly marked the way. It seemed to Don that the dogs had taken them into the woods a good two miles from the motel parking lot on the scent of these mental patients when the trees suddenly thinned up ahead in the distance, and then Don could make out the silhouette of Brad and the dogs as they stood on a crest of a rise above the ravine. When he climbed up the hill to join them, huffing and puffing, Brad nodded and Don pulled out the antenna on his portable radio.

"Fourteen to base. This is fourteen, over."

"Go ahead fourteen, over."

"The suspects have been trailed to the railroad tracks approximately two miles southwest of the motel. The dogs have reached a dead end, here, over."

At the state police post, Bob Brooks was busy on the phone, going over the freight train schedule with a supervisor from the Soo Line railroad. The dispatcher walked up, waving his hands frantically. "Hold for a minute, please," Brooks said into the phone. The dispatcher informed him of the radio report. "Good," said Brooks. "The suspects did board the train, just east of the Louisiana Pacific yard. Can you tell me where the boxcars were going, particularly the empty ones? I see. Can you get me some numbers? Then call me back as soon as you can. Fine."

Brooks walked out of his office and stood next to his desk sergeant, a hefty man with an enormous waistline working on a gigantic breakfast plate that he had picked up at the little restaurant next door.

"Bill, where would two lunatics go? How far would they take that train?" The sergeant looked up from his heap of scrambled eggs and scowled.

"I think they'd ride that train forever- least until it, you know, disconnected. Then they'd be forced to hop on another."

"I agree. They'd feel secure on that train, as long as it kept moving."

"And then they'd become, you know, paranoid."

"Right. And they'd have to expose themselves- unless they were able to switch trains easily. Damn-it-all! We're facing the fact that they could just about be anywhere by now."

"All you can do is alert everyone along the line- and, you've already taken care of that, Bob. Search every railway car, hope that somebody out there spots 'em. This Brahms should be easy enough to identify."

"I'm leaving for Negaunee right after lunch," said Brooks. "I'm confident that this Von Himmler is holed up somewhere right now. Our job is to flush his ass out. It sure looks like we'll all be on eighteen-hour shifts until they're brought in. Son-of-a-bitch!"

"Things are tough."

"And let's pray there are no more killings."

"We'll keep getting bad press," said Bill in disgust. "Always get your bad press when there's a killer on the loose. Particularly, an escaped killer."

"And they thrive on that retarded angle," Brooks said, tightening his fist. "Makes us look like a bunch of incompetents."

"Blundering fools," added the sergeant. A buzzer sounded over the post's loudspeaker system.

'Commander Brooks, line two.'

Brooks leaned over the sergeant and snatched the phone. "Brooks speaking. What!?" Bill could always tell when his boss was nervous about something. He'd run a hand through his hair, and he was doing that, now. "Be right over."

"What is it, sir?"

"The hospital. There's some poison missing, they think. I'm going over there. Talk about blundering fools!"

Bill toyed with the remaining eggs with his fork. "Let me know what's going down."

"I'll call you," said Brooks, on his way to the door. "And call my wife, please. Tell her I need clothes packed for four days. Tell her I'll be picking them up in an hour."

"Good luck, commander."

Brooks waved, and then he was gone.

At the Bancroft Funeral Home, Von Himmler, with the help of the powerful Brahms, casketed the two young accident victims and placed them in separate slumber rooms on the main floor. The corpses had both been tagged with the full legal names of the deceased. This was much to Von Himmler's comfort when he took it upon himself to fill in the large, black signboard in the hallway with their names, using the white plastic letters and directional arrows that were stored in a wooden tray in the office.

When Von Himmler re-entered the slumber room in the east wing, he found Brahms, looking longingly at the body of Julie Marcotte, his dumb eyes filled with pathos. Brahms was attired in the same green hospital smock, still damp from having been scalded in boiling water and then wrung out by Von Himmler in the kitchen sink. "Master, she so pretty. She pretty, pretty, pretty girl."

"Yes, Brahms, she is beautiful."

"Mebee I stand here and watch. Mebee just two hours, I watch." Von Himmler rolled his eyes.

"Later, you big oaf. But now, you have important work to do. Bring Bancroft's body downstairs."

"She as pretty as girl I kiss, 'member?" babbled Brahms. "That one real pretty." He cracked a slow smile, as though relating a male conquest, revealing the bad teeth.

"Bring that body down here, now!" bellowed Von Himmler. Brahms took one final look at the peaceful expression and satiny skin on the girl's cherubic face, and then he plodded slowly toward the stairway.

Von Himmler walked into the office and looked at his gold pocket watch. The florists, who had called while he was scrubbing Brahms' filthy clothes in the kitchen, would certainly be there within the hour. Two truckloads of flowers were on the way from Marquette. He could hear heavy footsteps on the stairs above. Brahms was returning with the body. Then, the telephone rang.

"Bancroft Funeral Home."

"This is Irene Wagner, from the Mining Journal. I'm calling to confirm the funeral arrangements for Gerald Higby and Julie Marcotte for our Sunday edition."

"Of course. I can help you, ma'am."

"I just spoke with Mr. Higby. He indicated the funeral would take place at ten o'clock Monday morning."

"Yes, that is right. At the school?"

"At the Birch Public School. Fine then, sir. Just wanted to be certain. We always confirm arrangements when they're out of the ordinary. We want to be positive that our obituaries are as accurate as possible."

"Of course you do. Thank you for calling." Von Himmler placed the receiver back on its cradle. A bolt of excitement bored through him. He crossed his arms and hugged his sides, swiveling his hips in the sheer rapture, the joy, the delight, in seeing his plans unfold. This was something that went way beyond avenging his father's death. This was his one opportunity to show mankind that the world was deficient, hopelessly flawed, incorrigible.

His own father had always sounded an optimistic note regarding man's destiny. He was blinded, like so many others, in the belief that the application of science could heal the wounds and scars caused by man's inherent defects. Wolfgang knew that this was not possible. The noble attempt at racial purification by the Nazis had ended ignominiously enough. Consequently, if he had the power, he would simply flood the planet in the Mosaic tradition. The God that Wolfgang had no reason to believe in had made one great error of omission. He had failed to cast Noah and his sons into the same, violent, black waters into which He had pitched every other earthly man.

Brahms appeared in the office doorway. He carried the undertaker's corpse like he would a big baby doll, clutching it to his chest. Von Himmler supervised the placement of the body in the trunk of the white Dodge parked in the garage. "Now Josef, I want you to go straight to the kitchen, and make lots of sandwiches. You will be staying upstairs all day. This afternoon, the townspeople will be arriving for the visitation. They will be coming to see the two bodies. They will be visiting the pretty girl. Understand? Now, you make sandwiches and go upstairs, and stay there!"

"I will be good boy. There are donuts? Glazed donuts? Jelly, jelly, jelly, I love jelly."

"All that you can eat. In the kitchen; Now go! The florists will be here any minute!"

Erin Cronin carried in the lunch tray to her decrepit mother-in-law like usual, seated in her wheelchair in the parlour. She was busy with the spy-glass. "Mom, it's almost eleven. Time for your broth and your sandwich."

"Glory be!" announced the old lady, "Mr. Rutledge is working up quite a sweat, hey?"

"Lots of people will be at the funeral parlour, mom. He wants his yard to look nice, out of respect for the dead."

"I saw something that wasn't all that respectful at the funeral home, this morning." Erin, half listening, looked out across the avenue, past the wrought iron fence, where two florist's vans had pulled up in the drive. Great armloads of flowers were being carried into the funeral home by two young men.

"What was that, mom? What was it that you said you saw?"

"I saw Mr. Bancroft, running about the house, naked as a jaybird, I did!"

"Mom!"

"Big, naked, and erect!"

"Mother Cronin! I don't want you talking that way in front of your grandchildren! Now eat your lunch."

"Thank you, honey." And then, after wheeling forward and sniffing the contents of the sandwich, she exploded angrily. "What!? Tuna fish!? Another tuna sandwich!? I'm sick and tired of tuna!"

Wolfgang Von Himmler had never seen so many cut flowers in all of his life. Two truckloads had been delivered to the funeral home and divided up between the two slumber rooms containing the dead teenagers. He stood in the doorway of each room, looking carefully at the way the flowers had been arranged by the deliverymen. The pungent aroma given off by the colorful sprays seemed to fill the first floor with sweet perfume. Everything was now ready.

Von Himmler approached the big bay window in the east wing stealthily, and then he peered into the neighbor's yard next door. A barrel chested man attired in khaki work clothes was raking a large pile of fallen leaves onto a big, white sheet. As Von Himmler watched, the man lifted the four corners of the sheet, gathered them into his hand, then he hefted the bundle onto his shoulder and headed toward the rear of his house.

"Mr. Sam Rutledge," said Von Himmler softly, "so we finally meet again, after all these years." The blue eyes, absorbing the refractive image of the man through the large pane of glass, reflected twin rays of pure hatred back out into the yard.

When Bob Brooks met with Dr. Drake at the state hospital, the blue haired head administrator offered him a chair in his office, so that the commander might sit and relax while the good doctor hunted down the building superintendent who had first reported the poison missing from one of the storage rooms in the basement.

"No, Doctor Drake, I have got to see this for myself. I need to know the type of poison, the shape of the missing containers, and how the poison could be utilized by Von Himmler, if indeed, he does have it in his possession."

"We'll go to the storage area in the basement together, then. Mr. Truman told me he would be somewhere down there, in the general vicinity."

Drake led Brooks through the hallways until they came to a service elevator. "Things seem to be really bustling around here," deadpanned Brooks, noting the empty corridors.

"First Saturday of the month is visitor's day. Family and friends come to see the patients from eight in the morning til seven at night. There's even a spaghetti dinner in our cafeteria. I don't suppose that you could take time out from your busy schedule to stay for our dinner. I highly recommend our garlic bread."

"Afraid not," said Brooks, "but thanks. Maybe next month; Hopefully, I can come see Brahms and Von Himmler, back safely in their padded cells. I'll even bring the chianti."

The cellar of Newberry Joy was every bit as dank, dark and musty as Brooks had imagined. A labyrinth of shadowy hallways, illuminated by a scattered, inadequate network of naked light bulbs, led to numerous storage areas, utility rooms brimming with fuse boxes and electrical leads to nowhere, and rows of cells fitted with heavy, reinforced wooden doors. Brooks considered that, were the entire cellar to be suddenly plunged into total darkness, even a sane man, in feeling his way along the cobwebbed corridors and spring soaked outside walls in an effort to get out, would, in short order, be driven to madness.

"Years ago, these rooms were reserved for the most disturbed patients," said Drake, pointing at one of the rows of cells. "The idea was to keep the wildly dangerous subjects out of the wards above. That way, they wouldn't be able to infect the general patient population."

Drake led him into a large storage room. Brooks was pleased to see that the interior had been remodeled, equipped with fluorescent lighting, and kept clean and dust free. "The poison was kept in this room," said Drake, "along the rear wall, there."

Brooks could readily see that there was quite an inventory of heavy duty cleaning supplies- degreasers, floor waxes, window solvents, mop buckets, floor polishers, and a rug and carpet cleaner. There was a light knock at the door, and a stocky man with a short, butch haircut, wearing a dark green janitor's uniform greeted Brooks. "Hi Bob! Been a while. Nice to see you." The two men shook hands.

"Rod Truman! you're lookin' fit."

"You two have met, I see," said Drake.

"Been years," replied Brooks. "We used to bowl in the same league together."

"Until he got his big promotion, and decided he didn't have time for us common folk." Truman pointed at an empty shelf along the rear wall. "We didn't notice this, Bob, until right before Doctor Drake called you- the missing poison, that is. One of the workers came in for some window cleaner, and he noticed that the room had been gone through, I guess you'd say. Well, Perry came and got me right away. We went back in and looked for anything that might be missing. Didn't take long to realize that all of the poison was gone. I reported it to Doctor Drake right off."

"And what type of poison is this, Rod? And what do you use it for?"

"Prussic acid. We use it for delousing. It can also be effective for rodent control."

"Delousing- you mean lice, right?"

"A lice infestation," replied Drake dryly, "is a rarity. But in an institution of this size, it would spread quickly if not brought under immediate control."

"When delousing becomes necessary," added Truman, "the infected ward is evacuated and sealed off. Whoever is assigned the job wears a gas mask. It takes only a short time to treat a very large area. It is a gas, and we have a special hose and nozzle that connects to the end of the canister. It's some pretty powerful stuff. When the treatment has been completed, we open the windows and ventilate for a few hours. Lastly, we mop everything down, and she's ready to go again."

"How much of this prussic acid did you have, Rod?"

"Five canisters. You really don't know from year to year just how much of the stuff you're gonna need. We're probably lucky if we go through one, to tell you the truth."

"How big are they?"

"They're cylinders- and they hold, I believe, twelve pounds. They're about, oh, this long." Truman held his hands slightly less than two feet apart. "I can double check our inventory sheet for you."

"Was there a sign of forced entry into this room?"

"We believe a key was used," said Drake. "One of our maintenance men has reported his missing. I have a locksmith coming out this afternoon to change the lock."

Brooks fastened the clip on his pen to the inside pocket of his blue blazer. "I'm glad you called me right away on this. Let's just hope that our escapees aren't carrying the missing poison with them. Maybe you inventoried wrong, or something. When we mix unstable personalities with something this deadly, you could say that every man, woman, and child within five hundred miles of here is at a calculable risk."

Drake seemed to scoff. "I'm sure, commander, that we'll all get through this without suffering grave consequences," he said. Brooks shot him a cold glance.

"By the way, Doctor Drake, will you be attending the funeral, Monday?" Drake looked perplexed.

"What funeral might that be?" he asked, wincing slightly.

"Jeffrey Gobles' funeral. You know, the boy from Eckerman? It seems to me we've already suffered grave consequences, doctor." Drake looked down at the floor. Rod Truman looked at Brooks grimly.

Brooks made the one-hundred and ten-mile drive from Newberry to the Negaunee state police post located just west of Marquette in record time. He left his emergency lights whirling most of the way and reached speeds of well over one-hundred miles per hour on the sparsely traveled roads. One constant pervaded his thoughts as he concentrated fully on the road ahead; If this Von Himmler did have prussic acid in his possession, he was sure to use it, or at the very least, to make the attempt.

But, what method would he use to deliver this poison? It was particularly unsettling to think that he might attempt to introduce it into some large department store somewhere, and Brooks knew that Von Himmler would have, at that moment, already arrived at whatever destination he had chosen, as long as it was somewhere in the upper Midwest. A sense of extreme urgency gripped Brooks. He had always prided himself on his ability to keep a cool head at even the most disturbing times during his twenty years with the state police. But this situation had become something the likes of which he had never had to face.

Art Franklin, commander of the Negaunee post, met Brooks promptly the moment the latter arrived. Franklin was thin and gaunt from an ongoing bout with an undisclosed illness and was in the last year of his career with the state police. He was slated for retirement the following March.

"Robert, always nice to see you." They shook hands.

"Art, you're looking as spry as ever." Franklin led him into his spacious office. Brooks' quarters at Newberry were cramped in comparison. They settled into a pair of brown leather chairs that looked out into the post's parking lot. Brooks noted the great number of dark blue cruisers out there. His own Newberry fleet of eight vehicles suddenly seemed wholly inadequate.

"Robert, I received a call a few minutes ago from Lansing, regarding the prussic acid question. The news could be better." The old man looked at him gravely.

"Go ahead, Art, hit me with both barrels. What are we up against?"

"Prussic acid is also known as hydrogen cyanide. Its use is limited primarily to the medical field."

"Treating for lice and such," said Brooks. "I already got a lesson in prussic acid from the maintenance foreman at Newberry Joy." Franklin nodded.

"Hydrogen cyanide was also used by the Nazis- at the concentration camps." Brooks was stunned. "This gas was their great discovery. Apparently, they stumbled upon it quite by accident. As you might imagine, it has a devastating impact on human beings. This gas is one of the most lethal compounds made. Used properly, and it is safe, and extremely effective, in controlling pests. Used in a confined area, either by accident or by design, and it is highly fatal. It causes paralysis of the respiratory system in human beings."

"Art, Wolfgang Von Himmler is, of course, a German. I don't like the sound of this- not at all. Hydrogen cyanide, the Nazis, and a psychotic, old German. This is eerie- more than a coincidence. Art, my skin is crawling."

"Robert, we've got the FBI working with us now, too. Because of the possibility that the state line has been crossed with this horrific poison, Lansing jumped at the chance to get the Feds in on this. They've got all the information available from the Soo Line which you had sent through regarding the train schedules and the destinations of the freight and they're coordinating with all the local departments up and down the line."

"Art, that's a relief to me, a big relief. Personally, I feel that they're already in Wisconsin, or even Illinois, by now. I wouldn't tell that to our own troops, though. This is mission one in the U.P. If the suspects are still in the peninsula, somewhere, I want the state police to nab them, not some local dick." Franklin couldn't help but notice the deep, dark circles under Brooks' eyes, which seemed, by their very presence, to give more definition to the worry lines drawn across his face.

"Robert, let's get you checked into the motel first. Then, we're going for a bowl of chili, you and me. We just need to get you away from this, for a hot meal. Sound good?"

"Sounds good," echoed Brooks hollowly.

At three-thirty Saturday afternoon, Wolfgang Von Himmler, dressed to a 'T' in Herman Bancroft's black suit and red tie, greeted the immediate families of the deceased and took them on an initial private inspection of the displays. The Higbys and the Marcottes seemed very pleased with the work that had been done. Tina Higby, numb with sorrow, took Von Himmler aside, away from all the others. She was homely in her blue frame glasses, round face, and short, unhealthy red hair.

"Mr. Bancroft, Ed told me that it was your idea to have the funeral at the school. I can't tell you how much we appreciate all that you have done for us. I know that this is exactly what our Jerry would want." She blotted her eyes with a white tissue. "He was very involved with the school, you know. He was in plays, and, he was the star on the basketball team."

Von Himmler took her damp hand into his. "He sounds like he was a wonderful young lad. I know that my cousin, Herman, was deeply troubled by the accident. He was crushed when he had to leave town. It was the first time that I ever saw him cry." Tina touched the edges of her red hair, and then burst into tears.

Ed Higby came quietly up behind his wife, and placed his hands on her shoulders tenderly. "John, Ducky Deneau, the school board president, will be stopping in at about five. He's got the key to the school for you. He told me to tell you that the school is at your complete disposal, I think that's how he put it. Ducky has got a way with words, that's for sure. Anyhow, if there's anything they can do, you be sure and ask 'em. He said they already got the stands lowered, the chairs set up on the gym floor, and they set up the speaking platform. I think you'll be happy with what they got done over there." Von Himmler nodded slowly.

"Thank you, Mr. Higby. You have no idea how much Herman and I are in this community's debt. And did I tell you the good news? Herman promised to be back tomorrow night- late."

"John, I know what Herb told you last night, and I'll back him up two-hundred percent on this, we're all in good hands, right with you." Tina nodded in agreement. Von Himmler blushed, and a clump of gray hair fell across his forehead.

"I will be in the office, in case I can be of any further assistance. There are some last minute details still to be ironed out."

"I'll be sure and tell the Marcottes, John," said Ed, who then turned with his wife, and rejoined their entourage in the foyer.

For the next hour, Von Himmler remained sequestered in the funeral home office. Right after he had first seated himself in Herman's chair, the phone rang, and he answered. A young girl wanted to know the hours of visitation. He explained them to her. A minute later, it rang again. Then again; More dumb questions from more dumb people followed; After a short while, he put both of the phone lines on hold. He opened the metal file box, took pen and paper, and began jotting notes. He looked at the card entitled, 'Employees- Part Time and Temporary,' and studied the short list of names.

There was a steady murmur from without. It became more intense as the afternoon waned. It was the kind of low murmur one comes across in crowded theatres or restaurants. Von Himmler ignored it. There was a sharp rap at his door. "Come in."

A chubby, clean shaved man with curly blonde hair and a pug nose, dressed in a blue sports jacket and tan pants, eased through the door and smiled. "One heck of a crowd you got out there," he said, thumbing back toward the door as it closed. "You must be John." He offered his hand, saying, "I'm Ducky Deneau, school board president. Ed had told me last night about your plans to use the school for the service on Monday."

Von Himmler took the hand, smiling. "Yes, Mr. Deneau, I was told to expect you. My idea to use the school, it turned out, was a good one, considering the size of the crowd and-"

"Don't be so modest, John! I think it's a terrific idea. I've declared no school for Monday, obviously, on account of the funeral. Jerry Higby was quite a hero around these parts, you know. And there wasn't a prettier girl in town than Julie Marcotte, either. I think going to the school will help all concerned feel a little bit better about it all." A car horn beeped out on Birch Avenue. There was apparently a major traffic jam in front of Bancroft's.

"Mr. Higby told me that you have prepared the gymnasium well." Ducky pulled a blue rabbit's foot key chain from his sports coat pocket. One key was attached.

"Things are basically set over there, John. Here's the key to the school. This will unlock all doors in the vicinity of the gymnasium." He handed it to Von Himmler. "And if there's anything else that you need, you be sure and call me." Ducky tossed his business card onto the top of the desk. "My home number is on my card, there."

"Thank you, Mr. Deneau. I shall not hesitate to call." Von Himmler looked at the card with interest. Ducky was a Certified Public Accountant.

A boy of perhaps thirteen opened the door to the office and entered abruptly. "Hey daddy, mom wants you to come and see Jerry."

Von Himmler could see that the boy was dressed in a white shirt and dress slacks and he wore a tie that was identical in color and style to Ducky's.

"Son, I want you to meet the funeral director."

"Where's Mr. Bancroft? Mr. Bancroft took me on a tour of his operating room last summer. I seen where he gets the bodies ready, where he sucks the blood out."

Ducky shrugged at Von Himmler, as if to excuse his son's brash behavior. "Jackie, this is another Mr. Bancroft- Mr. John Bancroft. Come over and shake hands with the man." The boy grabbed Von Himmler's hand and gave it a single, hard shake.

"Dad! C'mon!"

"Now son, you're being rude to Mr. Bancroft."

"No," Von Himmler broke in, "I know that young people are very impatient these days." Von Himmler was most understanding. He patted the boy on the back, fighting the urge to scrape the acne off of his pubescent face. "You had better get going, Mr. Deneau."

Ducky backed toward the door, with his son tugging at him once more. "Remember John, if there's anything that I can do, make sure you call. You have my number."

"Yes, I will. And thank you again, Ducky." The door closed after them. "Ducky fucky," said Von Himmler.

Red Tomlinson, his wife, Connie, and Sam Rutledge walked across Sam's front lawn together on their way to the funeral home. They reached the wrought iron gate and headed up the narrow brick walkway to the front entrance. "Sure got a big crowd in there," said Red, looking into the bay window. He reached for the door handle, but at the same moment, the big door swung open. Red stepped back. It was Bob, bartender at the Sawmill.

"Red! Hi, Connie! That you, Sam?"

"Just leavin', Bob?" asked Red.

"I think so. Thought I'd get some air. Anyhow, I'm not much for funeral parlours. The flowers sure smell pretty in there, though."

Connie Tomlinson, a thin woman with knobby wrists and dishwater blonde hair smiled at Bob and then stepped past her husband and into the foyer.

"You workin' tonight, Bob?" Sam asked.

"Like always. It's gonna be busy, but quiet, if you ask me."

"Red and me will drop by after."

Bob looked up at the twilight sky. "Clouds moving in- bet there will be rain tomorrow. The day after Kennedy was shot last year- it rained like hell."

"Yep, you can smell it in the air." Sam put one foot into the doorway. "Guess I'd better be headin' in with Red and Connie."

"See you later, Sam."

Sam caught up to the Tomlinsons as they chatted with Ducky Deneau's wife, Millie. "Herb's doing okay, but poor Sandy, she's kind of a mess. Well, wouldn't we all be? Hallo, Sam! Haven't seen you around much lately."

"Evening, Millie."

"It's gettin' to be close to deer season," Red explained. "Sam's been awfully busy up at camp."

"I suppose you men can't wait to take your deer. I'm so glad that Ducky never took up hunting. Our school takes up most of his spare time as it is."

Sam made his way into the east wing. A set of french doors was propped open into the room where Julie Marcotte was laid out. There were twenty-five to thirty people crowding around Herb and his wife, Sandy. Sam walked right up to the casket and a shudder passed through him. He had known little Julie so well- she used to sit on his knee back when her dad used to work for Rutledge Logging. And, he'd watched her grow up to be a beautiful, young woman. In time, Sam was sure she would have put Birch on the map. She was a natural at acting and had a wonderful singing voice. She looked older, somehow, lying there. She really had passed on- he could hardly believe it.

"Sam, I'm glad you could come."

Sam opened his arms and gave Herb a big, fatherly hug. "I'm so sorry, boy. How's Sandy?"

Herb's eyes were moist and red. He looked up at big Sam and drew strength. "She's been sedated. She hasn't accepted it, Sam. She's not so well just now."

"None of us have accepted it, Herb. Now listen, if there's anything I can do, you just ask- and I mean anything."

"Might just take you up on your offer, Sam, what with the new undertaker filling in and all."

"What new undertaker?" Sam asked sharply.

"Herman Bancroft's cousin from Chicago. His name's John."

"I hadn't heard."

"Ed Higby was told Herman's expected back tomorrow night."

Sam scoffed at that. "Good. I don't like the thought of some stranger comin' in and doin' the buryin' in this town. That should be left to one of us Birchers." Herb tightened his lips together. "She's a beautiful girl, Herb. They say the good die young." The grieving father rested his forehead on Sam's shoulder.

"Thanks for coming, Sam," he managed, his voice cracking. "This is the toughest weekend we'll ever face."

"And just look at this big crowd of all your friends and neighbors. The town is with you, Herb. But you must know that already."

A solitary figure in the sea of otherwise familiar faces of townsfolk made his way slowly into the east wing. Sam studied the man with interest. The hair was gray and combed back, the black suit he wore was unusually baggy, and the cheeks framing the big moustache beneath the wire rim glasses were sunken and hollow.

"There's the new undertaker," whispered Herb. "He's been real helpful."

Von Himmler stopped and eyed Rutledge for a moment, then came forward, wearing a slight smile. "Mr. Marcotte, how are your family members holding up? This is a hard time, I know."

"My wife, she's pretty broke up. The doctor has her on tranqs. It's been tough- real tough."

"I am sorry." Von Himmler looked at Rutledge. "We have not met." Sam looked into the steel, blue eyes. This man looked almost emaciated, but his eyes were strong.

"Sam Rutledge," Sam said, offering his hand. The undertaker looked down at the hand, and then took it, briefly, a twinkle in his eye.

"I am John Bancroft. Herman flew out of town yesterday. He asked me to come and help during his absence."

"Doesn't seem like something old Herman would do. Oh well, he's always been a strange sort, anyway." Sam displayed a toothy grin. "I've been the next door neighbor for many years. There's always been comings and goings at all sorts of queer hours over here. It's not nothing too out of the ordinary, then, hey? You're just another comin', and Herman's just another goin'." He leaned forward to whisper privately into Von Himmler's ear. "You ever been in any of them scary movies, pal? Hey, we're stoppin' at the Sawmill for a drink after- bet you could use a cocktail, huh?"

"Never," replied Von Himmler. "I am not a drinking man. There is no time for such frivolity."

"That's understandable- I was probably out of line for askin'." Rutledge looked down at the baggy pants, hanging awkwardly on the tops of the shiny, black shoes. He placed a hand over his mouth to hide his sudden smile. A giggle would be inappropriate at such a solemn event, particularly while in the company of the father of the deceased. Rutledge turned his back to Von Himmler. "Herb, I better stop and pay my respects to the Higby clan- it's gettin' late."

"Go Sam, by all means. Thank you for stopping by."

"Mr. Marcotte," said Von Himmler, "I will be in my cousin's office if I can be of assistance." Von Himmler turned with a bow and followed Rutledge into the hallway at a safe distance.

Later that evening, after Von Himmler had seen the last of the many mourners out through the front door, he took a deep breath, turned and then leaned his back against the doorframe. The day could not have gone better for him. The community had readily accepted him as a viable replacement for Herman Bancroft. Why, he had that Board of Education President practically eating out of his hand.

He slowly walked into the east wing slumber room and opened the guest register, which the Marcottes planned to take home with them the day of the funeral. He looked up and down each page until he had honed in on the name of one particular visitor. There it was, the signature of Sam Rutledge.

"Sam Rutledge, you are condemned to death for the cold blooded killing of Doktor Horst Von Himmler!" he shouted. "The execution shall take place on Monday, six October, ten o'clock in the morning in the gymnasium at Birch school. All those attending are reminded to wear their gas masks." Von Himmler strutted through the house, his arms held high. "Herr Doktor Pfanmuller! Make room in the after life! I am sending you more of the human ballast which you desire!"

Down the street in the Sawmill, Red and Rutledge sat up at the bar, the both of them gripped with melancholy. The place had filled up when visitation hours ended, but the mood was so somber that most folks didn't stay for more than one. Behind the bar, Bob was now drunk. He had already broken four glasses, and as the hour grew late, he had begun to slur his speech.

"This town is dyin', and that's the God's truth," said Red. "Christ Almighty, why did they have to go and take Julie Marcotte?"

"The girl had talent," added Sam, sharing another jigger of Yukon Jack with the bartender. "Always thought she was gonna make something of herself- you know, put Birch on the map."

Bob dropped his chin onto the top of the counter. "Give me one a' yer cigs, Sam." Rutledge popped one from his vest pocket. This was the first time he had worn a suit and tie since Easter Sunday.

"Face it," continued Red, still on the same tack. "Factory's been closed for years. Sam, the logging 'll only last as long as you do. It's come down to this- no jobs, no hope. The young people either move away or end up quitin' school. Most everybody's collectin' either unemployment or welfare. You know what? I'm gettin' real depressed." Red knew he was not the most articulate man in town. He gulped from his Old Style, satisfied that he had made his point.

Rutledge was half-smiling under those deep, black brows of his. "Come on, Bobby, one more shot. I gotta get the hell out of here."

Bob was dunking two Alka-Seltzer into a glass of beer. "Hey R-r-red! Here's a toast for ya, boy! To our li'l town. Gonna be a ghost town, jus' like all the res'! To dead Birch, Meeecheegan!"

While Red, Bob and Rutledge were holding their private wake at the Sawmill Bar, Von Himmler stealthily left a side door of the funeral home, crept across the lawn and then entered the house next door. As usual, Rutledge had left his front door unlocked.

The only sound in the darkened house was the tick, tick, tick of the grandfather clock in the living room. Von Himmler turned on his flashlight and searched slowly through the main floor of the house. He disturbed two mice in the midst of their meal on the kitchen countertop. They scurried into a black corner, behind a canister set that probably hadn't been touched since Mrs. Rutledge had been alive.

Wolfgang was careful about pointing the flashlight away from the windows as he moved through each room. He made his way down a hallway and entered Rutledge's den at the rear of the house. That was where he finally found the gun cabinet.

CHAPTER NINE

Sunday morning dawned cold and rainy. A low pressure cell had moved in from the Canadian prairies during the night. On its way from out of the west-northwest, it had picked up additional moisture off of Lake Superior. The rain riding the accompanying twenty mile per hour winds lashed at the windows of the funeral home, acting as a powerful sedative for the exhausted Von Himmler, who remained deeply asleep well past his normal wake up time.

Finally, he opened his eyes in the Bancroft's big bed, finding himself in the surprisingly gentle clutches of Brahms, and he was at once grateful for the giant's bath and tooth polishing which had taken place the previous morning. Von Himmler wriggled from beneath the great left arm and arose to face the day.

As each hour now passed, he knew that Brahms had become an increasing liability to the ultimate success of his murderous plot. Their published descriptions in the newspapers and on television certainly must have been seen by more than one of Birch's residents, so that the big lumberjack's appearance in the town, were it to occur in a moment of carelessness, would certainly subject the both of them to immediate apprehension by the authorities. Von Himmler was reasonably sure that his own tracks were covered, at least for the duration of the time window that was necessary in order to carry out his dark plans. Brahms, on the other hand, had served out his usefulness, however faithfully, and required prompt disposal to insure the completion of the mission.

Late Sunday morning, then, as the community gathered together in its churches to spiritually come to grips with the accident on County Road 550, Von Himmler pulled out of the garage in the white Dodge, with Brahms hidden carefully in the rear seat. The rain pelted against the windshield. He drove slowly through town, past the IGA, and then swung out to the main highway. He turned north, following the directional arrow toward Lake Independence, and about a half mile up the road, he suddenly pulled off onto the shoulder.

"Brahms, take the wheel. I will now teach you how to drive." Josef threw open the rear door, climbed out into the hard rain, and then jumped into the driver's seat. He rammed the right side of his head against the edge of the roof, so eager was he to take this driving lesson.

"When driving a car, there are two foot pedals which you must know how to use, my boy." Von Himmler looked over at his student.

Brahms' head was wedged at an awkward angle against the headliner, due to his abnormal height. "First, press that pedal. No! Hold it down with your foot. Good. Now, the lever, here, move it across to the 'D'. Good. Look for other cars- be sure there is no other car coming. Now, hold the steering wheel, and press that pedal. Slower. Slower! Slow down!! Lift the foot up! No!!"

Brahms had accelerated to well over sixty miles per hour. Then, he hit the brakes so forcefully that he locked them up, causing the car to spin around three full rotations on the wet, oily road surface. They came to a halt in the oncoming lane, directly facing potential traffic that might be headed south.

Von Himmler again looked over at Brahms, ready to berate him for causing this near death experience. But, Brahms wore such a wide smile, with his tongue flicking back and forth at the corners of his mouth, like that of a lizard; The teacher could not bring himself to undermine such enthusiasm.

"Happy!" cried Brahms, "I happy and free!"

"Good, Josef. Why don't we give it another try? Not so fast this time." Brahms eased his foot back onto the accelerator.

"Happy! Happy! Free!!"

Jack Stratton called the Soo Holiday Inn's switchboard and was courteously connected to the room of Gloria Shutz.

"Good morning," Gloria answered.

"Hi, this is Jack, you know? From the state police?"

"Hi Jack! You're the guy from the roadblock, right?"

"Correct. I thought that I'd call you to see if you still wanted to go out for coffee. Still interested?"

"Very interested!" she exclaimed. "But I need some time to get ready. How about if you meet me in the lobby downstairs, here; Can you give me about forty-five minutes?"

"I'll be there," said Jack, trying his best not to sound over eager. "I hope you you won't have any trouble recognizing me."

"Oh no," she replied, "I think I remember you. You've got the big, ugly scar on your face, right?"

"No, I'm the guy with two bodies from the waist down."

"You have a heck of a tailor, then," she said with a laugh. "Maybe I should go out with him for coffee!"

"I better let you go, Gloria. Be seeing you, soon."

"Okay Jack, bye." Gloria hung up the phone and looked into the mirror above the desk. "Oh my God!" she yelled, "forty-five minutes!"

Roscoe Stokes, a state police trooper working out of the Negaunee post, pulled into the Birch IGA lot and quickly entered the store through the steady rain. He picked out a package of cream filled chocolate cup cakes, and a pint of milk and set the items down at the register. A lady in a blue smock, busily stocking cigarettes into a rotating display case, stopped her chore and walked on over to the counter to help him.

"No alcohol sales until noon," she said, waiting for a reaction from the officer.

"Very funny. I should be so lucky to have this Sunday shift." He winked good-naturedly. "Morning, Jill."

"Hello, Trooper Stokes. You shouldn't much care about workin' today, eh? Rainin' too hard to do much outside."

"Wonder if it's raining like this down in Green Bay? Football Sunday- that's where my heart's at, today- with those Packers."

"Lions and the Packers? I'll go with the Lions."

"You are a funny one." He paid for his snack and balanced the cupcakes on his forearm. "By the way, have you noticed any strangers in town? Anybody odd or unusual?"

"None to speak of," she replied. "All the fishermen are gone for the season. Too early for the deer hunters; Bear season's over."

"There are two escaped mental patients on the loose." He held a sheet that was adorned with photos of Von Himmler and Brahms up for her to see. "The younger one, there, he's six-foot seven."

"You better go and check your Packer locker room for him, hey?"

"I guess."

"No, I haven't seen the likes of them around here. And I've worked the whole weekend, no thanks to Doc."

"If there's anything suspicious, or anybody who you might want checked out, give us a call. The rumor is that they're in Wisconsin, but you never know."

"I'll keep on the lookout."

Doc Morgan, the store owner, walked in from the butcher shop. "Howdy officer, what brings you to our neck of the woods?"

"Hi, Doc. At least it's not an accident this time. That was a bad scene the other night."

"The whole town's in a state of shock," replied Doc.

"I was explaining to Jill, here, about the two mental patients."

"Saw that on channel six last night. They killed that boy in Eckerman, too bad."

"I better get back out to the car. They'll be radioing me, no doubt. Remember now, if anybody suspicious turns up, or if somebody spots that monster hitchhiking, you call us right then. They are two very dangerous characters." Roscoe saluted and walked out.

"Maybe we should have told him to stop at the funeral home," said Doc, after the officer had left. "I'd say that Herman's cousin is kinda shaky. At least he didn't serve coffee and donuts last night like we expected."

"The thought crossed my mind," said Jill. "But I was thinkin' that having a police car at the funeral home would upset the Marcottes and the Higbys. There'd be rumors startin' about somebody doin' something to one of the bodies. Heaven knows Sally couldn't take nothin' else. She's gonna end up in the hospital, herself, when this is all over."

"Poor Sally," said Doc.

At four o'clock in the afternoon, once again there was a great influx of townspeople into the confines of Bancroft's. The steady rain continued without. This time, Von Himmler was more visible, waltzing through the hallways and the smoking areas, mingling somewhat, bestowing greetings on a selective few. His confidence was peaking.

The immediate families of the deceased were keeping a stiff upper lip. Sally Marcotte was a sad exception. Under heavy sedation, she spent much of the time seated in a folding chair in the corner of the room where her daughter lay, staring fixedly at her casket. Every so often, her vacant look would give way to an expression of great anxiety and discomfort, at which time a loud wail would sound throughout the funeral home, lasting only briefly, and then she would again be silent for another indefinite period.

A gray haired man attired in a clerical collar stood talking with Herb Marcotte as Von Himmler made his rounds. Herb pointed at him, then the man nodded knowingly and proceeded toward Von Himmler. "Mr. Bancroft, I am Reverend Sterling."

"Good afternoon pastor." They shook hands.

"A pleasure meeting you, Mr. Bancroft. I've been in close contact with both the Marcottes and the Higbys. They've kept me apprised of the schedule for tomorrow."

"I am pleased that you will be pronouncing the eulogy, sir."

"Thank you. You know, this is a very difficult time for our little village. The highway has claimed many lives over the years, but this accident has had a tremendous impact. My congregation was in tears this morning."

"Pastor, may I have a word with you, in private?"

"Certainly, Mr. Bancroft."

Von Himmler led him down the hall, and then into the office. He shut the door, saying, "I will see to it that the coffins are in place on the gymnasium floor by eight-thirty tomorrow morning."

"That would be appreciated. By the way, when will Herman be returning? Herb said something about tonight. He's expected back late, I take it?"

"Quite late, I'm afraid. He shall be with us in the morning."

"Well, we'll require all of his expertise to bring this program off smoothly. We'll require all of your talents, as well." Von Himmler looked amused.

"That is correct, pastor. I will need all of my talents and experience. I also wanted to ask you, there is no police department here in Birch?"

"Nope. We used to have a full time department years ago. Had a mayor, too. As our population has fallen over the years, we reverted to a township government. We do have a constable in Powell Township, but you rarely ever see him. He's the park ranger up at Lake Independence. Name's Ned Baker."

"Thank you, pastor. We might have the need for a traffic control officer." Von Himmler took a step toward the door. "All will be in place in the morning, then."

"Will you have need of pallbearers early in the morning? I can pass the word around."

"That will not be necessary. Herman has a troupe of part time employees. I will simply put them to work at first light."

"Splendid, then. You know, Ed Higby said that even with Herman gone, we're in good hands. I can certainly see what he meant."

"Thank you, pastor. Thank you very much." Von Himmler opened the door for the minister and wished him well. Then, alone again, he took hold of the metal file box and just as he opened the cover, there was a soft knock at the door. "Come in, please."

A man wearing black horn rimmed glasses with gray hair took one step inside the doorway and stopped cold. "Where's Mr. Bancroft?" he asked. Von Himmler did a double take. At first, he could have sworn that this man was his own Dr. Katz.

"Herman is away this weekend. My name is John Bancroft. I am Herman's cousin from Chicago."

"I didn't hear that Mr. Bancroft had a cousin, not on his dad's side. I thought he told me his dad was an only child." He gave this odd man with the wire rim glasses a suspicious look. Wolfgang kept his cool.

"You're quite mistaken. My father was in the funeral business, too. Who are you, may I ask?"

"I'm Charlie."

"You're- Charlie Beaver?" Von Himmler rose to his feet. Charlie looked even more suspicious. "Mr. Beaver, I was just picking up the telephone to call you. Herman told me that you have been of great help to him over the years. He told me that I could count on you when the chips were down."

Charlie dropped his defenses. "Herman told you that?" Von Himmler reaffirmed his statement, and then went on to explain that Herman was out of town due to the reading of their aunt's will. Charlie relaxed, glowing with pride. He'd had no idea that Mr. Bancroft had relied upon him so. Maybe, just maybe, he would ask for a raise when Mr. Bancroft returned.

"Charlie, would you be available for work early in the morning?"

"Why sure, whenever." Charlie limped to the edge of the desk. "What time do you want me?"

"Seven A.M. We will begin by moving the caskets over to the school."

"I know how to use the transfer table," said Charlie proudly. "It's adjustable. That way, we can slide the caskets in and out of the hearse."

"And you will be expected to drive the hearse tomorrow, Charlie."

"Me?" he asked in amazement, "heck, no trouble at all."

"Good, then. I will see you at seven." Charlie charged to the door, gimpy leg and all.

"See you bright and early," he said excitedly, and then he left.

Von Himmler opened the telephone directory, searched the listings, then picked up the phone and dialed. "Hello," he said, "Ned Baker? This is Bancroft's Funeral Home calling."

"Right," said a man with a smooth, tenor voice, "what can I do for you?"

"I am sure you have heard by now about the funeral for the two youngsters at the school tomorrow morning here in Birch."

"I was planning to be there. You need somethin' special?"

"Mr. Baker, I was instructed to call you to ask if you could be there, in uniform, to provide crowd control."

"I guess I could." The voice hesitated. "Crowd control? I don't know. I'm sure I could help out. I got an emergency flasher for the top of my pickup. Sure, I can be there. Don't you want the state police to handle it?"

"No, Mr. Baker, the families prefer someone local."

"I'll be there, then. But I'll be in my ranger uniform- don't have any kind of police uniform. What time?"

"Eight o'clock," said Von Himmler.

"And who's this speakin'?"

"I'm John Bancroft."

"See you in the morning, John. I'll look you up."

Von Himmler shivered with excitement. It was nearly midnight, and the surrounding homes were dark and silent. He was out in the garage, where he picked up an armful of old burlap bags and tossed them aside, exposing his trunk that he had hid there. He unlatched the trunk, and opened it carefully. In it were the five canisters of lethal gas, assorted old garments, an extra pair of glasses, a jumble of prescription medicines and hypodermic needles, and a small, brass torch connected to a disposable tank of propane. He had turned the lights on in the garage, and now he searched for, and found, Herman Bancroft's caulking gun and three tubes of caulk. He took these items, the caulk and caulking gun, the torch, and a small spool of plumber's solder, and placed them inside a cardboard box and carried it to the hearse. He turned off the garage lights, grabbing a stray screwdriver within reach of the light switch, then walked over and opened the garage door. He started the hearse and backed out carefully into the driveway.

He drove directly over to the Birch school. Passing by the Sawmill Bar, he noticed that there were two cars parked in the exact same spaces in the lot next to the bar that they had occupied, from what he could remember, on both Friday night, when he'd first arrived, and then again on Saturday morning, when he'd seen them a second time while on his way to the grocery store.

From what he could gather, the entire town was sound asleep. He pulled up to the school entrance that was adjacent to the gymnasium and shut the engine off. Outside, the rain had stopped, and a howling wind whipped through the streets and up between the houses of the village, drying up the pools of rainwater and hardening the muddy moraine. Von Himmler unlocked the door, and then carried the cardboard box into the school.

Inside, the corridors were dimly lit. Just off to the right, at the bottom of a spacious stairway, a pair of steel doors was propped open wide, leading directly into the gym. Von Himmler looked at the door latches, and then held out the key that Ducky Deneau had given him and inserted it into the lock. He turned it, and the bolt slid out smoothly. The gymnasium, then, could easily be locked, and as Ducky had said, this was a common key that would enable Von Himmler to access the entire school. He turned the bolt back in, pulled the key out and stuffed it, rabbit's foot and all, into the bottom of his trousers pocket. Finally, he entered the gymnasium with the box.

The nightlights created shadows, but Von Himmler could easily look about him. "Are there any echoes, here!?" he shouted. Reverberations and echoes bounced around the old gym. He walked up to the podium, and then stood behind it, facing the empty rows of bleachers.

"I am in command here!" he shouted triumphantly. "I am one of the architects of the master race! I am one of the Reich builders! Isn't that right, Pfanmuller?" Von Himmler snickered with insanity.

He walked behind the platform and tested the two doors marked: MEN'S LOCKERS; WOMEN'S LOCKERS. The doors were locked shut. He picked up the solder, unwound it, then took hold of the torch and lit it. He attempted, as best he could, to heat the door lock and melt the solder into the keyhole and into the crevice above and below the latch on the men's door. He repeated this same procedure on the women's door. He loaded one of the tubes of caulk into the gun and trimmed off the very tip of the tube with his pocketknife. Then, he caulked heavily around the frame of each door, sealing them both tight.

He walked around the parameter walls of the gym, closing any air ducts, torching and soldering the latch mechanisms, and sealing them with caulk. He smiled as he did this. "American bastards," he whispered hoarsely. The entire job took no more than ninety minutes.

As he ambled from the gymnasium, he hooted and cackled giddily. He had a half tube of caulk still left in the gun, and this he hid under a long, wooden bench located in a corner just inside the entrance to the school. He closed the school back up, locked the door, then carried his supplies back out to the hearse.

Driving back down Birch Avenue, Von Himmler stopped in front of the Sawmill. He took the screwdriver out into the wind and walked around to the front of one of the cars left parked there in the lot. The car had state of Wisconsin license plates. He removed the front plate, then scurried around to the back of the car and took off the rear plate as well. Then, he returned to the hearse and drove straight back to the funeral home's garage.

Once inside, he again closed the garage door and turned on the lights. He searched for, and located, a large, red, six-gallon gasoline can that sat on the floor next to Herman's power mower. It was practically full. He carried it over and set it next to the trunk.

At three o'clock Monday morning, Von Himmler was back in the funeral home office, seated at Herman Bancroft's desk. Soon, it would be time to wake up Brahms. He'd chosen to allow the lumberjack to remain until two hours before dawn, at which time he would be sent on his way in the white Dodge, to fend for himself. Von Himmler was granting him this one opportunity to return to his native Canada, knowing full well that this could jeopardize his own plans. His only alternative would have been the clean execution of his loyal servant. 'If he was American, I would want to see the brain,' Von Himmler had thought while comparing the pros and cons of letting Brahms live. Canadian citizenship, then, had been the determining factor.

His random thoughts drifted back to his lab work at Eglfing-Haar. He wondered what had become of his many brain specimens in the cellar, there. Invading American troops had surely confiscated them- and destroyed his exhaustive documentation no doubt! Dirty human ballast scum! They will soon pay!

At Herman's desk, then, Von Himmler began to write upon a sheet of notebook paper feverishly. Now and again, he would mumble something and then slam his fist down on the desktop. It was a speech that he was writing, although he was doubtful he would have the opportunity to deliver it. The phrases were familiar to anyone whom had ever skimmed through a copy of 'Mein Kampf'. The words, the sentences, the paragraphs, all contained the pounding rhetoric of manifest destiny, physical and mental superiority, and the savage degradation of a people, and this time the target was the American people. Von Himmler was working himself up into a foaming frenzy deep in the night. He wrote and rewrote, and then he rewrote again until the first gray mists of morning cloaked the countryside.

"Brahms!!" he shouted wildly. "Brahms!! Get up! Come down here!" Von Himmler stood at the base of the stairs, shaking. Up above, the big knee hit the floor with a resounding thud. Brahms soon appeared, making his way unconsciously down the stairs.

"Brahms! There is no time to waste. Go straight to the garage. You must leave at once!"

"I go in car?"

"Yes, you will go in the car you learned to drive yesterday. Remember, Josef, what I told you, yesterday? Remember what I taught you about the big, green signs?"

Brahms closed his eyes. Von Himmler became impatient. "I look for S-S-T-E. I look for arrow. I follow."

Von Himmler's wild look softened. His big, dumb pupil had learned his lesson well. "Excellent, Brahms! You are going home, to Canada."

"Canada," echoed the lumberjack, "rivers, hills, big trees cut down, logs and lakes." He pulled at his long, stringy hair.

"Yes Brahms, home to Canada. Now come to the garage. Come with me, now." Von Himmler led him through the kitchen. He felt almost fatherly as he picked up the white box with the cellophane top that housed the streusel from the counter and carried it into the garage.

"You will like this streusel, Brahms. It is the best in town. My mother used to buy these for me. I cannot eat it, now."

Von Himmler started the Dodge, and while the engine idled, he removed the license plates and replaced them with the Wisconsin plates that he had stolen during the night. He opened the garage, and backed the car out into the driveway. He motioned frantically to Brahms. "Time to go!"

The lumberjack plodded over to the driver's side door, then turned and faced his master, who had climbed from the vehicle and stood tensely in the drive. "Home," he said slowly, "home to Canada."

"Get into the car, Josef, and don't hit your head so hard this time. Wait for me. I will lead you from town in that other car." He pointed at the hearse. "Follow me."

He led Brahms through town and out to the highway by the first real light of day. To the early risers along Birch Avenue, it must have been an odd sight, indeed. The big white hearse leading the little shiny, white car in some mock procession; Brahms did seem able to operate the Dodge in a way that would not cause undo attention. Through his rear view mirror, Von Himmler kept a close eye on the car behind. At one point, he pressed down on the accelerator of the big hearse in an evasive maneuver. Brahms had unexpectedly pressed down on his own gas pedal and had nearly plowed into the rear door of the hearse.

When they had traveled roughly a mile out of town, Von Himmler pulled onto the shoulder, and waved Brahms on. As he drove by, the lumberjack seemed to be smiling, his head tucked at that awkward angle against the headliner. Von Himmler watched until the Dodge was out of sight, then he U-turned, and returned to the funeral home.

Back in the kitchen, Von Himmler paced nervously. It was nearly twenty of seven. He never had gotten any sleep. His whole being was burning with anticipation, as though he had been pumped up past the danger limit with powerful amphetamines. He did not bother fixing breakfast. His stomach was knotted and twisted, recoiling like a serpent within the walls of his abdomen.

He went into the garage. He rechecked the pearl handled thirty-eight caliber revolver, the double-barreled shotgun and the big deer rifle which he had taken from Rutledge's gun cabinet during the previous evening. The three guns were loaded and ready. He covered them with burlap and went back into the home, again. He spent the next few minutes watering the flowers in each slumber room, and then he closed each casket securely.

At two minutes to seven, Charlie Beaver arrived. "Morning," greeted Charlie. Von Himmler only stared at him. "Did Mr. Bancroft show up last night?" Charlie wobbled his thick black glasses.

"I am afraid not. His flight was cancelled. You know how that goes."

"You bet. Windy today, ain't it? Hope those tents in the cemetery don't up and blow over, whew!"

"You're familiar with the high school?"

"'Course," responded Charlie somewhat indignantly.

"Good. You told me yesterday that you know how to use the adjustable table- the lift, to move caskets?"

"No problem, John." Von Himmler handed him the rabbit's foot key chain.

"This is the key to the school. Use the door in front of the gymnasium. You may take the caskets, one at a time, over to the school. As for the flowers, you will obviously have to make a number of trips. The lift, incidently, is located in the garage, beside the hearse. The car keys are in the hearse."

"I'll get right on it," said Charlie.

"If you require any assistance, please let me know."

"Everything's got rollers on it these days," said Charlie. "The caskets roll in and out of the hearse. Only time I might need a hand is when I shove the caskets off the display stands in there." He gestured toward the slumber rooms. "By the way, want me to take them display stands over to the school?"

"By all means. And Charlie, I shall be upstairs."

"Good deal."

There was a firm knock at the front entrance. "Should I go and get that, John?" asked Charlie.

"No, I shall see who it is." Von Himmler stepped into the foyer and then opened the front door. A stocky man dressed in a brown uniform with a matching Canadian mountie style hat stood waiting in the morning breeze. Von Himmler flinched.

"Ned Baker," he said with a nod, and a tip of his hat. Von Himmler recognized his voice from their phone conversation. "You must be John?"

"Yes, Mr. Baker. You will have to excuse my reaction. I wasn't expecting you for at least another hour." Ned walked on in. The ranger was one of those men who had aged particularly gracefully. The skin on his face, especially at his cheeks and the sides of his high forehead, was shiny smooth and healthily tanned. He had a glow about him. His brown eyes and pleasant facial features sat low in his skull. When he removed his hat, he exposed a silvery brush cut, the hairstyle that he had worn throughout his adult life.

"I'll tell you, I was up early this morning. Thought I'd just swing by and see if I could be of any use. Pretty slow up at the park this time of year."

"Thank you, constable."

Charlie smiled and winked at Von Himmler. "Maybe he could give me a hand with the caskets, and the flowers, even."

"Oh, no, I couldn't ask-"

"Why not?" interrupted Ned, spinning his hat boyishly. "I've got lots of time before things get busy down the street."

"If you insist," said Von Himmler.

"This way, Ned," ordered Charlie, turning on his heel and making for the garage, "I'll show you what we're s'posed to do."

Wolfgang Von Himmler stood before the mirror in the second floor bathroom, clipping his moustache meticulously. Satisfied, he lathered his face and shaved. The razor blade made a sound like new sandpaper against a fresh cut hunk of pine, as it passed over his chin and cheeks. He set the razor down. His face was a naked pink, soft as a new baby's bottom. One and one-half inches of thick, gray whiskers were all that remained of the once bushy moustache, matted squarely beneath his nose. His steel blue eyes, glazed with madness, welled with the tears of blinding hatred. A lifelong passion for vengeance, having grown more twisted with each passing decade, ravaged what was left of his soul.

There was a commotion downstairs. Ned and Charlie were back for a load of flowers this time. The two caskets were already in place, over at the school. Von Himmler could hear them shuffling back and forth from the garage to the slumber rooms and then back, again, until they had jammed the back of the hearse with flowers. He listened for the now familiar roar of the big V-8 engine, and when the hearse pulled away, he walked down the stairs and headed for the garage.

Jack Stratton lay back on the bed in Gloria Shutz's motel room. He had just placed the phone back on the receiver following his call to the Newberry state police post, having informed the sergeant of his sudden illness.

He had immersed himself all night in the powerful libido of this wonderful, new woman whom he had just met. She had this game, this little routine, and Jack was thrilled just to play his part in it.

She came out of the bathroom, and Jack knew that it was time to close his eyes again. He closed them, leaving one eye open just enough to clearly see this attractive, naked blonde with the nice, firm tits, jiggling toward the bed. He couldn't believe it. She was bringing the towels, again. Jack had lost count. This was either his seventh or eighth such treatment since shortly after midnight, when the two of them had left the 'Locksview Lounge' down near the lobby and retired upstairs to Gloria's room.

She carried an armful of big, white terry cloth towels, dripping wet, to the bed. These, she had first soaked in the bathtub, in ice water, then wrung out hurriedly, and now she was once again bringing them to her lover in order to treat his body.

Jack tightened his muscles, anticipating the placement of the freezing towels on his bare skin. Gloria spread out the towels across his upper torso, his stomach, his thighs, and even his legs. As she performed her work, and as Jack began to shiver, her nipple rubbed slowly across Jack's lips. He knew by now to keep his lips pursed, despite his urge to lick and to suck and to nibble. While he continued to cool, she played with him, caressed him, and teased him. A ringing bell sounded from the direction of the locks, located just two-hundred feet from the motel. The bell was a signal that one of the locks was either opening or closing, and Jack had heard the bell from time to time throughout the long night.

Gloria lifted the towels off of Jack, and rubbed her palms over him. She climbed on top of him, and rubbed her body over his, her nipples hardened from the friction as much as from the cold. Then, abruptly, she mounted him, riding him into the dawn of day, his skin slowly returning to normal temperature.

For his part, Jack fought the instinct to thrust out his hips, preferring to be obedient, to give in to her needs and wants. She lay down on him, licking his cheek and moving back to his ear with flicks of her tongue. "Don't move, you big stiff," she whispered heatedly, "don't move a muscle."

Charlie Beaver slowed to a stop in order to drop Ranger Baker off on Birch Avenue, out in front of the funeral home. They had completed the delivery of the remaining flowers and had arranged the sprays around the caskets in the gymnasium. Charlie was a self-described expert in such matters. "You head on in," he said to Ned. "I got to park the hearse back in the garage and unload that lift. Tell John I'll be there in a jiffy, eh?"

Ned climbed from the hearse and gave the passenger door a good, hard slam. He was thirsty. All of the lifting and hoisting and arranging had parched his mouth and throat. He stood out on the neatly edged sidewalk and waved at Beaver as the vehicle sprang forward, then he passed through the iron gate toward the funeral home's entrance, licking his dry lips.

Von Himmler was pacing like a caged animal when Ned came through the foyer and started down the hallway, past the now empty slumber rooms. "You have finished," Von Himmler said in a monotone, slipping a hypodermic into his suit coat.

"Nice moustache," said Ned with an innocent smile, mopping his brow. "We got her done. Guess I could use a cold glass of water. The other fella'll be in here pretty quick- he's finishing up there in the garage."

Wordlessly, Von Himmler led him into the kitchen and handed him a glass, then turned on the faucet. Ned leaned over the sink, filling, then emptying the glass impatiently. "This sure takes a long time to get cold, don't it? My God!!" Von Himmler plunged the needle into the base of the ranger's neck, and then pumped in the clear fluid with a strong squeeze.

"You will do exactly as I tell you, Mr. Baker." The glass dropped from Ned's hand and shattered in the sink. Von Himmler gripped him by the shoulders and spun him around. His strength was surprising. Ned looked full into the hypnotic eyes. "You will follow my every instruction. You will obey my every order. My voice is your unquestioned commander. Do you understand me?"

"Yes," Ned said, wincing. Beaver entered the kitchen from the garage.

"We're all set up now, Mr. Bancroft. Damn! That was a big, big job, you know it? How about our wages?" he kidded. He looked at the park ranger and his light mood left him. "Hey! What's wrong, Ranger Baker? You sick or somethin'?"

"Haul him down! Hold him down!" shouted Von Himmler without warning. Ned tackled Beaver and wrestled him to the floor, stuffing a knee into the small of his back. The heavy black glasses spun across the green and black-splotched linoleum floor. Von Himmler patiently measured out the thiopental.

"Jesus! Mercy! Get the hell off me, you sons of bitches!!" Von Himmler knelt down on one knee and calmly injected the drug into the base of Charlie's brain.

Josef Brahms passed by the Newberry exit without incident, heading east on Highway M-28. His mouth was stuffed with the coffee cake that Von Himmler had given him. Starting out so early in the morning had enabled Josef to drive through Marquette before the city's streets had clogged with the usual Monday morning traffic. As the miles rolled by, Josef had become more and more skilled at aiming the car, especially at high speeds. This newfound adeptness with the steering wheel had all but eliminated his early penchant for drifting across the width of the roadway from one shoulder to the other terrifying oncoming drivers in the process. Fortunately, the highway was practically void of traffic. Josef next whipped right by the

Eckerman restaurant where just Friday morning, he had committed what would prove to be his final senseless murder. He paid no attention at all to the hand painted, full color picture of the famous sweet roll. Besides, the eatery was closed on account of Jeffrey Gobles' funeral.

A few miles east of Eckerman, the first road sign indicating, 'Bridge to Canada' loomed. Brahms recognized the large, block letters. "Canada!" he screamed in a high pitch, "home to Canada! I go home, now!" Josef pressed the accelerator to the floorboard.

Back in the funeral home garage, Von Himmler had reopened his trunk, and carefully emptied its contents out onto the concrete floor. This allowed him access to the secret compartment in the very bottom of the old box. He lifted away the false bottom, and brought out a white linen hamper containing a jacket, a pair of trousers, a shirt, and a hat. Next came out a pair of lineman's style boots. He carried these items, along with the pearl handled revolver, up to the Bancroft bedroom.

Once in the upstairs bathroom, he wrapped a towel about his neck, then moistened a washcloth and held it up to his forehead. He shook a bottle of black theatrical hair dye, which he had mail ordered with Dr. Katz's approval while he was confined to the state hospital, and sprayed an even coating over the top of his head. He wheezed as he breathed the fumes. He repeated this same procedure on the sides and back of his head, then dabbed his forefinger into the still wet substance and smudged it into his little moustache. He wiped his face and ears with the damp cloth, and then stood back, admiring his haunting reflection.

He walked into the master bedroom, where Ned and Charlie, drugged and hypnotized, stood waiting for their orders. "When I walk into a room, you will stand at attention!" cried Von Himmler. Charlie and Ned both jerked up stiffly.

Von Himmler stripped off his suit coat, slacks and shirt, and slowly slipped into the German officer's uniform that had been stored in the hamper. A knight's cross gleamed at his throat, and a pair of swastika patches were sewn into the shoulders. The black boots glimmered in the daylight. The hat he placed upon his head was black and gray with a wide leather band, adorned with a silver eagle perched atop a wheel emblazoned with another smaller swastika. The final touch was the pearl handled thirty-eight, which he jammed into his belt line.

"Both of you! Beaver! Baker! Wait for me in the kitchen! I will have more instructions for you. Then, we shall attend the funeral service, together."

"Yes sir," they replied smartly in unison, and then marched obediently toward the stairs.

By nine-thirty, the Birch school's gymnasium was half-filled with townspeople. The hundred folding chairs set up on the shiny maple floor were already mainly spoken for. The two families of the young accident victims congregated solemnly around the caskets and the podium. The incredible array of fresh flowers encircling the caskets and overflowing atop hastily erected folding tables nearby were, in themselves, an awesome spectacle.

Reverend Sterling stood in a tight group of several men just inside the entrance to the gymnasium. He was fidgety, and already damp with nervous perspiration. "The services may begin at ten o'clock sharp," said the reverend, synchronizing his wristwatch with the time displayed on the school's wall clock. "Tom, here, will be opening things up this morning." Tom Franklin, the school's principle, was running his finger along the bridge of his nose and smoothing out his eyebrow. "That's right, reverend. They were both topflight citizens, and among our most talented students, both inside the classroom and out. They will be sorely missed."

Dave Cronin, who lived directly across Birch Avenue from the funeral home, nudged Ducky Deneau with his shoulder. "Your gym looks real nice and shiny, Mr. President."

"Thanks, Dave. This has required an all out effort since late Friday night, when Ed Higby called and asked if the gym might be available. I'll tell you, putting this thing together demanded more stamina than if you had to make love to a whole houseful of good lookin' whores!"

The snickers from that group of men, excepting a stern faced Reverend Sterling, cascaded to the four corners of the cavernous room. Dave Cronin sheepishly gazed across the way, into the first row of wooden stands. There was his wife, Erin, seated between his wheelchair bound mother and his two children, scowling with disapproval and patting her hand on the empty seat beside her.

"I better go and sit with the wife before all the seats are gone," he muttered. "See you, guys."

Ducky Deneau looked about the floor of the gym, searching through all the familiar faces without result. "I wonder if John Bancroft needs a hand with something? I haven't seen him, have you, reverend?"

"I haven't seen him at all this morning."

"Charlie Beaver told me Herman's flight was cancelled. He didn't make it."

"Pretty windy," said Sterling.

"I'm headin' over to the funeral home," said Ducky. "You and Tom, you start this thing when it's time."

Sterling gave a nod toward an older woman, saddled with osteoporosis, hunched on a stool behind the electric organ that had been brought over from the Lutheran church. She commenced playing, 'Rock of Ages'. "That's what we'll do, Mr. Deneau," he said. "Tom, let's make sure the mike is set right. We can't have any feedback, today." The principle and the minister headed toward the podium.

Ducky walked briskly up Birch Avenue, sidestepping the parked cars and pedestrian traffic. "Morning, Jean, morning Frenchy, hello there, Donna, how are you?" He nodded and smiled warmly like a good politician to passersby, and by the time he'd gotten to the Sawmill Bar, the groups of neighbors and acquaintances had thinned to but a few last minute stragglers. Up ahead, Ducky could easily make out the white sign on the funeral home lawn. At that moment, the bell in the Lutheran church's steeple began to toll.

A green Ford pickup was parked directly in front of Bancroft's, on the opposite side of the street. Ducky walked close to it, sure that it must be Ned Baker's truck. 'Wonder what Ranger Baker's doing here?' he asked himself. Then he remembered. That was Ned carrying the last of the yellow and white carnations up near the podium in the gym. Ducky strolled up to the front door of the funeral home and walked right in.

"Hey John! Service is about to start!!" he cried, proceeding down the long hall. He found Charlie Beaver and Ned Baker standing at attention in the kitchen. "Good morning, gentlemen. Everything's in prime shape over at the school; Great job, setting up those flowers! Where's John?" Then he heard the clip clop of heavy shoes descending the staircase. Ducky stepped back into the hallway and looked toward the stairs with his best smile. Then he froze, a look of utter bewilderment turning the corners of his mouth down. "Hitler!" was the last word on Ducky's lips before a thirty-eight caliber bullet whistled through the middle of his forehead, spattering a good deal of blood and brain tissue onto the wall behind.

Jack and Gloria were snuggled together cozily in their motel bed when the civil defense siren at the locks began to sound. Jack had been dozing, and looking back upon it later, he was sure that he had been conscious of a crash just before the siren wailed. The trooper sprang out of bed and opened the room curtains wide.

"Jack! I'm naked!" Gloria whined. Jack could see that there was a definite commotion down at the Poe Lock, the newest and largest of the five locks that together comprised the world's busiest lock system. As Jack stood watching, a city police car, a Soo Locks security car, and a fire truck all converged at the scene.

"Gloria! Get dressed! It looks like there's been some kind of accident down at the locks! Hurry!"

Jack wouldn't allow Gloria the time to put on her bra, so she held her left arm across her sweater for support as she and Jack trotted the two-hundred yards to the sight of the mishap. Jack dragged her through the growing crowd until they were right up against the protective fence that had been constructed to keep the tens of thousands of annual visitors safely away from the sheer, seventy foot drop into the often turbulent waters below.

Jack could see that a car had come right down Ashmun Street at a high rate of speed and the driver, for reasons unknown, had just kept going, past the dead end, and had hurtled a set of guardrails, several rows of safety railings which were designed to keep the tourists from bunching up too tightly against the fence, and, finally, had landed the car on the fence itself and now it hung precariously out over the lock, threatening to plunge down, taking the fencing with. The driver, Jack could see, had, sadly, kept on going, breaking through the windshield and, apparently, landing way below, in the forbidding, gray waters of the lock itself.

"Where's the driver?" Gloria asked, looking around in the growing crowd of the store clerks and their customers who were pouring over to the scene in droves from the adjacent downtown business district.

Jack pointed out the big hole in the windshield to her, indicating where the driver had exited. "Poor devil," he said.

"Think he's dead?" asked Gloria, cupping her breasts in the cool air.

"I'm sure of it, doll face. At least he went quickly."

"Everybody back!" yelled a city policeman. "Rope off this area! All civilians back! Rescue underway! Everybody back!"

Jack held out his badge. "Jack! What the hell are you doing here? Aren't you working out of Newberry?" The policeman gave Gloria the once over, noting her uncombed hair and generally disheveled appearance. He concluded the obvious- these two must have just jumped out of the sack together.

"Got the day off," Jack replied.

The car, a white Dodge, hanging as it was, threatened any rescue boat below which might stray too close to the western wall of the lock. "You think the car might end up in there?" asked Jack of the officer.

"Hope not. What a mess we'd have, then. There's a wrecker on the way, now. We'll pull it off the fence right away!"

"You're lucky this isn't a warm July day," said Jack, gesturing at the growing throng of curiosity seekers. "I've seen this many people, and more, standing at the fence when it's nice out."

"We woulda had some folks losing their heads, that's for sure," said the officer.

Gloria tugged at Jack's sleeve and said, "you know hon, if that car didn't have Wisconsin license plates, I'd say it was my bosses' car. Looks just like it."

"There are lots of white Dodge sedans around," Jack answered. "I see 'em out on the road every day."

"Wait a minute, Jack! Look at the dealer stamp- on the back of the trunk!" Gloria said with a start.

"Northern Motors, Marquette, Michigan," Jack read aloud. "It's from your neck of the woods, alright, doll face. I wonder who this guy is?"

"We're running a check with Wisconsin, now," added the officer.

The wrecker arrived, was quickly backed up through the crowd, and then hooks and cables were connected to the rear axle of the balancing sedan. The car was slowly pulled back and away, easing the strain on the fence. One guy in the crowd started yelling encouragement, and right away the other onlookers began clapping and cheering as the car came lurching and rolling towards them.

"That was sure easy," said Gloria, swiveling back and forth at the waist in a feeble attempt to keep warm. The cheering subsided.

At about that time there was a great shout that arose from out of the lock, where a U.S. customs patrol boat had anchored, searching for the body of the unfortunate victim. "Hey, it sounds like they already came up with the body down there," said Jack. "Gloria, this isn't very pleasant. Why don't we just go back to the motel?"

"Jack, I'm a mortician, remember? Dead bodies have no effect on me whatsoever. I work with them every day. Let's stay! This is exciting!"

Jack and Gloria found themselves in the small group of gawkers permitted around the car while the police searched for personal items and other clues. "You can rule out alcohol," said one of the officers, his head wedged under the rear seat. "This guy sure liked to eat! What a fuckin' mess, eh?"

The city policeman applied a hammer and a big screwdriver to the trunk lock. Jack and Gloria had shuffled in beside him. "Here goes!" announced the officer, enjoying a glance at the front of Gloria's sweater, at the tight outline of her hard nipples in the pink knit. The trunk lid popped open wide, and Gloria let out a spine tingling scream and then fainted dead away, managing to direct herself into Jack's strong arms as she fell. Lying sideways, folded around the rim of the spare tire, was the moldering body of Herman Bancroft, his mouth and eyes crudely sewn shut.

Reverend Sterling, his elbows braced on the top of the podium, spoke calmly into the microphone, eulogizing Julie Marcotte and Gerald Higby. Now and again, he sponged his forehead with a damp, blue hankie. Before him, in the first two rows of folding chairs sat the Marcotte and Higby clans. Their loved one's bodies rested in softly padded caskets of identical design, one to each side of the podium. Sally Marcotte, seated in the first row despite the advice of her physician, stared blankly at the moving lips of Reverend Sterling.

As anticipated, the gymnasium was filled to capacity. There was a numbness in all of those faces in the wooden stands where an entire town now sat. Many in the audience wept openly. Many were saddened to the point of despair by the reality of premature death exhibited upon the tragic stage before them.

"....As brothers and sisters under God, we can only lift up our hearts and comfort our neighbors who must withstand the weight of such a heavy loss..." The reverend choked on his words. He stood open mouthed, aghast. The townspeople, so intent on the steady consonance, the comforting resonance of his voice were startled. Through the open doorway and into the center of the gym walked Charlie Beaver, carrying five green metal tanks like an armful of firewood. Four or five steps behind Beaver, Ned Baker paced, a center fire deer rifle held firmly in his hands.

"What is this? Some kind of a bad joke!?" cried Red Tomlinson.

"Just a minute!" said Sterling firmly over the public address system. "Gentlemen, your actions are most inappropriate. Please find yourself a seat. Have some respect for the dead, please!" Some in the crowd applauded sporadically. Charlie nestled the canisters up together in the middle of the floor, standing them up like gigantic bowling pins. Then, there was a loud gasp through the crowd. The clapping stopped.

Wolfgang Von Himmler, attired in full Nazi regalia, goose-stepped into the gym, holding a double-barreled shotgun. His eyes sparkled with wild excitement, his madness shining through for all to see. Here was the runaway winner of the annual Halloween costume contest come into the gym three and a half weeks too early. In but a few scant seconds, the deep look of mourning and pity on that calm sea of six-hundred faces had been washed away by a surging tidal wave of shock, terror and disbelief.

Red Tomlinson, leaving his seat in the stands, made three long jumps in order to reach the main floor, and then sprinted toward Von Himmler at breakneck speed. "Fucking Adolf fucking Hitler!! I'll knock your fucking block off!" he snarled. The shotgun was quickly brought to bear, and as Red launched his stocky body in a flying tackle at Der Fuhrer, both barrels unloaded their twin charge of high powered buckshot, and Red fell bleeding, mortally wounded, to the well polished, hard maple, gymnasium flooring. Von Himmler reloaded the gun.

"Samuel Rutledge! Private Samuel Rutledge!! I am Adolf Hitler! I am here for you! You killed my father!!" hissed the strange voice loudly.

The townspeople screamed and panicked. Some stood, some took a step or two toward the exit. Three members of the Higby family tried the locker room doors to no avail. "Baker! Use that gun on the next person who moves!" Spittle foamed on Von Himmler's lower lip. The crowd settled back, mesmerized by the unfolding drama.

"You!" he cried, pointing into the stands and cutting short his prepared speech. "Everyone of you! You are the human ballast that we Germans call Americans! Carpetbaggers! Thieves! Trash! You are to be an example to the rest of the world! Yours will be a permanent solution!!"

Some in the gathering looked back toward the podium to Reverend Sterling for a response. He was still holding both hands over his ears, recovering from the deafening blast of the shotgun. He quietly stepped to the back of the stage.

Sam Rutledge stood up in the stands, then made his way down the bleachers until he reached the main floor. He walked slowly toward Von Himmler. When he had advanced within ten feet of the madman, he stopped and stared in shock. "You were the boy?" he asked. "You are the doctor's son?"

"From half-a-world, and half-a-lifetime away, I have come for you, you scum," he hissed.

"Take me, then," said Rutledge, offering himself up for sacrifice by dropping defenselessly to his knees. "I give myself up to you. There shall only be one more death. Go ahead, blow my head off." Von Himmler smiled, pointing the barrel of the gun directly at Rutledge's nose.

"Baker! Beaver! Come here!" Charlie and the ranger left the gas canisters and joined with Von Himmler and Rutledge in a curious circle. Von Himmler pulled out the thirty-eight and, training it on Sam, gave up the shotgun to Charlie. "Take this gun and point it at the tanks. Wait for my next order."

"That's my own gun!" Rutledge announced, bristling. "Charlie! What the hell are you listening to him, for? Ned? For God sakes, why are you a part of this?"

"It is the affect of thiopental, injected into their brains," said Von Himmler. "They shall come to their senses, in another hour or so." He circled behind the kneeling Rutledge, brought the pistol up, and then smashed the side of the gun across his right temple. Rutledge dropped forward, onto his face. The townsfolk gasped collectively.

"Cover me!" Von Himmler now ordered Ned. When they had reached the double doors together, Von Himmler turned and pistol-whipped him, dropping him at the doorway. He quickly unjammed the doors and turned full toward the hushed crowd. "Beaver!!" he screamed at the top of his lungs. "Fire!!!"

The shotgun barrels exploded in a volley of thunder, piercing and mangling the canisters. The deadly gas poured out of each tank like convicts pouring out of some old, dark prison, ready to greet the fresh air. The hiss of escaping gas became obvious to each and every mourner. The effects of the poison on the doomed was clearly visible.

Von Himmler locked the gymnasium doors, slipped on the gas mask, and then sealed the door cracks with the remainder of the caulk that he had left under the wooden bench nearby. Beyond that door, the cries and screams of anguish were horrible beyond description.

Men, women, children; An entire town was in that poisonous room, a whole town was in there, in the throes of a suffocating death. Six hundred human souls at that moment scrambled up a mounting pile of bodies toward the ceiling. The more fortunate amongst them stood on the heads, necks and legs of their neighbors, just to enable them to breathe for a few seconds longer. They formed a flesh and bone sculpture, and only the devil could lay claim as the artist. Hundreds of bodies piling high in the gym; A pyramid of blood; A tower of hair, and teeth, and lips.

Through the deadening layer of rubber stretched now over his ears, Von Himmler determined that all human sound had ceased from within. He went and propped open the outside door, and slowly pulled off the mask. He walked out into the schoolyard, looked up at the cloudy sky, tears streaming from his wild blue eyes. "Father, you are avenged."

In the gymnasium, under one edge of the death pile, there was a movement. A life sign; Then, a struggle, and a body breaking free of the mass; There was a desperate squirming, a wriggling, and then, he was on all fours like a bear, and a man, by the blind instinct of self preservation, threw himself headlong into one of the sealed air duct vents like a human battering ram, breaking through, somehow, and breathing the good air on the other side in a short, insufficient series of inhalations.

Rutledge, his head and shoulders thrust into the sheet metal enclosure, for many minutes just lay there, breathing those shallow, painful breaths. He never looked back into the gym, but instead, pulled the rest of his body into the duct. He slowly moved forward, away from the horror, on hands and forearms, and then he drew his legs beneath him and managed to slide onto his back. More rest and recovery; Then, with all of his remaining strength, he brought his feet together and kicked at what seemed to be a screen covering another vent in one of the hallways and then he heard the clanking of the grate as it broke free and bounced across the tile floor. He slid out of the sheet metal duct feet first and landed hard on his buttocks. His legs had just seemed to give out, as though they were not legs at all, but twin sacks of flour. He pulled himself down the hallway and out to the school entrance.

The outside door was propped open, as though to air out the place. The bastard, then, might still be there, somewhere. Rutledge thought he could hear the scuffing of shoes or boots out on the sidewalk. As he reached the door, he heard what sounded like a 'poof!' followed by a great rush of air, and immediately, the loud report of a pistol shot.

Rutledge crawled out toward the street, and then witnessed a scene which he would first describe a half hour later, when the state police came, and then over the course of the next several weeks, he would describe it again, over and over, to other state police investigators, to a team of police psychiatrists, and even to the FBI.

It was the sight of a big, red gas can, tipped over on its side, of Rutledge's own pearl handled thirty eight, lying beside it, and next to those two items, the body of the lunatic Von Himmler, dressed in his Nazi uniform, going up in bright, hot flames.

CHAPTER TEN

Dick took another drink of brandy, and sank back into the soft, yielding, velvet couch. He pulled off his bifocals, and massaged the deep indentions on either side of the bridge of his nose. The grandfather clock ticked away at this, the blackest hour of the long night. There was nothing to be said. Anything he might try to say to Rutledge would come out all wrong.

For his part, Rutledge emptied the last four ounces of the bottle into his glass and took a swig. He looked over at Dick with his beet red eyes. "Fifty years after, and this happens. I swear to God, I tear myself inside out most nights. The brandy helps."

"The whole thing's been kept- secret?" Dick asked softly. Rutledge nodded slowly.

"They got to everybody, I guess. Some folks ended up with lots of money. I ain't sure who they paid off- Gloria Shutz and the Bancroft family, for sure. Red's brother- he was outta town when it happened. Me? I spent the winter in Nevada- not been feelin' so hot lately." Rutledge struggled to his feet, then walked across the room and pawed at some papers on his secretary. He picked through a large stack of mail, and then retreated back to his spot on the couch with a handful of envelopes and periodicals. "Life jus' goes on, Dick." He started through the pile.

Dick sat in stunned silence. Rutledge had indicated that on top of everything else, the government had cloaked the crime from the general public by plugging any potential leaks with wads of money. The whole story was one outrageous nightmare come to life. The events in Dallas in November, 1963 in many ways paled in comparison to this, the most hideous of crimes.

"Doctor bills, hunting and fishing magazine, heavy equipment catalog, electric bill. Shit, I kept all the lights off, I unplugged the frig, set the house at forty-eight degrees to keep the pipes from freezin', and here's a fifty-five dollar electric bill. They must a' let a man in to read the stinkin' meter. Wonder what he thought about this ghost town? Fuck!"

"I'll help you sort through the mail tomorrow, Sam. Come on up to camp tomorrow- in the afternoon, when it warms up. We're camped in the usual place- closest tent to the fishing boats." Dick realized that it was well past three. "Hope the grandson slept through," he said. "I better get going. I don't really want to leave you alone like this, Sam."

Rutledge ignored the last statement. "We'll take my truck. Where's your car pulled up, again?"

"Along the fencerow. I drove until it got swampy." Dick felt cold. "You know, I remember Ned Baker real well. He used to give me fishing tips. Yesterday afternoon, the girl in the store up there told me he had died. She didn't say how- probably doesn't even know. That's why I was in the cemetery tonight. You won't believe it, Sam, but I was lookin' for his headstone."

"And you found it," Sam said, jingling his keys. "He's buried with all the others. I ain't sure who identified the bodies. I wasn't in any shape to do it, I can tell you that. I think when they decided to keep everything quiet, they used my front-end loaders and my backhoe and got the job done quick. I was thinkin' they collected all the ID's and made a list from those. I don't know."

They walked through the house toward the rear door. "You've been back for two nights, Sam?"

"In this house two nights. Stayed in a motel in Marquette for a week. Made a couple day trips. I broadcast that grass seed first day I came back. Came up right away, didn't it?"

Dick did not care to discuss it further. He followed Sam out the back door and headed for his garage. Rutledge walked like an old man. Dick looked over at the outline of the funeral home, lighted by the moon against the night sky. His heart fluttered.

Rutledge drove Dick back to the gate and unlocked it, then proceeded down along the fence line, back toward where his car was parked. "I'll be stoppin' by the lake tomorrow," Rutledge said, his voice heavy with alcohol. "Maybe you can cook us up some fish. I'd like that."

Dick's thoughts returned to Todd, sleeping soundly, he hoped, back in their tent. "Good, Sam. Come by about four. That'll give us enough time to fill up the stringer."

They slowed near Dick's car, and Rutledge powered his truck through the soft ground in order to turn around. They shook hands. Dick wiped a tear from his own wrinkled cheek in the darkness.

"Thanks," said Rutledge. "Life's been empty. I been kinda hollow, I guess you'd call it. Thanks, eh? It feels better to talk to someone- someone who knows."

"It always is, Sam. Remember, I'm your friend, for life." Rutledge coughed again.

"You better hightail it back to that grandkid of yours. See you tomorrow, hey?"

Dick walked to his car and started the engine. Rutledge was waiting, making sure that Dick was able to get out of the soft stuff in his sedan. Dick followed his tire tracks through the high grass, back out to the gate, his friend following. When he reached the gate he paused for a moment, then rolled down his window and gave Rutledge a final wave.

He hit the highway and drove at high speed back toward Lake Independence. After listening to Rutledge's incredible story, he felt numb. His mind was mush. There were questions surfacing in his head. Among them, was why the judicial system had failed so in dealing with a dangerous monster like Von Himmler. He was institutionalized, but there could not have been a serious attempt made to uncover the real motive behind his barbaric murder of Toivo Ahonen. If that motive had been divulged, or if the case had been brought properly to the public's attention, certainly the state would have taken the steps necessary to classify him as extremely dangerous to society, and then locked him up in a padded cell somewhere until he'd rotted away.

How incomprehensible, that a frenzied night of alcohol induced activities by three young soldiers in Koblenz, as tragic as they became, would, nearly a half-century later, prove to be the sole cause for the annihilation of a small, northern town, a somewhat backward place where its residents, for the most part, accepted their station in life, enjoying the simple pleasures provided for time immemorial when God molded the natural wonder of the Upper Peninsula.

The crimes that long ago night were dastardly, Dick admitted, as he drove the white striped highway. Many a day he had spent during the prime years of his life, asking what more he could have done to temper the activities of that fateful night. What more could he have done the night an innocent man, a man so worthy of life, a kindly doctor, had been so savagely beaten and murdered. The prostitute- she was way beyond repair when Dick had reached her. The actual infliction of her head wound and the details surrounding it had always been concealed by Rutledge and Toivo. Dick had never really wanted to know, for that matter.

Dick had concluded that their experience in the war together had sent Rutledge to the brink of insanity. And, Toivo had always been a follower, and he was content to march in line behind Sam, stepping smartly to the cadence of Sam's increasingly bizarre plans and actions.

A small, furry creature scurried across the road in front of Dick, and he hit the brakes reflexively. It seemed somehow pointless, to save the life of this raccoon or skunk, after having just been made privy to the fact that the entire population of a village had been gassed, then the bodies heaped into a common grave by the government, intent upon covering up this pernicious act, the horrible act of this satanic, mass killer- he who had tracked his prey halfway around the world over forty-six years. And what of the terrible death of the beautiful Thomas woman back in Ohio? Dick had more than a sneaking suspicion that this Von Himmler had been responsible for that murder, as well.

Dick was dolorously drunk from the brandy, and as the unrelenting pictures of Rutledge's graphic descriptions of the heinous crime passed through his mind's eye like an old newsreel, a feeling of fright took hold of him, bringing an icy sweat to his face and a loathing to his soul with the realization that, somehow, he would be next. After all, originally, it had been his own idea to seek out a neighborhood doctor all those years ago in Koblenz. If this human monster was capable of reaching out from the captivity of his debilitating mental illness to strike in such awesome fashion, could he not now break the bonds of the grave to complete this powerful, single-minded quest?

Dick felt there was a sudden movement in the rear seat, saw it, he was sure, out of the corner of his eye. He cried out, and stuck his arm and hand behind the bench seat, feeling nothing but air. Dick shuddered, and knew that he must be very drunk.

He completed the drive without further incident, monitoring his racing pulse, and when he finally pulled his car into its parking place next to the tent, he let out a sigh of relief.

Things seemed as he had left them. With a mindful swallow, Dick unzipped the tent flap and found Todd all curled up in his sleeping bag, snoozing soundly. Dick secured the tent flaps, and crawled into his own bag, which he had already occupied briefly much earlier that evening. He soon felt warm and secure, and normally he would have fallen asleep within moments. But, the Birch story just overwhelmed him.

The brandy, at any other time, would have sent Dick into a deep sleep all by itself. But the strong dose of alcohol, mixed with the hellish visions of mass execution, had him on the jagged edge of pure fear. And, he was completely exhausted, considering that his long day had commenced with a ten-hour drive, and then he had set up camp, had gone fishing, had a few beers with dinner, and finally, ended up late nighting it with Rutledge. He was very uneasy, and could not put this matter to rest, even until morning. He tossed and turned, and he even pictured what Toivo's death had been like. Gruesome.

And then he heard the crunching sound made by the disturbance of one of the little gatherings of twigs and unraked fall leaves somewhere off in the darkness, out beyond the buttoned up flaps on the tent. It was the type of crunching noise made when a man tries to move soundlessly through dry woods- a man lacking the skills of a good hunting guide. Dick sat right up, straining his ear inside the tent. Another crunch followed. He put on his glasses. Someone was out there- moving slowly in the direction of the tent. If this person was to circle around, it occurred to Dick that the intruder would be able to make his final approach through the silent sand without so much as a peep. He and Todd would be sitting ducks. There was another barely audible crackle, closer this time. Dick reached for his windbreaker and felt in the pocket for his screwdriver and pliers. Damn! He had left them in Rutledge's entryway- on that goddam table. He took hold of the flashlight and held it tight in his fist.

The moon, still bright high in the western sky, projected a pattern of well-budded branches against the ceiling and side of the tent. Two more crunches and it sounded like someone was standing at the back of the car.

Dick's breath had quickened to the point that he was gulping air like a fish in order to remain quiet. He thought about the long pole Von Himmler had used with the razor sharp point in order to suspend Toivo up near the ceiling of his gas station. Rutledge had told him all about it. With a weapon like that, the madman could aim for a likely spot in the center of the tent from ten feet away and thrust it like a spear, through the canvas, through the sleeping bag, and into Dick's vitals. Or worse, into Todd's;

Dick heard another noise, looked over at the side of the tent and saw the shadow of the head as he moved in closer. Dick was paralyzed with dread. He would not die without a fight. He forced himself to his knees, maneuvered toward the tent flap, tried to take in a deep breath, took hold of the zipper, and ever so slowly pulled it up. He was surprised how quietly it moved in his quaking fingers. He had given the track a treatment of three-in-one oil the previous fall, before putting the canvas into winter storage. He stopped just above the top of his head, still kneeling.

Taking the flashlight into the palm of his right hand again and squeezing it with all of his might, then cocking it back in order to deliver a roundhouse blow, Dick took hold of the outer flap cord with his left hand, which was tied in a simple bow knot, and prepared to mount his own pre-emptive strike. 'God help me,' he thought, looking back at Todd. He yanked on the cord, sprung up from the door of the tent and catapulted himself out into the night with a growl.

The deer looked up at him, no longer chewing on its mouthful of grass. The ears pushed up, fully cupped. It made a "whoooh!!" sound, turned, then crashed and thumped back into the depths of the woods. Dick, falling to his knees, could see the white flag jerking back and forth through the shadowy forest like a slalom skier slipping in and out of gates. Dick was so overly exhausted that he crumpled right to the sandy ground with a heavy sigh and just laid there for at least a quarter hour. Finally, he managed to crawl back to his bed. "The motherfucker's dead," he said.

When morning mercifully came at last, Dick was positive that he hadn't slept a wink. He climbed out into the cool morning air, and was greeted by some of the thickest fog that he had ever seen, anywhere. He cooked breakfast, and then roused Todd gently. "Breakfast," he said, "pike and eggs, eggs and pike, orange juice, toast, hot chocolate- good morning!"

Todd stretched and groaned, and then started his day. "You sleep good, gramps?"

"Like a log," lied the grandfather. "After the dishes are done, I'm thinking about driving into town." Todd looked very disappointed.

"Awe, gramps! I thought we were gonna go fishin' some more- I don't wanna go into town. We were in the car for two whole days. Let's just go fish. Go into town tomorrow." Todd looked at him hopefully.

"Tell you what- this really can't wait. I have to go. But, if we check in with that nice girl at the store, maybe I'll let you stay here and fish from shore. Mr. Rutledge is coming this afternoon for dinner. Now mind you, you are not allowed in a boat by yourself- is that understood?"

"Sure gramps, thanks a lot! I promise, I'll be good." Dick rubbed Todd's scalp with his fist. "Ouch! Hey! When did you talk with your friend Mr. Rutledge?"

"On the phone last night, after I checked in with your grandmother."

"Did he tell you why there's no town, now?"

"He started to tell me. Now eat your breakfast, boy. We'll talk about this after you show me just how much fish you can eat."

"It's a deal, " said Todd. He picked up his dixie cup of juice and slugged it down.

While Todd finished his breakfast, Dick opened the trunk of the car and got out Todd's fishing pole and one of the tackle boxes. "I'll get your line ready," he said. "You need a bobber about three feet up from your hook." He fastened the little red and white bobber to the line. It took him much longer than it normally would have. His hands were shaking. "Now remember, if you hook a big one, bring him up slow and run him onto the sand. Those pike have sharp teeth so keep your hand away from their mouth."

"I know gramps."

"All you need now are the worms- they're over at the base of the tree. If the sun comes out, keep 'em in the shade."   Todd nodded, his face full of egg yolk. Dick left his own gear in the car, to keep it out of the moist air. It had always been his habit to put the poles and tackle boxes back into the trunk each night. This forced him to keep everything organized. Fishing tackle could become such a jumbled mess. Before closing the trunk, Dick took out a wrench from his toolbox and headed for the boat. For a second time he recalled that he'd already left his pliers at Rutledge's place. He would have to remind himself to get them back.

Maybe Sam would just bring them when he came.

He climbed to the back of the boat and loosened and removed the two spark plugs from the boat motor. It isn't that he didn't trust Todd to be a good boy, but doing this would insure him that the boy couldn't be overcome by the temptation to try and start the motor while his gramps was away.

After pulling the two plugs, Dick returned to the picnic table, where Todd was just finishing his last bite. Dick just knew that he would have to pay a visit to the state police post. It was the only way that he might achieve peace of mind. "Let's get the dishes done, young man. Then, we'll stop by the little store."

After cleaning up, Dick and Todd drove over to the camp store together. When they walked in, the girl was leaning over the bait tanks, which looked like a row of old laundry tubs, and she was netting out the minnows that had died during the night. She flipped them off of the seine and into a waiting plastic bucket.

"Good morning," said Dick. The aeration pumps droned steadily, keeping the water moving in the tanks and bubbling in oxygen.

"Oh, hello," she said, "it's a foggy one today, hey?"

"I'll say. I think it's about the thickest that I've ever seen."

"Can I help you?" Dick placed his hands on Todd's shoulders.

"I just thought I'd ask- now don't mistake me, we don't want to be a bother, but I have to go into Marquette this morning for a little while and my grandson, here, wants to stay around."

The girl smiled a warm smile and looked at Todd. "I think that can be arranged," she said. "I have a chore or two around the store, here, that needs doing. You don't mind being paid in candy bars, do you, guy? What's your name?"

"I'm Todd. And I'll get paid in candy bars!"

"I told Todd, here, that he can fish from shore if he would like- after he's done working, of course. He knows he's not allowed in the boat without an adult."

"Gramps, I know!" protested Todd.

"I'll keep him busy for a little while. Then, he can go fishing. Is that okay with you, Todd?"

"Okay!"

"You know," said Dick, "I feel very foolish. I didn't catch your name yesterday, miss."

"Donna." She turned and hung the net up on a nail above the tanks. "And yours?"

"I'm Dick, excuse me, again." He turned slightly red. "Donna, thank you so much. I'll be back around lunchtime. Perhaps you'd like to have fish dinner with us tonight. My friend, Sam Rutledge is coming by. You may know Sam."

"No, afraid I don't. I'm a student at Northern Michigan University. I worked here part time last summer. This will be my first year full time."

"You've got yourself a great job, then, Donna. This would be a wonderful way to spend the summer."

"I like it," she said.

"Well, if you're not busy, plan on stopping at our campsite around five. The fish'll be cookin'."

"I just might take you up on that, Dick. Thanks for the offer." Dick opened the door to leave. "Okay Todd!" she barked, "the porch could use a good sweeping."

"Yes, ma'am!"

Gramps couldn't help but smile as he headed for his car. Todd was sure to impress Donna with that inherited work ethic running on up the Chapman line. In fact, Todd had taken the push broom and immediately began to sweep with extra effort. 'Must be that northern air,' Dick thought. Then, his thoughts dragged him back to Birch.

A fifty-minute drive found Dick at the Negaunee state police post located out approximately ten miles west of Marquette. He approached the desk sergeant and then was led into the spacious office of the post's commander by a well-dressed young woman. She turned out to be the commander's secretary. "He'll be with you shortly," she said. "I'm sure he'd very much like to discuss the case with you. Would you care for a cup of coffee while you're waiting?"

"Thank you, I take it black." Dick stood at the window as the secretary retreated, closing the door behind her. He looked out into the parking lot, at the row of deep blue state police cars, ready and waiting in the fog. This reminded him of his last visit to a doctor- a check up by a cardiologist over the winter. Dick had been experiencing some discomfort in his chest. He recalled being led into a tiny examining room by the receptionist, and then he waited and waited for the doctor. For the longest time, he listened to footsteps, to muffled voices, looking at his wristwatch impatiently, wondering all the while when the doctor might finally show himself. He later had told Lucy that anyone seeing that doctor with a perfectly healthy heart to begin with would most likely leave with a bad one, just from the nerve wracking wait.

The door opened again and the lady smiled sweetly, held the door, and a much younger man than Dick had expected walked in with two styrofoam cups of coffee. "Mr. Chapman, your coffee, sir."

"Thank you," Dick said, eyeing the blue blazer with the band of stripes at the shoulders that the man wore.

"I'm Bob Brooks, commander of this post." Dick shifted the coffee from his right hand to his left, in order to grasp the firm handshake.

"Dick Chapman," he said, "a longtime friend of Sam Rutledge. I'm here because of the Birch case." Brooks grimaced.

"My secretary mentioned that. You're a friend of Sam Rutledge, you say?"

"I've known Sam for nearly fifty years. We were in the Great- er, World War I together. You see, I know exactly why this whole thing happened- God awful as it is!" Brooks set his coffee on his desk. He studied the man standing before him up and down. He looked to be about the right age- middle sixties.

"You've seen Mr. Rutledge, then, since he got back into town?"

"Just last night. I came up for the walleye opener from way down in southern Ohio- have been for many, many years. I always camp up at Lake Independence and then always get together with Sam over a few drinks. I am shocked by this, I can't begin to tell you; What a travesty! What a goddam nightmare! I didn't sleep last night, I can assure you."

Brooks noted that the man's coffee cup was shaking, and that he had grown ghostly pale. He placed his hands gently on Dick's left arm and carefully lifted the spilling cup away and set it down. "I don't think you need coffee, just now. A shot of bourbon would probably be more like it. Your name came up, Mr. Chapman, in my numerous conversations with Sam Rutledge."

"You're very kind. I don't suppose I do need any coffee right now. I was up drinking with Sam last night- kind of a wake, a very grim one."

Brooks invited him to sit in one of the stuffed leather chairs in front of the window that he had inherited from Art Franklin. "You know, Mr. Chapman-"

"Please call me Dick."

"Dick, I was involved in this case from the word, go. I was the commander over at the Newberry post last fall- that's where Von Himmler first escaped- from the state hospital, there."

"And now you've been moved here? Transferred?"

"Art Franklin, the commander here, retired in March. They offered me the job. Nicer office, so I accepted. The pay's a bit better, too."

"What did Sam tell you about his link- our link, really, with the man who did this?"

"He told us about the war incident- about the unfortunate death of the German doctor. About the injuries to the child Von Himmler; He filled you in about Toivo Ahonen, and the manner in which he died?"

"Sam told me last night."

"Mr. Rutledge was shocked when I first told him about the details surrounding the murder in St. Ignace. He had lost contact with Mr. Ahonen over the years. He had heard that Mr. Ahonen had been killed, but thought that it had occurred during the commission of a robbery."

"And that was my understanding, also. I used to stop and have lunch with Toivo years ago, when I first started coming north. I guess I dredged up bad memories for Toivo. He began to cut our visits short. He would make excuses for not wanting to see me. Finally, I just let him go. Then, ten years ago, Sam told me that May he had heard that Toivo had been stabbed during a robbery attempt."

"The St. Ignace police chief, and the chamber of commerce president, working together, withheld the actual details of your friend's killing from the public. They offered up the robbery story. Pure fabrication- and the judge was in on it, too, I might add."

"And what is so tragic, commander, is that I know, if either Sam or I had just heard that name, Von Himmler, we would have come forward with a motive for that terrible killing. My God! This could have all been avoided!" Dick's forehead was beading with sweat.

"Obviously, revenge was the motive. I have spent many a sleepless night, myself, since last fall. My wife and I are separated. This has been, and continues to be, a great strain on all of those involved." Brooks reached into his breast pocket and pulled out a cigarette. He lit it and puffed deeply. "One of our troopers who was assigned to check out the Birch area the day before the mass murder has been in a psychiatric ward since Christmas. He couldn't get rid of his guilt until it just ate him alive. There are many, many scars.

"You understand, Dick, that the real story will never come out. The government has deflected any media attention away. Birch is just another Upper Peninsula ghost town, as far as everybody around here is concerned."

"Could it serve a purpose, to tell the world what happened here?" asked Dick.

"Dick, the order to maintain the secrecy of the operation in Birch apparently came from the highest level of government."

"You mean the President?"

"These are uncertain times, Mr. Chapman. President Kennedy had been assassinated just ten months before. I was told that if a lone man, as psychotic as Von Himmler was, were capable of carrying out so horrific a mass murder with such calculation and precision, when the news crews came in and Huntley-Brinkley had the film footage for our nation to see, the American public would react nervously at best. Why, it might even spawn a wave of such crimes throughout the western world."

"This man was insane."

"He was a monster, Mr. Chapman. I was permitted to view the FBI file on this man back in February. As a youth, he was kicked out of medical school. He joined up with the Nazis in a bizarre capacity, worked at one of those experimental medical centers- like the ones they exposed during the Nuremburg trials. He lived with his mother again until she died in, I believe, 1953. He obtained the necessary papers, and came over here, to the U.S., in the summer of '54. They believe he drifted, until he ended up in St. Ignace the following spring. He originally had the names of you three soldiers- must have gotten them from the records of the military tribunal they set up in Koblenz, following his father's death. Probably searched through archives and old military records to trace your home addresses. I would imagine that as cunning as he was, digging up that kind of information wouldn't prove to be too difficult. I'm rambling, Dick. You'll have to forgive me."

Dick thought of putting forth his theory on the unsolved murder in his hometown. There was something gnawing at him, though, and he had to ask. "He is dead, is he? You're quite positive that he is dead?"

"He is dead, Mr. Chapman. Rutledge told you of the suicide?"

"Yes, that he soaked himself head to toe with gasoline, lit a match, and then shot himself in the head just as he blew up into a ball of fire."

"I'd say that was accurate. Incidently, that was also the way Adolf Hitler went, more or less. You knew he took on the Hitler character?"

"Appalling, Commander Brooks. You took lab tests of his remains?"

"Routine procedure," Brooks said, tapping out his cigarette. "Fibers at the sight of the suicide matched precisely with fibers found in Von Himmler's celebrated trunk. Scorched pieces of a partial plate from the upper denture matched hospital dental records exactly. The fiend is very dead, the Michigan State Police attest to this."

"And the story- do you actually believe, commander, that the actual story will never come out?"

"I don't know that it will not. Personally, I haven't spoken with a single investigative reporter," Brooks jested dryly. "Our government has invested a tidy sum into the project. It has worked so far." Brooks cocked his head slightly and looked Dick in the eye. "I have the authority to make any and all arrangements that may become necessary."

"They won't have to pay me to keep quiet, commander. I'm getting to be an old man. I'm not one to cause a row. I just had- you know, questions."

"And you came to the proper place, and I'm the right man."

"You're allowing Rutledge to remain in his house? I'm surprised, under the circumstances."

"Dick, your friend is dying. I'm sorry to apparently have to be the one to tell you. Lung cancer- nothing more they can do. He spent the past six months in a veteran's hospital out west- in Nevada. Had part of his lung removed. The decision was made to let him live out his life in Birch, and he agreed to adhere to certain guidelines."

Dick looked off into the fog, again. So Rutledge had cancer, terminal cancer. It was not possible for Dick to deal with it all.

"He- he sure wasn't too happy about the size of his electric bill, when he saw it last night," said Dick, relieving some of the tension in the air. "He figured fifty-five bucks was a bit much to operate the furnace fan to keep his pipes from freezing. I'm sure he had a freezer plugged in, and whatever else. The man's got a big, big house."

"And he seems to have a good friend. You're a good guy, Dick. I'm one hell of a judge of character."

"Guess I won't dispute it, then. One more thing, commander."

"Shoot from the hip."

"The grave up there- I suppose the idea of a mass grave bothers the dickens out of me."

"That was a decision from way upstairs. They flew some military personnel in from the air base south of here by helicopter. They got the job done with the heavy equipment that Rutledge used up there. I stayed away that day, and that's about all I can say about it. It was a sorry situation. Look at it like one of those ocean liners going down- those people never get a decent burial, either."

Dick, still seated in the chair, looked outside, again. "Geez, that fog is still as thick as pea soup."

"You'll be driving in it, so take it slow, Dick. You look very tired to me. Why don't you take a little nap here on my couch. I can even offer you a fresh pillow from the closet."

Dick arose from his seat. "Thanks, but I have to get back to my grandson." He shrugged his shoulders and said, "well, that should do it. I'm feeling a little better, I think, anyway." Brooks handed him a business card.

"Here, if anything comes to mind, you call me, collect."

"Okay, commander." The two men shook hands. "I invited Sam up to the lake for supper, this evening. I think I might stop in and see how he's feeling. He didn't tell me about the cancer."

Brooks walked around behind his desk and opened the top drawer. He reached in and brought out a key, offering it to Dick. "Here, you'll need to unlock the main gate if you plan to just drop in on him."

"Thanks, that would help. I walked way around the fence line last night to get in. An old, dead pine had dropped on the fence and bent it way over- I think this will make it a little easier on me."

"I should say. I'm sure Mr. Rutledge will appreciate your concern."

Brooks watched the older man slump his shoulders slightly. He held out his hand. "Nice meeting you, Mr. Chapman. You've got my card. Don't hesitate to call me at any time."

"Thank you, commander. Thank you for everything."

Walking back out to the car, for just a moment, Dick pictured himself in the midst of a terrible, endless dream. 'If only I would just wake up. This is really all just bullshit.' But he knew full well now that there was no turning back- that this was the new reality.

As Dick drove north toward Birch, the idea that his nightmare was at an end seeped into him, even though his raw emotions fought the concept. He did recognize the fact that he would feel no real relief until the passage of time lightened the burden- this knowing of how and why six hundred innocent human beings had perished in official silence. Dick understood that he, himself, was that one unique individual who chanced to be in a certain place at a certain time, so as to allow him to witness the historical events which now enabled him to grasp this whole story objectively, even while reacting with great emotion. This was his living paradox, of sorts- his analytical objectivity shining through despite coupling his horror, his grief, and his deep despair.

Several times on the road north, just when the fog appeared to be lifting, Dick would cross over a hill or follow a curve through the forest, and the thickest mist would re-appear, hanging in the still air.

Dick thought about Rutledge, about the cough and the cancer. While Dick struggled to accept the surreal, Rutledge was in the process of living out his last days in an empty world devoid of purpose. His world was of shadow, of memories gone bad, life turned to stone. What could Dick do to help his old war buddy? Not much, he was afraid. Rutledge had hit rock bottom. Only Rutledge could transform his shattered existence and move in some semblance of direction. Only he, and he alone, could place the tragedy of his life into a rational perspective, and then go on, somehow, like before. Hunting, fishing, a rework back into the natural cycle of his life; Rutledge would go on living for a while, of that Dick was sure. Rutledge would never be one to fall upon his sword, his pride would carry him until the cancer took over completely.

Dick could offer friendship, if nothing else. He could be there for Rutledge- be there to listen when he sounded out the pain from the depths of his soul, be there when death was looming close, to offer comfort, to offer hope, to offer whatever support that he could muster.

This might be Dick's other purpose, then. He would continue to take his grandson camping and fishing, continue teaching him to live in harmony with nature, providing the boy with a frame of reference that he would one day rely upon when handing down a like experience to his own children and grandchildren. That of itself was important to Dick. And now, another duty beckoned. Dick would step up to counsel a fellow mortal soul who was already half way down the rocky road of terminal cancer.

Dick wondered if Rutledge really was planning to stop up at camp later for the fish fry. Having spilled his guts out until the wee hours, having dug up every last detail of the horror which he had so vainly tried to forget, would he really be up to another visit, particularly if the conversation might just lead to more of the same?

This terminal cancer that Rutledge was riddled with- why, that was a matter that they had not even addressed. More grief, more sorrow, more helplessness; 'He's sure paying now,' thought Dick, 'he's paying, but good.'

When Dick reached the Birch turnoff, he slowed down and headed toward the gate. It might do Rutledge good to sit around the campfire in the fresh air, even on a clammy and fog shrouded day such as this. He would just stop off and give Sam a kick in the ass, like any good friend should.

The gate was chained and locked, and so Dick used the key that Brooks had given him. Once he pulled the car inside, he took a moment to re-secure the gate. He was positive that Rutledge would be home. Since it was going on noon, he was sure to find him up and around, even if he had slept in a little. He hoped that their lengthy conversation together hadn't taken too much out of him, or had him depressed.

Dick drove slowly past the empty shell of the IGA and then turned onto Birch Avenue. The fog obscured the roofs on many of the houses. It seemed to be even thicker in the area surrounding the little town, as though nature were providing an added covering, as if to occlude the sight of this wretched disaster.

Dick pulled up and parked in Rutledge's driveway. The cold air did send a fresh chill through him as he made his way up to the big front porch. Maybe it was too cool for the camp dinner, after all. Dick certainly didn't want Rutledge to start coughing due to this cold, clammy air. That is something he would discuss with him. The weather forecast sounded more favorable later in the week.

Dick rapped on the large oak door. Neither a sound nor a stirring could be detected inside. He knocked again. Dick wondered if Rutledge might still be sleeping. He tried the knob. The door was unlocked, so he entered.

The house felt warm and dry. The grandfather clock's pendulum swung softly, barely issuing a tick as it passed back and forth. "Morning, Sam!" greeted Dick loudly. "Good morning! Hallo!!" The only sound he heard was the rush of hot air through the heating ducts issuing from the forced air furnace down below.

Dick walked into the kitchen. The place was cluttered with dirty dishes, pots and pans, cans of food, and empty eggshells. A stack of bread had been pulled out of its plastic wrapper and left to sit on the countertop by mistake. Dick took a minute and carefully loaded the bread back into the bag and folded it closed before it became stale. It looked as though Sam had eaten quite a breakfast. Perhaps as ill as he was, he had eaten and then felt sick afterward, and had laid back down in bed. Dick imagined that his friend must have become increasingly weak and nauseated as the cancer had taken an increasingly firm hold.

Dick assembled a pile of dishes on the counter and then took them in both hands over to the sink. When he looked down casually into the bottom of the ceramic basin, the dishes fell out of his grasp and crashed to the floor, sending pieces of broken china and shards of glass to the four corners of the room. Dick let out a loud wail.

A detached human hand, knotted into a loose fist, lay in the bottom of the kitchen sink. The hand was big and meaty, and Dick never even considered that it could belong to anyone besides Rutledge. It was so shocking to see it, and yet Dick studied it with a morbid fascination, examining the rough edges of bloodied skin and flesh where it had been neatly severed from the wrist.

Dick stepped back from the sink, and now he turned and dashed through the house, the shock wearing thin and a sensation of panic, of mortal terror, taking hold of him. He gasped for air, searching wildly for what must be left of Rutledge on the first floor, and, after finding nothing, he ascended the staircase up to the sleeping quarters.

Dick cowered and quaked, and approached the master bedroom

despite the overwhelming instinct to flee. The door was closed. He placed his hand on the doorknob, fought again to regain his breath, and then threw the door open, letting out a yelp of fear.

The sight was absolutely appalling. Horrid; Dick was gripped with revulsion, and yet, again, as with the hand in the sink, he could not look away. There was Rutledge, skewered somehow on a length of metal pipe, his head and shoulders wedged up against the ceiling. He was nude. Dick could see that a hole had been drilled through the rafter, and a rope had been fished from the attic and had been knotted below Rutledge's armpits. Dick looked up with dread at Rutledge's pale face, at the unfocused, bulging eyes staring lifelessly down upon him. And there was the stump where the right hand should be. The rug on which Dick stood seemed spongy. He looked down at his feet and saw that the carpet was soaked through with blood. All of his blood had run down the pole, draining Rutledge completely.

Dick stared at the white legs, all goose flesh, the great barrel chest, now bluish-gray with death. He looked upon the face, studied the features. In their contorted state, he could barely recognize that this was, indeed, Rutledge, whom had been impaled. And Dick knew what this meant, and he knew just what he was up against, and he trembled with renewed terror.

Then, a voice, very faint, came out of that death mask of a face. Dick practically went through the ceiling. "He's going- going- to-"

Dick watched the puffy, blue lips. He did detect an almost indistinguishable, imperceptible movement of the mouth. "Sam! I'm praying for you, Sam!"

"In-dep-en-dence." Rutledge had issued a final breath of a warning. Then, his mouth dropped open.

Dick felt a sudden stab of pain in his left forearm. It traveled up into his shoulder. He held his left elbow and took a final look at his old war buddy, tortured to death on that stake. "Father in Heaven, accept his soul in Your mercy, oh Father. Make him a soldier in Your Heavenly Host. Amen."

"Oh My God! Todd!" Dick cried. He held his left elbow and ran back down the stairs and out to his car as quickly as his aging legs would allow. He was shaking, and was at once thankful that he had left the car key in the ignition, which wasn't normally his custom. He couldn't imagine trying to stick that key into that hole in his frantic state.

He revved the engine, throwing the car into gear. He peeled out of the driveway like a teenager, and then pushed the gas pedal down to the floorboard. When he approached the fence gate, he aimed for the chain and closed his eyes, then felt the mild impact as the car surged through the barrier, leaving Birch in its wake.

The eight minutes that it took Dick to drive from the gate to the Lake Independence campground turn off proved to be the most agonizing span of time that Dick had ever spent. Though the deep throb in his left arm worried him as it now spread into the center of his chest, all of his available faculties were pinpointed upon the grave danger that Todd now faced, and the potential opportunity his grandfather might have to alleviate the danger. Dick was driving as fast as the dense fog would allow. 'The hand,' Dick thought, 'was the one Rutledge set on my shoulder just last night, when he surprised me at the cemetery.' He also now knew that Von Himmler had been in the house with them the previous night, listening as Dick described in detail the location of his campsite. 'That must have been Ranger Baker that got cremated,' he thought. 'Von Himmler got away.'

"You want me!?" screamed Dick aloud, grimacing from the tightening pain in his chest, and just managing to keep the car on the pavement in the blinding fog, "you can have me! Don't touch my grandson! God, please don't let him touch my grandson!"

Dick reached the turn off and slammed on the brakes and turned the wheel hard to the right, squealing the tires and throwing up a shower of gravel as he hit the dirt trail. He careened along the campground road, oblivious to any of the other campers. When he spied Rutledge's pickup truck parked alongside his very own tent, he slowed to a stop and turned off the engine.

Still holding his left arm, he walked stealthily through the campsite, peered into the tent, and then looked down toward the beach. Their boat was nowhere in sight.

Dick fought through the sand until he stood at the water's edge. The fog enveloped the lake and did not permit him to see very far out upon the waters. "Todd!! Boy!! Gramps is here!! Todd!!"

Dick cupped his best ear and listened for a response. Then, he heard a child's voice. "We're out here, gramps!" it said. "Mr. Rutledge came to take me fishin'. He couldn't get the motor to work!"

'Oh my God!' thought Dick. 'The fiend- what is he up to?'

"Todd!! I'm coming!!" Dick stomped back through the sand to his car and opened the trunk. He brought out his rod and bait casting reel, and then opened up his tackle box and picked out one of his favorite lures- a large red and white daredevil spoon with a big treble hook from its supposed place of honor in the top tray of his box. Dick connected the lure to the high-test wire leader and then headed for the grouping of rowboats pulled up on the beach. He took a final look out into the lake, and seeing nothing, pushed one of the boats into the water and, grasping his pole, shoved off onto the calm waters.

The pain seemed to be receding somewhat, and Dick was able to take both oars firmly and then he began to stroke, awkwardly for the first few pulls, and then he found his rhythm, and began gliding surprisingly smoothly out onto the fog bound lake. He pulled steady for a minute or two, and then he cupped his hands to his face, yelling, "Todd, where are you!?" He was trying to throw his voice, to camouflage his position. He listened intently to the quiet.

"I'm out here!" Todd answered, from somewhere in the mist. It did sound to Dick like the voice was considerably closer. "Gramps! This isn't Mr. Rutledge! He's scaring me!"

Dick aimed the bow of his boat toward the voice. He rowed hard for a short time, until the pain in his chest tightened, again. Then he set the oars up out of the water so that the paddles rested on the stern. He cupped his hands again, and directed his voice toward shore, not so loud this time. "Todd! Todd, boy!"

"We're out here, gramps!" Dick could tell that he had again moved in the right direction. He didn't care for this game of chess that they were playing- with his grandson, the helpless pawn.

Young Todd cowered in the back of the boat, one hand on his fishing pole, trying not to look at the man who sat in the middle boat seat, handling the oars. The man was facing him, wearing a dirty, round ranger hat, an even dirtier, old brown coat, and a pair of heavy lineman's boots. He wore a full gray beard and moustache, which together served to at least partially hide the gaunt, wasted face, a face which looked like wrinkly, weather beaten skin stretched over skull bone. Todd was especially frightened to look at his blue eyes, which seemed to have been transplanted from some wild animal, gleaming as they were from the malnourished, yellowing eyeballs. His mouth housed no teeth, so that, when he smiled at Todd, he looked all the more hideous and death like.

"When I was your age, Todd, your grandfather and his two friends knocked at our door after we'd gone to bed. They forced themselves into our home and they killed my father."

"Gramps! Help!" Todd screamed, and then the terrible man, looking like he had come directly from some skid row in hell, let the oars set in the water, and he drew a gleaming hunting knife from beneath the moth eaten coat.

"Shut up, boy! Shut your mouth!"

Todd sat frozen, too afraid to move. His heart pounded in his young chest. The blue eyes now looked like little, blue flames.

And then Todd, who remained seated there without moving so much as a muscle, heard a faint, 'whup', and as he dared look at his deranged abductor, holding that sharp knife, there was a clinking and a fluttering as a big daredevil spoon took a secure hold about the skinny neck, the big treble hook sinking into fabric and flesh, way past the barbs, and then in one utterly fantastic movement, it was as though an invisible hand had gotten a hold of him and jerked him viciously overboard. Todd closed his eyes but heard the loud splash and then felt the icy lake water slap his face. When he opened his eyes, the man was gone!

Dick slowly reeled in the slack in the heavy monofilament line that he had so expertly, so desperately, cast out. He observed the angle of the line deepen into the water as the heavy clothing and big boots dragged Von Himmler down to the silty lake bottom. He applied gentle pressure to his rod tip, and he felt the great weight of the man deep below, his rod tugging a bit as he apparently struggled in agony at the bottom of the lake.

"Gramps! You got him!" cried Todd, paddling slowly toward Dick in the other boat. "I think he was gonna kill me." Dick looked up, but kept the gentle pressure on the rod, and as he counted the seconds into minutes, all of the movement and motion halted.

"Can I come aboard with you, gramps?" Todd had brought his boat right up along the side of Dick's. Gramps let out some slack, and then set the rod down so that it extended out over the bow, and he strained to help

Todd climb aboard. "Gramps! You're sick! You're all white!"

Dick looked down at his fingernails, and saw that they were turning a purplish blue. He knew that he was having a heart attack. "I'll be alright," he said. He lay back, his shoulders resting in the bow, and he held the rod, again. He tightened up on the line.

"Think he's dead?" asked Todd. "Is he drownded by now?"

"Yes, I'm sure of it," replied the grandfather. "He had to die, Todd. There was no other way."

The two of them presented an odd scene in that boat in the fog. They were sitting there, staring at the tip of the rod that had now stopped twitching and pumping up and down. The fog was so heavy as to not permit them to see the shore, so even Dick wasn't sure which way was back.

Dick lifted his rod with what little strength he had left. "It's been five minutes, at least," he said. "I've been counting. He's a drowned rat." Dick, still lying back, began to pump and reel, pump and reel. "Feels like the biggest fish, ever." Todd looked alarmed.

"Gramps, just leave him down there. I'll row us back to camp. You need a doctor."

"Naw, the police'll want the body," replied Dick. "It's not hard to bring up- it feels like it wants to float. I'm feeling okay. If it's the last thing I do, I want to tow this bastard back to shore."

Dick brought the line up with the great weight still connected and then struggled to more of a sitting position. "I don't think he's there!" he cried suddenly in disbelief, seeing that the treble hooks were intertwined with the laces on the big boots, and snagged to the fabric of the coat.

There was an explosion of water at the very front of the boat, and a hand and an arm latched around Dick's neck and bent him back as though he were a sapling, his head and shoulders stretched out over the water. "Chapman! I kill you!" hissed a raspy voice from near the waterline.

"No!" cried Todd. "No!! Stop it!!" The boy picked one of the oars up and pulled the pin from the oarlock, then scrambled to the front of the boat with it. He looked down and saw the death grip which the fiend had around his grandfather's neck, and saw that the peculiar position which his grandfather was in, all bent back like that, would not even permit him a chance to struggle- it was as if he were paralyzed, completely helpless. Todd then located the toothless mouth, which was opened wide as it breathed in heavily to fuel the attack. Todd raised the butt end of that oar up above his head like a spear, aimed for the black hole between the gums, and, just as he was about to launch his weapon, a loud shot rang out, the ugly head exploded in a shower of red, the arm released itself, and the attacker slipped quietly beneath the surface of Lake Independence, again.

EPILOGUE

Dick lay on the litter in the back of the ambulance, an oxygen mask pressed over his nose and mouth. Todd knelt beside him, happy that some color had returned to his grandfather's face. The tips of the fingers were once again pink.

Bob Brooks climbed into the back of the ambulance on one knee. "How's he doing?" he asked Todd.

"They say he's gonna be okay," replied the boy. Dick gave Brooks the thumbs up sign.

"I was plenty worried when we got him in off the lake," said Brooks. "Don't try to talk, Dick. Just lay there, still, and keep breathing that good air." Dick held his palm out and gestured at the commander.

"I imagine you want to know how I managed to show up," said Brooks. Dick nodded slowly.

"When you mentioned that electric bill, I got to thinking about it- got a hunch. I just decided to take a drive up this way. Happened to have my rifle with me. By the way, I'm sorry about Mr. Rutledge. I radioed for an ambulance- they should be there by now." Dick nodded, again.

"While you're in the hospital, if you don't object, the boy, here, can stay with me- at least until your family arrives from Ohio. I've been meaning to take a few days off. Maybe he can help me explore the great north woods. Okay with you, Dick?"

Dick nodded and gave Todd a wink.

"Break it up!" said the ambulance attendant. "Commander Brooks, we're going to need him, now. Do you want to ride with your grampa, son?"

Todd took Dick's hand firmly into his own. "You bet I want to," he said. "I'd go anywhere with my fishin' buddy!"

Printed in the United States
21970LVS00003BA/340-366